THE
CRYING
HOUSE

BOOKS BY B.R. SPANGLER

Where Lost Girls Go
The Innocent Girls
Saltwater Graves

THE CRYING HOUSE

B.R. SPANGLER

Bookouture

Published by Bookouture in 2021

An imprint of Storyfire Ltd.
Carmelite House
50 Victoria Embankment
London EC4Y 0DZ

www.bookouture.com

Copyright © B.R. Spangler, 2021

B.R. Spangler has asserted his right to be identified
as the author of this work.

All rights reserved. No part of this publication may be reproduced, stored in any retrieval system, or transmitted, in any form or by any means, electronic, mechanical, photocopying, recording or otherwise, without the prior written permission of the publishers.

ISBN: 978-1-80019-718-3
eBook ISBN: 978-1-80019-717-6

This book is a work of fiction. Names, characters, businesses, organizations, places and events other than those clearly in the public domain, are either the product of the author's imagination or are used fictitiously. Any resemblance to actual persons, living or dead, events or locales is entirely coincidental.

To my friends and family for their love, support, and patience.

PROLOGUE

Thirty Years Ago

He heard the front door thump close with a sharp blow that rattled the walls. His ears filled with the shuffle of her work shoes against the linoleum as she entered the kitchen. Then came the smell of grease, carried on her clothes and hands and her hair, picked up from the diner where she waited tables. Frozen, his tiny heart pounded, its pace hastening to keep up as panic gripped his little body. Mommy was home.

The liquor cabinet was next. She opened it, a bottle and glass clanking, accompanied by a low grumble about the piss-poor tips and the stinking fishermen who gave her pennies for the plates she served. Her mood was bad, adding to his terror. He heard her drinking. Heard the subtle moan when she finished the first, and then heard her tip the bottle against the drinking glass for another.

He searched his bed, examining the corners, seeing that the sheets were tight. He inspected the blankets next, making sure he folded them exactly as she'd showed him. Maybe he'd go to bed. If she thought he was sleeping, she'd leave him alone. But his bedroom window was bright with daylight. He got up onto his toes, his being able to see over the sill since he'd turned seven. There was fire gliding across the bay, the sun still setting. His bedtime wouldn't come until he could see the first stars.

Going to bed early never stopped her before. The last time he tried it, he hadn't been able to see for days; the salt she put in his eyes causing them to burn. He'd rubbed them hard, but that only made it worse. Much worse.

"Why are there dishes in the sink!" Her hollering bounced up the stairwell and down the hall, her shrill voice piercing his ears.

The kitchen, he thought with frantic alarm. *The sink.* He'd forgotten about the plate he'd used for his sandwich.

"Get down here!" she yelled, slapping the dish against the sides of the sink. There was only the one, but she'd made sure to make it sound like there were dozens. "Now!"

Jump, he thought wildly. *I could jump from my window.* If he was hurt, maybe then she'd leave him alone. If he was dead, she'd have to leave him alone.

His feet moved toward his bedroom door, her voice exerting a power over him he couldn't understand. She could make him move. She could make him come to her. And make him kneel as if there was magic in her voice. He thought of the television show. The one with the snake in the basket and the man wearing the orange turban. He only had a flute, but with it he could charm the snake, control it. That was magic. Maybe that's what his mother could do.

"Coming," he heard himself answer, a sting in his eyes, an ache riddling his body while he tried not to shake. He was already crying from the fright and could barely manage the words. "I'm coming, Mommy."

He heard the closet door open then. He heard the burlap sack being dragged across the kitchen floor. It was the rock salt, and it dried his tears in an instant. He stopped and dared to touch his knees, feeling the papery bumps beneath his pants, the scabs from before—the cuts still healing. He hoped they wouldn't open this time. It hurt the most when the scabs cracked and peeled from his skin. The salt hurt something awful.

Another moan. Another tip of the vodka bottle, its stout neck touching the top of her glass as though a ritual of hers. She might add some orange juice now. She usually did that. "Hurry!" He heard the tick of rock salt hitting the floor—his mother setting the stage for him. "If you don't hurry, I'm going to add an hour."

Every part of him told him to hide, to go into his room and disappear. But he hurried for her, the panic growing like wildfire, his little feet racing.

"I'm here, Mommy," he answered and entered the kitchen, salt crunching beneath his shoes.

She eyed the floor, the milky white and gray stones between them.

"Well," she demanded, and drank her juice.

He said nothing more and rolled the bottom of his pants until his knees showed, the creases and scabs becoming itchy when the air hit them. He stood still a moment, hesitant to lower himself. There was nothing to lean on; she'd never allow it. With no easy way to do it, he whimpered as he inched closer, lowering himself to kneel onto the rock salt. It must've been magic. A dark and ugly magic. He was in her control, and he did as she commanded. He was the snake in the basket. He grimaced and cried silently to himself as his mother watched. When he dared to look at her, he saw the satisfaction crawl onto her face.

"Good. You stay like that. Cleanse your soul."

"Yes, Mommy."

CHAPTER ONE

Twenty-One Months Ago

Tina Sommers had never felt so cold, a misty cloud in her breath, ice needling her fingertips, and her toes felt like wooden stubs. A harsh gust lashed at her bare neck, locks of golden hair flailing about her head as she tugged on one of her tattered sneakers. There were holes in the top and on the sides of them, the miles of frozen ground behind her proving too much for the worn canvas. She clutched her jacket, the joints in her fingers aching as she tightened the flimsy fabric around her front and tried to hide inside it. Another wave of wintery air struck as icy slush spilled off a passing truck, pelting her from head to toe. When it was gone, her shadow returned to the snow-covered ground, the streetlights casting an orange glow over the roadside and turning her alabaster skin the same color. It was the last place in the world she thought she'd be this evening.

She gazed at the distance ahead, her insides squeezing. Her jacket fell open, the zipper torn, her throat closing around a sob as a tear stood on her cheek, its stinging cold in an instant. Tina cursed herself for not being better prepared, for not having planned. But there was no time to plan, no time for any of it. He'd touched her again, and that was enough. Anger stirred, her body tensing. She should have seen it coming. The way he was looking at her differently. His gaze wandering inappropriately. Tina shivered, but it wasn't from the cold January air. It was from disgust.

"I'm done with this place," she said, her teeth chattering hard enough to make her jaw ache. Her sights were set on Virginia Beach where her father lived. Nothing would stop her. Domed lights lined the highway, each of them one-hundred and twenty-two steps from the other. She knew the next one was another forty steps. Tina hoisted her backpack up onto her shoulders, wishing she'd filled it with more than a couple of changes of clothes, and added a few dollars to her pockets. She'd make it work, though, the nearest road sign offering a respite, a place for her to get warm before she continued.

She wiped her eyes, reading, "Rest Stop Next Right Five Miles."

Her heart sank. Five miles might as well have been one hundred. From her pockets, she uncovered her hand, the freezing air slicing her fingers. She made a fist and held out her thumb and practiced hitching it over her shoulder like she'd seen hitchhikers do in the movies and on television.

A car drove by, brake lights flashing, her heart walloping with the promise of getting off her feet, of sitting in a warm seat. Cloudy puffs of car exhaust spewed from the tail pipe, the noxious fumes sticking in the back of her throat, the idea of hitching rides feeling suddenly wrong.

When the passenger window lowered and a woman's dark brown eyes showed in the mirror, Tina saw a person appear in the rear seat, a gloomy shadow, the sight of it frightening her and changing her mind. She waved at the car, recalling a story about a woman and man luring young girls into their vehicle, and then feeding them drugs before trafficking them for sex. Tina waved her hand and backed away.

"Suit yourself!" the woman yelled, the passenger window gliding up as the tires peeled a layer of ash-colored slush.

Alone again, Tina tucked her hand into her pocket, a shiver holding her hostage. She shrugged her shoulders forward, taking the first of the steps that'd lead her to the rest stop. "Suit yourself," she said with teary sarcasm, the regret laboring in the cold, making her rethink her status. Was it more dangerous to stay outside or dare the safety of a stranger's car?

It was at least three miles before another car slowed, a truck this time, the height of it eclipsing the sedans and coupes which had been the popular fare traveling this stretch of road. The truck slowed until it was crawling, its tires crunching, the slush freezing as the night grew long and the temperatures fell. By now, Tina worried she wouldn't survive. Her fingers and toes were riddled with pins and needles. They'd find her half frozen to death, a picture of her on the morning news, legs and arms wrapped in gauzy bandaging, the headlines reading *snow-covered teenager in critical condition—amputations unavoidable.* She glanced at her hands, the tips of her fingers having turned oddly white, even in the orange cast by the streetlights.

"Looking for a lift?" a man asked from inside the truck's cab.

She said nothing, the window above her head and too far for her to see. "Wha—", she tried saying, her lips and cheeks stuck in place. Desperation played in her head, the warnings of being cautious easing.

"I said, you looking for a lift?" the driver asked again, the top of his bald head showing through the window's opening. She saw him then, his face round, cheeks plump, a heavy white beard that gave him a festive, holiday look. The man's eyes were a warm hazel color and recessed beneath bushy eyebrows. Tina didn't feel a threat like she did with the other car but remained careful. From the cab, a touch of heat reached her. The cozy smell of food came with it, her stomach growling. She glanced at the driver and then to her tattered sneakers, cringing at the thought of the miles remaining to the rest stop. Tina said nothing, her mother's voice sounding alarms in her

The Crying House

head about strangers—the words spoken a million times since she was old enough to understand them. *But the cold.*

The man must have sensed her reluctance, his continuing, "It's okay. I'm one of the good ones."

"I'm headed to Virginia Beach," she said, her mouth stuck. She pegged her foot behind one leg, her toes absent. She contemplated the offer, inching closer to the truck's radiating heat. "Would you be heading in that direction?"

"The Outer Banks," he answered, leaning close enough to peer down. His gaze drifted from her head to her feet and fixed on her shoes. "Listen, the temperature is dropping fast. It's only going to get colder and too dangerous to be out here, let alone walking. I can take you part of the way."

"Could we stop at the rest stop?" she asked, struggling to lift her arm and point down the road. "I think it's about two miles ahead." Anticipating heat, Tina moved toward the cab.

The driver agreed, his saying, "Sure, the rest stop it is. I gotta hit the head anyway."

The truck's passenger door opened, warm air gushing and wrapping around her like a warm blanket. The driver's hand appeared, pale fingers dancing in the dark, offering to help her. Tina's feet clumsily found the places to step as she climbed inside of the cab. When she was in the seat, she stayed still a moment and let the warm air from the vents wash over her. The cab's console was different than expected, the dash looking like a video game with computer panels perched beneath the windshield and behind the largest steering wheel she'd ever seen.

"You want to get the door?"

"Yeah, certainly," she answered, catching herself staring. When Tina closed the door, she was out of the cold but shook nonetheless.

"You'll warm soon," he said, shifting gears, the truck bucking as it went from first into second and then to third.

Her eyes closed, the harsh ache riddling her body fading, she drifted cozily into the path of hot air pouring from the vents, warming her head and face and feet. "That feels good."

"Another minute and you'll forget all about the cold," he said, turning knobs to the right and cranking the thermostat.

Tina's stomach let out a growl and she braced her middle, the sound embarrassing. The driver heard it. Tina tried covering it up with small talk. "How long before we get there?"

"Well, it's more than two miles. It's at least four by my count," he answered, working the shifter, his knee bouncing on the clutch pedal. "Chicken soup?"

"What's that?" Tina asked, realizing she'd only walked another mile. She looked outside, falling snow flying sideways and ticking against the window's glass. There was a foot of it plowed and piled against the side of the road. She wouldn't have made it. Not four more miles. Not even one. Her stomach growled again, the pit of it empty and gnawing her. "Soup?"

"The red thermos next to the console. The big one," he offered, Tina following his hand, his finger pointing to it without his eyes leaving the road. "Do you see it?"

"I got it. Are you sure?" she asked, the outside of the canister warm to the touch. Tina held it between her hands. "I don't want to put you out."

"Nah. Go for it. I can grab a burger at the rest stop," he said. He turned and eyed her a moment, looking up and down. Jokingly, he patted his gut, a noticeable paunch between the seatbelt straps. "You look like you can use it a heck more than me."

"Thank you," she said. And without hesitation, Tina unscrewed the thermos cap, steam rising onto her face; the smell of chicken soup bringing warm memories of a family she had once, long ago: her mother and father who liked to cook together on Sunday afternoons while she and her little brother played on the floor in front of the television set. The broth was still hot, the taste salty, her hunger overwhelming as she drank a mouthful and felt it warm in her chest as noodles slid down her throat.

"I hope you like it," the driver said with a smile that reminded her of a favorite uncle. "I made it myself."

"It's good," she said, gazing through the window where another hitchhiker struggled to take a step, his legs sunken to the knees, his feet disappearing inside a mound of packed snow. Like her, his clothes were thin and hung loose, a hooded gray sweatshirt barely covering his head. For a moment she thought to tell the driver to stop, to let one more inside with them and to share in the warm ride and the delicious soup. But there was only room for two and she had to be selfish. She couldn't go outside again. Tina raised her hand as if waving goodbye to an old friend, a fleeting moment of guilt passing like the snowflakes falling between them. The boy waved in return, Tina turning away and facing forward, her belly warming and her hands cradling the thermos.

It was the last time anyone ever saw Tina Sommers alive.

CHAPTER TWO

Pink. Not just pink though. Whatever it was, it seemed to glow fluorescent as sunlight peeled the dark from the morning horizon. *A jacket?* I thought, believing I was alone in entering the last of a five-mile jog. Sweat teemed on my skin, and an autumn chill nipped the air while I hurried to close the distance to a goal I'd been after for more than a month. Eyeing the coastline through a salty mist as it curved into the sea, my sight reached a group of abandoned houses that marked the end of my run. Beneath one of them, a bright pink flag waved as though someone knew I might reach it today and had set it there as a finish line for me to cross.

"I'll make it," I said, blowing out the words with a huff. I thought of who might have put it there, how sweet the gesture and how I couldn't wait to thank him. In the weeks since I'd ventured out before daybreak, this was the furthest I'd gotten. Waves lashed at the beach, the surf tumbling and erasing the footsteps that had been there before mine. I pushed harder, faster, my sneakers planting wet kisses as sea foam raced by me. "Today, I'll make it."

A stitch ticked inside, halting my stride briefly. When I tried to run through it, a spasm struck, the bite warning me to slow down. A doctor's voice rang in my head with nagging disappointment. I stopped to catch my breath. Walloping drumbeats thumped in my chest hard enough to feel in the pit of my throat. The doctors had been adamant in their instructions for me to take it slow, telling me that it might be as long as six months to a year before I'd feel the way I did before, feel like I had before my life was nearly cut short.

I took to my knee, the wet touching me with a chill. The fall season had settled on the east coast, the summer already a memory. While the seasons may have changed, the impact of the summer would be with me for some time. It'd be with all of us. Another chill raced through me. But this one rose out of a dark memory.

Inhaling through my nose, I slowly let the air out of my mouth, timing it to the breaking waves until the ache in my chest eased. A northeasterly wind blew through me; the swells growing—the tips of them frothy white as they folded and collapsed in a foamy tumble. Goosebumps bloomed on my bare arms, and I started running again, trying to catch my earlier pace.

The sky brightened with heaping clouds, their edges crisp and blazing with warm colors. I eyed my finish line, the flag. Or was it a jacket? My curiosity was roused. Finding anything around the abandoned houses was odd since I didn't expect to see anyone for miles. I could feel a smile, knowing I wouldn't be able to help myself. I'd have to investigate. It had been almost two months since I'd investigated anything. A best-case scenario here was that I'd put my detective skills to work and solve a lost-and-found mystery.

The closer I got, the scarier the houses looked. The beach was sharply crooked, which put the sun behind some of them, their silhouettes casting ominous shadows; the shape frightful like giants that had been stilled by the night. I was sure if I stared long enough, I'd see one of them move.

Originally from Philadelphia, I call the Outer Banks my home these days. Cut by an inlet of the Atlantic, the narrow chain of barrier islands stretches along the coast of North Carolina. Famous for its beaches, marshlands, and wildlife reserves, and an endless number of wading birds, this is also home to the sloping golden sands of Big Kill Devil Hill where two brothers made their historical first powered flight.

There are the lighthouses too, reaching for the skies above the shoreline. They're a huge attraction when the population explodes in the early summer months. But when the seasons change, the lighthouses empty, and the ferries and bridges grow thick with traffic for the annual pilgrimage west to the mainland. For me, this is home regardless of the temperatures or the time of year, and I couldn't imagine living anywhere else. I've come to enjoy the colder months, the quieter months, the island's beauty shining through unencumbered.

A gale pushed me sideways as I continued on toward the abandoned house above it. When I'd first arrived in the Outer Banks, I'd asked a Marine Patrol major, Jericho Flynn, about the vacation homes. He'd shared how they'd once been like crown jewels, stilted beach palaces for the rich. He'd also talked of the millions some of them cost, and about the sea levels rising, the beach erosion, and the increasingly violent storms. He'd said that seemingly overnight, the tides reclaimed the houses, and that meant everything was gone, including the white picket fences.

I'd only seen pictures when the homes were in their prime. And to see them now showed that it didn't matter how big or how fancy they had once been. The sea showed no mercy. It didn't discriminate. The pilings that supported the structures did survive though. For now, anyway. The thick stilts were driven deep into the beach, some of them paired together for additional support. But they were showing signs of wear; the tides lashing twice a day, every day, causing them to lean derelict with the threat of toppling.

Breathless, my heart pounding, my ears ringing, and my brow drippy wet, I reached the first of the houses and doubled over to

The Crying House 19

heave. I felt terrible and wonderful at the same time—the great contradiction of exercising. I was winded and sick inside and out, but I'd reached my goal and that's what mattered. The hot pink color turned out to be a jacket after all, and I tagged one of the sleeves like it was a streamer dangling over a finish line. I raised my arms in a quiet celebration for an audience of one: a lone seagull hovering above a sand dune and swaying sea oats nearby.

I'd show those doctors a thing or two and prove them wrong, prove to them I could return to working full-time sooner than expected. A thought came to call Jericho, my wanting to hear his voice and to celebrate with me. The two of us had become a couple soon after our first meeting. And in my time living here, he'd become the closest person in my life. He was my soulmate. The love of my life. Being a detective in the Outer Banks, it also helped that he was a major in the Marine Patrol too. There was a time when he'd also been the sheriff, which has opened more doors than I can count.

I read my phone's screen, itching to share my great news. The signal bars blipped on and off, the screen warning of a poor signal. I was out of cell range. I scanned the area, another pair of seagulls gliding effortlessly above the tall grasses and the dunes. A gust blew through me, the jacket flapping, loose boards rattling. No phone company was ever going to put a cell tower all the way out here. Not without a few residents. I'd have to wait, my celebration staying with me for now.

I took to one of the pilings and leaned against it with my shoulder, resting where the sunlight had warmed the wood. My attention shifted to the jacket. It was clean and new and not at all something anyone would have left behind unless it was by accident. I lifted it from the bottom, a sea breeze ballooning the insides. Beneath the collar, I saw the jacket had been hung. It wasn't here by chance. An errant wind hadn't caught hold and cast it a mile or more like a kite, loose fabric snagging a chunk of splintered wood. The jacket was placed here.

Around my feet, I found evidence of a party: a gathering of sunken beer cans and empty bottles labeled *hard lemonade*. Teens perhaps? High school kids probably, kids without a place to go and finding privacy in the deserted properties. I recognized the place for what it was, having been young once, my friends and I using a small patch of woods with rutted dirt paths and a trickling creek that swelled with stained water whenever it rained. We called it the clump, and it was nestled between our homes and a nearby shopping center. The clump was where we'd spend Friday nights, blowing off the school week, playing tunes from a handheld radio with a wire hanger for an antenna. We danced and smoked cigarettes and drank warm beers that tasted terrible but made us feel like rock stars.

What we didn't have in the clump were empty houses, leading me to think that who'd ever left the jacket behind might still be here. They might be inside. Today was early Saturday morning, the first days of October, and the kids had been back in school for the new year for the last month. Friday night lights had brightened the high school stadiums yesterday for their season opening football games. The timing was right for a party.

Would someone go inside though? I gazed at the underside of the house, the lumber black and green, stained by the sea and years of exposure. Standing three stories high, there was no siding or roofing tiles anymore: the wind ripping away the vinyl and plastic and asphalt shingles years before, the ocean gobbling every bit of it. I peered around the side, the windows open cavities, black holes; the sight of them giving me pause as though I'd just approached a haunted house on All Hallows' Eve.

Stepping around the litter, deciding to look inside, I stopped dead when I saw it. On the third piling to the left of the pink jacket, stray hairs dangled loose, anchored in the wood. And beneath them, a thick swath of blood.

The hairs were nestled between splinters, a tangle of chestnut-colored hairs that lifted and fell with a breeze. On the ends I saw tissue, the hairs having been ripped from someone's scalp. High on the piling, and facing away from the ocean, they'd been preserved, the blood dried by an endless sea breeze. But for how long? How long would they last?

In my career, I'd learned to recognize when a scene showed signs of an accident and when it was a crime. I glanced over my shoulder at the pink jacket, and then again at the blood and hair. An assault had occurred here. The possibility of a confrontation was whispered to me on a breeze. This was evidence I'd found. This was a crime scene.

CHAPTER THREE

The blood, hair and bright pink jacket spun up a thousand questions. This was the last place on earth I'd expected to find anything, especially with the waves breaking yards away. The site was both surreal and morbid and had me searching the beaches for anything that strayed from normal. I found nothing. What about inside the house?

When I was certain there was nobody else around, I began to take pictures, moving fast to preserve the scene as it was before going into the house. Like I said, I wasn't one-hundred percent sure what I had yet, but I had to investigate. A part of me hoped it would turn out to be nothing at all, my imagination gone wild. Yet, there was also a part of me that wanted a new case, craved for a new case the way I craved a sugar rush. That way I could show everyone I was better now, better than before.

Out of habit and fearful reservation, I ran the tip of my finger over the scar on my arm. It had been put there by a notorious serial killer, her driving a prison shiv deep enough to sever vessels and nerves. I'd almost bled to death but had survived the attack. The real damage she'd inflicted was what she'd set into motion: a series of events that would disrupt our lives like a hundred mile an hour train wreck. The scarring left behind was raised and shiny and fired tingles up and down my arm whenever I touched it. The doctors said the scar would eventually fade. I could only hope. While it had been almost two months, I still felt her doings every waking moment.

I shook it off, reminding myself of a promise to get back into form. Reframing the scene with my phone's camera, I flipped on the flash, the light beneath the house broken between daylight and shadow. I took another series of pictures and saw the blood was glistening as sharp light bounced from the patch. It wasn't as dry as I'd initially thought, and I had nothing with me to collect and save it. If this was a crime scene, then I needed to get a team out here fast. But first I had to assess what it was I'd found. The last thing I wanted to do was cry wolf on my return to being a full-time detective. A detective crying wolf was apt to get demoted. I couldn't step back at this point in my career. It was forward or it was nothing at all.

With my notes app, I jotted down the vitals, including the remains of alcoholic beverages strewn beneath the house, a description of the hair and the blood, along with the time of day and the location. With the location of the hair, I noted the possible height as well, which was at least a head above mine, close to five foot ten, possibly six feet. Tall and maybe female, based on the type of jacket and the looks of the clumped hair. I typed *long wavy strands with a chestnut color*. Unlike the blood, the hair wasn't going anywhere. The patch of it was stuck deep in a crevice of splinters.

With the cold air, I'd brought gloves and put them on, wanting to explore the pink jacket. In the jacket, I found nothing except that it was clean, and the fabric appeared to be dry. That told me the time of the incident may have been late last night or hours before I'd set out for my run. Any later and the change in tide, the sea spray would have dampened the jacket and possibly erased the bloodstains. As I moved toward and under the house, above me there was a hole in the floorboards, a large gap where there'd once been a staircase, my standing in what was likely a carport, the driveway gone, its gravel swallowed by the sea like Tic Tacs. My phone showed the cell service's bars flickering between low and none, the signal strength continuing to be abysmal. I had to go inside, but hesitated, knowing I shouldn't go it alone. I couldn't make a call even if I tried though, and what if someone was hurt? I could help them. Maybe they'd left the jacket behind on purpose, going inside to stay dry?

With my phone secured, I found a makeshift ladder beneath the hole—loose boards that had been nailed into place—each step a wobbly exercise, my balance slipping as the nails screeched and the wood shifted against my weight. Easing up into darkness, I found a rope tied off to a wall stud and hoisted myself, climbing into the house.

Inside, I was met with a musty smell joined by sour beer and urine, the odors overwhelming and making me gag. The view was gray as though a thick veil had been dropped in front of my face. I squeezed my eyelids and then opened them wide. I didn't move again until my sight adjusted enough that I could see in the dim light.

I'd entered the lower level, the sound of the ocean bouncing in the empty room, the walls clear of plasterboard. There was sharp light bleeding through the wall's seams as ocean winds rustled the house. Anything of value had been ripped out and taken, leaving behind a shell. From the looks of the room, I'd climbed into what was once the kitchen where granite counters had been, their sturdy perches still in place but empty of the expensive stone. On the floor, a scatter of cans and bottles, some newer and strewn amongst the old. Shelves built into the wall held thick cream-colored candles, their wicks gone, the wax melted and draping in long sculpted curves that hung over the lip like old curtains. This was definitely a place where the kids came to party, and it was a big step up from the clump I'd spent time in years ago.

Blades of sunlight filtered through the empty windows, dust shimmering in their path, the house's frame sighing noisily with each wind strike. When I felt the movement, I squatted instinctively, bracing for a fall. None came, though, and I made my way into a dining room, the ceilings vaulted, the daylight shining on unopened cases: a stash of alcohol for future parties. I searched the floors, using my phone's light where the sunlight couldn't reach. I found more mildew, my foot sinking where the floor felt soft and spongey, rot eating at the house like a slow-growing cancer. It wouldn't be long before it collapsed and got carried away by the waves, like Jericho had said.

In the living room, the ceilings were two stories above me with a gaping hole where a window had faced the ocean. The sun ducked behind a patch of clouds and draped the room in shadow, forcing me to rely on my phone's light. Across from me was an old fireplace—the brick and mortar pitted and crumbly like powder; the mantle and decorative surround in a lean with paint flaking and stirring. The firebox inside was stacked with dozens of candles, a parade of them arranged in rows, some newer and full, but most spent or half spent with mounds of wax drippings beneath. The hearth was covered with candles too, the used wax hardened and hanging off the edge.

When the sun reappeared, the clouds lumbering west, the window was like a light box and showed every inch of the room. My heart shot into my throat when I saw the body.

CHAPTER FOUR

A blade of golden light shone directly on her face, illuminating her wavy hair—the same color as I'd found in the patch of blood. There was a deep gash on her head, close to her hairline, which ran ragged. Her chest wasn't moving, and I pressed my fingers to her neck, my hopes of finding life were gone. Deep disappointment reared its ugly head. I sat back on my heels, knowing from the feel of her skin that she was dead. I lifted my fingers, rubbing my thumb and forefinger, the touch undeniable; she'd been dead for at least a few hours. Having been fooled once before, I put my ear to her mouth, and concentrated on hearing, maybe feeling a shallow breath. But this was death.

With the injury to the girl's head, I jumped back to my feet and listened carefully to what the house had to tell me. If someone was responsible, they were likely long gone by now. Winds battered the eastern walls, the house moaning, the rusting nails whispering up and down the stairs and through the halls. I only heard the voices the house spoke and heard none of the words a killer might say to me. I was alone. Satisfied, I returned to the body with my phone in hand.

The girl was tall, the location of the injury confirming the height of the blood and hair on the piling. She was in her mid-teens, naturally pretty and wearing some makeup on her eyes and lips. She wore a windbreaker jacket, but this one was a navy-blue color and a different brand than the pink one. Her jeans were a faded denim and had a tear in the knees, but not like the designer jeans with the rips and tears I see kids wearing these days. This rip wasn't intentional. It was from whatever happened outside. The gash on the side of her head was an inch long, the opening clotted, dry like the blood on her shirt collar. I found no other blood though. There was none on her neck, or on her face. A wound that deep would have bled heavily. Someone had cleaned the blood.

Her color was sheet gray, though she wasn't entirely cold to the touch yet. She wasn't warm either. Her skin had that papery feel though. The kind that only the dead have. I looked at my phone, hoping for a signal, hoping the height of the house's first level would help bring me in range of a cell tower. I was in luck, finding one bar that gave me a wink whenever I moved left to right. I had a body and couldn't proceed until I had a crew out here to process the scene.

I got to my feet, giving myself a moment, my heart racing, the bitter taste of adrenaline in my mouth. There were stairs leading to a second floor, the wood rotten, my weight causing it to sag, threatening to drop me onto the beach below. I stepped up on the hearth instead, gaining a foot of height to help me get a signal to my phone.

"Hello?"

"Dr. Swales?" I said, asking, her tone hesitant. She might not have had my number in her contacts. "It's Casey White."

"Casey!" she replied. "What a treat. It's early, dear. What can I do for you?"

"I'm sending you a text with coordinates."

"Coordinates. Is this a treasure hunt?" she joked.

I glanced around at the abandoned house, a touch of disbelief coming, considering where the day had taken me. "Doctor. It's a body. Female, adolescent. Could be an accident; but could be murder."

"Are you safe!?" she asked, raising her voice to a shout. "Casey?"

I tensed, hearing her guarding voice, the concern in it. I'd been through the one level, as well as beneath the house. But I hadn't been upstairs. "There's a second floor. It hasn't been secured. But I believe I am alone."

"I have the text." I heard her cup the phone's mouthpiece and yell in a southern twang, relaying my coordinates to her assistant Derek. "Hang tight. We'll come to you."

"My cell connection is bad. Can you call Jericho for me?" I asked. With the beach location, the house on the beach sitting in the water half the time, this could be in the Marine Patrol's jurisdiction. "I'm inside one of the abandoned houses."

"Marine Patrol and locals, along with my team. I'll make all the calls." I heard the mouthpiece shuffling again as she relayed more instructions. "Casey, you're okay?"

"I'm fine," I said, assuring her. It was sweet that she worried. "But please hurry."

"Keep your phone where it can get a signal," Swales said and then hung up.

I did as she suggested, putting my phone on the mantle, propping it between two candles, the signal strength ticking another notch for some improvement. I returned to the body, kneeling next to the girl, her eyes closed, a peaceful look on her face. This was the hard part. The waiting. The teams would be here soon, though, and when they arrived, we'd process the body with rigor and formality.

Until then, I could do nothing except keep her company. It wasn't the first time I'd kept the dead company. I'm sure it wouldn't be my last either. I resisted the urge to touch her, to begin my investigation as my head began to fill with questions. An undertone of sadness rose like the tide. Who was this girl? What happened to her outside? Did somebody want her dead? And the jacket? She had a blue jacket. Had her killer worn the bright pink one?

CHAPTER FIVE

Seagulls called noisily and boots sloshed in the water as Jericho yelled over the breaking waves while steering the Marine Patrol boat onto the shore. Along with his partner, they were first to arrive, the boat's motors throttling down as they secured the bow. The sun had reached mid-morning and the clouds that had clung to the coastline moved on and brought daylight into the rooms. In the endless drift of salt air, the autumn season was carried. There was the scent of leaves piled on lawns and wood burning in a fireplace. It was one season ending and another beginning. There was the touch of warm and cold air brushing my cheek too, a subtle warning that winter was coming soon.

"Over here!" I shouted to the men who were dressed for the colder air and for the trek over the ocean. They were plump with cushy jackets and pants, a dry suit, the Marine Patrol protective gear that swished whenever they moved. I watched as they approached, their hands carrying flashlights, my texts to the team including a message to bring them. With the shuffle of feet in the sand, I lowered myself and waved an arm for them to see me. "Can you see me?"

"Got ya!" Jericho shouted, grabbing my fingers abruptly and giving them a tug. "Don't fall."

"You!" I yelled, jerking my arm as my balance tipped. "Always trying to scare me."

"It's fun," he said, appearing beneath me, my phone's light shining on his upturned face. His expression turned serious when looking at the pilings. Brushing the whiskers on his chin, a frown formed around his blue-green eyes. "This structure doesn't have much time left."

"You think it'll collapse soon?" I asked, tensing with concern for our safety.

"It won't be today," he answered. He shook his head, his salt-and-pepper hair hanging limp beneath his Marine Patrol hat. He'd let it grow long the past couple of months, the look taking a few years from his age. He butted one of the beer cans with the tip of his shoe, adding, "If there are kids coming here frequently, we have a safety issue."

"One is still inside," I said and motioned to the wood boards used as ladder rungs. Jericho gripped a board, twisting his wrist once, freeing the board with ease, the nails losing their hold. I shrugged, saying, "It was strong enough to hold me."

"Well, you're as light as a feather," he said, tossing it to the ground. "Stand clear."

I did as Jericho said, making room at the opening. With a single leap, his fingers appeared on the floor's edge, their tips white. The top of his head appeared next, his face red and veins on his neck like swollen rivers. He let out a gruff breath, straining as he hoisted himself inside. I grabbed the back of his safety vest and pulled, his body sliding forward until he was next to me.

"You okay?" I asked, rubbing his back while he stayed on all fours.

"That used to be a lot easier," he said, winded. "It's the gear I'm wearing."

"Yeah," I agreed, nudging his middle and mocking, "Probably the gear."

"Funny."

"Listen, we've got a team coming." The humor gone, I had to figure out the logistics of the scene so we could process it. "They can't all climb up here like you did."

"I'll have a ladder set up for them," he answered, standing up to face the opening. "Tony?"

"Already on it, boss," his partner yelled, having heard us. The sound of a car approached, his attention shifting. "Looks like the medical examiner is here."

There were footsteps then, the marine patrolman leaving. I heard car doors opening and closing, and the chatter of Dr. Swales discussing some procedure with her assistant. We were alone and I went to Jericho's side, his putting his hand on mine. I felt him staring and took advantage of the moment, laying my head against his shoulder.

"Not the morning you expected?" he asked.

"Well, I made my running goal," I told him, lifting a celebratory hand in the air in contrast to the sadness I felt inside about the young girl lying dead.

"I'm really proud of you, Casey." His lips brushed my forehead with a kiss. He lowered his eyes to meet mine, a warning in them. "But please don't push too hard. The doctors—"

"I know what they said." Suddenly feeling sensitive about it, I covered the scar on my arm, and asked, "Just support me. Okay?"

I brushed his cheek softly. He cupped his fingers over mine, closing his eyes. "I will."

"Tell you what," I said, nudging him until he was looking at me again. "When we're done here, you can drive me home."

"Are you looking for a boat ride?" His face lit up, knowing how much I liked the speed of the boat, especially when there was wind driving whitecaps. I nodded eagerly. "You got it."

"When you two are done chit-chatting, would you mind helping an old woman?" Dr. Swales yelled impatiently, her voice rising and falling with a southern twang.

"Hey there," I said, peering down. She was small, but from where I was, she looked absolutely tiny. It might have been the winter wear:

an enormously poofy coat with rolls, and her head tucked inside an oversized wool hat.

"Hey yourself," she said, rocking back and forth, teeth chattering. "I'm cold and I'm cranky."

"It's not much warmer inside," I warned as Jericho's partner threw up a rope. We took hold of the ends and strung them through the framing where the granite counters had been installed. With a few seaman knots and some cleverly woven connections, the rope held securely.

"Tony, thread the wood planks to make ladder rungs," Jericho instructed.

"Got it," he answered.

Minutes later, I held Dr. Swales's hand and arm, guiding her inside while Tony stabilized the ladder.

"I can't seem to get warm." Her breath was shaky, her body shivering. Instinctively, I put my arms around her, thinking she wouldn't mind. "I guess it's all part of the experience."

"Experience?" I asked.

She shifted her wool cap, tufts of frizzy hair covering her ears, her glasses fogging. "Age, my dear. It's all part of the experience of getting old."

"Oh." I understood, and then countered, "You're not old."

She looked to Jericho, head nodding, "Sometimes I feel as old as the earth." She gazed at the walls and floor, taking in the sight, her expression grim. "Now, the reason we are here. I understand you have a body?"

"I do," I said, confirming and took hold of her backpack, a sea-green denim with yellow initials, M.E., embroidered on the outside. I tipped sideways, the weight of her gear nearly pulling my arm out of its socket. "Follow me and be careful. Some of the flooring isn't secure."

"You take the lead," she said, getting behind me. "I'd think we both want to get through this without injury."

When we were settled, Dr. Swales prepared her place next to the body as though it was a station at the morgue. She opened her backpack and placed her equipment neatly in a row, handing me a pair of latex gloves, our sleeving them on together and snapping the wrists in unison. There was focus and concentration on the scene.

Heavy footsteps paraded to and from the body, members of the police securing the sight with the help of Emanuel Wilson from my team. He towered over the others, his size giving me worry. Emanuel had once been a professional basketball player, and was a detective these days, working with me in the Outer Banks. With his height and weight, I didn't want to risk his falling though the floor. Jericho noticed, caught what was concerning me and gave me an indiscreet nod, telling me we were okay.

"How's your wife?" Swales asked as we got started, her question catching Emanuel's attention. "And the baby?"

"Resting and well." He looked uncomfortable a moment and glanced at me before continuing. "They're home now, thanks for asking."

"I'm so happy for you guys," I said with a smile. We were silent then, their trading eyes that were sad and familiar.

Jericho and I had lost a baby recently. An unexpected pregnancy. When the moment edged on unbearable, I assured them I wasn't fragile, that I was fine. "Listen, if you guys ever need a babysitter, you can call on us."

"Sure, I will." There was a look of elation, of relief. "We'll definitely take you up on the offer. Thank you."

"Now, let's see what we see," I said, turning our attention back to the girl.

"Any evidence of foul play?" he asked, his voice a deep baritone. Unlike Swales and I, beads of sweat sat on his upper lip and at the ridge of his dark hairline. He held open a glove, blowing into it, the fingers inflating.

"There's blood on the piling below," I answered. "A head wound that could have been accidental, but we can't rule out assault."

"The piling. I saw that. I can process it while you guys work here?"

"Yes. Do that," I said, agreeing.

Dr. Swales shined a penlight into the wound, studying it, and saying, "There could be splinters here which will support the find outside."

"And this," I said, lifting the girl's left hand, the knuckles with abrasions and bruising. "Evidence of assault, that she fought back."

A patrol officer approached, jerking the front of his coat closed. "Pink jacket outside?"

"I think it was left there," I answered. "Considering the trash around here, the owner might have been drunk and forgot it."

"And the rest of the house?"

"I haven't gone beyond this room," I answered.

The patrolman's radio squelched as he triggered the microphone and spoke into it, giving instructions to search the remainder of the house.

"Poor thing," Dr. Swales commented, pulling my attention. There was sadness on her face which was out of character for her. I'd worked with Dr. Swales since first arriving to the Outer Banks, and she'd always been stoic and professional. Swales tore her wool hat from her head, a ball of frizzy grays appearing in a poof. Her brow lifted and her lips went pencil thin. She began to shake her head, mumbling, "I'm tired of it. Of this."

"Understandable," I said, uncertain of how to console. "You've put in more years than all of us combined."

"That I did," she answered, her eyes weepy. With a rattle in her sigh, she peered over her shoulder to see who was in the room with us. When she was sure we were alone, she turned back. "Listen Casey, I wanted to let you know that this is one of the last for me."

"What?" I sat back from the body, wanting to answer her with immediate objection. But I had heard a rumor about a retirement and didn't know who it was. Until now. I went with a canned response I'd heard others use. "No? You're too young."

She smirked and side-eyed me with a wink that sparked. "Dear, I was already old when the Outer Banks was young."

"Retirement?"

Swales ran her fingers through the girl's hair, prodding the scalp. "I've seen my share. It's time."

"I hate to see you go," I said, taking pictures of the girl's knuckles, finding the same bruising on the other hand.

Swinging her penlight, Swales lifted each eyelid, their color gray. "Pupils are normal in size."

"Are you thinking it's a brain bleed?" I asked.

Swales cocked her head. "Are you looking to replace me?"

"You know you're irreplaceable," I said. "If one of the pupils is larger, it might be from bleeding in the brain?"

"Correct." Swales turned the girl's head and shined the light on the injury. The wound showed thin splinters embedded at the edges. "This appears to be superficial. I'll know more when we perform the autopsy."

"Did you set a date?" I asked, a dull ache in me, hating the idea of this job without her around.

"Not yet. I think I'll take it case by case." She motioned for help to roll the body. "Let's see what we've got on the other side."

I reached across the body, taking a firm hold of the shoulder, saying, "Lift."

Rigor mortis had set in, the body sounding with the tell-tale signs, and stiff like a board. While I held her in place, Swales examined the neck and spine, lifting the jacket and shirt to note anything outstanding. A more thorough autopsy would be scheduled before the body was transported. "Looks like we're clear back here."

Before lowering the girl, I searched her back pocket, having seen an outline on her jeans. From it, I pulled four cards that were seated together. We lowered the body to read the cards, finding one to be a debit card—the bank a local branch name I recognized. There was also a driver's license and two school IDs.

"Her name is Jocelyn Winter," I announced to the room, turning heads, seeing recognition sweep across those working the scene as a name was put to the face of the victim. "She lives on the west side of the island, and she is seventeen years old."

"Her poor mother and father." Swales shook her head and made a tsk-tsk sound. "Too young. Hadn't gotten a chance to live yet."

Jericho knelt next to me. "High school IDs?" He took one of them, the header reading, *East OBX High School*.

"Why are there two school IDs?" I asked, confused. The second high school ID showed her picture and all the same information, but it was for *West OBX High School*. "I don't understand."

"I think I can explain," Jericho answered. "West High was flooded early last year."

"It was lost like these houses," Swales added. "The township attempted a cleanup, but there was too much damage, and significant erosion was discovered in the foundation."

"So the building was condemned?" I asked. "What happened to the students?"

"East High is their sister school," Jericho continued.

"And major football rival," Swales added.

"The school is on higher ground on the other side of town."

"They combined the schools," I said, my mind already picking up on what they said. "A rivalry, you said?"

"For as long as the schools existed," Dr. Swales answered. She looked the girl up and down, continuing, "A friendly rivalry, but I can't imagine it coming to this." A puzzled look fell over her face. "That's not what you're thinking? Is it?"

I took the high school IDs and placed them in an evidence bag. "Who knows what went on inside the school once the students were thrown together. Their rivalry might have traveled the classrooms and hallways."

"Terrible if that's it," Swales said.

I searched the girl's other pockets, moving the body for the access. "Help me here."

"I got it," Jericho said as he and Swales obliged, shifting the girl enough for me to double and triple check every pocket again. When I was done, I sat back, dumbfounded. "What are you looking for?"

"It's missing," I said, voice muted while I scanned the floors and fireplace.

"What's missing?" Jericho and Swales asked in near unison.

"The girl's cell phone." I expected to find one, the outline printed in the girl's jeans telling me it couldn't be far. When I couldn't find it, I texted Nichelle with instructions to start digging into the girl's cell phone location.

A shuffle of footfalls came from the floors above, a commotion alarming us, the house rattling, the ceiling overhead threatening with a sprinkle of debris. Jericho bolted to his feet, yelling up the stairs, "Everyone okay?"

"Detective!?" the officer shouted down the stairwell, his shadow cast on the wall. "You there?"

"I'm here," I yelled.

"I think we've got a second body up here," he said, his voice breaking.

"Think?" Dr. Swales asked, raising her voice, annoyed. "Male? Female? Adolescent?"

"I… I don't know, ma'am?!"

My gaze shifted from Swales to Jericho and then toward the stairs.

"I've never seen anything like it before."

CHAPTER SIX

Swales's assistant and another from her staff took custody of the teen's body; a zipper closing as they secured Jocelyn Winter in a black body bag before carrying her out of the abandoned house and to the morgue. I had my doubts about her death being a result of foul play. Then again, I'd been wrong before when assuming anything this early in an investigation. My initial thoughts were that this was probably a case of a school kid party that had spiraled out of control. Take some raging hormones, pour in alcohol, sprinkle teen angst, stir the pot, and poof. A few beers later, they'd dance a little harder, clap a little louder and fight a lot meaner.

At first glance, the injury to the girl's head might have seemed only skin deep; the fight ending; the partygoers moving indoors as the night grew long. But I suspected there may have been a deeper injury that caused her death. For now, we'd found everything we could at the scene. An autopsy was scheduled, Swales opting to stay with us, curious to see what the officers discovered on the upper levels. When prompted, they weren't certain it was a body. But they were quick to say they weren't certain it wasn't either.

Before the move upstairs, I had to take care of some logistics and called my station to touch base with Detective Cheryl Smithson, her conferencing in the sheriff and the district attorney. Nervously pinching the side of my jogging pants, Jericho noticed as he waited with Swales. A phone call shouldn't have put me on edge, but this one did. Any dealings with Cheryl Smithson put me on edge. She'd worked for me the last year and had been promoted to lead detective when I'd taken on the more pressing role of a recovering victim.

It was how Cheryl's promotion came to be that rubbed me the wrong way. She'd stooped low for gain, which came at the cost of others; namely, Jericho. I could never trust her again. As much as it pained me, the phone call had to be made. Jericho mimed a grin and encouraged me to do the same, motioning with his fingers, repeating until I finally reciprocated. He could be goofy like that, and I loved that he was.

When it was my turn to speak on the conference call, I explained the case of Jocelyn Winter, adding my assessment of it thus far. I went on to explain the investigation of the property, the possible discovery of a second body on the upper level. As the voices went back and forth, I noticed the plywood beneath my feet was sodden and mushy, any evidence of footprints absorbed into the grain like a sponge, impossible to recover. It was another strike on this case, adding to the complexities.

The discussion moved to who should lead the investigations. My stomach grew heavy, but an edge of competition tensed my muscles also, telling me to jump on it. Just as I was about to speak, Cheryl interrupted to tell us she'd traveled south to visit with family and was at least six hours away. Heaviness weighed on me while the sheriff and DA chatted amongst themselves, their voices a buzz in my ear, my phone warming due to the poor cell connection. They understood there was a gap in coverage. As they spoke, Cheryl also mentioned sending a new hire from her team to help. My brain tipped with surprise. I was more out of touch than I thought, not having heard the news about a new hire.

Ours was a small station and the number of staff and senior lead detectives was few. In fact, it was just one when considering I wasn't back to full-time yet. I'd submitted all my paperwork and had sign-off from the doctors. Every muscle in my body tensed as the sheriff and district attorney discussed and debated. I'd been itching to get back into my work, but with the itch there were nerves too.

Like riding a bicycle, I heard in my head. *Yeah right.*

"We'll need a lead on this case," the district attorney said.

"Casey?" the sheriff asked, letting out a heavy breath. "How are things?"

"Things?" I answered his question with a question. "You mean, how am I?"

"Are you getting your strength back?" he asked.

"If it helps, I finished a five-mile run this morning and have never felt better," I answered him, a slight lilt in my voice—a tell when I'm bending the truth. I'd finished, but the never feeling better part was a stretch.

"That's excellent to hear," the district attorney said. "It's great to hear you're doing well."

"Well enough to take the lead?" I asked, blurting the question without a thought, my competitive nature coming through.

"Give us a moment, Casey," the sheriff said, the discussion continuing without me.

After a minute of waiting and worrying the phone call was going to end abruptly, the DA and sheriff returned and opted for me to take the lead, officially restoring me to a full-time status. Maybe it was my competitiveness that won them over. Pride swelled in my chest as I gave Jericho a thumbs-up. In Cheryl's absence, they also requested I run the scene for the second body, if that's what it was upstairs. All findings would go to Cheryl for her to assess if there was a case. I agreed, a small knot in my throat making my voice hoarse. There was a flutter in my gut from the butterflies waking after their nap, but I was eager to get off the call and to get to work. I suddenly felt out of place, glancing around, realizing how I must look with my hair pulled back and wearing a jogging suit, a pair of running shoes that were months old and showed miles of wear.

It is what it is, I thought, and told myself I'd change the first chance I got.

I had more pressing things to worry about. There was a body upstairs. What else were we going to find? And while I was strong enough to return to the role I was meant for, I'd had no idea it was going to be today. I also had no idea the day would include facing anguished parents and telling them the news that no mother or father should ever have to hear. Later that day I would have to tell them their daughter Jocelyn had been found dead.

CHAPTER SEVEN

The stairs to the second floor gave us pause; the first four steps rotten enough for Jericho to insist we not use them. While the steps were shoddy, the hand railing held secure enough to the wall and stairwell for us to climb around the rot and to the fifth step.

"Feels sturdy," Jericho said, bouncing up and down next to me, the step groaning beneath us.

"Really?" I asked with a hard stare.

"What?" he muttered, extending his arm for Dr. Swales. "I was testing it."

Swales gave the path we climbed a look, her stature on the short side, which made her unable to reach us without help. When she saw Jericho's hand, she looked to me. "Mind holding him?"

"We have you," I said, taking hold of Jericho's jacket, squeezing until my grip hurt. He guided Swales up the side, nearly lifting her as she joked about being dropped and what the county would owe her in a settlement. "You're not going anywhere."

The remaining steps were noisy, the planks of wood dry and undamaged. The sun had climbed high, brightening the rooms, spilling daylight into the darkest corners, warming the house enough to put a bead of sweat on my upper lip. When we reached the second floor, Jericho took the lead, inspecting the boards, ensuring they were solid. I surveyed the hallway, the walls holding some of their original forms, the drywall surviving the elements, the trim finishings and the baseboards remaining intact. The door frames and crown moldings across the ceilings were also untouched.

"Clearly, the kids haven't been up here. If there was a party downstairs, I wonder why?" Swales asked, drinking in the details, mouth agape at the ornamental woodwork.

"The steps," I suggested. "If they were coming here at night, they'd only know the first handful of them were rotten."

"They assumed all of them were bad," Jericho went on to say. He gave us a brief look over his shoulder. "Whoever they were, it's good they weren't up here."

"Which room?" I asked a waiting patrolman; his leather belt creaking, his nylon jacket swooshing as he held his thumb upward and pointed.

"On the third floor."

"There's another flight?" Swales asked, breathing hard as she cleaned the fogged lenses of latent dust.

"The place gets better as you work your way up," he said, wiping his brow.

"Lead the way, officer."

I held my phone's light, shining it onto the floor before each step. The house let out a moan as though protesting us, the winds batting it, the lean seeming to get steeper as we climbed higher. I braced the walls when a gale rattled the roof, making me sway as though I was in a boardwalk funhouse. I reached in front of me, Jericho taking my fingers in his.

"You're sure we're safe? We're not going to topple into the sea?"

"This house isn't going anywhere." His voice came with a reassuring squeeze. The second stairwell was narrower and dark. He raised his voice then, "Dr. Swales, you okay back there?"

"Don't you fret or fuss about me," she said sharply. I looked behind me, seeing her pause while she gazed up at us with a weary look. "But I could use a hand to hold."

"You got it," I said, offering my other hand, the touch of her fingers soft, the three of us with our arms draped.

The third floor was a large attic with dormers cut into both sides of the roof. The glass windows were still in place, protecting the room from the elements, preserving what the officers found. The ceiling angled hard and pitched thirty degrees from center. The structure was bare wood and free of moisture and rot. With the daylight coming through the windows, I tucked my phone away, my attention fully caught by what the officers had found.

A sheet covered what appeared to be a body, the outline of it showing through the fabric. As they moved closer, there was an odor that reminded me of the sea, but it was different. Swales detected it too, her nose up, sniffing the air.

"Do you guys smell that?" she asked with a look of curiosity, the mystery of the find intriguing her.

"We noticed that," the patrolman said, his forearm draped in front of his face, the smell bothering him. It wasn't overpowering, but maybe it was the idea of a corpse, his taking the smell as a body decomposing.

"Salt?" I answered, uncertain. "But it can't be from the ocean. Not like that."

"I think it's coming from the body," the patrolman said, squinting.

Swales was first to approach, her nose staying in the air. "It's definitely a salt base. And correct. The smell is emanating from the body, if that's what we're looking at."

"Note the location," I said, Emanuel joining us, his taking short breaths as he ducked his head to clear the rafters. "Placement appears to be in the center of the room."

"Did you notice the position?" Jericho asked.

"Other than the middle?" Emanuel said, answering with a question—his head sweaty, brow gleaming.

I took a moment to see what Jericho saw, orienting myself parallel to the body, noting where the ocean was, along with the sun. "From head to toe, it's facing east to west," I said, taking to a knee, studying the find.

"Accurate to a degree," Jericho added, his phone in hand. "Same as my compass."

"So, what do we have here?" Swales said, kneeling next to me, next to what could have been remains of a mummy from a museum or a gag prop from a seasonal store. She took her glasses from her face to clean them again, the air more humid.

"Is it real?" I asked, still uncertain what we were looking at. Handing out gloves, I sleeved my fingers with latex, watching Swales and taking any cues from her. I'd run the scene but knew to give her as much allowance as she'd need. "Where do you want to start?"

"I'm not sure where to start." She held out her hands, assessing the scene and what was once a white bedsheet—the color dingy, possibly offering us a timeline if it'd been new when brought here. Not an inch of flesh showed, the wrapping meticulous, care taken. "The head," Swales answered, cocking her head.

"Let's first decide if this is a prank?" I suggested. "You know, maybe the older kids at the party telling the freshman tall-tales about a mummy upstairs."

"I never thought of that," the patrolman said. "Halloween's not so far away."

While the idea was sound, the sheet, the outline's shape—that told me this was real. "I've got my doubts though. Halloween or no Halloween."

"Me too. If it was some kind of joke, I'd think there'd be more here," Emanuel said, inspecting the attic's corners. I watched as he took to the floor, rubbing his hand over the plywood. He held up his fingers, showing them to me, and added, "If I didn't know any better, this place has been cleaned."

"Booties, if you don't already have them on your shoes," I said, tossing the box to one of the officers, thinking a forensic search of the room could pick up a stray hair or other evidence. He caught the box and took a pair before passing it along. "Emanuel, take note, we have a room that appears to have been cleaned and a body that's been preserved in a garment."

"Got it," he said, snapping the elastic around his ankle. "You're thinking ritual?"

I half committed to the idea with a nod. "Definitely some ceremony here."

"Till this morning, I'd thought I'd seen it all," Swales said, chin in hand, cradling her elbow. She moved to the other side of the body, lowering for a closer look. "Fascinating."

"What do you make of this?" I asked her; Emanuel taking a picture from over my shoulder. I ran my finger around the outline, the stain bleeding through the fabric. "It's like there's an impression."

Swales said nothing at first, pinching part of the stain, the blemish leaving pale residue on the tips of her gloves. "We'll need to perform an analysis, but that smell?" Carefully, she put her fingers to her nose. "It's from the sheet. It is salt. Highly concentrated."

"Does a decomposing body leave behind salt?" I asked, feeling sure it didn't considering all the crime scenes I'd witnessed, but thinking perhaps the way the body had been wrapped meant salts and bodily fluids would bleed into the sheet. "Could the sheet act as a kind of wick?"

"Not like this." Though she shook her head, I sensed she wasn't sure. "I think it's time for a peek beneath the cover to see what we've got here."

Together we each took a part of the sheet, feet shuffling around us, eyes fixed with intensity.

"Ease it back slowly," Swales said, her tone teacherly. "I don't want to chance altering the state of what's beneath."

Her words gave me pause, an image of peeling skin flashed in my mind, slowing my hand. "I'll follow your lead."

"Easy does it," she muttered, inching the sheet away, folding it carefully, revealing the top of the head. Swales gasped, her voice rising, "Would you look at that!"

"What the hell is it?!" the patrolman shouted, feet scuffling.

"I need calm," I said, but felt the same. It wasn't revulsion, or maybe it was. It was definitely shock.

"What happened to her, him... that person?" the patrolman continued, his skin waxy, his color paling.

"In all my years," Swales said. "I've never seen this."

"Emanuel, get this," I said, holding the sheet in place.

His arms inched between me and the doctor, his phone in place to take a close-up picture of the face, its state like something out of a horror show. "Is... is it real?"

"I'm sure it's real. Presumed female with long hair, color is light blonde," I announced, thinking her hair was closer to an amber gold. The woman's face was sunken in, skin recessed and tight against the facial bones, her nose shriveled and her jawline and teeth jutting. As best as I could tell, the victim had no eyes. But I couldn't say whether they'd been removed or if they'd shriveled to nothing during decomposition. I'd seen my share of corpses, but this was unlike any I had ever seen at any stage of waste.

"Fascinating," Swales said with a huge look of awe. She hitched up, her face closer to the corpse, studying it, completely captivated.

"Fascinating?" the patrolman responded, his eyes fully round like saucers. "What the hell are we looking at?"

"Anyone?" Swales asked, searching our faces for an answer.

Jericho shook his head, "Afraid not, Doc."

"Me neither," I said.

Her focus shifted to Emanuel. He shook his head, saying, "Nuh-uh. Never!"

"I guess I'm the only one reading about the practices of Egyptian mummification," she answered, returning to study the body. "The salt! That's what told me what we have."

"Are you saying we have a mummy?" I asked. "I was only making light of it earlier."

"In a manner of speaking, yes. This is a mummy," she said, her eyes sparkling excitedly. "More specifically, it's a body that's been preserved," she continued and eased the covering down to the waist. The body was naked; the woman's breasts pancake flat. Her ribs protruded like her jawbone, each one showing distinctly.

"What do you think caused the staining on the sheet?" I asked. I wrinkled my nose. "Same salty smell too."

"Although there's no salt for us to see now," Swales said, pinching the powdery material on the sheet. "If I'm right, there had been at one time. We're looking at mummification through the heavy application of salt and other earthly materials."

"Is that possible?" Emanuel asked.

"Sure," Swales answered. "Ancient Egyptians harvested salt from dried lake beds and used it in their rituals when entombing their dead."

"Look at this," I said, taking a picture of the hands—the fingers skeletal; the nails trimmed and polished. "Speaking of ritual, there are signs of it here. This body has been prepared. Notice the hands, the placement of them across the middle, one hand placed over the other. And her hair, it's been washed and then neatly combed."

"Let's see the rest of her," Swales said and revealed the woman's midsection and her legs and feet. The patrolman panted with another gasp. "If you need to leave?"

"I'm fine," he said, sweat trickling down the sides of his round cheeks, color returning with ruddy blotches.

"The victim's toenails were trimmed and polished," I said, refocusing on the body.

"Her age?" Jericho asked. "It's hard to tell."

"I'd think it's impossible to tell with the body in this state," I answered, searching the mummified face. "She could be seventeen, or she could be seventy."

"I'll have an age when we perform the autopsy," Swales said.

"Her hair," I said, searching the golden locks. "I see no signs of grays, and the roots are natural, no hair dye used."

"Good eye, detective," Swales said, easing over the body with a light shining onto the face, the round beam centering on the mouth. Swales pulled the lips apart, the skin stiff like paper, showing the victim's teeth which were free of stain or blemish. "My guess, we're looking at an adolescent."

At that, my heart leaped into my throat. I searched the girl's face again, searched for a possible resemblance to me or to my ex-husband. But found nothing that stirred as familiar.

Fourteen years ago, when I was a uniformed police officer, my daughter was kidnapped from our home. I'd never stopped looking for her. With every case, with every victim close to my daughter's age, I couldn't help but give them a second and third look, seeking the smallest of clues that might become a miracle. There was none here though. Her blonde hair should have reassured me from the start, but I couldn't help but see Hannah everywhere, at least at first.

"We have a second case. We have a victim of foul play."

"That we do," Swales agreed, sitting back on her heels.

"Body preserved, potentially mummified. Her hair has been shampooed and combed. Her finger and toenails have been neatly trimmed," I said, making a short assessment. "While we can't tell with the salt on her skin, I'd bet her body was thoroughly washed too. The killer made sure to remove any evidence of his being with the victim."

"Linked to the body downstairs?" Jericho asked, kneeling next to me.

Unable to break my focus of the woman's face, the horror of what the mummification process had done, I answered, "They present differently. For now, I'm inclined to state them as unrelated."

"I'd have to agree," Swales said, laying her petite fingers on the victim's chest. "To reach this state, this body has been here for quite some time. The body downstairs is very recent."

"How much time?" Emanuel asked, scribbling in a notebook. "Month? Two or three?"

"More like twelve, maybe double that," Swales answered. "This body is preserved well enough that she could have been here even longer."

"It would have been less than four years," Jericho answered, offering a part of the timeline that we could use. He motioned to the house, the structure. "These homes were filled with families four years ago."

"The other homes!" I said with stabbing realization. "How many are there?"

"There's the six here," Jericho said. His face changed then. "You mean all of the abandoned houses?"

I nodded. "This victim shows signs of a ritual, of care, and of preservation. Couple these with the application of salt, the orientation of the body, and the proximity to the ocean. What if the killer is using the houses? What if there are more bodies?"

CHAPTER EIGHT

"Coming up," a voice called distantly. The sound was welcome and warmed me. It was Tracy Fields, a crime-scene technician I'd pulled onto my team the last year. She was accelerated. Scratch that. She was exceptionally accelerated. Tracy was one of those people who was born older. By the time I'd met her, she was already working on multiple degrees, and had most of the certification needed to become a crime-scene investigator. I barely remember what my interests were when I was around her age, but when she was just seventeen, Tracy already knew she wanted to solve crimes. While she could do anything, she had a knack for investigation. Law school was next, and I wouldn't be surprised if one day we were all working for her. Like I said, she was exceptional and older than her years.

"You okay down there?" No answer. "It's those first steps. You'll have to climb around them."

"Uhm. Okay. I think I see what you mean," she answered. I gave Jericho a look, his already leaving the attic to help.

"Jericho will show you the way," I shouted.

"It's great how much you've helped her, especially with Daniel gone," Swales said, a sad grin appearing. "She's a smart one."

Daniel had been our mayor, and before that, he'd been our district attorney. He'd also been one of Jericho's oldest friends and was Tracy's uncle. When he was murdered, I couldn't stop myself, and stepped in to help wherever I could. It felt natural to do. She was a bright young girl, with no parents left.

"Yes, she is," I answered, clearing my throat. I'd never been one to play favorites, but it was easy to do with Tracy.

"It's great that she's working with us again too," Swales went on to say, referring to Tracy's leave while I was absent. When I'd gone on medical leave, Cheryl had picked up most of my team. Unfortunately, that did not include Tracy, which put her without work while she continued her studies and certification.

"What do you mean?"

"I heard she's the new full-time hire."

"Tracy is the new hire?" I asked, a weight lifting, squashing a guilt and worry I'd carried for her since my leave. "That's excellent news."

"I thought you'd like to hear it." If anyone knew anything, it'd be Swales. I shouldn't have been surprised, but I was. She had a knack for keeping her finger on the pulse of everything and everyone's business.

"I'm here to work," Tracy said, appearing at the opening, face bright, blue eyes big and round, with Jericho standing behind her. There was a brief show of her dimples, which disappeared when her gaze fell on the body. She fumbled with a lanyard around her neck, jerking her identification from beneath a jacket zipper, the chain catching her chin awkwardly. She held it up for the patrolman when he approached. "I'm official."

"She's with us," I added, standing to greet her. Her identification badge was indeed official, showing her picture, along with the station's address and her position with the county. There was a sting in my eyes, the pride for her suddenly overwhelming. I opened my mouth to speak, my voice breaking, "I'm happy you got the job."

"Way to go kiddo," Emanuel said and gave her a thumbs-up. "You got a team yet?"

"Floater," she said, her chin high. She patted my arm affectionately. "I heard you're back full-time?"

"Wow! Word does travel fast." I gave Swales a look as the doctor made herself look busy.

"I guess that makes us all floaters?" Emanuel said, questioning who he should report to.

"I suppose it does." I wanted to relax his concerns. "For now, I'm the lead while on site. If we find enough evidence to support a separate case, Cheryl and I will split the responsibilities."

"Did I miss much?" Tracy asked and swung her gear around her front, unzipping her kit to fetch a pair of latex gloves. She sleeved them onto her fingers while drinking in the details of the room. She was eager to work, and I was equally eager to have her help.

"We've done our initial assessments," I said, leading her to the victim.

Tracy cringed and waved her hand. "What is that? Salt?"

"As best we can tell, the body was encased in fine salt in an attempt to preserve the body." I showed her the sheet, the outline, and the body.

"A cause of death?" she asked.

"Now you know better than that," Swales said with a scoff. "Also, congratulations and welcome aboard."

"Thank you," Tracy replied, a gleam on her face.

"No cause of death as yet, but I can tell you that the victim died elsewhere and was brought here."

"How's that?" I asked, moving to the victim's head, following the doctor's eyes, fixed on the area around the neck. Tracy retrieved her crime-scene camera and attached a macro lens with a ring flash. She struck the room with its harsh light in a flurry of test exposures, the batteries whining. She looked briefly at the rear display and adjusted the exposure as she knelt next to me. Near the victim's neck, there was a single injury: a three-quarter-inch incision lateral to the collarbone. I wasn't sure what it was but suspected that her fluids had to have been removed. "Victim was killed, and her blood drained?"

"Correct," Swales said. She pointed to the area as Tracy framed her camera and captured the image. "This incision is a textbook location. Whoever did this used a scalpel and then identified the common carotid artery and the internal jugular vein."

"They would have had a medical background?" Tracy asked.

Swales rocked her head with uncertainty. "Perhaps. But these days, most of the knowledge can be found online."

"With the vessels identified, they put tubes in place and created suction?" I asked, thinking of the search terms to send our IT expert, Nichelle Wilkinson. She had a knack for finding anything online, whether it was on the public internet or buried in the Dark Web.

Swales held up two fingers. "The first is an arterial tube. The second would be a drain tube." Swales gave the body a hard look, brow furrowed, glasses nearing the end of her nose. "Once the tubes were in place, the killer used an embalming machine to perform the drainage."

I looked at the remains, skin taut, a skeletal frame beneath. "But an embalming machine would have replaced the blood with embalming fluid?" I was certain the body would appear much differently.

"Can the machine use air in place of embalming fluid?" Tracy asked.

"This part I am unsure," Swales said, looking puzzled. "Generally, the arterial tube pushes embalming fluid while the blood is drained through the tube attached to the jugular vein. But in this case, there's no sign of fluids forced into the body. Only draining and then the heavy application of salt for the preservation."

"What does that mean?" Tracy asked.

Swales sat up, her hands balled and stuck on her hips. "It means that I've got my work cut out for me if I'm going to figure out what it is we're looking at here."

"What about water? Or saline?" I asked, grasping at ideas. "The saline is used in place of the embalming fluid and, over time, it would leech from the body, resulting in what we see here."

"Perhaps." Swales tapped her finger against her chin as she considered the idea. "I'll know more when I perform the autopsy. I can check the larger vessels."

I scanned the room, glimpsing at the quizzical faces, the questions mounting. "Whoever did this, and however they did this, there's a reason it was done this way."

When Tracy's camera flash struck the body, her concentrating around the hands, I caught the edge of something that had been hidden in shadow. I inched closer, waving to Tracy, an uncertainty showing with confusion. When she understood, she took another picture, saying, "Casey, what is it?"

"The hands," I answered with a short gasp. "I think the victim is holding something."

"Holding something?" Swales asked. "That's unusual."

"It certainly is." I didn't dare blink as Swales inched closer.

"Let's see what we have," she said, carefully lifting the victim's arm, to reveal a square piece of paper, the color of it tan like the victim's skin. "You're right. It's a folded sheet of paper."

The sight of the find came with a heavy feeling in my stomach. As Swales said, it was unusual. What did the killer place there? I held my breath as though diffusing a bomb, concerned that the parchment would turn to dust, maybe disintegrate when I touched it. "Could the salt leeching from the body make the paper brittle?"

Swales's eyes narrowed as she brushed her chin with the back of her hand. "I... I've no idea."

With the tip of my gloved finger, I nudged the thickest corner, the paper having been folded more than once. I heard the group exhale, peering up into faces leaning over, gathered around the body like medical students watching their first procedure. "It's okay," I said, assuring them. I chanced the next move, lifting the paper and opening it.

"Open it," Emanuel asked, his deep baritone resonating through the quiet room.

I lifted a hand. "I'm getting to it, but we need to be careful." I was sure the creases from the folds would crack and separate, the paper's brittleness giving me pause. But as the paper unfolded, the creases held. The building suspense ended with a collective sigh.

"What's it say?" Swales asked, the southern lilt in her voice rising.

I could just make out the words, the penmanship sharp and leaning to the right. "I've got a sentence… or maybe just some words."

"Go on, dear?" Swales asked. "Read it."

Peering at the page, the weight in my gut turning fluttery, I read aloud.

"*Distressing, calumnies, I, am, toward, affect.*"

"'Distressing calumnies I am toward affect'," Swales said, repeating me, and then light-heartedly added, "Anyone play Scrabble?"

"Or crosswords?" Jericho added.

"Distressing." I spoke the word, thinking it relevant to a number of motives like the state of the youth being in distress. That is, if the victim turned out to be adolescent. "These could be words indicating a motive?"

The whine of a battery charging rang in my ear: Tracy taking pictures of the paper before I preserved it in an evidence bag. "Your phone," she said. I handed it to her so she could take a picture with it, allowing me to send it to Cheryl and Nichelle, adding a massive clue to the mystery of our mummified body.

"Calumnies? What kind of word is that?" Swales asked. "Someone ask your watch or your phone for a definition?"

Jericho held up his phone. "Calumnies. It means slanderous."

"Like defamatory?" I asked, thinking there was a message that hinted at a possible motive. "I wonder if this was about a reputation?"

He shrugged, adding, "It could also mean misrepresenting."

It was the doctor's turn to shrug. "What about the other words?" she asked.

"I am and toward," Emanuel answered. "Maybe those are filler words? No meanings that might be indirect."

"Okay. We have a mummified body and a note with words. Words that together are not a sentence, but alone they offer some possible clues to a motive. The killer is disappointed with the young, the youth, believing them to be lazy?"

"Wouldn't they have just said so in a sentence?" Jericho asked, his face scrunched, telling me he didn't buy into the idea either.

"I know. It doesn't sound right." I took to standing, preserving the note in an evidence bag. "I don't think we have enough words."

"Enough words?" Emanuel and Swales said together.

"I'm sure it's already crossed your mind, but are you thinking this isn't isolated?" Tracy asked as she continued to photograph the victim's hands and feet; the skin on them was shriveled like the rind of dried fruit.

"There's more abandoned houses," Jericho answered.

"I don't believe this to be isolated." I texted more of the details to Nichelle, asking if there was any research into the words, possibly used in literature, a book that might be flagged by the authorities. "This note, the words, they feel like a part of—"

"A part of many." Swales leaned back and stroked her neck with a grimace. "Oh I hope not."

I cocked my head. "We'll know when we get to the other houses." Jericho held his phone up to let me know he'd been working the list. "Send them to us as soon as possible."

"It's going to take some time," he said.

I looked at the mummified remains, the girl's face, and tried to imagine who she was, what she looked like in life. I also considered the killer's perseverance and patience and the strength of his will to perform such an act.

"If I'm right, the killer believes he has all the time in the world. He believes he has all the time he needs to do something this atrocious to a person."

CHAPTER NINE

After a stop to shower and to change my clothes, my thoughts swirling with mummies and cryptic notes and two young girls with their lives stolen forever, I was back in my car for the drive I'd been dreading since I'd come across the pink jacket flitting in the breeze. My heart was on my sleeve and my stomach was tied in knots. I was going to Jocelyn Winter's home to visit with her mother and to tell her that her daughter was dead. Tracy joined me, using the time to catch up on the case, working on her laptop, relaying my queries to Nichelle about the two high schools, their rivalry. We needed to know who else was at that party.

Tracy sat quietly, wind blowing her hair around her face, eyes shifting from her laptop to the backside of her camera, which showed the mummified body on the tiny display. The images were being uploaded for Cheryl to review. She was returning to the station and would be briefed by Emanuel and Dr. Swales. I'd be lying if I didn't acknowledge the gnawing urge to jump onto the case of the mummified body. None of us had ever seen anything like it, especially a victim with a note from the killer. I wasn't clear if we had one or two cases, the evidence lacking, leaving us to work them separately until there was more. Jocelyn Winter's case took priority for the moment, until the team had identified the other victim. Since leaving the abandoned house, we'd learned that Rose Winter was a single parent, her husband, Jocelyn's father, deceased, killed overseas while serving for our country. We had nothing else to work with, only questions.

"Do I say anything?" Tracy asked, fidgeting with her identification badge.

I sensed she was nervous. "This is your first meeting with a family member?"

She gave me a hard nod, lips pinched thin and white. "Yes. First."

I looked at my rearview mirror, making sure the patrol car following was still there. They'd escort Jocelyn's mother after I delivered the news, taking her to see her daughter.

"Listen," I began, taking Tracy's hand briefly, "as a crime-scene investigator, asking family members questions is part of the job. But don't be alarmed if we don't get to ask any questions. Today is more about passing on the news."

"Okay," she said. "I can help investigate the girl's room if we're given permission."

"Just follow my lead." I swung the steering wheel hand over hand, exiting one of the island's main arteries. "If asked anything direct, remember to be tactful and respectful."

We passed East OBX High School, the one Jericho had mentioned, which had been made to serve students from both the east side and the west side of the county. Beyond the high school, the homes grew into large estates, the yards made up of manicured lawns and decorative landscaping. The houses were large, made of brick and stone, some with multiple floors and some stilted like the abandoned houses on the coast, their drives paved and long and lined with trees, a fancy mailbox at the gated entries with numbers and letters made of steel and fancily shaped. I'd been to this part of the county too, but only in passing—the area seemingly immune to crime.

We turned onto an elevated road, crossing over marshes and swamps, the smell of mud and peat thick and filling the car. Cattails edged the open water, sitting high along trees which leaned away from the banks; a scattering of red-winged black birds flitted from limb to limb. On the other side of the marshy lands the houses became a single-story ranch style, tightly packed side by side, the yards small, a narrow alley between them. We crossed the front of run-down properties next, the yards littered with rusted boat trailers and dilapidated lawn furniture; roof shingles sat askew, with windows boarded or missing altogether. We passed an empty lot with broken cinder block and turned-up earth piled in mounds, filling an acre, a brick sign close to the road the last remaining structure, reading *West OBX High School*. I knew then what the marshes were: a barrier, a line drawn between the classes; the students crossing it when West OBX High School was condemned.

We reached the location of a trailer and RV park, turning right once more, passing single and double-wide trailers, their driveways loose with stone and gravel, their foundations made up of old railway timber and cinder blocks stacked three high. My breath felt hot, my nerves waking, the hardest part of this job moments away. After we'd left the abandoned house, I'd changed into a business suit, wanting to appear as professional and as welcoming as possible. But regardless of how I dressed, there wasn't anything I could do, or say, to soften such harsh news.

"That one," Tracy said, pointing to a single, wide trailer, the outside well maintained, the siding white and pale yellow. There was a round glass-top table on the patio with two chairs, a small garden next to it with tomato vines clinging to a wood trellis, leaves wilted, their ripe fruits plucked, a bag of gardening tools and gloves bunched in the corner next to shallow steps.

I parked the car, the patrol car taking a place behind us. As I climbed out, the officer donned her hat and tipped it toward me, waiting for instruction. She'd accompany me for the meeting and, when I signaled, she'd escort Jocelyn's mother. The trailer door swung open, a woman resembling the victim appearing behind a screen door with rigid concern and fright on her face, her hand over her mouth.

Tracy came to my side as I dipped my head. "I hate this part."

"Where's my daughter?!" Rose Winter cried, the screen door slamming shut. The woman was in her mid forties and could easily be mistaken for an older cousin of the victim, her beauty impressive like her daughter's. She stood tall, her height like Jocelyn's too, her hair the same chestnut color and flowing at shoulder length. Her gaze was locked on us as we approached. Tears hung in her brown eyes and wet her cheeks. My gut was in knots, my feet heavy and my legs like rubber. I knew the endless ache she would feel the rest of her life. The woman raised her voice. "My girl didn't come home last night. Tell me she's okay?"

I opened my mouth saying, "Ma'am." A neighbor's door opened. And then another. I stepped closer, wanting to add privacy.

"Tell me!" she cried.

I extended my hand toward the door. "Ma'am, if we could go inside."

Her head swung back and forth, eyelids fluttering. "Mm mm. No!" Clutching the air, tensing, she said in a near shout, "Tell me here. Tell me now!"

I truly hated this part of the job. But it was a part of the job. There were no words that could diminish the pain this woman was about to endure. "I'm sorry, ma'am." My mind and voice shifting into autopilot, speaking the words we'd rehearsed, using the tones and intonations and body language we'd been trained to use. Tracy stood next to me, a tablet in hand, her expression like stone, her head moving in unison with mine. I went on to explain, "Ma'am, this morning, your daughter was found unresponsive."

"Unresponsive! She was found? Where?"

"At an abandoned house, ma'am. Your daughter was found alone; however, there was evidence of activity, a party, perhaps, that took place the evening before."

"She's dead! Is that what you're telling me?" Rose Winter cried over the sound of another door opening, a screen door clapping shut. I felt the stare of her neighbors, their venturing onto their stoops. "Who? How?"

"It's an ongoing investigation," I said, sticking to the scripted words, but then lowered my head. "Yes, ma'am. Your daughter was found dead."

"My baby girl," Rose said, losing the strength to stand, collapsing into a puddle of tears. I caught one of her arms as Tracy took the woman's other side. We eased her down onto the step as a next-door neighbor arrived. "Margaret, did you hear what they said!"

An older woman, her neighbor sat down, her hips filling the step as she took Rose's hand, patting the top of it. "I heard. I am so sorry," she said. The neighbor faced us, asking, "What happened... what can you tell us?"

"Ma'am, there was no immediate sign of what caused your daughter's death." I motioned to my head, adding, "There was an injury around her head. Beyond this information, we'll require our medical examiner to provide the cause of death."

"My girl," Rose cried, her color turning pale. She clutched her chest in a gasp, trying to catch her breath.

I knelt in front of her and held her hand. "Breathe," I said, afraid the woman was going into shock. "Take deep breaths."

Her eyes locked on mine, the sadness painful. "She's my baby." Rose let go and wiped her face, drying her cheeks and clearing her voice. Eyes red-rimmed, tears standing, her stare hard, she asked in a whisper, "Can I please see my daughter?"

I stood and motioned to the patrol officer. She joined us on the patio, the radio on her utility belt blurting inaudible static. The officer turned it off, saying, "Ma'am, I'm available to take you."

"Margaret?" I asked, directing my question to the neighbor. Her eyes were big with attention; her brow high on her forehead. "Would you be able to accompany Ms. Winter."

"Certainly," she said, swiping at her tears. "I've known Jocelyn most of the girl's life. I'll do whatever I can."

"Thank you." Margaret helped Rose to her feet, the two wobbly, leaning against one another. "And ma'am, it would be helpful if we could take a look in your daughter's room."

"Her room?" Rose asked, confused by the request.

"It might help us understand where, or who, your daughter was with last night," Tracy answered, her focus on me briefly before returning to Rose Winter.

"Yes, yes!" she answered. "Please, do whatever you need to do."

The patrol car was gone a moment later. Through the rear window, I saw Rose Winter's head on the shoulder of her neighbor, the life she knew ending with the news I delivered. While it was the worst part of the job, it helped fuel the investigation—filling the tanks, so to speak, driving me to find the truth.

The inside of the house was quaint and homey. A small family room was to my left with a loveseat and recliner. A television was hung on the wall, a glass-covered square coffee table at the center of the room. I walked by a corner hutch, its shelves clean of dust, each of them carrying dozens of pictures with the victim and her mother, the backgrounds in them showing their travels. They'd been more than just mother and daughter. They were friends. One picture stood at the center, a portrait of the victim, her smiling for the camera. I grabbed my phone and took a picture for us to use in our team meetings.

A kitchen hung off the rear, a single table against the wall with cans of tea and a half-filled jar of instant coffee. Beneath the jar, a scatter of brown crumbs and a dirtied spoon, a half a cup of coffee, the outside of it cold. We made our way through a short hallway, finding Jocelyn's room: a string of decorative lights running across the ceiling; the head of her bed covered with pillowy stuffed animals; a hot-pink accent wall with movie posters and plaques and ribbons of achievement for academics and sports—the school's name, *West OBX High School* embossed on them.

Tracy went from one to the next, reading each award.

"Did you find something?" I asked.

"None of her awards are from the other school. None with the name, East OBX High School," she answered. "Just from her old school, the one that had to close due to flooding. Being a senior, her last year, I'd think she would've continued in extracurricular activities."

"Colleges like to see activities. Make a note of it." I circled the bed to her closet, the sliding door ajar where I saw clothes typical of a girl her age. A thought of the awards and activities came to me. "It might be because nothing was available after the schools merged?"

"I suppose," Tracy said, unsatisfied with my answer.

I moved to the victim's desk, the corner of it carrying a stack of schoolbooks. "It's also possible, the victim lost interest in the activities."

Tracy eyed the wall of achievements, unconvinced. "Seems odd to have this much interest and then call it quits."

On the girl's desk there was a laptop, closed, the lid covered in colorful stickers, their names foreign to me, my thinking they might be the names of video games or rock bands. "Tracy. Do any of these look familiar to you?"

Tracy joined me, running her fingers over the stickers, "This one," she began, and nabbed a picture with her phone. "This one too. Alternative rock bands. But I don't know the others."

Instinctively, I opened the top drawer, finding a spiral notebook inside, the wire kinked, a pen clipped to the front cover where the girl's name was penned in fat cursive handwriting, loops in the letters shaded with red and green and blue. I suspected what it was before opening to the first pages. "I think our victim kept a diary."

"Open it," Tracy said, voice heightened. She came close to my side, our hovering over the pages, my leafing through them, each showing a date at the top, sometimes a header with a topic, followed by paragraphs written in the same handwriting as was on the cover. The rows were tightly filled and broken by an occasional doodle. Some of the pages were sparse, mostly blank save for a few lines to note the day and a melancholy mood or a grade on a school exam.

Dear Diary, I got an A- today on my lit paper. A minus. I know it's an A. That Mr. Dodge, he's a tough grader.

On other days, the pages were two and three deep, her writing about the new school, writing about new people, and new classes.

Dear Diary, I don't think I like our new school. I don't think the other kids want us here either. Like, it's hard to even go to my locker without getting a look. And it's not just the other kids. I seen them from teachers too. Diary, I wish we never had to come here.

"What's on the last page." Tracy asked, pawing at the diary. "Could be something there?"

I flipped to the victim's last diary entry and read the top line. "Looks like she added this yesterday." Shock stole my voice then, disbelief reigning as I tried to make sense of the first sentence, which read like it had been written for us to find.

Dear Diary,

My name is Jocelyn Winter. If you're reading this, that means I'm dead.

CHAPTER TEN

"She must have known?" Tracy said, reaching across my lap, taking hold and turning it over to show the previous page. "I mean, that's the only explanation."

The surprise of the words had left me stunned. "I've never had a case with the victim knowing they were going to die."

"Can we take it with us?" Tracy asked, pinching a corner, and eyeing the diary like it was a top ten bestseller. "I… I can read it tonight for you and summarize all the pages."

When she pulled on the metal spiral, I held onto it with a firm grip. "Tell you what, give me a day or two with it first," I said, quelling her fancy. I fanned the pages, seeing disappointment on Tracy's face. The volume of writing was larger than I'd expected and made me think twice. "Tell you what, I'm a horribly slow reader. I'll see how far I get tonight and then turn it over."

"What's the rest of the last page say?" Tracy asked, our moving to the girl's bed, the mattress sagging, a stuffed elephant tipping onto its side.

"It reads: *Dear Diary, My name is Jocelyn Winter. If you're reading this, that means I'm dead. Michael invited me to tonight's party. He told me that I'd be safe with him there. I do like him. I like him a lot. But can I trust him?*"

"Michael," Tracy said, writing down the name. She tapped the end of her pencil against her lips, eyes wandering around the girl's room. "The victim isn't sure she can trust him?"

"Jocelyn must have felt threatened?" I scanned the girl's bedroom walls, searching for anything with the name Michael.

"Read some more," Tracy said.

I read on: "*Michael told me that Grace wants to be friends. He says they asked me to go to the party to say sorry for what happened at school. I don't believe her. I know it's a trap. It's not Michael's fault either. He likes me. I'm sure of it.*

"*When Grace and her friends attacked me, she said that the next time they would end me. I know it might just be a threat, but I believe her. I'm afraid of her.*

"*This might be a dumb idea, but I want to see Michael. And the minute I come home, I'll write another page. If we kiss tonight, then maybe I'll write two pages.*

"*But if you have my diary, and if you're reading this, then that means I never made it back to my room. That means, Grace and her friends did end me.*"

"There's mention of a previous attack." I motioned to Tracy to make a note of it, realizing I was holding onto a very strong lead, as well as having a list of suspects. "This establishes there was a history between the victim and a girl named Grace."

"And Michael too," Tracy said. "I mean, just because Jocelyn likes the boy, doesn't mean he isn't responsible. She asked if she could *trust* him, that it was a *trap*."

"That's true. It could've been Grace and Michael together," I said, touching the page, the lettering; the paper dipping and rising with the last words from Jocelyn's pen. "I suspect we won't have to look too hard to find who was at that abandoned house."

"May I?" Tracy asked, tugging the diary again. I handed it to her, taking my phone and writing the names and a text message to Nichelle.

"Nichelle will search the high school systems," I said. "We'll have a list of students to interview soon."

"It's hard to believe," Tracy began, leafing through the page. "Kids killing kids?"

"I know." The idea of it disgusted me. Violence at their age, it was unsettling and made me sick to my stomach. "It happens way too often."

"Casey! Look at this," Tracy said, voice rising. "There's an entry from her first day at the new school."

Dear Diary,

I am mudborn. I've never been called mudborn before. I didn't even know what that word meant before. Not until today. Or did I? Maybe I've always known, but never knew there was a name for me. Mom does the best she can. We have what we have, and that's all of it. I'll never have what the other kids have. I hate the new school too. And Laura hates it also. The halls smell funny and the food tastes different. The other kids look down on us and treat us like we are trash. At the cafeteria, a whole table of kids told us to go back to the swamps where we belong.

"Laura," I said, adding the name to my list, sadness for the victim creeping up my spine with a chill. I knew what it felt like to be treated like an outsider. I think everyone feels it at some point in their life. "This sounds like persecution. It sounds like the school merge was awful for them."

"There's a poem," Tracy said, slowly turning the page, easing the loose paper into the spiraled edge. "The victim calls it *Mudborn*."

I shook my head, saying, "Mudborn. That word again." I added it to the notes on my phone, highlighting and setting it in bold lettering. "I don't know the word. What does the poem say? Maybe there's a clue in it?"

Against my mother's words, I like to walk the soggy marshes and wade barefoot into the still waters. I like to feel the mud squish between my toes and feel velvety cattails brush against my wet skin. I like to float in the company of dragonflies and migrating monarchs. And I like to smell the dangling honeysuckle and the lotus blossoms.

Where others only see swamp, I see beauty. I see it in the reedy grasses topped with swaying fronds. I see it in the herons, their stilted legs reflected in the surface ripples. I hear it in the sounds that are my private orchestra. And I feel it in the soft currents crawling toward the ocean, driven by moon tides and turning over the bogs that are made up of the mud which is said to course through my veins.

I am mudborn.

"Mudborn," I said as Tracy closed the diary. I thought back to the houses with the manicured lawns and the paved drives. "We drove across a shallow bridge, over marshes and swamps. Did you notice?"

"Uh-huh," Tracy answered. "I noticed the change from those bigger houses near the school."

"It was a big change." I went to the plaques and ribbons, Jocelyn's consistency of winning first and second place for her previous high school. "This may go deeper than just some school rivalry."

"A hate crime?" Tracy asked.

I gave Tracy a hard look, the mention of a hate crime having dangerous ramifications, its potential like a bomb that needed to be handled with care. "Let's keep it to ourselves for now. At least until we know more. If we're to propose hate as a motive, we better be damned sure of it."

Tracy rattled the diary. "Casey, if it was hate, I don't know how we don't run to the top of the tallest hill and shout?"

I sat down and put my hand on the diary. "I'm not saying we don't," I answered, keeping my voice calm. "We just have to be absolutely certain, make sure we haven't misinterpreted anything, or jumped to a conclusion that could potentially ruin an innocent life."

Tracy rocked her head. Her agreement reluctant. "I won't say anything."

I pushed the diary toward her, and said, "You go ahead and read it first."

Her face brightened. "Really?"

"Report every finding," I instructed. "I want details. Understood?"

"Understood."

"And the words from the note we found—"

Tracy wrinkled her nose. "—on the mummified body?"

I touched the diary, the idea of a connection being possible. "Be on the lookout for them. Note any occurrences in the diary's pages."

While we finished the investigation of Jocelyn's room, I learned more about who the victim was. Jocelyn Winter was a sweet, ambitious, and admirable girl with an amazing future. Like Tracy, a part of me wanted to find the tallest hill and scream at the top of my lungs, rage stirring—every picture of the victim, every written page giving me a glimpse of a life shortened, a life stolen. That's not how we did things though. Our way was to find the truth, to clear the path to it, and to bring justice for the victim. At times, and quite often, it was painful and cruel, and it almost always felt terribly unfair. But it was how we worked. We'd taken an oath and had sworn to uphold it. It was how we lived.

CHAPTER ELEVEN

We returned to the station to do the paperwork for the Jocelyn Winter case. I followed Tracy inside, my steps heavy, the station's smell strong and powerful enough I thought I could taste it on my lips. I swiped at the tingle running through the scar on my arm, my days on leave having put distance between me and the station. Until stepping inside, I hadn't realized just how much. This was a good thing though. I was back and everything about it felt new again. There were goosebumps and excitement tickling my insides, and while I felt anxious, I gladly drank in every detail that met my eyes.

I stopped when I reached the small wooden gate separating the receiving desk from the offices and cubicles. The surface of it was cool to the touch, smoothed by decades of use. A moment was needed before I could cross the barrier, making things official that felt like it was fresh out of the academy, my first day on the job. I was thrilled and scared at the same time, a hot mix that was a welcome change from my day to day of recuperation and physical therapy.

The benches lining the walls held a few souls: a pair of men with scrapes and bruises on their faces and arms, their wrists in handcuffs, their eyes tired and bored as they waited to be processed. Instinctively, I searched their hands, saw their knuckles which were puffy with red welts that'd turn black by this evening. From the looks and the smell, I doubt either would recall why. The rest of the benches were empty, which matched the vacant sound of the station too, the usual typing and low chattering drone a memory of the earlier hours.

"Quiet day, Alice?" I asked, cradling the gate in my hand.

"Detective!" the station's desk officer said, her voice pitchy with surprise. She appeared from behind the counter, a bonnet of salt-and-pepper hair pinned in a bun. "I just got here for the night shift. Haven't even had my coffee yet. It's really good to see you back."

"It's good to be back," I told her, the men on the bench rousing to the welcome. I nudged my head toward them, curious.

"From what I was told, a scuffle on the boardwalk," she said. "Don't expect much else going on. Though I did hear you had a heck of a day."

"I did," I said and found the bravery to step into the station and close the stout gate behind me. "Alice, you have a good shift this evening."

"You do the same," she said and disappeared behind the counter.

I made my way to the sheriff's office and got a quick handshake as he welcomed my return, along with a fast sign-off, an approval to continue with the investigation into Jocelyn Winter's death. While I didn't call the death a murder just yet, he agreed it was suspicious and warranted our further investigation. From there, I weaved through the maze of cubicles and offices, popping my head in on a few folks I'd come to know since joining the ranks in the Outer Banks force, their sharing looks of surprise and welcoming handshakes and hugs.

I was never one for close contact and did my best to keep the welcomes at arm's length, my sights set on my desk. When I reached it, I powered on my computer and monitor, wiping my hand across the black panel, cleaning it of the dust that had accumulated while I was gone. Across from my desk, Tracy was already sitting in her chair, her head lowered, her focus fixed on the pages of Jocelyn's diary, one finger gliding across the girl's handwriting, the other taking notes on a tablet, occasionally slurping from a straw, a sea of empty diet cola cans strewn across her desk.

Behind me, Nichelle Wilkinson was hidden by towering monitors, the top of her ruffled brown hair in motion. She specialized in all things technical, and she was also the first person I reached out to whenever we needed to research or to access a system, whether it was public or private. I peered around the corner undetected, her cubicle walls made up of a new collection of cats in comical cartoons she'd torn from magazines and newspapers. Her calendar showed the month of October, a pair of fuzzy kittens sitting on pumpkins in celebration of the upcoming Halloween night. She'd added to her collection of pictures since I'd seen them last: a half dozen newspaper clippings, each mentioning our achievements, the cases we'd won. The scar on my arm ached with dull remembrance, forcing me to recognize the story that was missing, the one I didn't win. I lived though. Survived. And some would call that a win.

"Well, are you going to say hello?" Nichelle asked, jumping up and wrapping her arms around me. Her body was warm and soft, and her bushy hair swallowed much of my face, tickling my cheeks as she squeezed me tight. I returned the hug, warming to it. She pulled back a moment later and planted a dry kiss on me, saying, "I missed my neighbor and friend. Tell me you're back full-time?"

"I am back full-time," I said, her doting brown eyes bigger than I thought possible. She jumped up and down excited by the news. "Did you get any names?"

"Business already?" she asked, her mouth in a pout. She winked with a smirk. "Of course, I did."

Nichelle rolled her chair, the wheels squeaking as she plopped onto the seat, her fingers tackling a keyboard, the names appearing across the screen. "From the looks of it you had no trouble?" It was a polite question, my already knowing her penchant for working around formalities to fulfill my requests. These were students though, and they were minors, underage. As such, I had to be careful. Caution

The Crying House

weighed on a sigh. "Nichelle, you didn't break into anything. Did you?"

With her brow raised and fingers splayed across her chest. "Who me?"

"Nichelle?" I asked, not sure if she was kidding.

She sneered, answering, "It's all good. The school accommodated my request. I mean, with the case on the news, I mentioned the investigation and had something in my inbox before I got off the phone."

"Was it a lot of students?" I asked, wondering how much work we were looking at.

"Lucky for us, most of the students from that high school leave their online profiles public."

"Online profiles?" I asked, uncertain how she'd used them.

"I'm using them to make a who's who list of anyone that might have been at the party," she answered, refreshing her screen to show the results.

"This is good," I told her, seeing multiple names, including quite a few students with the first names Michael and Laura. One name on the list stood out: Grace Armstrong. "Is that the only student with the name Grace?"

"She is," Nichelle answered. She raised a finger, light brown and tipped with neon green nail polish, pointing to the name. She paused, her expression changing. It was a look I'd seen before. A dangerous look. "Say the word and I can get to digging, bring you more data."

I hesitated, and considered Jocelyn's diary entries, the history mentioned between her and Grace. We might need what Nichelle offered, especially if we were to question the students. "For now, stay above board," I answered, cocking my head, warning her. "But see if you can dig anything up on an incident that occurred in the school. It was recent and occurred between Jocelyn Winter and Grace Armstrong."

"I'll get on it," Nichelle said, keys rattling again, her eyes fixed on mine as she blindly typed. "I'll text you when I've got something?"

"Yeah," I answered, adding, "Also, I'll want your help at the high school."

"Back to school?"

"I'm coordinating an interview with the victim's classmates."

"Say the word," Nichelle said, her focus drifting to her screens.

"And get back to me on that," I said, turning away, Jericho's voice coming from the front of the station, "as soon as you have something."

Before I stepped away, Nichelle asked, "Anything about the other body?"

"What have you heard?" I asked, answering her question with a question, peering over the cubical walls, searching for a flash of bright red hair, wondering if Cheryl was back from her trip. By now, she'd surely have made a formal comment to the press. That was her thing. The press. The limelight. She loved it.

Nichelle glanced at her calendar with the Halloween pictures, her gaze returning to me. She folded her arms and leaned in closer, hushing her voice. "Was it... was it really a mummy?"

"It was," Jericho said, joining us, and putting on a face full of fright, playing into Nichelle's fancy for Halloween. He'd changed out of his Marine Patrol uniform, replacing it with denim and flannel: a staple look when he was off duty. To me, he had the handsome look of a lumberjack, especially since adopting a five o'clock shadow that'd never know the time of day. It was always there, and it always looked great. Turning serious, he added, "It's a first, and we're all hopeful that it is the last."

"That reminds me," Nichelle said abruptly. "I have the other list you—"

"The list of abandoned houses," I said, finishing for her, facing Jericho, and asking, "A joint venture across our teams?"

Nichelle rummaged through a stack of books and printed papers, muttering annoyances about the clutter until she found the list. "Got it!"

I held the page of addresses and pictures, the count of them higher than I'd expected. She'd gone the extra mile and added a column with the geo-tagged information, providing a latitude and longitude as well. Reviewing the map coordinates, I understood their need, some of the street addresses no longer relevant. "This isn't a few houses," I said alarmed by the number of them. "We're going to need multiple teams."

"Then we tackle it with multiple teams." Jericho took a picture of the list. "I'll forward to my team so we can prepare."

"Nichelle let's also review this with the fire department since they'll have tracked the properties too. Might be the list is shorter now?"

Jericho held his phone, a reply showing. "The formalities are under way for a house-to-house search. The marine patrol will pair up with you guys."

"Field trip?" Nichelle asked. "I've been eager to get out there."

"It is," I told her. As I scanned the list and thought of the mummified body and the overwhelming smell of salt, I added, "You might not like what you find."

The day ended, the bodies discovered delivered safely to the morgue, Emanuel working with Dr. Swales while Tracy read the diary and Nichelle researched Grace Armstrong and a previous altercation with Jocelyn Winter. I'd completed all paperwork needed to officially put me back on the payroll again. Now, my fingers laced with Jericho's as we walked the boardwalk. I'd made a promise to join him this evening, and to help him pick out a retirement gift for Dr. Swales. Two slices of boardwalk pizza and a colorful snow-cone that turned my lips blue, I was content, but the cases nipped at my thoughts, especially some of Jocelyn Winter's words.

"I was told this place is good for gift shopping." Jericho put his hand behind the small of my back, leading us toward a boardwalk store with a sign reading, *Clean Living*. Another sign read, *All Products Locally Sourced*. "We should find something in here."

"I'm sure she'd like a gift certificate?" I said, offering an idea. I wanted to continue walking, the sun dipping for the night, the evening bringing with it a chilly autumn breeze.

"Not the doc," he said, squeezing my fingers. We stopped at the store opening, his facing me, pleading to go inside with him. "Come on, it'll be fun."

Reluctantly, I agreed and followed him into the store. The scent of perfumed candles and potpourri was strong, the place small with shelves along walls and a few in the center. They were stocked as though nothing had been sold all year, every inch of them filled. On one shelf, jars short and tall, their insides golden with honey, lighting making them bright and showing honeycombs inside them. I picked up one of the jars, holding it for Jericho to see. "Does she have a sweet tooth?"

Jericho regarded the find, picking a jar for himself. "Not sure if she does. But I do."

"That's a good choice," an attendant said, his square glasses oversized for his narrow face, his eyelids droopy. He was a middle-aged man with a thin manicured beard, lean and tall, his pants and shirt pressed neatly, tidied like his hair, which had been combed back to reveal a dark widow's peak. He picked up a jar, holding it as though posing for us. "May I recommend a creamed clover honey as well. Sourced locally, of course."

Jericho took the second jar, inspecting it a moment before shaking his head. "I don't know if she likes honey."

"Ahh. This is for a gift?" the attendant asked; Jericho nodding. He waved for us to follow and led us to another section of the store, the shelves lined with jars of powders and soaps. He offered us a jar, the contents like grain with shades of green. "Does she like to take baths? It can be quite exquisite when done right."

"I'm sure she does," I said, not knowing how it could be done wrong. I wanted to make a joke, Jericho catching the look on my face. I fought the urge and picked up a jar to read the instructions instead. "*Toss into your tub for the most relaxing soak.*"

"That sounds easy enough," Jericho said, his interest waning. He eyed his watch, adding, "That'll work."

"Shall I box two for you?" the attendant asked, smiling and showing a pair of front teeth which appeared capped, their color sharply different from the others. "It's fifty percent off for the second jar."

"End of season sale?" I asked.

"Precisely."

"Could you gift wrap them for us?" Jericho asked.

"Yes, sir," he answered, his voice quiet as he bowed and left us alone.

I glanced around, a question festering. "Jericho, have you ever heard of the word, mudborn?"

"What's that?" he asked, looking surprised, as though a ghost had just whispered a secret into his ear.

I could see the word registered with Jericho. I could also see from the look of him that it was something dark. "Jocelyn Winter. It was written in her diary. The kids at the high school—"

"They called her mudborn?" His brow furrowed deeply, his scratching at the scruff along his jaw. "I haven't heard that word in years. I'd thought it'd been lost."

"But what does it mean?" I was beginning to understand my initial concerns, understand what Jocelyn wrote in her poem. "It's derogatory, isn't it?"

"It's a stupid and mean-spirited word," he answered with a huff, taking my hand. He was quiet as we made our way to the store counter. I nudged him, wanting more. "I hated that word when I was growing up. I still hate it."

"It refers to the part of town Jocelyn is from?"

"The other side of the tracks, so to speak," he answered. "But in this case, it's the west side, which is where the marshes and parks are… and where the swamps are too."

I nodded, repeating, "The kids at east high school versus west high school. They live on opposite sides of town. Living in the mud."

"It's about rich kids being idiots." A scowl showed on his face.

"Did the rich kids have a name too?" I asked, wondering what the kids with less might have called their counters.

"The burghs," Jericho said, handing the attendant his credit card. "I'm not sure of the origin though."

The attendant held the card, answering, "It means bourgeois." He returned Jericho's credit card and motioned to a book of crosswords, a thesaurus, and a dictionary next to the cash registers. "I like to do crosswords. The word is French and means well off, the middle to upper class."

"Makes sense," Jericho said.

"Still, the way the kids use the words, makes them both ugly," I said, thanking the attendant.

We exited the store with a birthday present for Dr. Swales, the gift-wrapping silver and purple with a poofy bow around the box. The wind had picked up, clearing the boardwalk's foot traffic, leaving us mostly alone as we continued the evening. "Which were you? I mean, you grew up around here. Were you a burgh or a mudborn?"

"Neither really," he answered. "I grew up somewhat in the middle."

"That probably explains why you're so good with everyone," I said, complimenting as I pulled him close to me, inviting the quiet to join us on our walk.

"You're not so bad yourself." Jericho leaned over, giving me a kiss, helping to quiet the ugliness of the day.

The last of the sunlight disappeared as though a switch had been flipped, the boardwalk lights coming on, their colors amber and gold like the honey jars, like the mummified girl's hair. The moon was nearing full, cratered like the victim's face, the textures like crêpe paper. Only, the moon was pink as it hung just over the edge of the ocean like a giant eye watching our small part of the world. I thought of Jocelyn Winter and her being called mudborn, and how that must have made her feel. Death is always sad, especially when it's been an accident. But if her death was a product of hate, then it was beyond tragic.

The news stories would begin soon, and my next steps might include getting ahead of them. They'd consume the airwaves and feed a community scorned, a dangerous rage growing. And with it, a cold fear driving into anyone they thought responsible.

CHAPTER TWELVE

It was three in the morning when the call came in—the room pitch black, my feet cold as I threw the covers off me. Jericho let out a short snore, the mattress shifting as I sat up. Hands outstretched, fingers splayed, I had to feel around the dark while the fog in my head cleared. For a moment, I couldn't recall where I'd laid my head to sleep for the night. When the room was before me, I could just make out faint images of the bureau and the nightstand, my phone placed screen down, and I knew where I was. When the ringtone stopped, a text message came next, my phone buzzing, a crisp line of light escaping the sides.

"Who is it?" Jericho's voice was sluggish, his words sodden with sleep.

"Sorry, I'll get it." I clutched my phone and swiped at the bright screen, squinting, the afterimages green. "We're at your place?"

"All night," he answered. "Come back to bed."

"I woke up confused."

"Sleepy," he said, his hand finding me to rub my back. "Who was it?"

I dared a look, eyelids half shut. "It's from Dr. Swales. She texted: *I need you at the station.*"

Jericho sat up. "Is she okay? What time is it?"

"It's three thirty in the morning," I answered, scrolling through earlier messages to see if I'd slept through them. There were none. "I don't know what it is."

Jericho was up and out of bed, his phone in hand, swiping. "Just you," he said, the sleep gone from his voice and replaced with concern. "Casey, give her a call and make sure she's okay."

I dialed the doctor's number, worried, having never received a call from her in the middle of the night. "No answer."

"Text?" Jericho asked, shoving his leg into his pants. His worry was growing, leading me to the same, Dr. Swales being one of our closer friends.

"Wait, babe, she's typing," I said while watching dots bounce on my screen. A moment passed, our bodies frozen in the gray light. "She texted: *I'm searching an old case. You need to see this.*"

"Which case?" Jericho asked as he sat on the bed and kicked the pants from his foot. "Are you going in?"

I texted back,

I'll see you in a few.

"I guess that answers that."

Once I wake up, I can never fall back to sleep. Jericho can drop his eyelids and be asleep within a heartbeat or two. I wished I could do that. If not for Dr. Swales, I would have woken up soon enough anyway, the poem Jocelyn Winter wrote renting time in my mind. Her words were beautiful and haunting, and deep with meaning and definition of who she was. She was mudborn. And she embraced it.

On my way to the station, I made one stop at an all-night quick mart for a heavy dose of caffeine. I usually drink my coffee black, but this cup needed a taste of some sugar and cream to soften the bitterness, the harsh bite making me cringe. When I got to the station, I made my way past the evening arrests, the benches full of slumbering bodies. While most of them slept away their troubles, a group of women were still ripe with party fever, their words slurring, eyes droopy, their laughter rising and falling in cackling fits.

"Morning, Alice," I said, seeing her labor over forms and folders from behind the counter. Bright-eyed and wide awake given she was a few hours from the end of her shift. She gave me a wave and smile. "Have you seen Dr. Swales?"

"She's downstairs," Alice answered and ran a pencil back and forth through her hair. I waved a thank you, a smile creeping onto my lips as one of the drunk women cracked a joke about a man she'd been dating, his being impotent, her telling him there were no hard feelings. The ladies roared, but Alice didn't laugh, scolding them instead. "Keep it down!"

The basement, I thought, my smile disappearing in an instant. I made my way to the steps, hesitating before grabbing the banister. The place gave me a creepy vibe. The stairwell was narrow, and the steps creaked as I descended to what had been converted into a storage area. I ran my hand along the sandstone and plaster, the touch of it cool and damp. As I ventured lower into the room, a surprising tune rose through the dim light. It was Swales humming to Helen Reddy's "I Am Woman," a song I knew from the seventies; a favorite my grandmother used to sing. I took a moment to listen, the doctor's voice fetching memories I hadn't had in years. The doctor could carry a tune; she reminded me of my grandmother's singing, a familial gift that had been passed down to my mother but had ungraciously missed me.

When I reached the bottom of the stairwell, I entered an open space with floor-to-ceiling shelves that were lined with case files sleeved in plastic. Round bulbs with thick filaments threw amber light and cast shadows onto the water-stained floor and showed me the room's recessed corners where spiders liked to nest. Some renovations had been done since my last time down here: the walls fresh with paint; the air feeling drier—runs of duct work across the ceiling and walls.

"Over here," Dr. Swales said, her voice coming from the end of a shelf. She wore a pair of old-fashioned headphones, a shiny metal band dividing her frizzy hair which made it stand tall. She waved to me, rocking a dance step in her green crocs while singing, "I am woman!"

"Yes you are," I answered with a smile, the tune carrying in my head. I tugged on one of her headphones, the wire leading from the orange cushion to a handheld tape recorder with the name *Walkman* on it. "You know, music is all digital now. You can download it."

"Nah." She put on a serious face. "I already have a great music collection. Why would I buy it twice?"

"Good point." I held up my phone to show her the time. "What's the urgency?"

Swales stuffed her Walkman and headphones into an oversized bag and shoved a case file toward me. "It's about the mummified body."

The floorboards overhead groaned as morning traffic entered the station, dust drifting into the light. The plastic sleeve was old and covered in the same dust; the manilla folder's jacket labeled with a date that was thirty years earlier. "This case is decades old. Victim found in the same state?"

"Not quite. But it's the salt," Swales said and pushed the folder into my hands. "I didn't recall the similarity until I got to the morgue."

"How about the MO?" I asked, doing the calendar math in my head. If the case was connected, the killer would have to be much older. "Shortcut this for me."

Swales pulled a thermos from her bag, the canister ancient. She poured herself coffee, the smell strong, and then offered to refresh my cup as we pulled up a pair of fold-out chairs and opened the file.

"It was my first year," she began, her eyes narrowing with a smile. "Ironic when you think about it. Considering retirement, and this new case possibly being my last."

"And your first case involving salt." I drank the coffee offered, the taste of it warm and pleasant.

She opened the folder and spilled old crime-scene photographs onto the table. "The victim was female. A mother. Her name was Connie Jamison."

"And she was mummified?" I asked, picking up a color photograph, yellowed by the years since. The picture showed what looked like the interior of a garage. At the center was a pinewood box that was the right height and depth for a coffin, but it was too short to fit an adult. "The victim's legs were folded?"

"Correct," Swales answered. "The husband, Gerald Jamison, he stuffed her body in the box, pushing the woman's legs up to her chest before encasing her in salt."

I searched the other photographs until reaching a mugshot, a picture of Gerald Jamison, the lighting harsh, his face cratered with pock marks and riddled with frown lines. "Were there more?"

Swales gave her head a shake. "Just the one. His wife. He left behind a son though."

"Tell me about the scene." I was hoping her memory recalled more than just the salt.

She sighed and drank a mouthful of coffee, her earlier energy waning. "It was a long time ago, but I do remember the smell. I hadn't thought of the case in years."

"Until the smell yesterday," I commented, leafing through the paperwork which listed Gerald Jamison's conviction for second-degree murder and abuse of a corpse. He was sentenced to life in prison without the possibility of parole, the judge calling his acts particularly heinous. "Are you thinking it's a copycat? That someone might have picked up on the old case and mirrored the mummification?"

Swales dipped her head and raised her shoulders. "I wouldn't know." Capping her thermos and gathering her things, she added, "I thought it might help for you to see though. The memory woke me up and I had to come in and find the file."

"How about words? Like the ones we found written on the note?"

Her lips thinned as she searched her memory. Swales shook her head. "Not that I recall. But I'm sure if there were, it'd be in the file."

I braced her arm with a squeeze, appreciating that she called. "This is a huge help. Especially since the case is new and we've got nothing but a body and a note to work with."

"Speaking of which, that body isn't going to autopsy itself." Swales readied her Walkman headphones, adding, "I've got to get back to the morgue."

"Any findings yet?"

Swales made a tsk-tsk sound, her eyes narrowing as she wagged her finger. "Casey, you know better than to ask. But I will tell you when the autopsies are scheduled. I'll call?"

"Yes, as soon as you have something. Sooner?" I joked.

Swales pushed the headset onto her head, pressing play on the tape recorder as she spun around and hummed, her voice rising with the steps she climbed, leaving me alone with the case file.

I turned my attention to the details, taking a picture of the court filings and some of the crime-scene photographs, sending them to Nichelle with a request to build a profile. I wanted to know where Gerald Jamison was these days. While he was in his mid thirties when convicted, possibility of release would only come if he was pardoned or if his sentence was commuted to a fixed term. A lot can happen in thirty years.

In the folder, I found Gerald Jamison's handwritten confession. The pages were from a legal pad, aged and crinkly like the photographs; a round coffee stain on the first page which had turned black, probably left there by the interviewing detective. At the bottom, a signature, scrawled haphazardly, the name unrecognizable.

I skimmed the pages. Gerald had admitted to having built the pine box and placing his wife inside, and then covering her with loose salt. He'd also written that the salt had come from his truck—his job being a driver for a salt manufacture and his having access to large quantities.

I read on, Gerald providing the date when he'd built the box, and an explanation of his wife falling down the steps and hitting her head. He explained how he'd come home one evening from his truck route and they'd argued, and then his seeing her lifeless body at the bottom of their staircase, a large pool of blood on the floor, an injury to her head. Afraid of how it would look, since they'd had the police to their house in the past, Gerald decided to hide his wife's body, using the salt to mask the smell of decomposition.

Second-degree murder? The district attorney was able to convict the husband of murder without premeditation, citing it a result of the argument. The signed confession was submitted as evidence, the DA having enough to convince the jury. There were also previous accounts of the couple arguing—the neighbors submitting affidavits and taking the stand to testify under oath. There were the husband's fingerprints on the stairs along with the pinewood box he'd built and then placed his wife inside, covering her with more than five hundred pounds of salt.

Past visits from the police

I texted Nichelle, adding to the earlier message. There was history of the police at the Jamison house. Who else lived there? There might be police records that could offer us some names.

See what you can dig up.

I found nothing in the old case about a note, about words like the ones we'd discovered. But I did find a name. It was the name of Gerald's employer: Salt Mineral Incorporated. I wrote it down and texted it to Emanuel. Thinking of our mummified body, could the sheer volume of salt required be more than someone can pick up at a local market? With catering companies, restaurants, and commercial uses, I'd think anyone could buy just about any amount of salt needed. Where did the salt come from? My gut told me that if we found the source of the salt, we'd find the killer.

CHAPTER THIRTEEN

The station's conference room was airless and stiff, the team scattered, Tracy and Nichelle sitting with their faces aglow by laptop screens. Emanuel and a few others stood around and watched their phones or gazed out the window, a soft breeze carrying autumn leaves to fall against the glass. The team looked like mannequins, but that changed as soon as I entered the room, their eyes falling behind me, waiting to see what would happen when Detective Cheryl Smithson arrived.

I clutched my hands, my palms growing itchy and damp. This was the first meeting with the two of us working together again. It was inevitable, and given our history, it was apt to be rocky. I knew I'd have to learn to work with her again, but that didn't mean I had to like it. In a recent previous case, Cheryl had dragged Jericho's name through the mud, and it cost him dearly. It cost him an election and almost his home. Cheryl was motivated for Cheryl alone—a rocky expectation was an understatement.

I'd already learned Cheryl was unhappy with the arrangements, and that she'd made sure everyone was aware of it. While I'd have preferred it if there was just one lead overseeing everything, that wasn't the case. Those ranking above me and Cheryl, particularly the newly elected mayor, had suggested that we co-lead the investigation of the mummified body. Given the addition of the marine patrol and the growing list of abandoned houses, I understood their reason and agreed to the arrangement, regardless of how uncomfortable it might be for the two of us. For now, I told them I'd play nice. I'd do so no matter how much bile rose to the back of my throat.

The room's low chatter hushed when Cheryl arrived outside the conference room, heading in our direction. The sight of her was surprising, looking older than I knew her to be, looking professional. She was dressed more formally than she used to, wearing blue slacks and heels and an expensive beige blouse. It was more than the new clothes though. Cheryl entered the room with a swag in her shoulders, her head held high, and a strut that was sturdy with confidence. She smiled pleasantly, greeting the room, but her grin faded when she saw me, her eyes firm as she dropped a bag onto the conference room table. I sensed the annoyance, her cheeks turning red like her hair.

The wide loopy curls swung around her shoulders as she pivoted so her back was turned away from the room. She took to my side, the smell of lavender shampoo wafting, her mouth near my ear, her breath hot. In a forced whisper, she said, "Just so you know, I made a formal objection to the mayor about our co-leading this case."

I stood in silence, unsure of what to say. I thought I could actually feel the anger coming off her body like steam rising from a hot spring. She was fuming, and I eased back to put some room between us. I felt a snarky bark coming and couldn't hold it in. I commented with a shrug, "You'll try to keep up?"

Emanuel sat closest to us and cupped his mouth to hide his smile. Cheryl balled her hands, closing her eyelids briefly as she took a breath. When she let go, the flush in her cheeks faded. "Well," she said, spinning around to face the group, "shall we get started?"

"Yes," I answered. I decided that'd be the one sardonic moment between us. There was a mummified body and the murder of Jocelyn Winter. With autopsies scheduled, and lab results pending, those were more important. "We shall."

"Where are we?" Cheryl asked.

"We have two bodies, one surely a homicide, and another that's more of a question," I said, opening the meeting. "First, Jocelyn Winter, a high school student. Her body was found with a single injury to the head. I've started work on this case with Dr. Swales."

"Has a cause of death been determined yet?" Emanuel asked.

Reluctantly, I had to shake my head.

"Accidental?" Cheryl asked.

"We'll hear from Dr. Swales when there are autopsy results. But I've requested permission to interview classmates." Before the team followed with another question, I added, "And since this may not be a homicide, we'll concentrate on the second body."

Cheryl plugged the video cable into her laptop. The screen at the front of the room showed the pictures of the attic, the mummified body at the center. "In the report, there was mention about the orientation of the body?"

Tracy raised her hand, the sight of it bringing me back to why we were really here, the pettiness set aside—absurd when considering we had an unsolved murder. I also needed this. I needed to be with my team and hadn't realized how much I'd missed it. "What do you have, Tracy?"

"I'm leaning on an idea about the pyramids," she said, holding up a color print with two pyramids, the sun low on the horizon, its placement directly between them. "Ancient Egyptians and mummification. I'm proposing the body's orientation from east to west and it's centering north to south in the room was purposeful, possibly in similarity to the locations of the great pyramids."

"The pyramids?" Cheryl asked, her tone glib. Tracy put her hand down but kept her head up. She'd been on the receiving end of Cheryl's first reactions before and knew what to expect. "What else do we have?"

"One minute. I'd like to explore the idea." I got caught in Cheryl's stare, but ignored it. There was definitely something in the placement of the body and it needed to be explored. "Tracy, what's your thinking?"

There was hesitation, but I urged her to continue. "I got this house's position using a sitemap I found in the county archives. The foundation was built to sit in perfect alignment along the cardinal points of north, south, east, and west. The accuracy is to a tenth of one degree."

"How did you take the measurements for accuracy?" Nichelle asked. "The property documents only included location data."

"A maps app I found online," Tracy answered. "Along with their tools."

"Nice," Nichelle complimented. "Send me the work and I'll confirm it."

"If I'm understanding this, the killer selected *this* house, believing it was special?" I asked.

"That's what I think. The great pyramids are royal tombs and I think we can look to them for reference."

"For the list of abandoned houses, let's prioritize the searches based on their alignments." Cheryl asked, catching on to where Tracy was going.

"That's the idea," Tracy said. "We'll know where to search first."

"That's good," I told her, seeing a dimple flash. "We have the marine patrol to work with in the search. Adding priority to the list is valuable."

"I suggest developing a map in advance of the house-to-house search also," Cheryl said.

"I'm on it," Tracy offered.

"Nichelle will help with the alignment validation," I said. Nichelle gave a nod, agreeing.

"And the note? The words?" Cheryl asked, rapping her knuckles against the table, bringing the room's attention back to her.

"No outstanding leads yet." With my laptop plugged in, I showed the words on a second monitor. *Distressing calumnies, I, am, toward* and *affect*. "But work is in progress."

"Nothing?" she asked with a strong tone of disappointment, forced and purposeful. Like her stare, I ignored it.

"We are exploring famous literature, novels that have been linked to serial killers and flagged by the FBI," I answered, assuring her there was work in play. Looking at the words on the monitor, an idea came to me, and I decided to run with it. "We might also be able to use the words to find relationships across them, a pattern."

"Age, education level," Emanuel said, catching on. "That sort of thing?"

"Exactly. We could determine a level of education based on these words. It would give us an indication of who we are looking for."

"What else do we know about the killer?"

I moved to the monitor, chin in hand as I envisioned who it was we were searching for. "I'd suggest a male, but that's solely based on the history and statistical data—the majority of murders that include ceremony and orchestration being committed by men. I'd also suggest middle-aged, educated given his knowledge of chemistry and biology."

"The incisions?" Tracy asked. "To drain the victim."

"Some training in medical school. Possibly a dropout," I said, throwing the ideas to the room. "It's a start of a criminal profile."

"Good. Keep with it." Cheryl rapped her knuckles again. I found the sound of it, the gesture even, very annoying. "Now, how about the salt? From the preliminary reports, there was salt used?"

"Correct," I answered. "Dr. Swales believes it was a key component used in the mummification—"

"Nichelle!" Cheryl blurted, talking over me. Nichelle's brown eyes were large with confusion. "I want you to reach out to Swales and start researching the salt."

"We've already got Nichelle working the abandoned houses, the real-estate and housing permits and postal addresses, and—"

"Nichelle can work multiple tasks," Cheryl said, facing me.

"Guys?" Nichelle raised her hand. "I'm literally right in front of you."

Nodding her head toward Nichelle, expecting agreement, Cheryl continued, "You'll begin an investigation into the salt."

The bile I'd held down earlier rose to the back of my throat. I needed to find patience and took a breath. "I suggest the team's work garner their strengths." As I spoke, the mayor and sheriff walked by the conference room, watching us through the glass. I remembered the one thing I didn't like about this meeting room—it was a fishbowl. All glass for anyone to watch. I could see they were gauging our progress. I faced Cheryl, softening my voice, and dipping my chin. "Listen, try it my way? And if you're not happy with the progress, we'll change things up."

Cheryl shifted her weight, grinding the tip of her shoe against the floor as though stomping out a cigarette. She regarded my words, my request, and finally relinquished. "Fine. We'll try it your way. You want Emanuel to work the salt?"

With her approval I squared my shoulders with the table, stealing back some of the space so that I was closer to the center. "Emanuel," I said, raising my voice to sound more forceful. "Other than the residue on the sheet, there are no salt samples recovered from the body."

"But the reports of a smell?" Cheryl asked.

"Swales believes the bodies were encased in salt. It was removed after mummification, and the skin leeched the residue onto the sheet," I explained, voice remaining forceful, masking the fact that I didn't fully understand the science yet.

"If the salt came from the bodies, wouldn't there be some on the sheets?" Cheryl asked, pitching her hand on her hip. "I mean, you reported smelling it."

"Sure, you can smell the ocean too, but what was leeched isn't enough for a sample," I said. "With the lack of it, let's move on to identifying what we can."

Emanuel flipped through his notebook, the size of it miniature in his hands. "Without any samples, what do you suggest?"

"Arithmetic," I answered. Heads lifted from behind laptops and phone screens. "Actually, all of us can do this one."

"You want to know how much salt was required?" Tracy asked.

"Exactly," I answered. "That means, we use what we do know to calculate the amount of salt needed to mummify a body that is roughly the same size as the victim."

"We already know the victim's height," Emanuel said, catching on. "I'll get an estimate from Dr. Swales on an estimated body weight."

From the corner of my eye, I could see Cheryl shaking her head. "What does knowing the victim's weight get us?"

I scanned the table, Nichelle's brow rising: an answer waiting for me to acknowledge. "Nichelle, you want to share?"

Nichelle leaned forward, her cat mug in hand. "Knowing the weight will help us identify where the killer could have purchased salt in large quantities."

"We're assuming the volume used to mummify a body is going to be large," I added.

"I've already confirmed none of the local markets sell in large volumes," Emanuel offered.

"He may have purchased the salt online? We'll have to expand the search," I explained to Cheryl. "And look at salt mines and suppliers on the east coast that sell in bulk."

The Crying House

"To cover a person entirely, encasing them in salt would have required hundreds, maybe a thousand pounds." Tracy showed a fifty-pound sack, purchasable online. "But they would need twenty or more to do the job."

"Emanuel can also explore if it's possible to buy larger quantities and have it shipped," I said, nodding toward him. "I think we've got the gist of what we need to know about the salt. Let's move on."

Cheryl stepped to the side of the conference room table, close to where she used to sit when working for me. "What's next?" she asked.

"The sheet." I motioned to Nichelle, a picture of the sheet appearing on the monitor as I paced the front of the room. "It came from somewhere. What's the thread count? Was it expensive or generic, something available at a local department store?"

"I'll take that one," Cheryl answered, surprising me. "I know a little about sheets and thread counts."

"Does salt go bad?" Nichelle asked, the screen refreshing with a review of our field report. "Also, why wasn't there any salt found on the body?"

I looked at my hands, my fingernails, and then Cheryl's hair, the luster, and the shine of it. "Like Tracy said. This house was special. The killer selected it to place his victim. He'd prepared her, cleaned her hair, combed it. He'd given her a manicure and I'd say as part of his ritual, he cleaned every bit of salt from her skin beforehand." These were only suggestions. It was likely I'd remain uncertain until we heard it confirmed by the killer.

"Mummify the body, prepare it, position it," Cheryl said, thinking aloud. "That's a lot to do in an abandoned house without getting caught."

"What if the abandoned house isn't where the body was mummified?" I proposed to the team. I thought of the challenges we had getting inside, and then climbing up to the third level. But then

I thought of the ocean. "It had to be elsewhere. With that much moisture in the air, mummification would be impossible."

Cheryl looked to Tracy. "What else did you find out about the ancient Egyptians?" she asked, a slight tone of sarcasm in her voice.

"Well," she began, tapping her keyboard and searching through her notes. Although I hadn't assigned it directly, I'd posed the question about us not finding any salt and the mummification. I expected she would have investigated it. "To answer Nichelle's first question, salt is a preservative which means there's no chance of spoil, no fungal or bacterial or yeast or any microbial growth to take place. But for the mummification process, an arid location is a requirement."

"The killer had to have performed the mummification elsewhere. When it was ready, he moved the body to the abandoned house," I added. Cheryl joined me at the table, refreshing the screen to another picture of the attic and the outline of the body on the sheet. I went to the screen and motioned around the sheet. "As we can see here, there is salt residue staining the sheet."

"You mentioned leeched?" Emanuel asked. "What is it from?"

Tracy stood, her chair rolling behind her. On her screen there were pictures of chemical elements. "Salt doesn't contain water, which is why it's such a great preservative."

"Then where did the stain come from?" Cheryl asked.

"It's from the body," I answered, my tone flat, the idea of how mummification works a bit unsettling.

"The Egyptians used what's called natron, a natural salt and ash mix that they harvested," Tracy answered, swiping the mouse to show a series of pictures, each of them exhibiting a different stage of the mummification process. "Salt is a desiccant, a chemical that is really good at removing water from things."

"That confirms the killer needed a dry location." I stared at the stain on the sheet, struggling to stomach the discussion. "It also helped to prevent decomposition."

Nichelle cringed, saying, "Nothing for nothing, but that's gross."

"Can any type of salt be used?" Cheryl asked.

"That's another part of the investigation. I've asked Tracy to research it," I answered.

Cheryl lifted her chin, understanding, and said, "Tracy's findings along with Emanuel's will center our search on the source of the salt."

Shifting topics, I held up a picture of the victim's face. With the sight of it came gasps from those who hadn't seen it yet. "The hardest question we have to answer is the victim's identity."

"How?" Emanuel asked, shoulders hung in a shrug. "With the body in such a state, is it possible?"

"With such a drastic change in the face, it's unlikely to resemble anyone." I held another picture, changing the angle. "To complicate things, Dr. Swales has been unable to recover any fingerprints. There might be dental records. Maybe DNA recovery. But both will require significant time."

The sheriff and mayor walked by the conference room a second time, the direction opposite to their first. They were checking on us again, the interruption nagging at the back of my mind like an itch. Reluctantly, I offered them a nod and saw Cheryl do the same, her sharing in the sentiment, the two of us finding common ground in wanting to be left to do what we do—investigate murder.

"Reconstruction?" Nichelle said, voice wavering with uncertainty. She scanned the room for agreement, adding, "Of the face. Like they do with skeletal remains."

I was familiar with the technique—having used it in previous cases—applying computer models to put flesh to bone and create a picture of a victim long after they'd died and their bodies had perished. "Now you're talking," I said. "Get with Dr. Swales and start researching what's needed."

"Awesome!" Nichelle rubbed her hands together vigorously. "I just installed new GPUs which will cut the modeling time by half."

The meeting went on another thirty minutes, the conversations going around the table, my confirming a direction and instructions with each member of the team. And though Cheryl would never admit it, I could sense the appreciation from her; a smile coming slowly, her eyes warming graciously when I sought her approvals for the assignments. Setting our differences aside, it was guidance that I offered and, with it, we made progress.

As the morning exited to midday with the sun shifted across the sky, daylight bleeding through the windows, some of what was tasked began to come together. I centered on a list of the abandoned houses, the count growing, the conference room's large screen showing a satellite map image so that we could determine their positions relative to the cardinal points of north, south, east, and west. And as Tracy had suggested, more than half held an accuracy of better than a tenth of one degree, which was like the first house. I couldn't help but think that where there was one body, we were sure to find more.

When the time came for a break, I revisited the Jocelyn Winter case, the words from her diary sticking in my head the way a tune on the radio will sometimes follow throughout the day. I borrowed the diary from Tracy, taking it to my desk alone, my feet up and leafing through the pages with care, as though my fingertips were touching her spirit and reading her thoughts, her writing bringing me emotionally close to the victim—which was dangerous grounds for me. It was dangerous grounds for any detective.

"Is that the diary?" Nichelle asked as she returned to her cubical.

"Tracy told you about it?"

"Any chance I could give it a read?" I dipped my chin, questioning the relevance to the tasks given to her. She saw this, and added, "You never know. There could be something in there about her cell phone."

"Nothing yet?" I asked. "No signal?"

"Other than I confirmed Jocelyn Winter's phone does exist." Her focus stayed locked on the diary. "I'm working with the phone company, and we have tracking enabled. If the phone comes online, we'll get a ping and have a location."

"Keep on it," I said, and held up the diary. "I'll give this back in a few. You and Tracy can work through it. I asked Tracy about the note and the words. If you see them anywhere in the diary, let me know."

"Will do," she said. "I'm cross-referencing with famous literature as well." I gave her a thumbs-up as she went to her cubical.

While I didn't have any solid evidence that one murder was related or unrelated to the other, there was still the possibility the killer of the mummified victim had been interrupted by the teen. Did Jocelyn and her killer's paths accidentally cross? The questions were many, mixing into a jumble like voices, the noise making it impossible to distinguish the one I needed to hear. When my phone rang with a text message from the mayor, I knew it was about Jocelyn's case.

My screen read:

Jocelyn Winter. The school interviews are approved.

Her text meant we were going back to high school. We were going to meet Jocelyn's classmates.

CHAPTER FOURTEEN

Sixteen Months Earlier

Beth Fremont hitched her thumb over her shoulder, an eighteen-wheeler passing, a cloud of hot exhaust and road dust pelting her bare arms and face. She closed her eyelids and mouth, cowering as the gust stung her skin and buffeted her body like a flag struck by a stiff wind. A cloudless sky, the sun was high and baking the top of her head, the road's blacktop dancing as heat shimmered above it in a watery mirage. It was four in the afternoon and the heat had been unrelenting since she'd set out this morning. She searched ahead and behind for a cell tower, her phone's service dismal, and found none. But the time was accurate, her gut wrenching with learning she'd have to walk another ten hours before she reached the beach.

A full day of walking, a small price to pay for a week in the sand and sun, she thought casually and recalled her mother's fun stories about hitching rides across the country when she was her age. Beth slowed as she suddenly blanked when trying to hear her mom's voice. It had only been a few years, but she'd been warned this would happen one day. She couldn't remember the sound of it, her heart sinking when the intonations were gone, the tone missing. There was the way her mom's funny laughter pitched high: she heard it, but it was faint, the memories fading. "I miss you, Mom."

She faced the oncoming traffic and walked backward heel to toe, poster board on her front, the sign with big black marker letters reading, *Wildwood Senior Week*. Maybe she'd get lucky and some of her school friends would drive by and stop for her. A lot of them said they were going to the beach too. It was the end of their final year of high school, the week at the shore a tradition, a pastime for the kids before going off to college. Just because she couldn't get a ride didn't mean she couldn't go.

Beth pitched her thumb again, thunder rumbling as though she'd accidentally cued it, an oncoming storm unexpected. Hitching seemed like a good idea the day before, her father adamant about her not traveling. He was especially adamant about her not taking the car and driving on the highway. And though she loved him, he'd changed when her mom died, making life at home with him unbearable.

The morose thoughts came as the footsteps she counted crossed another thousand. *Maybe it would be different if Mom had died from cancer. Maybe Dad wouldn't treat me like this if it had been some other slow-growing disease?* It was a bad traffic accident though, and just because it happened to her mom, didn't mean it would happen to her too. After a week at the Jersey Shore, she'd head south to the heart of North Carolina. There, she had a job at her cousin's restaurant waiting for her. It would be a fresh start. Then she could show her father she was able to take care of herself. Heck, she might leave Philadelphia behind for a year, maybe more. College could wait.

Plump raindrops struck the top of her head, cooling her scalp in an instant. A breeze sliced across the highway, dropping the temperature ten degrees, making her pause, recognizing the dangers that came with a strong front. Beth peered into the sky, the sun's brightness in jeopardy, a distant wave of black and blue clouds marching toward her from the west. She sifted through what she'd brought in her backpack: her clothes and bathing suits, along with bags of personals. What she didn't have was a rain jacket, a windbreaker or anything for bad weather.

Then she saw the line of hard rain, the color of the trees dimmed by the thick downpour. Lightning split the sky, searing the air, and causing the hairs on her arms to stand on end. A thunderous, Godlike boom shook the ground and reverberated through her, as though a short earthquake had struck the ground, the colors of her *Beach or Bust Wildwood* sign beginning to run, the letters drippy like the black mascara around her eyes. Another hot blade forked across the sky, splitting open the clouds with clashing color, the air concussed with instant thunder, making her scream with startled fright.

"Shit!" she shouted harshly as steam rose from the pavement and crawled around her legs. The heat dissipated fast and would turn her cold soon as rainwater seeped through her clothes. Another volley of fast lightning strike came—Beth shielding her head with her sign. "Oh shit!"

She edged to the side of the road, climbing down the embankment until she was shoulder high to the road, hoping the dip in the ground might protect her. A horn blared from above, the insides of a car she knew from her school packed from window to window, the glass fogging, the familiar faces a blur. She'd missed a ride. Rainwater dripped into her eyes, her hair flat against her head, her clothes drenched and clinging to her skin. The sky was full gray, as though a dingy blanket had been thrown over her part of the world. There was no sign of the sun returning, no return of the heat.

Her toes wet, her feet beginning to slosh inside her shoes, Beth made her way back to the road and to the gravelly shoulder, her wrinkled thumb in the air, rainwater dripping from her wrist. She was willing to take any ride now. Rain pelted her head and arms, ran down her face, and sprayed from her mouth. She held her arm out, stretching, her skin bright white in the gray light, the plans for a tan coming to mind, warming her with fond thoughts of sleeping on the hot sand.

The Crying House

It'll be worth it, she thought and chanced a step closer to the road. Traffic was light, her taking backroads to escape the risk of getting picked up by the cops. A single truck appeared in the distance, its headlights on and flashing once to signal seeing her. There was nobody else coming, and Beth held the sign, peering down at it, the words and letters a sloppy mess.

"Useless now," she muttered and tore it from her neck, tossing the sheet of poster board to the roadside. In the sign's absence, Beth realized the stormy rain had bled through her shirt and bra, the clingy sheer fabric showing everything. A flush of embarrassment bloomed on her neck and face as a Ford Bronco slowed and stopped for her, its windows fogged, the inside of the cab hidden. The passenger door swung open, a man appearing, his look was soft and not at all like she'd expected. In a voice that was calm and carried quietly, he asked, "I bet you'd love to get out of the rain?"

When his eyes shifted to her front, she covered her chest with her arms and answered, "Yes, I would. Thank you." Before entering the truck, Beth turned her back to him, placing her backpack against her front. Horns blared, a sedan careening past, followed by a cloudy spray, dousing the truck and tearing loose a tarp in the truck bed. The corner closest to her flapped violently, whipping the air with a snap as she continued to follow the passing car, wondering who was inside, the rear window soaped with the lettering, *Senior Week*.

"Would you mind tying that down," the driver asked.

"I got it," she said, taking hold of the loose bungee cord, tugging on the veiny yellow and green rope until the tarp stopped flapping, the corded line cutting into her palms. Beneath the cover, she glimpsed a half dozen burlap sacks, the ends of them sewn shut, an odor of salt strong enough that she could taste it. She looked briefly at her hand, a rope burn in her palm, answering, "It's the least I could do."

"I can't afford to get them wet," he said, peering up at the sky. "It'd ruin everything."

"Everything?" she asked, curiously, while settling into the passenger seat and placing her feet to the sides of a large blue and white cooler.

As Beth closed the door and wiped the rainwater from her face, the storm pelting the cab's roof and windshield, he answered, "Yes. Everything."

Beth Fremont never arrived at her cousin's restaurant. There were no reports of her arriving for senior week either. Concerned, her cousin contacted Beth's father and the police. Reports were made, and a missing persons case was opened in her name. Beth's identification was circulated to every police station and to every firehouse from the north to south along the east coast.

For a while, a *Beth Fremont Missing Person* flier waved, tattered and frayed, on a telephone pole. From sunrise to sunset, and throughout the evenings, the wind picked at the flier, pelting it with the beach sand Beth had desperately wanted to touch. The tiny grains struck like bullets, beating the once sturdy paper, causing it to grow weak, the ink fading. Then came the day the flier's hold finally failed, the wind taking Beth's picture and her name, the two soon forgotten.

CHAPTER FIFTEEN

It was Monday morning, the Outer Banks quiet the day before, a few of us working what we could, taking advantage of the downtime to research and refresh. A news story flashed on my phone about Jocelyn Winter's mother having attended Sunday Mass, the church filling to capacity, the sermon with a heavy tone of injustice, of hate and the crimes brought against one of their own. The press lapped it up like horses at a trough.

With permissions that started in the mayor's office and the school district's superintendent, the East OBX High School principal, and their guidance counselor, I found myself walking the halls of a high school by mid-morning. It had been years since I'd last stepped foot inside a school, but much of it was the same, even the smell, which was a mix of books, cleaners, and a faint scent of the cafeteria's square pizza slices. Reflections of the ceiling lights bounced from a smooth stone floor as I passed rows of red and blue and yellow lockers. Across an archway of a connecting hallway, there were curly streamers, a decorative poster beneath it, the student body celebrating a homecoming dance. I came to stop at a showcase with thick wood shelves and glass, carrying plaques and trophies along with pictures of the football teams, the years dating back thirty or more. In the more recent team pictures, there were framed newspaper headlines highlighting football games won over a school rival—West OBX High School.

A student bumped me as she rushed down the hallway, searching her bag, a school ID swinging from her hand while she tracked the time on a clock above the lockers. As the bell rang, the classroom doors swung open, the students pouring into the hallway where I stood with Tracy and Nichelle, their flooding every available inch of space in an orderly stampede. There were the fastidious kids, the ones with their heads down, hands clenched to the straps of their backpacks, feet a blur as they sped past us. There were the jocks, walking carefree, joking and goofing as teachers prodded for them to get a move on. One slowed to give Tracy a smile, mistaking her for a student, his eyes leveling with her station identification as his mouth parted with a slight gasp, surprise casually showing on his face. Tracy flashed a bashful smile as he hurried on with his friends, and she made herself busy swiping errantly at her phone's screen. There were the girls who owned the school too. I recognized them immediately. They followed nobody and took their time, glancing around and speaking closely while using their phones every couple of minutes. It was in that pack I saw the student we were most interested in—Grace Armstrong. I confirmed it with a look at my phone, Nichelle providing us with pictures she'd found online.

"So, this is high school," Tracy said, the hallway around us emptying. I looped my badge and its lanyard around my neck, motioning to Nichelle to do the same. Tracy triple-checked her new identification, the picture of her face bright with a smile, which is exactly how I would've expected it to be. "I've only seen them in the movies."

"Hold up a second," Nichelle said, her hand in the air, fixing a hard stare, trying to digest what was said.

"You were homeschooled?" I asked.

"Uh-huh," Tracy answered, dimples showing as she drank in the details and watched the students. "I didn't even go to kindergarten or pre-school."

"And you have *never* been inside a school?" Nichelle asked, head dipping with disbelief.

"Nope. Never." Tracy knelt to touch the floor, pressing her palm against it. She went to a locker next. "I mean, I've seen them in the movies and on television, like the movie *The Breakfast Club*. Just never been inside one before."

"*The Breakfast Club?*" Nichelle asked with a laugh. She peered over her shoulder at me. "You believe this one?"

I tried to hold in the laugh, but somehow learning she'd been homeschooled her entire life didn't come as a terrific surprise. "Well, now is your chance, Tracy. Take your time to look around."

As the two went on ahead of me, I read a text message from Cheryl. She'd requested the return of Tracy and Nichelle before two this afternoon. I'd borrowed them for the day with permission, taking them off the case of the mummified body to help interview Jocelyn Winter's classmates. There were potentially hundreds of students to consider, but we'd narrowed our focus on names from Jocelyn's diary and students from her class. For now, I ignored the text, showing Tracy and Nichelle a copy of Jocelyn's schedule.

"Can we see the library?" Tracy asked excitedly. "Do you think it'll look like the one in the movie?"

"Yeah," Nichelle answered. "I'm sure you'll see it has books like the one in the movies."

"It just so happens, the library is where we will be today." A second bell rang, echoing with a sharp clap, the hallways empty, save for a few late students running as classroom doors shut in unison.

With the students in their homeroom classes, we walked alone as a voice bellowed over the school's speakers. Tracy flinched. A low gravelly voice, throat clearing, a heavy breath coming before a long pause.

"It is with heaviest of hearts, I am saddened to report the death of one our own. The school has lost senior classmate, Jocelyn Winter. This is a traumatic loss. For today, first period is a free period. Your homeroom

teachers, school nurses, and your guidance counselors are available to anyone who needs to talk."

When the announcement ended, the hallway quieted again, echoing the sound of our footsteps. We said nothing as we passed the classrooms, the student faces showing through the glass, shock in their eyes, some crying, some raising hands, most on their phones.

By the time Tracy had finished her touristy exploration of the school, we'd already entered the third period of the day. Jocelyn's class for that period filed into the library, the students taking to the center where they were told they had a free period. We were given the library's audio room, a fifteen-by-fifteen-foot room with soundproofing pads that were planted on the walls in checkerboard squares. There were shelves of audio equipment, including reel-to-reel tape players and turntables that played vinyl records, along with a modern fare of CDs and computers that I assumed were used for mixing digital tracks. A table had been placed for us at the center of the room with three chairs on one side and across from a single chair.

For the student's security, the parents of Jocelyn's class were notified in advance, agreeing to have the school's guidance counselor participate, her sitting in the corner closest to the door. She wasn't much older than me, late thirties maybe, her hair brown and stringy, wearing horn-rimmed glasses, her skin waxy and shiny. She wore a beige blouse with ruffles in the front, and a pair of pleated blue pants. In one hand, she held a clipboard with the names of the students we were to see. A cup of tea was in the other, the paper teabag label sitting on the outside, an orange-pekoe flavor.

"Next student?" she asked, opening the door.

"Yes, please." She nodded, leaving the three of us alone. "Let's hope number five has something useful for us."

"When do we get to talk to some of the students from Jocelyn's diary?" Nichelle asked, her laptop showing a spreadsheet with a list of student names. "I don't have the class roster, just the student names."

"I hope it's soon," Tracy said, eyes dulled with boredom.

"The school visit losing its luster?" I asked, joshing her.

Perched on her elbows, her chin resting on her hands, Tracy pointed above the door to a clock with a red second hand that ticked with each second. "I'm not kidding you, but I could've sworn I saw that clock's minute hand jump backward a full minute before the end of last period."

"School clock," I said, sharing a laugh with Nichelle. Tracy looked on us with confusion. "Boredom can trick your eyes."

"Officers," the guidance counselor said, a student to her side—a pretty girl with dark brown hair and eyes the same color, her skin like the color of wheat, her arms red from recent time in the sunlight. "This is Laura Sumter."

"Hi Laura," I said, putting on a smile. By the end of the day, my cheeks would be sore from forcing them. "Have a seat."

"Am I in trouble?" she asked, voice shaky, and her approach cautious.

"Trouble?" Tracy asked, answering the question with a question as a means to entice a response. "Why would you ask?"

Laura shrugged as she eased into the seat. "Maybe for being at the party."

"No trouble at all," I said, assuring her, and trying to settle her nerves. "I'm sure this morning's announcement was difficult to hear?"

"We already knew," she answered, her voice trailing as she looked away nervously. When her focus returned, she added, "I mean, with the news on TV and all."

"Understandable you would have heard about Jocelyn." I stayed silent a moment, wanting to see if she'd offer more. When she said nothing, I asked, "You mentioned the party?"

"Uh-huh," she answered, chewing on her upper lip.

"You were there the entire time?" I noted her name with a check next to it.

Laura twirled a lock of hair around her finger, tugging on it as she regarded the question. She glanced at the guidance counselor; the woman nodded with encouragement. "Most of it." She held out her hands. "A lot of us were there. Homecoming and all."

"Did you know Jocelyn Winter?" I kept my eyes with hers, gauging her reaction to my question.

The corner of Laura's mouth curled into a smile, briefly, and then thinned. "Sure. We've known… I mean, I knew her all her life." Tears appeared, standing a moment before she swiped at them. Her voice breaking, she said with a whisper, "We… we were friends."

"And neighbors?" Nichelle gently asked. I could see she'd looked up Laura's address: across the street from Jocelyn. The girl nodded silently.

"Laura, do you know if anyone would have reasons to want to hurt your friend?" Tracy glanced at her notebook, the question being one of the few I'd given her to ask.

The girl's eyebrows furrowed as she shifted in her seat, her expression changing to one that gave validation. "Yeah. Like, everyone there knew there was going to be a fight."

"The fight." I touched my head where Jocelyn's injury was located. "What can you tell us about it?"

Laura mirrored my motion, raising her hand before placing it in her lap. "Jocelyn and Grace Armstrong," Laura answered, offering the name eagerly. "And Grace's friends. They jumped Jocelyn, but only pushed her around."

"Since you live on the same street, did you go to the party together?" I asked.

Laura shifted uncomfortably again. "Well, yeah," she answered, tugging on her hair until her finger went white. While the audio room was tempered cool, Laura's forehead gleamed, a sheen of sweat. "We almost always went to them together."

"Them?" Nichelle asked. "The parties?"

"Uh-huh."

"Did you leave the parties together too?" I asked, wondering how Jocelyn ended up alone.

"Some of the time." Laura shook her head, adding, "But not always."

"And that night? What time did you leave the house?"

Laura's gaze drifted to the ceiling as she considered the hours. When it returned, she answered with a shrug. "I don't remember. But it was late. I remember the tide was coming in because my shoes got wet."

"Then the tide was out when the party began?" Tracy asked, jotting a note, a glimpse of a timeline on her tablet.

"Uh-huh," Laura said. "Tide was low when we got there."

"That means you were there for at least six hours?" I recalled the tidal charts I'd reviewed when I first arrived at the abandoned house. The tides would also help establish timing, tell us exactly when the beach beneath the house was free of seawater.

"That sounds about right," she answered. "High tide at midnight."

"Midnight," I said, repeating it while I wrote it down. Laura knowing the tide sounded strange, but I'd learned to expect it. That was life in the Outer Banks, and it separated the locals from the visitors.

"Tell us more about the fight." I noted the clock and then peered through the glass toward the classroom of students waiting their turn. "Was anyone else involved?"

Laura's nerves were getting to her, fingers clutching and tugging, her glancing at the guidance counselor again and waiting for the nod that it was okay. Reluctantly, Laura answered, "It was mostly Grace." She tried to swallow; her mouth was dry. She sipped water, the room stifling quiet, the sound dampening on the walls absorbing everyday sounds like sponges. "Yeah, Grace."

"Did you try to stop it?" Tracy asked, her words met immediately by a look of guilt.

Tears brimmed in Laura's eyes, the guidance counselor taking to her side and offering a tissue. "It's okay to answer," the woman said in a soothing voice.

Laura shrugged, saying, "I would've… but I was afraid. I was afraid of Grace and her friends."

"That's understandable," I said, hoping it would help. It wouldn't though. Looking at the girl's unwashed hair and dark circles beneath her eyes, she'd been holding onto what happened and her friend's death. The guilt of not helping was suffocating her. "As best as you can, tell us what you saw."

Laura wiped her face. "We were partying, and everyone was having fun. Michael brought his radio, so some of the kids were dancing. I was talking to my friend Kat when I saw Grace and her friends corner Jocelyn."

"What was Jocelyn doing at the time?" I asked.

Laura peered over her shoulder to look into the library at her classmates. I tried following, tried to see if Grace was there. When she turned back, she answered, "She was talking to Michael."

"Michael?" Tracy asked, voice lifting, the name registering from the diary pages.

"Michael Andros," Laura answered. "He was Grace's old boyfriend."

"Boyfriend?" I asked, surprised, and wondering if that'd been included in Jocelyn's diary. "And he and Jocelyn were friends?"

"Well yeah," Laura answered with an *as-if* expression; the knowledge of the two expected to be known throughout the world. "It's why Grace fought with Jocelyn."

"It's why?" I asked, but heard a motive developing. "Grace and Michael were a couple?"

"Yeah," she answered, showing another *as-if* expression. "For like the last four years."

"Until Jocelyn started going to their school?" Nichelle asked; Laura confirmed.

"Grace and Michael became Michael and Jocelyn?" Tracy asked hurriedly, drinking in the school drama.

"It started earlier this month," Laura answered, reading into Tracy's enthusiasm as though the two were gossiping.

"We should move on to another student," the guidance counselor said, tapping the face of her watch. Tracy frowned at the disruption. We finally had something to work with. On cue, Laura was on her feet, responding as if the school bell had rung.

"One more question," I said, Laura sitting down. I handed her a piece of paper: the words found on the mummified body.

"*Distressing, calumnies, I, am, toward, affect?*" The corner of her mouth turned down with a frown.

"Do you recognize these words?"

"Nuh-uh," she said, standing again, eager to keep to the guidance counselor's cue. "Maybe on a spelling test." She handed me the paper and headed to the door.

"Laura?" I asked. Her hand on the doorknob, she hesitated before turning around. "Please."

I got up, stretching my legs with a lean and moved toward her. She saw my arm extended, my hand perched with my card between my fingers and plucked it from the air. "I'll call if I remember anything else."

"Do that, please," I said. "Thank you."

As she left us alone, the guidance counselor said, "Next, we have Bobby Brice."

I studied the clock over the door and saw the minute hand jumping backward as Tracy had described earlier. It wouldn't stay that way, though, and it wouldn't buy us the kind of time we'd need to interview all the students. "Let's skip ahead," I said.

"Skip ahead?" the guidance counselor asked, scanning her clipboard.

"We'll talk to Grace Armstrong next."

CHAPTER SIXTEEN

I'd need more coffee before we moved on to interview Grace Armstrong. The guidance counselor left the room. In the far corner, the principal had put a square table, setting it up with coffee and tea and bottles of water for us. There were baked goods too, but I couldn't eat, my stomach feeling sour. My mouth was dry and my eyes tired. I'd still not caught up on sleep from the previous day, when Swales's three a.m. text message woke me for a meeting in the station's basement. I counted the students waiting their turn. The number would easily take us into the next day. Half could be eliminated, and we could get lucky with Grace's interview. Would we get a blubbering confession?

"You two," I said—Tracy and Nichelle huddled close, their backs turned, my coffee refreshed and sweet-smelling steam rising. I went to the table, their paging through Jocelyn's diary—"I want everything you find that's been written about Michael Andros."

"Are you thinking jealousy?" Tracy asked.

"It's one of the oldest motives." I took my seat, the hardness of the school chair uncomfortable. "But Grace and her friends attacking Jocelyn? That was coordinated, whereas jealousy is usually a spur of the moment. Tracy, what other ideas should we explore?"

"There's the rivalry," she answered.

Her phone rang, taking her attention, a text message arriving on my phone at the same time. It was from Cheryl, the text requesting that Tracy return to the station sooner than two, their needing her help with the maps and the abandoned houses, the setup for the search becoming a larger effort than expected. "I'm sorry, Tracy, but I think your school day has been cut short."

"Really?" she asked, frowning as she gathered her things. "I was just getting into this."

"I'll catch you up later." Nichelle patted her back, her hand out, palm up, fingers in motion. "The diary."

"Shoot." Tracy grunted, handing it over. "Can't they figure out the maps. It's not that hard."

"By the way, Cheryl just needs you this afternoon."

"I can stay?" Nichelle asked me.

"Looks like it," I answered. I put on a stoic look I thought might help Tracy. "Feel motivated."

"Sure," she said, not buying into it.

"Cheryl is asking for your help. That's a good thing."

Tracy twisted her mouth, one dimple showing, her saying, "I suppose."

"Text me any findings," I said as she made her way to the door. I thought by now Cheryl would have had the search of the abandoned houses secure, the teams prepared, a schedule established. But she didn't. As much as I wanted to step in and drive both cases, I had to feed her some rope and let her do her own thing. I could only hope she wouldn't hang herself with it, or one of us for that matter. As Tracy was about to leave, I added, "I'll make sure you're with us when we search the houses."

She shot a wave in our direction as the guidance counselor returned with Grace Armstrong. A pretty girl, her hair a brunette color that was on the shorter side. She wore thick eyeliner that accented her eyes and had deep red blush painted high across her cheekbones. She carried a petite Gucci backpack—brown leather and tan canvas, two gold letter Gs embroidered on the front. I was stuck on her bag which would have cost me a few weeks' salary, probably more. I think it was the earrings that threw me the most though. They were diamonds, a carat each, and threw sparks whenever she turned her head. They were real and they were expensive. And worst yet, Grace Armstrong knew it. As she entered the room, she took a moment to follow Tracy's exit, sizing her up, a look of distaste on her face. At once, I knew we were going to have a hard time of it with her.

"My name is Detective Casey White," I said, handing her my card, though I had my doubts she'd hold onto it. Grace took the card, eyeing the front of it before dropping it inside her Gucci bag. "This is my colleague, Nichelle Wilkinson."

"How do you do?" Nichelle said, offering her hand.

Grace accepted the handshake, keeping it brief, answering, "I guess I'm fine." She took a seat, bringing her bag around front and sitting it on her lap. "Can we make this quick?"

"Do you have somewhere to be?" I asked, already knowing her schedule, our having access to it.

"I do," she answered, a knee bouncing as she ran her finger along the zipper of her bag.

"We'll do the best we can." I had no intentions on keeping to time. The girl was nervous, but not as nervous as Laura Sumter had been. Her placing the Gucci bag on her lap, and the way she gripped it tight, told me she needed to feel guarded. "Let's talk—"

"She was alive when we left the party!" Grace blurted, fingernails digging into her bag, the tips of them picking at canvas. Nichelle cast a look in my direction. Grace tensed and then relaxed, continuing, "That's like why we're here. Am I right? You guys want to know what happened to *that girl*."

"That girl?" Grace emphasized the words for a reason. "Her name was Jocelyn."

Grace eyed the table with the refreshments, licking her dry lips. "May I?" she asked, suddenly polite.

"Would you like some water?" I went to the table.

"Water. Yes. Thank you."

I handed her the bottle and sat down, giving the girl a moment to collect her words and wet her mouth. "Now. You were saying?"

"Jocelyn Winter," she began, and tugged on one ear, the diamond throwing a spark. "She was alive when we left the party."

"Where was this party?" Nichelle asked, helping to establish the location.

Grace side-eyed the guidance counselor; the woman's face like a statue, unmoving as she listened.

"It's okay," I said. "We are trying to understand what happened. Also, when it happened, and where it happened."

"The party was at an abandoned house," she said. "We've been using it all summer."

"It's easily accessible?" I asked, thinking about the tide and the trouble entering the kitchen.

Grace nodded, drinking the water. "Only when the tide is low."

"Did you speak to Jocelyn?"

Grace's gaze fell to the table, her hands around the bottle of water, bruises on her right hand, the knuckles scraped and swollen. When she caught me staring, she quickly tucked her hand beneath the table to hide it. "*That girl* had it coming," she said with a sneer; the guidance counselor peering up from her phone.

"Had what coming?" Nichelle asked, shifting in her seat as Grace Armstrong's true colors began to show.

"This was my year!" Grace declared, a frown forming. "I wish she'd never been here."

"You felt threatened by Jocelyn?" Her neck and face were without color, and no perspiration. The knee bounce from earlier had settled as well. She was in control. "You didn't like that she was at your school?"

"It's my school. But I didn't feel threatened!" Grace answered, insulted by the question. She reared up, angrily squeezing the bottle, and grimaced, saying, "She's a fucking mudborn."

"Grace!" the counselor said with a clap of her hands. "We don't use that language."

"A mudborn," I said, studying the girl as she eased back into her chair. There was no signs of nervousness or apprehension. And though my next question was reserved for the station's interview rooms, I had to ask it, "Is that why you killed Jocelyn Winter?"

"Detective!" the guidance counselor snapped; her voice dampened by the room. She began texting who I'd guess was the principal. "All questions are to focus on party attendance, participants, timing, communications with the decedent, and that is all," she scolded, my question falling outside the agreed boundaries.

I rephrased the question, "Grace, did you want Jocelyn gone?"

"Yeah!" she answered, her voice like a low growl.

"Grace, that's enough!" the counselor countered, clapping her hands again.

Ignoring her, Grace continued, "And I'm glad she's gone."

"Why?" I asked, knowing the interview was going to be over in a minute. "Why did you want her gone?"

"Because it wasn't fair!" she shrieked, her head shaking. "This was my year! I was supposed to be valedictorian! I was supposed to be the prom queen!"

"Grace," the guidance counselor said, her voice quieted. She stood behind the student, her bony fingers crawling over the girl's shoulder. "That's enough, dear."

I leaned forward, a diamond spark catching my eye, and demanded, "What else?"

"And because she took Michael!"

"Detective!" the principal said, entering the room, heaving a rattly breath, his face plump, cheeks red. He turned to Grace and composed himself. "Grace, that'll be all for now."

Like Laura Sumter, Grace stood without another word, her lips pressed tight. She swiped the bottle of water and began to exit the room, but cocked her head once more to say, "Like I said earlier, she was alive when I left the party."

"Thank you for your time." I eyed the principal and guidance counselor, a flash of guilt rising for having gone beyond the agreed terms to question the students. When Grace was out of sight, I told Nichelle, "Get everything you can about her and her friends."

"This was not the place!" the principal said, raising his voice in a huff, jowls quivering. "You were only to ask about participation at the party."

"I understand," I answered. He was right; I'd colored outside the lines. But sometimes we had to. It was clear we'd need to bring Grace Armstrong to the station. "It won't happen again."

"We only agreed to this with the mayor provided you would *not* put the school district at risk."

"Agreed. And it won't happen again." I nodded, his reprimanding as though I were still in high school. He raised a finger, wagging it at me, ready to dish more of his scolding. I stood, having heard enough from him. "With respect, sir, there is nothing more serious than murder. My job is to find the truth. Is that understood!"

Sweat gleamed from his bald head, his wagging finger in retreat. He pulled a handkerchief from his suit jacket and used it to wipe his brow. "Yes. Of course, Detective," he agreed, his voice and emotions diffused. "But if it's all the same to you, I think I'll stay around for some of the interviews."

"That's fine," I said, knowing we had a strong lead with Grace Armstrong. I asked the guidance counselor, "Can we see Michael Andros next?"

Before answering, she looked to the principal for approval, his giving it, "Certainly."

He patted his head dry, saying, "You know, the Armstrong family is generations deep, and the wealthiest in the area. They're going to come at you with a team of lawyers."

"I would expect them to," I answered. "Grace Armstrong is our number one suspect."

CHAPTER SEVENTEEN

It was just after the noon hour, the school kids gathering in the cafeteria along with me and Nichelle, the principal offering us a place to eat to save some time before we got started again. I stared at a square patty of gray meat between two buns, and a paper boat filled with soggy fries, the ends limp and unappetizing.

"Not to your liking?" Nichelle asked, scoffing down one of my fries.

"By all means," I said, the muscles around my mouth stuck with a grimace. "Please, help yourself."

"You don't mind?" she asked, lifting her eyebrows.

I'd also grabbed a side salad and a tiny cup of blue cheese dressing. That'd be enough to get me through the afternoon. "I'll split these with you," I said, snagging a greasy French fry.

"Look over there," Nichelle said, her lips on her burger, glancing briefly to the corner opposite of where we sat. Through the crowd of lunch tables, I saw Grace and two other girls sitting together along with a few others we had yet to question.

"I see them." I watched as they dared a look in our direction, heads popping up briefly, only to dip again, speaking from the sides of their mouths as though trading secret punchlines. "What's your take?"

"Me?" Nichelle asked, her mouth full, mustard and ketchup in the corners. She chewed fast, answering with a hard nod, "Definitely have to bring her in, but gotta do it right."

"Do it right," I repeated. "You mean with her lawyers."

A yell came from across the cafeteria, the abrupt noise giving me a start, the large room getting crowded, kids being kids, their letting off steam with the midday break. Students were staring. Entire tables without a word said, their mouths chewing while they watched me and Nichelle try to get through the meal. I hastened the pace to finish so we could leave.

"What's that?" Nichelle asked: the Jamison case file was sticking out of my bag.

"This is the Connie Jamison case," I said, searching my left and right and then behind us to make sure the kids couldn't see what was inside the folder when I opened it. With my arm, I shielded us, the first picture showing Connie Jamison, the eight-by-ten photograph in color, but faded with a green and yellow tint that spoke its age. The victim was shown in the homemade coffin made by her husband, the crate shortened, the bottom and sides of the box lined with a thick black plastic, her body folded awkwardly with knees pressing into her chest. But it was the chunky salt covering her body that I waved a hand toward. "Look familiar? It's one of Dr. Swales's first cases. A husband killed his wife and hid her body in the garage. He covered her in salt to mask the smell."

"Right. This is the case you texted me about." She searched her phone. "Here it is. Gerald Jamison."

"This is Gerald's wife," I said, handing her another of the yellowing pictures.

"He used salt too." Nichelle held her burger away from her face, giving the next bite a second thought. "But it's different. With our case, we only found residue."

"I gave that some thought. What if, in this case, Jamison got caught before he could finish."

"What if his wife was only the first?" she asked.

I cocked my brow, questioning, "What if she wasn't the first?"

Eyeing the handwritten confession. "He says here that it was an argument?"

"The medical examiner report showed death was a result of a cracked skull, a brain injury. *But* what if he was only getting started?"

"But?" she asked, hearing my reservation about the report. "What are you thinking?"

"It's the other similarities," I said. "It was clear his wife's fingernails were trimmed post-mortem, hands placed on her chest, and her hair was brushed neatly. There was care taken in the preservation of her body."

"Was there a note found in her hands?" she asked, skimming the pages, flipping to another, saying, "How about the incision around the collarbone?"

"Neither." I took a bite of food, thinking of the differences in the cases. "Killers change their M.O. as they progress. As they evolve."

"True." Nichelle pinched a page, pulling the confession from the file. "Confession sounds solid?"

"I haven't put my finger on it yet, but there is something off about it," I said, reluctant to agree to it being open and shut. "Not that it matters. With the confession, there was no trial, no jury. He was convicted and sentenced."

Nichelle shifted to a picture of Gerald Jamison, the man's stare cold, the picture dark. "This case does have similarities. And it does look like mummification with salt."

"There is one thing Gerald Jamison did that we could use to help us."

"Chase the salt," she answered.

"Exactly. That's the profile I want," I said, giving her direction. I thought of the team and added, "He was a truck driver for a company called Salt Mineral Incorporated. Emanuel is already researching it and others, but anything else you find out, send it to the team, and include Cheryl too. It's her case to lead. I'm just helping."

"Got it," she answered, side-eyeing a table across the cafeteria. "Our audience is growing."

I glanced to the other side of the cafeteria as I tucked the photographs safely away inside the case folder, a table of jocks staring but saying nothing. "I'm guessing the one in the middle is Michael Andros."

"Maybe," Nichelle answered, her attention lost to her phone. Nichelle sat back, the chair's plastic creaking. "For a profile, where do you want to get started?"

I perched an elbow on the table. "Well, this case is done, it's thirty years old, a husband tried and convicted. How about where he is these days? Prison? Home?"

"And if he's out of prison?" she asked. "Are you thinking about bringing Gerald Jamison in for an interview?"

"Not sure." I didn't think we had enough to question him. "See what you can find out. And his son? What happened to him after his father went to prison?"

"Got it. I dug up some police records already and will send them over," she said, typing the directions given.

There were more eyes on us, my sensing a rising concern, the glances, the low drone of chatter. Most of it came from the jocks, along with two other tables, my guessing all had been at the party and now they were afraid of the troubles that might come their way. They were alive though, and a classmate was dead. I could've stood up and made an announcement that would bring them relief, telling them we were only interested in recording a witnessed account of what had happened at the abandoned house. Instead, I stayed in my seat and chewed on the drab food and let them stew in their worries a little while longer. It was time that they had plenty of—a life's worth. What did Jocelyn have?

CHAPTER EIGHTEEN

"I really liked Jocelyn," Michael Andros said, his voice low, his dusky blue eyes wet and glassy—the boy from Jocelyn's diary; the subject of her affections. We'd also come to learn he was Grace Armstrong's boyfriend. That is, until recently.

He looked older than most of the students and could be easily mistaken for an adult with his muscular build and a face shadowed by a heavy stubble. He was also handsome with a chiseled chin and jawline, wavy light brown hair and a pensive look, as though stuck in a serious thought. "I was the last one with her too."

"Before we discuss that, could you tell us about the fight?" I asked.

"Between Jocelyn and Grace?" he asked, peering over his shoulder toward the counselor and principal. They gave their consent. "I didn't know Grace and her friends were going to do that."

"Do what?" Nichelle asked, seeking the details as she recorded the meeting. Michael swiped at a lock of brown hair, combing it behind his ear. "After the fight in the bathroom, Grace made like she felt bad and wanted to apologize to Jocelyn."

"As I understand it, Grace had you ask Jocelyn to the party?"

He blinked rapidly, not realizing how much I knew. He also had no idea we'd been reading Jocelyn's diary either.

Michael shook his head, gripping his hands, knuckles white, uncomfortable with the questioning. "Yeah." He shrugged apologetically, saying, "But when Jocelyn got there, Grace went after her."

"In what way?" I asked, wanting him to speak the details so I could corroborate his story against what other students had reported.

"It was mostly Grace," he said, wiping his forehead, the room warming with the door closed. "She was yelling at Jocelyn and pushed her."

"Pushed her how?" I motioned a shove, getting up from my seat, throwing my two hands forward. "Was it a push, a shove? One or both hands? Michael, was it a punch?"

He half nodded and shook his head, uncertain. "It was kind of like both. I guess?"

"Show us." I went around the desk, inviting him to stand. His taking the role of Grace as I took the role of the victim, Jocelyn. I had the unwanted attention of our peanut gallery too: the guidance counselor uncrossing and recrossing her legs, her neck long, craning to see past Michael. And the principal, his pouchy face blotchy and glazed shiny like a donut. Michael stood still, refraining. He was a head and shoulder above me, broad, his chest blocking as he squared his position in front of me. I insisted, raising my voice. "Show me!"

His hands were a blur, his palms landing flat against my shoulders. The strength behind the force threw me to the floor. He was over the top of me in an instant, an apologetic look on his face. "Oh man, I am so sorry. Sometimes I don't know my own strength."

"That's good. I'm fine." Michael helped me back to my feet, a pain rifling across my bum, the landing painfully hard like hitting a rock. When I was facing him again, I took his hands and placed them gently onto my shoulders. "So Grace pushed Jocelyn here?"

"Uh-huh." Hair fell into his eyes as he agreed, nodding.

"Was Grace first to strike?"

"Yeah. Grace was running when she hit her first... pushed her, I mean."

"Thank you, Michael." I urged him to sit down again as I went to my seat, a wrenching throb in my lower back. I made a note to myself to never ask a football player to demonstrate anything physical.

"We have reports that Grace was shouting something?" Nichelle asked.

"Mudborn," Michael answered. He grimaced at the sound of it, adding, "Man, I really hate that name."

"Did the fight escalate before or after the name-calling?" If we established name-calling before the physical altercation, it would show state of mind—Grace Armstrong demonstrating her position toward Jocelyn's status.

Michael shifted and took a deep breath. "Grace screamed the name before she ran at Jocelyn." A smile appeared, his brow rising. "You know, Jocelyn fought back. She got right up and pushed Grace. I didn't know she'd do that. But I guess she'd had enough."

"Then what happened?" Nichelle asked, inviting the story, wanting to hear more.

"Grace went ballistic! She was furious."

"And Grace's friends?" I asked. We'd established specifics as to Grace starting the physical altercation, but the remaining details leading to the fatal injury hadn't yet been mentioned.

"They helped Grace back to her feet." He waved his hands. "But then she was on Jocelyn, and I couldn't get her off of her."

"What was Jocelyn doing?" I asked.

Michael raised his forearms in a guarded position to block his face. From behind his arms, he answered, "She went like this. Grace was throwing her fists and hitting anything she could."

"Michael. Would you show us that again?" He raised his arms in a blocking position. On his right arm, there was a deep scratch stretching from the bottom of his wrist to the middle below the elbow. The edges of the injury were puffed red and swollen, oozing a clear fluid. "How did you get that injury?"

He angled his elbow, peering down at the cut. "I think it happened when I grabbed Grace to break up the fight."

"Grace scratched you?" Nichelle asked.

"It wasn't on purpose. Might have been a ring or bracelet or something?" He rubbed at the scratch as though he could erase it. "She was swinging wild like. I doubt she even knew she got me."

"We'll want to take a picture of that." Michael looked to the principal and guidance counselor, their nodding to me and giving Michael their consent again as Nichelle held her phone above the injury. "How did Jocelyn strike her head?"

Michael's composure changed, his shoulders slumping. "I couldn't stop what she did next."

"Stop what?" Nichelle asked, reframing the photograph, to take two more.

"Grace started fighting me to get loose. When I let go, she ran at Jocelyn, screaming," he answered. "She struck her really hard. That's when Jocelyn fell backward and hit the piling."

Michael stopped speaking, emotion catching his words.

"It's okay if you need to take a minute."

"We heard it. Everyone heard it."

"Heard what?" Nichelle asked.

He touched his head, the place where Jocelyn's injury was located. "We heard her head hit the wood. She went down like one of the guys after a bad tackle." He swiped at his eyes, voice breaking. "It's one of those sounds you can't get out of your head. I was so scared."

"What did Grace do?" I asked. "What did Grace and her friends do when Jocelyn was lying there?"

"Nothing," he answered, eyes bright with fright. "We all froze!"

A school bell sounded, its dampened ring inside the audio room still loud enough to make us jump. Michael recomposed himself, expecting to leave.

"And then?"

He answered, "Jocelyn got up."

"No more fighting after that?"

"Nuh-uh," he answered, moving to stand, eager to get to his next class. "Grace left her alone, like nothing ever happened. I can leave?"

"In a moment. What about Jocelyn's injury? It wasn't severe enough for her to leave?"

"Guess not." He chewed on his lip, searching for more to say. "I mean, I offered to take her home, but she insisted on staying, said she was okay."

"You mentioned the hit was like one of those bad tackles," Nichelle said as she brushed the side of her head. "Did she get sick? How about slurred speech?"

"You're talking about concussion symptoms." Michael propped his foot on his leg. "Coach showed us so we could watch out for it."

"That's good to know. And how about Jocelyn?" I asked.

"She was woozy at first." I leaned into his reply, listening for any evidence of Jocelyn exhibiting a symptom. He registered the reaction, answering, "But I watched her, and she seemed fine by the time I went home."

Michael glanced over his shoulder at the clock, moving to the edge of his seat. If Jocelyn wasn't showing symptoms of concussion, would a brain bleed still be a possible cause of death? If not, then Grace's attack did not end in murder.

"Before you go, can you tell us about your relationship with Jocelyn?"

A grim look came, his eyes watering. "I know we're young, but I really cared for her."

"And Grace?" Nichelle asked.

Michael frowned, saying, "It's complicated—"

"Uncomplicate it," Nichelle said.

The Crying House

"I went with Grace a long time, but Jocelyn," he paused to look at the principal and guidance counselor, their nodding for him to finish and leave. "With Jocelyn it was special."

He was up and at the door in a breath, my asking, "When was the last time you saw Jocelyn?" I was worried we hadn't established who the last person was to see Jocelyn alive.

Michael slung his backpack around, throwing an arm through the straps, seating it onto his back. "It was late. The tide was coming in, and I had to get up early the next morning for some fishing. Everyone had left. I offered to walk her home, but she wanted to stay behind, watch the moon or something."

"Stay alone?" Nichelle asked, walking to the door, and handing him our cards.

"The moon was full. I think she called it a harvest moon," he answered, taking the pair of cards and slipping them into his front pocket. "She loved to watch the ocean when the moon was out."

"Was there anyone else in the house? Did anyone go up the stairs?" I asked.

He frowned, answering, "Never. Those steps are rotten. That was a rule we had. We couldn't chance anyone getting hurt or we'd lose the place." Michael realized what he said then, his gaze falling to the floor. He looked at me then. "I thought Jocelyn was okay. I really did. Before I left, we'd been dancing and laughing. It was like the fight had been forgotten. We were all having a good time."

"Thank you, Mr. Andros," the principal interrupted, a second bell peeling the air, its twin ringing from the library. The principal raised his voice, "Go on now to your next class."

With that, our interview with Michael Andros was complete. But it wouldn't be the last. I needed more details about the fight. I couldn't trust that he was telling the truth about the stairs and the other kids not going to the second or third floor. At any age, curiosity was apt to get the better of anyone.

"Detective," the principal said, joining me at the table to hand me a paper slip, the face reading *Hall Pass*. At first, I thought it was a joke. When he saw my face, he motioned to turn it over. I did, and found Jocelyn Winter's name and a number, along with three more numbers. "It's her locker and the locker's combination."

"Thank you for allowing the request," I said, handing it to Nichelle. "We'll give it a search on our way out."

"Have your office call ahead next time and we'll set up the same arrangements."

"I will," I told him, nudging toward the door, Nichelle packing her things. "Thank you again for the time here today."

We said nothing more, the air between us remaining uncomfortable since Grace Armstrong's interview. I wouldn't be surprised if we weren't invited back, word of the exchange surely making the rounds of parents and the school board. But maybe that was okay. Between Jocelyn's diary, and the dozen accounts of the assault, there was more than enough evidence to file charges. I only needed the autopsy to confirm a cause of death, confirm it being a direct result of the fight. Then I'd arrest Grace Armstrong.

CHAPTER NINETEEN

Unlike the early morning bell, the late afternoon at the high school was quiet, the hallways empty. I held the note from the principal, Jocelyn's locker number and combination on it. We circled what I thought was the same hallway for the fifth or sixth time, the school building becoming a maze, our spinning in circles, turned around and lost.

"This way?" I said, voice edging with uncertainty, another row of red and blue lockers on each side of us, their numbers far out of range. "Haven't seen any yellow lockers? Was that in the connecting building?"

"I don't know," Nichelle answered annoyed and curt. "Lemme see that hall pass, you said two-fifty-seven?"

I handed her the slip. "Can you make out the last digit?" The principal's hands had been sweaty, his smudging the penciled figures, the locker's number questionable. "Number is two-fifty-seven, or it might be a nine?"

"A nine," she answered, holding the paper against the hallway light. "But... it could be a seven."

"It shouldn't matter though," I said as we stepped into a newer hallway, an annex connected to the main building, the air stuffy. I scanned the tops of the lockers, mumbling, "Looking for two-fifty-seven or nine. They'd be near to one another."

"I think this is the right place." She waved her hand toward a row of lockers. "I've got two-fifties on this side. This must be the hallway for the students that were from the old school."

"Here it is. Two-fifty-seven," I raised my voice, my exclamation bouncing as I gave a blue locker a knock. I rolled the locker's dial, touching the first two numbers and then rolling it back to sit on the third. As I jerked on the handle, metal clanked inside, but the latch stayed in place. "What gives?" Now I was truly feeling like I was back in high school as I rolled the dial again, entering the combination. The same results, metal clack. "Shit, I don't think he gave us the right combination."

"Here, let me," Nichelle said, my stepping aside as she produced a small pocketknife and slipped it in between the metal, and thumped the locker's combination dial with a bang. Almost instantly, the locker sprang open. She stepped aside, saying, "All yours."

I shook my head, stifling a laugh. "I really, never, ever want to know how you just did that."

"What?" she asked, putting on a look of innocence. "You mean you didn't get that as part of the academy training?"

"Umm. That's affirmative. But since the locker is open, let's look inside."

Inside Jocelyn's locker there was a stack of schoolbooks and notebooks, the kind with spiraling wire for a binder, the names of her classes written on the covers. There was a school project stuffed in the rear, made of construction paper which was rolled and perched in one corner. Another set of books was propped on their side, the binders tagged with labels I'd seen at the library, the Dewey decimal system still in use.

"Look at this." Nichelle took a picture, refocused, and took three more. On the locker's door, a large red heart, only it looked purple on account of the locker being painted blue. The initials M.A. inside the heart. "Michael Andros."

"Confirms what we already knew."

"Yep, confirms they were a couple," she added.

"There's nothing else here." I finished up, taking notes about the heart and Michael's initials. At the end of the hallway, a door leading outside had an exit sign above it. Through the narrow window, I saw a flow of bodies, a steady parade, and heard the booming voice of someone speaking through a loudspeaker. "What do you suppose is going on out there?"

Nichelle regarded my words, concern slowly appearing on her face. "Should we go see?"

"I think we should."

There was a parade outside of the school. Men and women carrying large signs above their heads with children skipping alongside them. Some held hands and waved colorful flags; some carried signs around their neck, their knees slapping the boards, the tops covering their chins. And on the signs, I saw pictures of Jocelyn Winter, her pretty face, her eyes bright and alive. They were friends and family and neighbors, a mournful song rising from the gathering, the count of them enough to cause concern for the students who were soon to exit the school. Nichelle nudged my arm, looking at the windows, faces hidden behind the glass.

"Who will answer for this child's death!" a man yelled, stepping in front of the crowd, his sign being one of the biggest, and reading, *Stand Up Against Hate*. That's when other men and women came forward, dressed in black suits and dresses, standing next to the first man and facing the school with signs that read: *STOP Hate Crimes* and *No One Is Born with Hate* and *Ignorance is Fear*.

There were others as more people arrived, a news van pulling up and parking, a reporter exiting to run alongside what was quickly becoming a demonstration. I clutched my phone and called the station for police support, "East OBX High School!" I said, telling them to send a squad car. It was only minutes before three in the afternoon and when the last school bell rang, the students inside would be leaving, Grace Armstrong and her friends amongst them.

"How do you think—" Nichelle began to ask.

"I don't know," I answered, tense with worry of what was going to happen. "But with as many kids who'd seen the fight, it wouldn't take long for word to get around."

"This is bad." Nichelle's voice was shaky as ten or more cars and vans arrived, the insides spilling, demonstrators piling into the crowd and blocking the path to our car, blocking the school exits. "Casey, this is really bad."

The chanting and singing gained until I couldn't hear anything else. I put my hand on Nichelle's back to guide her forward with me. She was shaking, her eyes bulging with terror. "It's okay, they're not here for us."

"Are you sure?" she mouthed, following my direction. I wasn't.

"Detective!" one of the reporters shouted, weaving through a couple of demonstrators, their dressed in their Sunday best, holding signs with the words *Mudborn* and *Burghs,* a huge red circle with a slash crossing through them. "Is one of the East OBX High School students a suspect in the death of Jocelyn Winter?"

Nichelle ducked behind me. I suddenly stood alone in front of the reporter and his cameraman, the demonstration closing around us, the people tightening until the view of the parking lot was gone. "This is an ongoing investigation." My voice drowned in the chanting. I raised it as loud as I could without shouting. "At this time, we don't have any details to report!"

"Can you tell us why you're at the school?" he asked, his lanky frame tall enough to stretch over two demonstrators, hand clutched around the microphone that he pushed near my mouth. His cameraman sat squat near the ground and pointed the lens up, the barrel rolling as he zoomed the focus on my face. "Does it have to do with the students at the abandoned house?"

"We are piecing together the activities taking place during the hours before Jocelyn Winter's death!" I answered, my throat hurting as I tried speaking over the crowd. "This includes interviewing students from Jocelyn's school."

Rose Winter suddenly appeared across from me, the cameraman pivoting the camera on her. "Who killed my child!?" she yelled, her cry galvanizing the crowd, the chants turning into a defining roar. Her arms were looped with two men, their carrying her weight as she broke down into a sob. Through tearful gasps, she yelled, "Which of these students beat her!? Which of them killed my girl?"

"Ma'am," I said, my heart aching—wanting to say anything that would sooth her suffering. But it wasn't possible. She stared at the reporter and then at us, hate beaming from her eyes: hate for the injustices of her daughter's death. "We're investigating every aspect of your daughter's murder. We will find the truth."

She shook her head violently, tears streaming. "Bring them out to me!" she demanded. The school's afternoon bell rang, releasing the classes, the students poised to walk into a cyclone of chaos. She raised her voice above the clamor, screaming, "You bring them out to me!"

Patrol car lights flashed, turning Rose Winter's wet cheeks red and blue. The principal and schoolteachers stood guard at the school doors and prevented the students from being released. Huddled close behind one of the teachers, the sunlight flashed on a Gucci backpack, the letters GG shining as Grace Armstrong went back inside. I think in that moment, if the mob knew who Grace was, they would have killed her on the spot. How long before her name was forever attached to the name Jocelyn Winter? How long before the details of the fight reached all the parents, including Jocelyn's mother?

CHAPTER TWENTY

It was four in the morning when my phone buzzed, my eyelids peeling open in a wide stare, the room an inky black, my believing it was a dream that must have roused me. A slow rumble came from deep inside Jericho's throat, his snoring light, the sound lulling me back to sleep. But it wasn't a dream and my phone buzzed again. I stared into the room until it turned gray and showed me the outline of a window and a bureau, the nightstand, and the shape of my phone.

"Who is it?" Jericho asked sharply, forcing himself onto his elbows. Concerned, he continued, "Is everything okay?"

I tilted my phone enough to see the screen, squinting at the sudden brightness, I read the name, "Dr. Swales."

Jericho let out a laugh and dropped his head back onto his pillow. His voice was muffled as he spoke into it. "This is becoming a thing."

"A thing?" I asked, putting my arm around him, his body warm, inviting me to snuggle closer. "I don't think she sleeps."

"Casey," he answered, his voice sleepy and without concern. He turned enough to reveal the side of his face and spoke from the corner of his mouth. "Feel honored. She thinks highly of you."

"That's nice," I muttered, using his body as a pillow, the weight of my eyelids mercilessly heavy. The darkness and Jericho were an intoxicating elixir, the moment staying a minute, maybe more. It wouldn't last though. As Jericho's soft snore returned, I opened my eyes, knowing they'd have to stay that way until I answered the doctor's call. If Swales was texting at this time of the morning for the second time, she'd found something. And for the second time, there was no way I was going to be able to go back to sleep.

My phone's screen brightened the room when I picked it up. Quietly, I held the blanket over my head, making a tent to shield the light so Jericho could sleep. Three text messages waited for me, all sent within the last fifteen minutes.

I'm up

I texted, and then scrolled up to read the name *Jocelyn Winter* and the words *Autopsy Findings*.

Good

Swales texted back.
My phone showed an ellipsis blinking like my tired eyelids.

Join me at the morgue. And bring me some coffee.

"You sure everything is okay?" Jericho asked, joining me beneath the covers, concern returning. "Swales?"

"She's fine." I cupped his cheek and kissed him, assuring him she was okay. "It's work related."

"Good," he answered, jumping out of bed.

"Where you going?"

"This is as good a time as any," he said, clearing his voice, the room growing bright as he fished something from the pocket of his pants. Confused, I said nothing as he returned, his hair standing in a tilt from sleep, a reserve appearing on his face that piqued my curiosity. "Casey?"

"What's going on?"

He knelt next to the bed, an endearing look on his face. My heart swelled with his gesture, a flash of dreamy memories from when I was a little girl, the visions filled with a gallant and romantic proposal. I cupped my hand over my mouth, apprehension filling me, my wishing he'd stand up and stop what he was doing. I wasn't ready for marriage. From his cupped hand, Jericho revealed a small jewelry box, the color of it black, the material velvet. I held up a hand and shook my head until my teeth hurt, wanting to try and save us from the moment. "Jericho, please—"

He didn't wait for me to finish, though, and opened the box, the inside of it lined with bright red satin, a key sitting in the middle, a heart-shaped keyring attached to it. "Casey. I love you and I want you to have this," he said, his blue-green eyes bright in the room's scant moonlight. A smile brimmed from ear to ear as he offered the box to me.

"I don't know what to say," I told him, trying not to sound confused. Being honest about the gift, the gesture, and the corniness, I answered, "You're giving me a key to your heart?"

Jericho stood, brushing his knuckles across his chin, his smile turning into a smirk. "That'd be good too."

"Too?" I asked, feeling more confused.

"Casey, it's a key to the house." He smirked, adding, "With Swales calling at all hours, you should have a key. You should live here, make this our home."

"Of course," I answered as quick as I could, trying to save face. Jericho had wanted us to move in together for some time, but I'd resisted it. I'd resisted it enough that it had become a sore point between us. My chest tingled and warmed, relieved as I wrapped my hands around his fingers. Without any hesitation, I asked him, "Are you sure about this?"

The Crying House

Jericho seemed to melt as the lines on his face softened. "Do you know that I still get nervous when there's a chance I'll see you at the station."

"What?" I asked and regarded the sweetness in his voice, his words casting a spell on me that put a lump in my throat.

"Do you know that I work the schedules so that our shifts are the same hours," he continued. His eyes were beaming as though he was seeing me for the first time. "I do that so we're not apart for more than a day."

"Come here," I said, coaxing him closer. I was ready for the next step with him. "I would love to move in together."

There'd been a time once already when we'd almost moved in together. Shortly before the attack that nearly killed me. It was before I'd learned the girl who I thought was my daughter was somebody else's girl.

The plans had been set, a spare bedroom ready, my apartment packed. It fell apart as revelation upon revelation about my daughter mounted, followed by escalating tragedies that pummeled the life I thought I'd had. I thought I'd found my missing girl, but it wasn't Hannah. When we learned her identity, we did the right thing and found her parents and reunited them. My heart was like glass and it shattered into a million pieces. I hadn't felt that kind of pain since the day Hannah was kidnapped. It devastated me. In my mind, she'd been snatched away again, taken, along with any hopes of my being happy.

But that was then, and I'd recovered since. I'd found my way to being the person I was. I couldn't imagine life without Jericho in it. I clutched his shoulders until his chest was against mine and kissed him hard.

He held up the key, his fingers pinching the heart-shaped ring, "Your key, ma'am," he said. I put it safely in my hand, excitement flourishing. "I love you, Casey."

"I love you too," I said, hugging him. I'd been thinking about us a lot and found myself staying with him most evenings already. I had my place and the computers, and Nichelle to help with the online amateur sleuthing, to continue the search for my daughter. But I needed more from life. I needed to live again. I gripped him harder as he let out a groan when I squeezed. "I love you so much."

"Easy," he said, exaggerating his struggles to breathe, groaning with a silly jest. He looked at me then, cutting the moment short. "You better answer Swales before she sends a patrol car."

"Right, she just might do that too." Jericho returned to his side of the bed, taking the covers and turning to his side.

I'll be there in a few

I texted back and then scrolled to her first text message, the words haunting.

Jocelyn Winter's cause of death. You need to see this!

The county's morgue held its own creepy vibe, making the station's basement feel like a walk in the park. In almost all my cases, a stop or two at the morgue was required, Dr. Swales filling in the blanks with the cause of death and the timing of it. Located in the basement of a township building, I stored my things in a locker and put on the required booties and gloves. I welcomed the addition of a heavy lab coat, having brought a sweater to wear beneath it to compete with the cold. Derek, one of the assistant medical examiners, held the coat for me as we faced a pair of thick resin doors, Jocelyn Winter's body on the other side. The lab coat was white and long and oversized for my build, which made it perfect to battle the chill that'd hit me when the refrigerated air hit us.

After the shock of the cold, it was the smell that struck next. Entering the room was like walking into a cloud of decomposing bodies mixed in a steel vat of chemical solvents. While embalming was reserved for the funeral homes, the decedents stayed in the morgue throughout the autopsy. They'd sometimes remain after while arrangements for transport to a funeral home were made. The room's refrigeration helped abate some of the decomposition, but it could only do so much. I'd probably wash the clothes I was wearing two to three times. Even then, the odor clung and permeated the fabric.

Derek swung the doors open; inside, the walls a freshly painted concrete and cinderblock, and clean of any blemishes. The autopsy tables and equipment shined in the overhead light, the stainless steel buffed just right; Dr. Swales insisting on a clean environment, having the room washed from floor to ceiling every day, sometimes twice. I held back a breath, taking the air slowly, sipping it until I could adjust.

"Are you coming?" Swales asked, her voice perky and loud enough to hear over the hum of the wall of refrigeration units with a dozen square doors, all of them closed. I wondered how many bodies lay in wait behind them. Swales snapped her fingers, saying, "Casey?"

"Sorry," I answered, approaching an autopsy table, a white sheet covering a body. Bare feet were exposed, their color a placid white, broken by stringy veins of blue—the signs of lividity more pronounced than when I'd first come across Jocelyn's body. There was a manilla covered toe-tag hanging askew from her left foot, the writing showing me Jocelyn's name along with the date of her death. The sight made me cringe, but I kept my face blank, staying professional. I never wanted to be laid out in such a way. Not with my feet bare and exposed to the world. And especially not in the cold. I know the dead can't feel a thing, but the idea of it seemed sad and without dignity. If I could, if I'd thought of it, I would have found Jocelyn's favorite socks in her bedroom and brought them to the morgue for her to wear. "Was death from a head injury?"

Swales held up her finger telling me to wait, her knuckles knobby and inflamed. I glanced at one of the scales hanging from the ceiling, the basin empty, the red needle on the face set to zero. I'd expected to see a brain or something but could see they'd already gone through some of the cleaning. Swales pulled the sheet down to just above the girl's chest, her skin sewn shut with post-mortem sutures—two lines of thick stitches running along her collarbone and a line straight down the middle toward her naval. The stitching was massive, and always unsettling, the pattern a crisscross that would never bleed and would never heal.

"Now. I have a find to show you. This was pretty subtle. We almost missed it," she said, her left brow higher than the right. She noticed my staring, and added, "Those? They're called baseball stitches."

"Not particularly pretty, are they?" I commented, my thoughts returning to the lack of dignity. But dead was dead.

Swales tilted her head and pushed her thick glasses into place. "What you're feeling. It's because she is so young."

And it was. Swales was right. "Yeah," I said, feeling emotional as I heard some of the girl's poetic words in my head. *I like to float in the company of dragon flies and migrating monarchs.* "She was a talented writer. Did you know that?"

Swales closed her eyes and sighed, her hand closing around mine. We said nothing, as though silently praying for the dead. "Casey, don't be annoyed with this, but there's a line we can never cross. I think you already know that."

"Yeah," I said, understanding her warning. "I know."

"Do the job, but don't let it get personal."

"I won't," I told her, clearing my throat. "What did you find?"

Excitement returned to her face. "Well. I'll tell you this was some kind of mystery." She lifted Jocelyn's hair where there was a cut across the crown of the girl's head—a straight line from one ear to the other. "Suspecting a brain injury, we removed the cranium, of course, and performed a brain autopsy."

"A brain autopsy?" I faced the scale. "Not just weighing them?"

"Much more involved. It's how we attain a definitive pathological diagnosis."

"And? Was it a bleed?"

Swales shook her head, her mouth pinched. "This child had a perfectly healthy brain."

At once I started looking at Jocelyn's body, searching for bruising and injury, believing we'd covered every inch of her in the field. There was nothing.

"Another thing to note is there's no evidence of sexual trauma. Jocelyn wasn't a virgin. But she wasn't raped or sexually assaulted the night she died either."

I nodded. It was a small mercy.

"What about this?" I asked, pointing to the injury on her head.

Swales raised her small shoulders with a shrug, her lab coat moving in a single motion. "Purely superficial."

"Really?" I asked. It wasn't Grace Armstrong's push that ultimately killed Jocelyn.

"Sorry to disappoint."

"Her heart?" I asked, grasping at straws, thinking of those stories I'd watched now and then on the news about a young life tragically ending too soon. "Was she sick?"

With her gloved fingers, Swales pried open the girl's mouth, baring Jocelyn's front teeth. Using a telescoping light above us, she shined a bright spotlight to let me see deep into the girl's throat. "Look at the front teeth."

I did as Swales instructed. The edges of Jocelyn's teeth were uneven, the image sparking a memory of pictures from Jocelyn's home. "That's not right."

"How so?" Swales asked, tilting her head.

"Her left front tooth is chipped. It shouldn't be." From my phone I showed Swales the one I'd taken at the Winters' house. "This is the most recent school portrait. She had perfect front teeth."

The corner of her mouth lifted. "Detective, have you ever considered this field for your profession? You'd make a fine medical examiner. Not as great as me, but a good one for sure."

"I don't think I could stomach it," I answered without regard for the idea. I took a picture of the chipped tooth. "Do we know if the tooth injury was sustained before the girl's death?"

"An exact time can't be determined."

I showed my phone again. "Then it could have happened any time after this picture was taken."

Swales held a plastic bag, a piece of tooth at the bottom, the size of it no larger than a grain of rice. "During my examination, I found this at the back of her mouth."

"Then this happened at the time of death?" I used the light on my phone to search the area around her lips, the skin abrased, a slight shade to it that hadn't been there before. "Is that bruising? There was no injury there before."

The doctor held up her hand, shaking her head. "Like I said, we almost missed it." Frustrated, I urged her to continue. "It's an ante-mortem injury, caused at the time of death. The killer held their hand over the victim's mouth." Swales peeled the girl's upper lip back far enough to show the underside where there was a deep incision. If Jocelyn had lived, the injury would have been significant enough to bleed.

"She didn't swallow the piece of tooth," I said, thinking I understood the timing and why the bruising wasn't there before. Jocelyn had already died before she could have swallowed it. "Her killer was still pushing on her mouth. Jocelyn was suffocated?"

"Look here," she said, jerking a spotlight into place, shining it on Jocelyn's face, which was eggshell white and clear of any blemishes. Swales pinched a lower eyelid, peeling it down. "It's faint, but there are signs of petechiae hemorrhaging."

"I see it," I told her, a crowd of blood-red pinpoints dotting the underside of her eyelid.

Dr. Swales covered the girl's face, my seeing the victim a final time, she said, "The victim was restrained, the killer large enough to have the advantage, to keep her from moving. With a hand covering her mouth, it prevented her from breathing adequately."

Her explanation had me thinking of multiple people being involved. One or two of them holding Jocelyn down by the shoulders, and another on top of her to cover her mouth. "Would there be any way of knowing if more than one person was involved?"

"With the lack of injuries to the rest of her body, I suspect it was one person, and it's possible they didn't know the poor girl was even in trouble. Let alone dying." I frowned at what the doctor had alluded as she gently pressed her hands along the sheet and smoothed the wrinkles. She fixed a hard look at the body, saying, "That is, until it was already too late."

"You're suggesting this *could* have been an accident?" I asked, a strong current of disagreement between us.

Peering up at me with big eyes, Swales answered, "Given the limited injuries, it does open the idea of an accident as a possibility.

In cases of intent, I'd expect the damage inflicted to be much more pronounced."

"I don't buy it," I said, sounding short with her. "Not after what happened at the party."

"I can offer the medical facts as an examiner. My opinions are based on my experience, and the many who have lain on my table before this girl."

"I understand," I said, wanting us to be on the same page. "I'd think the same, if not for the history the victim had with these other girls."

The doctor's face expressed sadness, a smile wavering. Swales understood what I was feeling. Her voice was glum, saying, "With the medical evidence we have, it could have been murder with intent. But with my experience, having seen these injuries, it was accidental. That's manslaughter."

She gathered her notes and handed a formal report to me.

"Doctor," I said, touching the white sheet, a stir of rage building for the girl's sweet life which had been unfairly cut short. "The DA will make the final call, but regardless of intent or accidental, whoever is responsible *did* kill her. That's murder."

Swales acknowledged what I said without a reply. And like a stone splashing water, my hard feelings toward those responsible were there and then they were gone. I was the assigned detective, and I had a job to do. I needed the evidence to prove my case. I needed a witness.

CHAPTER TWENTY-ONE

I made my way through the station, eager to catch up on the case of the mummified body, hoping Cheryl had made progress in addressing the abandoned houses, creating a list of them for us to search. On my desk, I found sheets of printed pages: photocopies with handwriting I recognized to be from Jocelyn Winter's diary. A Post-it note was attached from Tracy, telling me to read the pages.

Doubts were building about Grace Armstrong having killed Jocelyn. The two had fought terribly and done so in front of everyone at the party. But a brain injury was not the cause of death, relieving Grace of immediate responsibility in the direct connection to their fight and the injury to Jocelyn's head. The ideas of Grace and friends returning later on remained at the front of my mind, but I lacked the proof. I'd need the girl's whereabouts in the hours after the party. That left the killer of the girl in the attic—the possibility Jocelyn interrupted his visit.

A coffee in hand, my trying to rid the smell of the morgue, I sat and took a sip, and purposely stayed clear of my keyboard and mouse, leaving the computer to remain asleep while I read the diary pages. The first line caught me at once.

Dear Diary,

Michael kissed me today. It was everything I ever thought it would be. But then I saw Grace and she called me a mudborn whore.

If only that was the worst of it. Diary, when she attacked me, I thought I was going to die.

Michael surprised me first. He likes to do that you know. I was at my locker before lunch period when he snuck up behind me and tugged the ribbon in my hair. I knew it was him and played along. When he went to tickle me, I started tickling him back. We were laughing a lot and started to get like really close. I could feel his breath on my neck. It was exciting. I never felt like that with someone else. When his lips were on mine I stopped laughing. I think I might have stopped breathing. His lips were dry and they were soft and I felt the tip of his tongue touch mine. I didn't know he was going to kiss me like that and I kept my eyes open. That's when he opened his and we stared at each other with our eyes crossed. We started laughing again. Diary, it made me feel warm all over.

I can't wait to kiss him again. I was going to too and got up on my toes (I love that he's so tall), but then I saw Grace at the end of the hall. She was staring at us and I pulled away from him. Her eyes were mean looking and reminded me of the neighbor's dog, the one they had to put down for biting people. I knew she hated me, but now she was mad at me. She didn't say anything, but I knew she would when Michael wasn't around.

Grace caught up to me later, sometime after Calculus, I had to go to the bathroom so bad and couldn't hold it anymore. I should have waited until I got home though. If only I'd waited. I won't make that mistake again. I heard the door to the lavatory open and heard her voice, along with her friends, Missy and Clara. At first, I thought they were there to ditch class, and didn't know I was sitting in one of the stalls. Then they started kicking the stall doors, and I knew they'd followed me there.

The Crying House

"I know you're here," I heard Grace's scratchy voice. "Mudborn whore. That's what you are! A mudborn whore!"

"Mudborn whore," the other girls chanted, laughing giddily, turning on the faucets, going from sink to sink.

Why did they run the water?

I was scared and lifted my feet off the floor, thinking they'd pass, hoping they'd believe they'd made a mistake. I could see the girls through the crack between the doors. They worked at the sinks, taking wads of paper to plug the drains, steam rising and fogging the mirrors. I felt the outline of my phone and thought to call my mom.

"There you are!" Grace yelled making me jump, her peering down over the wall of the stall. She had a huge grin which turned serious, her pleading with a pouty face, "Oh Jossy, I just wanted to talk to you."

"Talk?" I asked, the sinks full, the hot water spilling onto the floor. I didn't want to show I was afraid. Not to her. "Okay. We can talk."

"Not like this!" she said, raising her voice as I pulled up my underwear and pants, careful not to stand up, crouching so she couldn't catch hold of my hair. She pinched her finger and thumb together, squinting, and said, "Just a little talk. A couple of minutes is all I'm asking for."

A frown crossed her face, steam rolling across the ceiling, the water running beneath the stalls and puddling around me. When I looked down at my feet, it was already too late.

"Get her!" I heard.

My memory is a little foggy after that. But I remember enough to tell you what happened diary. When I'd looked down, the girls grabbed me, their arms appearing beneath the stall door, their hands like claws, gripping my ankles, squeezing hard enough that I screamed. I tried to kick and stomp their hands, but it was too late.

"Let me go!" I shouted.

"Pull!" Grace yelled, the girls abiding her commands, jerking their arms together.

My legs flew out from under me, and thew me backward. I struck the toilet bowl hard enough to knock the wind out of me. I think that was the first time I'd ever had that happen to me. It felt like I was suffocating, the air was gone and all I could do was wheeze, but no breath would come. It was terrible. I think I blacked out for a second. Maybe more. When I came to, I was groggy and saw the bathroom's ceiling, the hot water on my bum and back. That's when they pulled me across the floor, sliding me over the tile. I grabbed for one of the stalls, but my hand was wet, and I lost hold when Grace screamed, "Stand her up!"

The bathroom spun around my head, the girls pitching me upward, their hands beneath my armpits, their fingernails digging into my skin. I still have the marks, scabs shaped like a crescent moon. My backside was soaked, hot water splashing and stinging my bare legs, my skirt dripping wet. "Please," I begged, woozy and too weak to fight.

Grace stood within an inch of my face, the top of her head just beneath my brow. I saw hate in her eyes as she stared. "You think you could just come here and take what's mine?"

"I'm not taking anything," I said, feeling like I was going to vomit. A spark of courage came from somewhere, and I moved closer, and looked down. "Maybe he wasn't yours to have."

I felt a slap then, the world turning bright with a flash, my head rocking sideways. My ears were ringing and there were tears standing in my eyes with the taste of blood on my tongue. "It's not just about Michael," Grace said in a whisper, her tone cold and vicious. Her friends squeezed my arms tighter and laughed like jackals when the pain made me cry.

"I can't control who Michael likes."

"But you're a mudborn," she said with a look of disgust. "Let's see if we can wash off some of that mud."

That's when they dunked my head, shoving my face into the hot water, holding me down, my head burning, my cheeks and nose and mouth on fire. I don't know how long I had my head in the sink, but at one point they lifted me up, one of the girls crying it was too hot. I was gasping for air, choking, and spitting up the water. They dunked me again. I kicked and pushed, and was able to get free, the back of my hand striking the bridge of Missy's nose. When I was up, I saw her tumbling backward, blood spewing down her face.

"Get her!" Grace demanded again, her voice shrill.

I pushed through them with everything I had, fingers clawing at me, scratching at my arms. I was weak but able to run. They were almost on me again when I reached the lavatory door, the hot water stinging my eyes which made everything blurry. When I opened the door to the sound of the hallway, the girls stopped. I looked back a moment, my heart pounding so much it hurt my chest. "Leave me alone," I managed to say, my voice hoarse.

Grace smirked at me as Clara helped Missy to her feet and shoved paper towels beneath her nose. "This isn't over."

"It's over," I said and held up my fist.

"Oh yeah," Grace said, pointing at me. "Next time, I'll kill you."

I put the pages down, understanding the ramifications of what Jocelyn had recorded in her diary. Her murder could be viewed as being premeditated, with it pointing squarely on Grace Armstrong. Grace and her friends must have gone back to that house after the party. Like Grace said: *Next time, I'll kill you.*

"You coming?" Tracy asked, surprising me, her appearing in my cubical. She saw the pages, and asked, "What do you think? It'll help make the case against them?"

"Possibly, but we need more," I said. "I met with Swales this morning. The head injury had nothing to do with Jocelyn's death."

"Really," she said, a look of astonishment: the same I'm sure I showed at the morgue.

"What was it?" Nichelle asked, her head popping over the top of the cubical wall.

"Swales called it postural asphyxia." I hoped they didn't ask what it meant, my still trying to wrap my head around it.

"Asphyxia, like they held her down so she couldn't breathe?" Tracy asked. I gave her a nod. "Maybe those girls went back after Michael left her alone?"

"That is what we need to determine. Does Grace Armstrong have an alibi?" I turned to Nichelle who'd been tasked with following up on the student's whereabouts after the party.

"I hit up the Armstrong household first," she said, flipping through her phone.

"And?" In my head, I was begging that there wouldn't be a discrepancy in the hours.

"According to her mother, she reported Grace being home at the same time Michael Andros reported that he was still at the house with Jocelyn."

"Damn," I muttered, picking up the pages—Jocelyn's handwriting encouraging me to find any holes in Grace's alibi. "Grace's mother probably wouldn't have had eyes on her daughter the entire night?"

"I've reviewed their property online. It's secure." Nichelle gave me a look I'd seen before, telling me that she didn't want to disappoint.

"What is it?"

"I don't think I can get access. It's one of the better systems."

The Crying House

"See what you can see," I said, hating that we might be going at this blind, incapable of finding a hole.

"I'll do the best I can."

I thought of the girl's Gucci bag. A security system was a reasonable assumption. "Security footage is important. Tracy, pick up the task to check the other students and their whereabouts."

"Will do," she replied.

I put the pages down, turning them over so that I couldn't see Jocelyn's words, her voice a whisper in my head that I couldn't quiet. It was her story. The bathroom incident was horrifying. On paper, Grace Armstrong was the perfect suspect. I only had to find the truth of the events leading to her death. Was Swales right? Was it an accident? Or was it intentional?

"You asked if I was coming?" I said, repeating Tracy's question. "Where are we going?"

"Oh, yeah." She held up a list. "You were right: the fire department tracks the abandoned houses. We compared the lists, reconciled them, and have a consensus. We've got houses to search."

CHAPTER TWENTY-TWO

Waves clipped the patrol boat, sea spray coating my hair and face, my gloved hands tightening around one of the boat handles. I was dressed for the ride, padded thick with layers of wool and flannel and nylon. I was prepared for the coldest of cold from head to toe. And yet, shooting across the ocean in the autumn months, I was still freezing, the ocean bite unusually vicious, my teeth chattering and muscles aching with an uncontrollable shake. But the drive was gorgeous and showed me the familiar sights I hadn't seen in a while. There was the bubbling of whales nearby. And birds on the water, some flying in a dive, fishing for their next meal. There were dolphins nosing the surface. And the sun was like a steel penny, tucked behind clouds.

Jericho was in the boat's pilot seat, his figure rock steady as we sped over a watery chop and rode past a patch of islands. Sea spray wet his face, glistening, and beading on his sunglasses; his thick coat and pantsuit were slick too. I looked on in awe, the sharp wind and colder temperatures didn't seem to faze him. He glanced over to check on me and threw the throttle into neutral, the boat coming off plane, stopping us in the middle of nowhere and leaving us to drift.

Jericho looked at the GPS display, and a red icon shaped like a buoy marker that showed the coordinates we'd set earlier. We were heading south to a cluster of abandoned houses, three total, a remote location that was only accessible by boat when the tide was high. The next low tide was near midnight, and with the list of houses numbering thirty-four, we had to search what we could in the daylight. "We've got another ten minutes," Jericho said looking downhearted, his voice sad. "Just wanted to stop and take a look."

I took his hand, his skin feeling dry and rough, beaten by the cold sea air. I sensed he was sad and asked, "You okay?"

"It's my home," he said, scanning the water, searching, pointing to the west. "There used to be a small beach over there. Now I can only see rocks. The Outer Banks is doomed if the sea levels continue to rise. None of the homes can survive the over wash from the waves, especially if the storms get worse."

"Hurricane season is here too," I said, facing a front of bad weather, the southern edge on the horizon covered in dark clouds, the color of them a deep purple at the center, fading to a morbid green around the edges. The storm loomed, haunting the Outer Banks with the threat of danger. "I didn't think we'd see this one."

"That's just the edge of it," he said. "Latest forecast has it turning north, north-west toward open seas."

"That'd certainly help. We don't want to drive back in that weather."

"Still, it's a rain shower compared to some of what will hit later this season," he said, the two of us staring as the boat lifted and fell with a swell. "Let's get going."

I put on a smile. "Did I mention how glad I am to get to work with you today?"

"No, you didn't mention it." My words touched him and helped to take his mind off the storm. "I'm glad to work with you too."

"Well, I am, so let's get there before I freeze."

Jericho punched the ignition on the console, firing the twin motors, a blue cloud of spent fuel rising, the wind catching it and spinning it into a whirlwind. I waved it out of my face and took the place next to him, steadying my hands on the rail, gripping it hard, knowing I had ten minutes of freezing temperatures to face. "Ready?" he asked.

"Ready—" I started but never finished, Jericho gunning the motors, launching the boat, the bow rising toward the clouds in an exhilarating rush.

Of the three houses we were to inspect, only one remained intact enough for us to enter. The two other homes were leaning beyond any safe approach, their roofs collapsed on the southern side, while the northern side of the houses were also in danger of complete collapse. The trusses were exposed also, the plywood and shingles gone, along with the windows and siding. The third house had been saved by the other two: the property nestled between them, shielded from the batting winds and the rising sea, untouched by the caustic erosion.

"It doesn't look all that bad," Jericho said, beaming a flashlight beneath the underside of the house. I exited the boat, seawater rushing around my feet, my toes dry, Jericho having insisted we wear the full gear, including rubber boots. I'm glad I listened to him, but the shoes felt biggish and klutzy. "We should be able to get in there."

"Who owned these homes before?" I asked, wondering if there'd be any merit in our investigating the previous owners.

"Nobody. They were condemned by the county." He kept walking, my following. "I mean nobody in the last three years or so. I knew most of the previous owners, but they've all moved away from here. I can't blame them for not wanting to live near the ocean ever again."

I joined him beneath the house, looking up at a black hole, the steps to enter the house gone. The pilings supporting the structure were sound, straight and sturdy; the sand at the base of them damp, but in place. "Guess we've got to climb." I jumped first, catching the lip of the entrance. I felt Jericho's hands on my bottom, pushing as I hoisted myself up and peered into the opening. I got my arms level as Jericho lifted. I yelled down, "A little more."

"How's that," Jericho asked, my foot in his hands as he helped me through. I lay on the wood floor to catch my breath, lungs stinging with congestion, the inside of the house dank, but absent of the littered beer bottles and cans we'd seen before. "Casey?!"

"I'm okay," I yelled back, throwing a ray of light onto bare walls and floors and wood studs that had fallen inward. "The inside is in bad shape."

Jericho's hands appeared next, his upper body seeming to float as he lifted himself, his eyes and face red with the struggle. I clutched his jacket and jerked on it to help, catching one of his legs and swinging it toward me. "I'm good," he said and wasted no time, beaming his flashlight and heading into the other room.

"Similar to the other model," I said, finding the layout the same with the kitchen leading to the dining room and then to a large den. "Even the steps are the same."

He kicked the bottom step, the wood soft and mushy. "It's rotten too." Without hesitation, he climbed around the steps, jumping to the fourth, the step sagging before he leaped to the sixth. "Careful, they're all bad."

I followed quicky, the house's main floor empty of any bodies, my hoping for none to be found. What if this was an isolated case? What if it was a family member, an accident, their afraid to tell the police and deciding to mummify the remains in ritual and dedication? It was possible. "Wait up," I said, reaching the second-floor landing. The remains of the house appeared much like a carnival funhouse—the walls and floors haunted by time and what exposure to the elements had done.

"I think we're—" Jericho began saying, but as he spoke the wood he walked on splintered with a sharp crack. The floor disappeared from beneath his feet. He gave me a brief look and raised his hand as his body disappeared from my sight, a cloud of brown dust shooting to the ceiling.

"Jericho!" I screamed, dropping to my knees with a hard thump, dread looming, my mouth filling with the taste of wood rot and mold. I flashed my light back and forth, seeing nothing but shimmering particles, fear driving me. For a moment, I swore my heart had stopped. A grunt sounded then, his voice weak and muffled. A dim shape moved below, surrounded by black timber. There was faint daylight reaching us from the outside, and I could hear the ocean waves breaking close by. He'd landed in the kitchen, not far from where we'd entered it. Groaning, my light shining on his head, Jericho rolled onto his back and squinted against the brightness. My heart eased. "Are you okay?"

He covered his eyes, coughing, waving at the heavy sediment drifting between us. "You gotta watch that first step," he said with a laugh—his humor a good sign.

I crouched as he shoved debris from his arms and shoulders. Inspecting where I was, I could see the floor was solid, untouched by the years of exposure.

Jericho asked, "What do you see?"

In the flooring, the floor joists showed signs they'd been partially cut. The floorboards had been cut too, the edges rough, a thick saw blade used. "Jericho we're not safe."

He beamed his flashlight, seeing the same.

"It's a booby trap?" Kneeling, he ran his fingers along the edge of the flooring that fell with him. "The saw cuts aren't fresh, but they're there. They're intentional. My guess is a handsaw, quarter inch, the kind used for trees."

Above the floor, a mark had been chiseled into the baseboard, a dot and dash that looked like morse code. "I've got a mark above the floor." I was suddenly scared to be in the house, studying the baseboards and door frames, wondering if I'd crash through the floor next. "Avoid stepping anywhere there's a marking in the wood that looks intentional."

"It's obvious?" he asked, shouting over the shifting lumber.

"It is. The marks are dashes and dots," I answered, recalling the use of morse code from a previous case. "You'll know it when you see it."

"Stay still while I get back up there," he said. "And call it in to the others. Something tells me this might not be isolated."

"Already on it," I said, turning on the speaker to my radio, static belting a squelch and squeal. "Come in. Come in."

"I got you," Emanuel answered, his voice hollow over the radio's speaker.

"We're at one of the properties," I said.

"We're about to enter one too," he said. "Anything yet?"

"Possibly," I said. "I believe the structures have been tampered with. We've got wood joists and flooring that's been partially sawed. They've been made to collapse."

"Everyone okay?" he asked, static mixed with the concern in his voice. I heard Cheryl's voice in the background, her asking the same. "Jericho?"

"He fell though the floor, but he's okay."

"Good." I heard Cheryl answer. Emanuel added, "Do you need us to send help?"

"Negative," I said. "Be on the lookout for a marking in the wood. Look for dots and dashes. I believe whoever did this put the marks, so they'd know where to step."

"And where *not* to step," Jericho added, his joining me, breathing heavy, his jacket with patchy charcoal black, a sleeve torn and spilling white stuffing.

"We'll be on the lookout for them," Emanuel said.

Jericho flashed a light onto the wall, searching, and stopped when he came across the markings. "Damn. That's not a coincidence."

"Did the first house have anything like this?" Cheryl asked, the radio breaking up.

"Negative," I answered. And followed up with, "Unsure actually. We didn't come across any."

"We'll be on guard," she said. "Over."

"We need to cross that," Jericho said, his light steady on the gap in the floor. "We'll have to jump it."

"Like Indiana Jones," I said, preparing to jump, stirring the courage to make myself do it. "I've got this."

Jericho held my hand as I leaped over the hole, my stomach shooting into my chest, the open floor beneath me a moment before I landed on the other side. He followed without hesitation, the two of us shining our flashlights with fervor, painting the walls and floors, seeking out the next booby trap.

When we advanced to the next level, Jericho shouted, "There!" On the baseboard there were similar markings to the first. We knelt and carefully inspected the floor—the surface appearing without compromise. "Smart move. All of the saw cuts were made beneath, from the lower level."

"With no ceilings, he had full access." I judged the distance, adding, "How far do we need to jump?"

Jericho's eyes grew round and big, answering in a mutter, "I dunno."

"There's no telling from here," I said, taking his hand as I plucked from my earlier courage to take the leap.

"What are—" he yelled, quieting as I launched myself as far as I could, Jericho letting my hand go, the oversized boots working against me, the tip of one catching the floor, my misjudging and landing in a tumble.

I came out of the roll, careening forward, sliding onto my knees and braced for the floor to collapse. My back ached as I held my breath, the floor creaking, the house groaning, the floorboards holding. I'd landed at the entrance of a room and peered inside. Daylight blazed through a west-facing window.

The room was the highest in the house and dry, like the attic from the first. The windows were still intact; the floors swept. And in the center, was what we'd feared we would find.

A shrouded body was placed facing east to west in what I could only assume to be a perfect orientation. I'd check the compass later to be sure. Just a tuft of brown-colored hair showed at the top of the shroud. The faint smell of salt told me we had another victim. Jericho waited patiently, his face smudged black from the fall, and giving him raccoon eyes. I leaned forward to where my feet and knees had landed and perched my flashlight with the battery end down to throw the bulb's light onto the wall and give him a reference point.

"Jump to here. It'll be safe."

"What's in there?" he asked, waving fine dust from around his head.

"We have another mummified body."

CHAPTER TWENTY-THREE

Chilled air struck the back of my brain, the thick resin doors swinging shut when I entered the morgue. Doctor Swales and her assistant gave me a courteous nod as they moved fluidly together, back and forth, getting ready for this morning's heavy work. Across from where I stood, three hospital gurneys sat side by side, the faint outline of the killer's victims beneath sterile evidence sheets. The body bags were already removed, along with the salt-laden sheets the killer had used, each of them carefully bagged as evidence, a forensic team receiving them—a tedious chore of scouring every inch in hopes of lifting evidence overlooked by the killer. Of our searches yesterday afternoon, the bodies were discovered in three of the abandoned properties, including the property Jericho and I had been in. We now had four mummified remains. Four victims. And no idea how long ago this began. The Outer Banks had a serial killer.

It was another early morning when I decided to come in, the sun just a glow, a warm tinge of light building in the east. I couldn't sleep. Even Jericho's low snore wasn't enough to lull me. I'd tossed and turned beginning at just after three, eyelids springing open, the moonlight skipping in and out from behind thick clouds while a steady wind rattled the trees. Fingerling branches batted the bedroom window, scratching the glass and haunting one of my earliest dreams: the one of a mummified body buried alive, the victim clawing at the coffin's lid, carving the killer's words into the wood. When I had enough, I gave up on finding rest, made my way to the quick mart for some stale coffee, and then onto the morgue.

I was here this morning to finish what we couldn't the day before. While the remains of the victims were discovered in different houses, miles apart in some cases, there was one thing in common with yesterday's searches. The tide. With a distant storm pushing west, the high tide rolled in with crushing waves. The search parties were in danger of getting stuck in the top floor of the crumbling buildings. Per my request, and with Cheryl's agreement, the teams cut their investigations short, and shifted into body recovery mode. It was a sound decision. Jericho and the Marine Patrol had insisted, and they took over securing the victims and delivering them to the morgue.

I shut my eyes as cold air pushed onto my cheeks and lips: a refrigerated mortuary door opening. My ears filled with rubber soles against the floor and water splashing against steel. There was the placement of instruments on a tray, metal clanking against metal. The wheels on a gurney squealed when being moved into position. A faucet trickled, water draining as someone opened a cardboard box and crumpled the cellophane wrapper. Derek and Dr. Swales chatted, their words short, their dance well-rehearsed, both knowing every move. These were the sounds of the morgue, necessary in preparing to perform the autopsies.

"Casey dear?" the doctor asked, jarring me from the silent moment. "You want to take a look before we got started?"

"If it's okay with you?" I asked, finishing my morning coffee and setting it aside. The room's resin door opened slowly, Tracy joining us, a camera in hand to record our findings. "Thanks for joining early."

"Morning," she said, her eyes puffy, hair sticking out the sides of a paper cap. "I've got my camera."

"Good. If I'm right, we're going to have more notes to solve."

Derek rolled the first gurney to the autopsy table. And though his size allowed him to easily transfer the body on his own, he motioned to my gloved hands while Tracy sampled the light to test her camera's exposure settings. "Care to help?" he asked.

"Yeah, sure." While I was always dressed for the morgue, layering in the protective gear per the doctor's standards, I'd never lent a hand like this. My face warmed and got tingly, my nerves edging. "Tell me what to do."

"Fingers beneath," he instructed while Dr. Swales readied a microphone and performed a sound check for the official autopsy recording. I looked into Derek's eyes, his brow raised, as he instructed me, saying, "And when you reach your palms, we can lift on—"

"One second," I said, sandwiching my fingers beneath the body and the gurney's bed, the evidence sheet tucked between, working as a layer to guard the decedent. "Okay, I got it."

"On one... two... three, and lift."

"Don't drop the body," Swales said, a smirk on her button-round face, Tracy joining with a smile. I was already anxious and tense, fearful of making a mistake, her commentary unnecessary. But it was also helpful in a weird and quirky way. The body was in the air, but our motions seemed slow, the room's refrigerated air feeling stiff, the scent of the salt irritating my nose and making me feel green. It wasn't the smell so much as what it had come to represent—a mummified body, a victim of a cruel and vicious demise. I followed Derek's lead, lifting and setting the body onto the autopsy table, the touch of steel as cold as ice. With the doctor's nodding approval, Derek removed the evidence sheet to reveal the victim. Dr. Swales didn't waste a moment and slid a single step stool into place, the feet shrieking as they dragged. With her height adjusted, Swales leaned over the victim, her tall hair casting a long shadow onto the victim's torso. "Female, and mummification evident." She braced the table for balance, a sigh following her words.

I couldn't tell the victim's age, but her skin was like paper, tanned and shriveled like leather that was tight to the bone, their jutting like boulders in the sea. The victim's eyes were gone too, or had possibly already decomposed, leaving dark, shadowy craters in their place. The victim's hair was an auburn color which had been combed straight, and a tight part cutting down the middle of the scalp. She was more skeletal than the first, leaving me to wonder if the process of mummification was longer in time to complete, or if this victim's death occurred earlier. There was no answering any of these questions until we had names, dates of their disappearance, or until we caught the killer. "Doctor, the hands, the fingernails and toes. Do you see? Tracy?"

Tracy photographed the hands before we touched them, saying, "The fingernails look like they have polish."

"Manicured," I said, noticing the sheen. "The killer gave her a manicure, possibly a pedicure too."

She focused on the nail beds, the camera mechanics rattling successively. "They grew after she died."

"Come again?" Swales asked, her face turning up, eyes bright and large. "The fingernails?"

"Uh-huh," Tracy said, moving to the toes, recording the pedicure.

"Quite the common observation." The doctor held her finger in the air and took a breath. "But, my dear. That one is a false study. It's not that the nails grow after death, but the nail bed, the skin around them retracts."

"I didn't know that," Tracy said, moving with the doctor, her waving Tracy toward her.

Dr. Swales put her fingers around the collarbone, shining a light onto the suture marks. "Signs of the same procedure, lines into carotid artery and the internal jugular vein."

"May I?" I asked, my concentration on the hands where I saw what I suspected would be present. A piece of paper was tucked beneath them—the corner of it barely visible. "We've got another note from the killer."

"Yes, yes." The doctor lifted the victim's hand to show more of the paper, the motion sounding like paper tearing. Swales slowed, Tracy gasping, our sharing a fear the victim's arm would break off if forced. Beneath her breath, the doctor said, "It's fine. Not too dissimilar than working with burn victims."

"I see the note," Tracy exclaimed, her voice muffled behind the camera while she recorded the activity.

The note was square, folded, the size of a matchbox, and it had yellowed with age.

Swales questioned, "What have they left for you this time?"

"I don't know if these are meant for us," I said, the words remaining a puzzle. Try as we might, we'd found nothing to give context to the first note discovered; the six words—*distressing calumnies I am toward affect*—seeming completely unrelated. "But, if there is something the killer wanted to say, we'll figure it out."

As the doctor slipped the note from the victim's hand, she looked up to me, her glasses fogging, and said, "I like the science. Cause of death is my puzzle to solve. You can have the rest."

Derek came around the gurney, brow raised, his forehead wrinkling against the tight crop of his hairline. I accepted the note, saying, "Let's see what this one says."

As I unfolded the note, the paper crinkling as it opened, I saw one of the first words.

"*Affect?*" Derek announced, his reading from over my shoulder.

I continued to open the note, showing more words, saying, "The words are *an affect I am toward abide.*"

Swales and Tracy repeated the words back and forth, explaining definitions, trying to source a link between them, debating if it was a complete sentence. The paper was in poor shape, fragile, the folds brittle, the feel of it like the victim's skin. Before placing it into an evidence bag, I sat the note on the empty gurney, taking pictures and sending it to the team. I looked to the two bodies, Derek seeing my interest.

"Affect, toward and abide?" Tracy searched her phone's screen. "As a sentence, it doesn't make any sense."

"Might be the killer wasn't trying to communicate a sentence?" I didn't want to admit it, but the words were as unrelated and confusing as the words discovered with the first note, repeating some of the same words but the meaning still obscured. "Let's get this recorded. We've got two more bodies to search."

With permission from Dr. Swales, Tracy and I helped Derek uncover the two other victims, allowing us to photograph and carefully remove the notes left behind by the killer.

And like the others, the notes were filled with more words: over twenty words in all. None of them full sentences, all of them a mystery. Some of the most frequent words used were *cleanse*, *situation*, and *respite* — but noticing this didn't bring me any closer to a meaning.

"What was it Laura Sumter said?" Tracy asked aloud, recalling the interview. "Spelling words?"

I could only shrug my shoulders, the four of us starting blankly, every definition, every synonym and antonym declared, repeated, and used to piece together sentence fragments that were as nonsensical as the words themselves.

Was the killer baiting us? Or had he left the notes for his own purposes? Were the words a map to more victims? Perhaps a map to his location, his identity? I took pictures of the notes with my phone to send to the team while Tracy did the same for our records. We bagged each while Swales and Derek went about their morning, continuing the autopsies. It was the cause of death that was Dr. Swales's puzzle to solve. With the notes in hand, the jumble of disconnected words whirling in my head, I had a sordid and haunting puzzle of my own to solve. The killer was speaking, and yet I had no idea what he was saying.

CHAPTER TWENTY-FOUR

I left the morgue with Tracy following, our going to the station to brief the team on the bodies recovered, three additional notes discovered in the victim's hands to join the first—the senseless words circling my brain like a wind picking up debris and stirring it aimlessly. Worry had me biting my lips, the uncertainties casting doubts to the directions to take this investigation. The killer's words were the key. We just needed to figure out what that was. I'd feel better once we convened to review: a team meeting scheduled for this morning, which would include Jericho and a few from his team. Cheryl notified the mayor, relaying the news, telling her that without question, the Outer Banks had a serial killer. I didn't share the frightening part though. The Outer Banks has had a serial killer for some time. Given the unknown ages of the bodies, there was no telling just how long.

A thick fog rolled into the Outer Banks that morning with a murky coat, white and gray with hints of blue. Drops of water suspended in the air became a light rain as we drove to the station, the oncoming headlights veiled and slowing the drive. By the time I reached the station's parking lot, the raindrops were swollen and cold, dousing my head and shoulders and setting a chill deep inside me. I shook with cold and tried drying myself, ringing my hair with my hands, dripping on my chair and desk, limp bangs flopping in my eyes and water running down my face.

I eyed the bathrooms, but wasn't fast enough, Cheryl stopping to see me before the meeting. "Don't you look like a wet rat."

"Morning to you too," I said, turning away to ignore her. I was used to her trying to get under my skin. *Trying*, I told myself, feeling uneasy. Cheryl did get under my skin, but I let it bounce off me as I eyed the heavy makeup she wore today. "We're not all waterproof."

She ignored the comment. "Listen, I've got a hairdryer. You're welcome to use it."

"Yeah," I answered, surprised by the offer. I looked over her shoulder, the cubical she sat at empty, no signs of use, the computer equipment removed, a coating of dust showing where the equipment had been. Confused, and realizing she'd moved, I asked, "Where are you sitting?"

There was a grin on her face. "I got one of the offices." The freckles on her nose were suddenly all I could see, unable to look her in the eyes, her status at the station leaping mine. "It's the one next to the corner office. You'll find my hairdryer in the bottom right desk drawer."

"Thanks," I said, cringing and wanting to tell her to wipe that smile off her face. I continued to pat my hair with a handful of paper towels I'd found, the paper bundle becoming a mash. "That's nice of you, Cheryl."

"Don't be too long." I watched Cheryl walk away, a stir of jealousy pinching. There was an air about her that spewed confidence. Although her getting an office bugged me, if I was being honest with myself, when Cheryl put her mind to it she could lead a team. But she was dangerous too. Her newness and her inexperience were apt to put my team's life in danger. Cheryl held her phone above her head, looking back at me as though she knew I was thinking about her. She added, "Fifteen minutes."

The Crying House

The clocks on the wall said it was quarter to nine. Jericho would be joining before long. Yesterday's discoveries were already frightening in their magnitude. The team was going to be blown away with what we found this morning. Tracy arrived with me and was already at work at her desk. She'd normally arrive with Nichelle, one following the other, the two having started to carpool, and even talk about getting an apartment together. Nichelle arrived alone, my saying "Morning," as she stared at me and shook her head. "Well the rain got you too."

"It did," Nichelle said, her hair frizzy, raindrops like jewels. "You guys make any progress at the morgue?"

"We did," I said, a paper towel falling apart in my hand. "By the way, we'll want to cover truck routes and anything else you've been able to dig up on the different salt mining companies found."

"Sure thing. I already started." Nichelle shoulder's slumped, her chin dipping as she took to her routine of switching on monitors. "I'll send what I have."

"Did something happen?" I asked, searching her face. I looked to Tracy, who gave me a shrug. "Nichelle?"

She hesitated and then propped her arms and head on top of my cubical wall. She was wet like me, her skin shiny like bronze, but it didn't bother her. She looked around, and when satisfied that we were alone, she said, "Cheryl wants me only to stick to the tech." She shook her head. "I mean, I know that's my role, but I like doing the research and being in the field too."

"I'll talk to her." I made the offer but didn't know if I'd be able to change Cheryl's mind or even overrule at this point. She may have had a good reason for reprioritizing Nichelle's role. "I can't make any promises. Okay?"

"Thanks." Nichelle slipped away from the cubical wall and went about her routine.

"You fared better than me, Tracy?" I asked, seeing a folded umbrella in the corner of her cube, the pleats dripping. I snatched some paper towels from her desk, doing my best to avoid taking Cheryl up on her offer.

Tracy flashed a dimple with a smirk. "Better than you." She opened a drawer and handed me a compact hairdryer. "This will help."

Finally dry, the conference room filled nicely with my team—that is, mine and Cheryl's team. Jericho and his team were on time, filing into the rear of the conference room. They were dressed in their Marine Patrol gear, some taking to seats while the remainder lined the walls. Cheryl wasted no time in getting things moving with a motion to Nichelle, who threw pictures of the victims onto the screen.

"Yesterday's house-to-house search has produced three more victims, all presenting the same as the first victim, giving us a total of four bodies recovered, along with four notes," Cheryl began, Jericho and some of his team looking to me a moment before shifting back to Cheryl. "We have no names so let's review what we do know—"

As Cheryl went on briefing the room, I opened my laptop and readied the pictures of the notes and the scanned pictures of the Jamison case. For the meeting, these were our best lead.

"—would you agree, Casey," Cheryl asked, my missing her question.

My neck got hot with embarrassment, Cheryl having noticed I wasn't paying attention. "Agreed," I answered, faking it to save face. I pivoted the discussion, asking, "But how can we be certain we found all of them?" The room was silent. I showed pictures of the four notes, the words genuinely looking like a school list of spelling words as

Laura Sumter had suggested. "Until we determine the meaning of these words, we won't know if we have found all of the victims."

"All of the victims?" Emanuel asked, unsure of what I meant. "You believe there are more?"

"Didn't we search all the properties?" Someone on Jericho's team asked.

"I don't think we have." Nichelle threw an updating list of properties onto the screen, a list she'd warned me about earlier. "I was able to reconcile our lists with the fire department, but then I came across an entirely different one which is used by the surveyor's office. I've highlighted in yellow the houses we failed to include in yesterday's search."

Cheryl went to the screen, the list of yellow highlights numbering close to a dozen. "Seriously? There are that many?"

"That many," Nichelle parroted.

"Why the discrepancy?" Jericho asked. "Township department red tape?"

"I'd already submitted an inquiry to the surveyor's office before we reached out to the fire department. Since the surveyor is responsible for the maps, the right-of-way, the annexations, that sort of thing, every entry requires a physical survey."

"The fire department gets an updated list after the surveyor's office has signed off on a property?" I asked.

"Correct," Nichelle confirmed. She shook her mouse, the arrows circling the new list. "*This* is the complete list of all of the properties."

"Shit," Cheryl grumbled. "We have more searches to do."

"Looks like we do," I confirmed, glancing at Jericho, thinking of the flooring, the impending dangers. We had to cover the booby traps before anything else, the priorities in the meeting suddenly shifting. "Team, that means extra caution. We don't know the extent of the traps the killer has set in the houses."

Jericho took to the center of the floor to better face both teams. "There is the very real potential for severe injury. We'll need to double up efforts and include full eyes-on surveys of the structure before advancing to the upper levels. Understood."

"Understood," his team said in unison.

"For the three additional victims, the properties had traps placed on the second floor," Emanuel said, passing around photocopies, the pictures showing locations of the compromised wood joists, the undersides, a quarter-inch-thick saw cut made where the second and third floor loads were most critical. "If you're not looking up, you'd never know what was waiting for you."

"Should we consider these dangerous enough to kill?" Cheryl's question stayed the room, the teams trading quick looks back and forth.

"Survivable," Jericho said, having fallen victim to one of them. "I don't believe murder is the intent."

"The booby traps are a deterrent," I said. "What do we know about the dash dot, markings? Is it morse code?"

Tracy raised her hand, a habit she'd likely never break. "No code. Nothing identifiable. I think they're just an indicator the killer used for himself. Like Emanuel said about the traps, these are also easy to overlook."

"Unless you knew to be looking for them." I took the video cable and plugged in my laptop, refreshing the screen with the notes. I hung my thumb over my shoulder, instructing the teams, "Write these words down, or use your phones to take a picture of the screen."

"Is there going to be a test," someone on Jericho's team joked.

"Potentially," I answered, a low chuckle sounding through the room. "These are the killer's words, and we have to decipher their meaning."

"Could they be related to the dash dot things?" Emanuel asked, a finger bouncing as he counted them. "Any correlation on the number of them?"

"None," Nichelle said, her face in a frown, brow pinched; the circles beneath her eyes telling me she'd been working during the night. "I've disassembled and rearranged the first note every which way there is, every permutation possible, including rearranging the letters and assigning numeric values to their positions."

"Nothing?" Cheryl asked.

"I haven't gotten a single thing." She thumped her finger on her mouse. "Not even a lead to work with."

Trying to sound hopeful, I said, "Well, we've got three more notes to add to the first. That might help."

"Might?" she questioned.

"For now, the team can help. That means all of us. Review the words and send in your ideas—"

"Assignment taken," Cheryl interrupted, lifting her watch.

I changed the screen to show the next item on the agenda: a picture of Connie Jamison. "For those who aren't familiar with the case, I want to present Connie Jamison."

"Thirty years old, Mrs. Jamison's husband murdered her, and placed her in a pinewood box, covering her in salt," Cheryl said, taking the lead.

"Where's the husband today?" Someone from Jericho's team asked.

I changed the screen to show the husband: Gerald Jamison's mugshot, the picture dated, his black hair receding, but long in the back and around the ears, the style outdated. "This is him." I tapped the keyboard, changing the screen to include a picture of the institution where Jamison was incarcerated. "Convicted and sentenced to life in prison. He's not our suspect."

"But you have someone in mind?" Emanuel asked, chewing on the end of his pencil. "You think the killer is familiar with this case."

"Possibly, but not a copycat," I said. "They may have gotten the idea from the Jamison case."

"Or from the Egyptians," Tracy added, her idea introduced before.

"Yes. And definitely the technique," I said, supporting her comment. Changing the screen again, the sound of gasps coming from the room as the face of the first victim appeared. "And it is the technique of mummification that's making identification difficult."

"I've been working on that," Nichelle said, her excitement lifting. She twisted around to face the room, asking, "Anyone play with those apps that make you look old or young?"

"I have," someone answered. "Can't say I've aged really well though."

The room sounded a quiet laugh. "Is the software good enough to make a face from that?" someone else asked.

Nichelle sat up. "I know it is." Her answer was spoken with optimism and passion, the technology in her comfort zone. "But it did take a combination of techniques to get something."

"You're talking about forensic art?" I said, asking, having used the technique to make a face from a skull. "You're combining software that de-ages with facial reconstruction?"

"That's the idea—" she began.

I raised my hand, picking up on her choice of words: *I know it is*. I'd come to recognize when Nichelle jumped ahead and started things on her own. It's why she stood above everyone in her field.

"Nichelle. You already have something!" I squinted with excitement, wanting to see what she'd done. She nodded enthusiastically while I handed her the video cable from my laptop.

"What are you talking about?" Cheryl asked.

"Watch this," I said, nudging her arm, wanting her to share in the excitement of seeing the team work their miracles.

As Nichelle prepared, she explained to the room, "Mind you, this is really raw. It's a first attempt. The computer modeling takes a lot of time, but the technique is solid. With Dr. Swales helping, we scanned the first victim's face after the body was received."

"But I didn't give her a task to do that," Cheryl said, commenting to me, but speaking loud enough to steal Nichelle's attention.

I put my lips next to Cheryl's ear. "Leading sometimes means letting go." I gave Nichelle a nod to continue.

"Once the facial depths were established, the bone structures measured, the software I applied performed a facial reconstruction."

"Show us," I said, a gush of pride rising.

Nichelle clicked her mouse, the screen refreshing with a woman in her late teens to early twenties. She had golden-blonde hair, almost yellow, and her skin was like ivory. Pretty with high cheekbones and a narrow chin, her eyes were round and big. I pawed at my mouth, pinching my lips, the image catching my breath. I knew this face, the sight of her unexpected. I let out a breath. "But what are you doing here?"

"Who?" I heard someone ask.

I stood to move closer—the face from a missing persons case out of my old neighborhood in Philadelphia. "I know her. I mean, I know her case. If I'm right, her name is Tina Sommers. Her father was a judge, and the case was in the press for months."

"A judge?" Cheryl asked. I saw Nichelle working her keyboard, typing rapidly.

"Judge Randall Sommers from Philadelphia." Nichelle raised her voice for the room to hear. The screen changed to a picture of the judge in his chambers—the desk, and surroundings grand—his daughter posing next to him. Her face showed similarities to the model Nichelle generated. "He has a place in Virginia Beach, and it was reported that his daughter was on her way to it when she went missing."

"Tina Sommers." My voice was low as I picked through my memories.

"You worked her case?" Cheryl asked.

"No. But I remember it. And I remember the girl's father claiming it was connected to organized crime, a powerful gang and retaliation."

"Proven?" a voice asked, my eyes fixed on the screen.

"Nuh-uh. Never substantiated."

Cheryl waved a hand. "Put up the picture you made of her."

Tina Sommers's face reappeared. "Bring up a map of the east coast." Nichelle added the map. I pointed to my hometown of Philadelphia and then to Virginia Beach. "Her mother, and the mother's boyfriend had claimed Tina ran away."

"Who did she leave with?" Emanuel asked.

"Nobody, and she didn't have a car either." I thought through the particulars. "No bus tickets or train tickets either."

"Put a marker on Philadelphia," Cheryl said, joining me at the map. Nichelle dropped the pin on the city and then added one to Virginia Beach.

Emanuel held up a note. "I've collected names of salt importers and distributors, along with mining and harvesting companies too," he said, handing the note to Nichelle. "One of those is local, but small volumes only."

She glanced at it a moment, then looked to me, saying, "He's got Salt Mineral Incorporated on here, Gerald Jamison's employer."

"Let's go ahead and add it. Put the others on there also," I said, wanting to see them all, wanting to see the proximity, determine any connection. Nichelle obliged, the pins forming a triangle, and at the center was a maze of twisting roads. It was the main arteries spearing the center that showed above the rest. "What if Tina Sommers was hitchhiking?"

"It says here that she'd disappeared in the month of January last year." Tracy clicked through a page on her tablet. "There was an east coast winter with reports of stormy weather."

"Yeah, but we're talking about a runaway," Emanuel said, challenging the idea. "I've known young boys and girls to leave their homes in every type of weather. No regard for the season or even their next meal."

"What about rest stops?" Jericho asked from the back. I'd almost forgotten his team was here. From the looks of their activity, they'd keep busy making plans for our next round of trips to the remaining abandoned houses. "Were there any reports of Tina Sommers being spotted at a rest stop?"

"A truck stop, I think?" I couldn't recall the details, hard as I tried.

Tracy held up her hand. "From the report, there was a sighting at a truck stop outside of Williamsburg, Virginia. Closed-circuit television. A short security clip."

Nichelle added a pin. The room went quiet, the location being an intersection for east coast traffic headed toward Virginia Beach and the Outer Banks.

"She made it all the way to Williamsburg?" Cheryl asked, mouth slack.

"When there's a will," Emanuel began with a sigh, "your feet ignore the distance."

Looking at the salt, the sources, "We've got this company in the Outer Banks." I gave Emanuel a look from over my shoulder. "But you said they were small?"

"Sea salt, harvest a couple hundred pounds a year."

"We'll keep a pin in it for now."

"What are you looking for?" Cheryl asked.

"Truck stops, like the ones when driving from here," I answered, pointing to the pin atop Salt Mineral Incorporated, tracing the roads from Philadelphia to Williamsburg and then to Virginia Beach. "From I-95 to route 64, it's the same roads traveled by the victim. We need to see the video at the truck stop."

"I'll get on it," Nichelle said.

"And I'll confirm distribution routes of any of the other importers or mining companies," Emanuel added.

"Collect driver names and their routes to complete the picture. In particular, I want the regional drivers, and I want to know if any live near Virginia Beach or the Outer Banks." I closed the Jamison case file and handed it to Emanuel.

"Yes, ma'am," he answered, taking the file and returning to his seat, where he gathered his laptop and an enormous coffee mug. He tipped his head toward the front, a courtesy for Cheryl to address; she returned it, agreeing to the work assigned.

"Nichelle?" I asked.

"Already on it," she answered, packing her laptop, understanding the urgency. "I'll be at the morgue with Dr. Swales. A few hours in the cold and we'll have a portfolio of photographs, multiple angles to feed the computer models."

"What do you think about a sting operation?" Cheryl said, her voice lifting. Emanuel and Nichelle stopped and turned around. Cheryl went to the screen, fingers splayed across the pins, her palm on the main arteries. She faced the room, hands clasped. "Let's run with the idea of a truck driver. He's an employee of the salt mining company, access to salt, and a route that brings him through Williamsburg. We can do more than just get the names. We can use a sting operation."

I didn't want to squash Cheryl's enthusiasm, but there wasn't enough data to support the type of operation she was proposing. "A sting?" I asked, trying to sound curious, as though I were asking her to elaborate. I sat on the edge of the table. "How would it work?"

"You mean, one of us hitching rides?" Emanuel asked, his eyes going to Nichelle, her age and beauty making her a natural candidate.

Cheryl shook her head. "I was thinking younger." Her words rang like a sour note. Cheryl shifted to the picture of Tina Sommers. "Someone closer to the victim's age. A similar skin tone and hair type too."

All eyes went to Tracy. My hands were in the air, words spewing from my gut before I could stop them. "That's a terrible idea!"

Cheryl snapped her head, eyes narrowing. "Maybe you could give me a moment to explain?"

"I get to go in the field?" Tracy said, hand raised again. "I'll do it."

"No!" Awkward silence crept over the room like a drifting haze. Attentions steered in my direction, leaving me to defend my position. I went to the map. "Yes, the Jamison case involves salt. We also have a salt mine to research. That's all it is. Research."

"It's the only lead we have," Cheryl said. She pivoted to Tracy, her heels clapping the floor. "Undercover?"

"This is a very bad idea." I'd raised my voice, putting myself out there. "Anyone could try and pick her up."

Cheryl pitched her hands on her hips. "What's your suggestion then?"

"Let the team do what they do. Emanuel will get more on the salt mine and the Jamison case. Nichelle and Dr. Swales will work on the identities of the rest of the victims."

"What do I do?" Tracy asked. I heard the disappointment. She was eager to do more.

"We have the Jocelyn Winter case to progress," I said. Jericho held up his sheet. "And… we're searching houses after this meeting."

"I could use the help," Jericho said, handing the list to Tracy.

Cheryl regarded the list as it passed hands. "Okay then. We'll sit on the sting operation. But the idea stays alive."

"Alive," I agreed with relief, eyeing Tracy as she worked with Jericho.

"If that's all, let's get to work." Cheryl gave her hands a clap, my heart skipping at the sharpness.

CHAPTER TWENTY-FIVE

Before we could leave the conference room, the newly elected mayor joined us. The sheriff stayed with her—the two eager to make my union with Cheryl work for them. With their company came instant unease with Jericho remaining in the room, his having run against the mayor, campaigning against her. I saw then why I loved him so, why he was admired by everyone. Without skipping a beat, he stepped forward first, taking her hand in his, wearing a smile as warm as the sun.

"It's good to see you, Mayor Stiles," he said, addressing her with the formality and reverence one would expect. The mayor greeted Jericho with the same respect he'd offered. "Is the office treating you well? Did I make the right decision bailing out of the race?"

She cocked an eyebrow and gave a soft chuckle. "Well. To be honest. I'll say, there are days when I wish you'd kept your name in the running." Julia Stiles was a tall, slender woman wearing a business suit that matched the office of her position. The mayor was a lawyer by trade and a leader in African American groups that had national ties. She was well liked and had a large following. "I wish I was here for a friendly get-together, but it's a visit about Jocelyn Winter and the storm that's brewing around her case."

I thought of the demonstration that had gathered outside of the school, the chants and picketing, the signs about hate crimes and racial inequalities. "Mayor," I said, taking her hand, her grip strong, her touch soft like velvet, "I was there. At the demonstration?"

"Mudborn and Burghs. It's not just the one," she said, eyes narrowed. She held her phone, angered as she shook it. "My office is getting flooded with calls, and reporters clamoring for statements."

Jericho searched beyond the conference room and toward the reporters. "Do you think it'll get picked up? Become a national story?"

I hadn't thought of the reach the demonstration could have. "Soon," the mayor answered. She pivoted toward me and Cheryl. "That is, unless you can tell me for sure this wasn't a hate crime? That'd squash it."

"Ma'am," Cheryl said, sticking her hand in front of the mayor. The mayor obliged, but her focus stayed with me. Cheryl motioned to the screen, the case of the mummified bodies. "I can give you a summary of the—"

"In time," the mayor said, interrupting Cheryl. "I'll need to know more about that case. But right now, I have to know where we're at with Jocelyn Winter."

"Her death is still being investigated." I hated that I had to simplify my answer, giving the mayor a canned response. Without reporters, I wanted to share the additional news. "Off the record?"

"Of course." The mayor motioned to an aide, telling him to close the conference room door. "Tell me."

"The cause of death was not a result of a brain injury, as we'd first suspected."

"But the reports of the fight? The reports of the girl's head injury?" the mayor asked.

"It was postural asphyxiation," Cheryl answered, taking the opportunity to jump in with an answer.

"She was strangled?" the mayor asked. "Explain."

Cheryl tugged on her fingers, a light flush appearing on her neck. "Well—"

The Crying House

"It wasn't strangulation," I interrupted, wanting us to be careful in the messaging. "The girl's position was compromised which caused respiratory failure."

"Who?" The mayor side-stepped and went around us to go to the screen. "Do you believe it was the same killer?"

"We haven't dismissed the possibility," I answered. "However, we have evidence of an assault that took place in the school."

"An assault… inside the school." The mayor braced the back of a chair, braced for news she already knew the answer to. "It involved the same girls?"

"Yes, ma'am," I answered, the story of the bathroom incident as strong a piece of evidence as any to sway a jury into believing Grace Armstrong was somehow involved.

The mayor slowly closed her eyelids, the pressure of the position weighing on her like an invisible weight. The conference room stayed quiet for the moment. When the mayor was ready, she approached me and put her hand on my shoulder, her brow furrowed, her voice low as she said, "Be right about this."

"Ma'am?"

"Before we bring a child into this station from that school, you have to be one-hundred percent certain." Her expression changed to one that was woeful and weary. "Once word gets out about this other assault—" her finger in the air, "—*and it will*, there's going to be a call for retribution."

"I'll be sure, ma'am."

"And this other case?" she asked, nudging her chin toward the screen. "I stopped at the morgue. I don't like what I'm seeing."

"No, ma'am," Cheryl answered. "But we have a strong lead."

The mayor's mouth parted, the strong lead a surprise to her. It was a surprise to me too. I wanted to tell Cheryl to shut it, to stop jumping to conclusions we hadn't reached. The mayor was smart, her surprise showing for just a moment. "How strong a lead?"

"I wouldn't exactly call it a lead, but it's an old case we're researching," I tried to explain, hoping to level the field and not set an unattainable expectation, which was a rookie mistake.

"It's a good lead," Cheryl said, sticking to her position and countering mine.

The mayor closed her eyelids slowly as she'd done earlier. "Take a breath," she said, but I couldn't tell if she was talking to herself or to us. When she opened her eyes, she addressed us both. "You need to do better. Work together better. When I ask a question, I want one answer. That means, you need to get on the same page."

"Yes, ma'am," we said in unison.

"What's next?" she asked.

"There's a handful of abandoned properties which we'll investigate this afternoon," Jericho answered, handing the mayor a copy of the list.

"Let's hope they're empty." The mayor tucked the list into her bag. She opened the conference room door, noise from the front of the station spilling into the room. "Hear that?"

It was reporters. Not just the few that perch in wait day in and day out. There were cameras and lights, a press conference being set up. "Yes, ma'am."

"With as many bodies as we've stacked up in the last couple days, I have to answer some questions. Normally, I'd request a lead detective to join me, but seeing how you two—"

"I can follow your lead," Cheryl offered, interrupting her.

"Jericho?" the mayor asked, voice sharp.

"Mayor?" he asked. He stepped forward, leather from his equipment creaking.

"I'd like you to speak about the abandoned houses, the Marine Patrol's involvement in search and recovery of the bodies."

"Yes, ma'am."

"As for you two," she said, dipping her chin and glaring, "you need to turn this *messtigation* into a proper investigation. Do better."

As Jericho and the mayor exited the room together, I could feel the heat coming from Cheryl, her misstep with the mayor costing her time in front of the camera. A warm smidgen of delight came with knowing she'd missed out on one of her favorite things—attention. As for me, I'd already had a lifetime in front of reporters and their cameras and thought the mayor was right in requesting Jericho's assistance. She was right about our getting on the same page. And she was right about us. We needed to do better.

I'd only been back at my desk a few minutes when an officer approached me, a teenage girl at her side. It was Laura Sumter. The girl looked nervously around to see Tracy and Nichelle, along with me, my card between her fingers. She held it up to give to me, like it was a hall pass needed to enter the station. The front of the station was busy with reporters, and the mayor and Jericho and I wondered how Laura made her way inside without being stopped.

"Thank you, officer," I said as she exited the cubicles and left Laura with us. "Here take a seat."

"I needed to talk to you," she said, finding the chair brought to her from Nichelle, sitting in it, crossing her legs, denim swishing, and then uncrossing them. She was as nervous as we'd seen her at the high school. She folded her arms, and I saw the sunburn I noticed before had begun to peel. As she tucked a lock of dark brown hair behind her ear, her eyes caught the light. They looked glassy, making me wonder if she'd been crying. "It's about Jocelyn."

I grabbed a pen and paper, rolling my chair across from her, spying a glimpse of Tracy leaning back to listen. Nichelle was close by too, the two of them having grown extremely fond of Jocelyn's diary. "I'm glad you came. Do you have more information?"

"That night—" she said, her voice shaky. "I got my feet wet when I was leaving."

"I remember," I told her. "The tide had come in around midnight."

"Yeah, right. I couldn't remember if I'd mentioned it or not."

I rolled my chair a little closer. "Laura, you didn't come here to tell me about the tide."

She shook her head, tears brimming. "It's about Michael."

With her comment, there was motion from Nichelle's and Tracy's cubes. "Michael Andros?"

"He was alone with Jocelyn at the end of the party," she said, offering an additional statement. "I saw him with her, before I went home. They were…"

"Go on," I said, encouraging her.

"Together!" she said, releasing the word as though she'd been holding her breath.

"Together?" I asked, knowing that could mean any number of things. "How so?"

"Kissing," she blurted, wiping her nose, visibly shaken. "I saw them kissing."

This wasn't anything we didn't already have. Michael had told us the same. I sensed there was more though. "Do you believe Michael could have harmed Jocelyn?"

She gave me a shrug, answering, "I don't know. I just thought I should tell you what I saw."

"How come you didn't mention this earlier?"

"The school bell rang," she said, quick to answer.

"About Michael, do you know him? Is he in any of your classes?"

Thick bangs fell into her eyes as she looked down at her hands, her voice soft as she answered, "Since we were kids, when he lived up the street from us."

"Michael Andros?" I asked, chair wheels screeching with Nichelle and Tracy inching closer. "He lived on your street."

A faint smile appeared, "Yeah. The three of us were always together." Her grin faded, a sad look returning. "But then his dad got that promotion and they moved east. We didn't see him again until our school was gone, and we started at West High."

She looked at her phone then.

"Do you need to take that?"

"It's my mom. She's waiting," Laura said, standing to leave. She turned to see Nichelle and Tracy, adding, "I wasn't sure if it would help, but I wanted you to know what I saw."

Before she could leave, I said, "One more question, when you saw Michael alone with Jocelyn, did you see Grace Armstrong and her friends anywhere around the property?"

Her mouth turning down, she answered, "Nuh-uh. Not that I could see." Her mouth crooked then, her sights set on the front of the station. When it returned to me, she added, "But I didn't stay very long after that."

"If you have anything else, please call." She held up my card, leaving, her steps rushed as she texted a reply to her mother. Laura Sumter was gone, the brief meeting a surprise. It wasn't often we'd receive a visit from a student, particularly alone, without a parent, and one who was close to the victim. Nichelle and Tracy joined me, their expressions riddled by the same news. "You guys heard that?"

"We did," Tracy answered.

"Should we bring Michael Andros in for more questioning?" Nichelle asked.

"Not yet. Keep in mind, he told us he was the last to be with Jocelyn. That wasn't new information," I said, additional questions forming around what Laura shared. "I think I'm more interested in our learning that Michael Andros was technically mudborn too."

CHAPTER TWENTY-SIX

It was low tide, the breaking waves receding into the ocean, the sun slipping from its perch to rest on the shoulders of the Outer Banks, the west glowing with warm colors. The sky to the east was clear, the hard angle of sunlight casting long, autumn shadows that stretched in front of us as we made our way over a sand dune and through swaying sea oats, our approaching the final abandoned house to complete the search of all the properties. I had Tracy on one side of me, and Jericho on the other, the day growing on us, the hours late, our having waited until the house was accessible again.

This one was the furthest of them all, the drive taking us to the northern tips of the Outer Banks. The beach erosion was fierce. A handful of the properties were no longer accessible by foot or safe to enter, even by boat. But this one looked similar to me, the model being the same, possibly designed by the same architect and builder. The stairs leading inside were gone like the other houses, the opening showing what might be a mudroom which should enter a kitchen. The roof held onto some of its shingles, and the east side of the house kept sheets of vinyl siding. But it was the upper floor that we were interested in. From below, I could see that a few windows remained, surrounded by plywood that looked soft, saturated. There was a hole in the roof too, the size of it significant as though a car had driven through. That alone might have been enough to urge the killer to pass on using this property. We had to confirm, though, and we'd know soon enough.

"This one doesn't look too bad," Jericho said, hoisting himself through the hole, groaning and grumbling about touching something wet. "Gloves guys. There's no telling what's been growing in here."

"Growing?" Tracy said with a look of disgust.

"It's fine." I got behind her, my hands on her hips.

"I'm not sure I can make that jump," she said, eyeing the opening. She shook her head, "Physical education wasn't a priority with homeschooling."

"You mean you didn't run laps around your living room?" I asked, seeking a smile. She offered a grin, but I could see the nerves.

"Up, up, go," I said as she held her arms, Jericho taking hold and lifting her, a loud buzz coming to my ears. "Did you guys hear that?"

"Hear what?" Tracy asked.

"I don't know," I answered, putting my hand on my gun, believing us to be isolated. I ducked, seeing nothing but the waves and sand and our footsteps from Jericho's car. Beyond the waves, boats motored in slow motion, their distance playing tricks with how fast they were actually moving. "Could have been the boats, the sound of them bouncing off the sand dunes."

"It's gone now?"

"Yeah, I think so," I said, Tracy's eyes staying large as the two of them lifted me to join them in the darkness.

"Flashlights," Jericho said, our lights clicking while we made our way through the kitchen and family room, knowing which way to go.

"Keep an eye out for any booby traps," I warned.

When we reached the stairs, Jericho took the lead, a stick in hand, prodding each one, thumping them. "Solid, no signs of rot."

"Upstairs." I pushed us to keep moving, eager to get to the top floor. When we reached the landing, I found the first marks, firing a warning with my hand raised, "Stop!"

"I see it," Jericho said, our flashlights converging on the floorboards, a dash and dot chiseled into the baseboard. "And there too." A second set three feet from the first—the killer marking the beginning and ending of his trap. Jericho leaped over the marks without warning, landing hard, his gear clamoring against the floor.

"Dude!" Tracy yelled with surprise, fingers spread on her chest. "Let us know you're going to do that, okay."

"Sorry," Jericho answered. "I will. You're next."

Tracy was more limber than I was, jumping without hesitation, landing in Jericho's arms. I tossed the equipment bags, readying myself to leap when a loud buzz filled the air again, the sound seeming to circle around us. I jumped, landing in their arms, saying, "Okay. Please tell me you guys can hear that."

"How can you not?" Tracy shrank back and scanned our surroundings. "Kinda loud to be boat motors that far from the beach."

We looked at Jericho, his having the most experience with outboards and inboards. He shook his head, uncertain. "Could be one of those tiny toters, a nine-horse-power motor."

I searched for more markings as we made our way to the top floor. The sound became more distant, leaving behind the crash of waves. I opened the tide app and read my phone. "Time check. We just past slack tide."

"The tide is coming back in?" Tracy said, pitching her toe into the floor, the wood bare, but dry. Her lips were moving as she worked out the time. "We've got two to three hours before the first water is beneath the house. Six hours and we can swim back to the car."

"I didn't bring my swimming trunks," Jericho joked as he took the lead to the attic. "Let's hope there's nothing—"

But he never finished, the sight of a body stealing his words—the three of us at the top of stairs, motionless, still like statues.

I'd hoped the last of the bodies was already discovered, but that wasn't the case. By now, any discovery might have been more expected, felt less shocking. It didn't though. The sight of the sheet and seeing the outline of a body filled me with angst and fright and twisted my gut into knots. My throat felt like sandpaper, my mouth drying with the faint scent I'd come to recognize as the killer's signature—his mummifying young women.

A terrible thought occurred to me then. While this was the last of the abandoned houses, had there been more? Were there homes that were no longer accessible, that had been washed into the sea?

The idea of there possibly being more victims, more victims that we could never find, haunted me.

"Who is this guy?" Tracy muttered, her voice breaking the silence.

"We're going to find out," I said with conviction.

The attic was identical to the others. The floors and walls were clean, too clean to have been from a lack of disturbance. The killer had swept and made the attic a place of worship, his temple established for the placement of his sacrifice.

"Tracy?" I asked, her phone still in hand.

"Already on it," she answered. "Dr. Swales says she can be here in thirty minutes."

"Good," I said, going to the body, the sheet whiter than we'd seen with the other victims. I took pictures with every step, recording it all. From head to toe, the body was positioned east to west—the killer sticking to his script—blonde hair spilling from beneath the sheet, the fabric's color, its luster, giving an indication this murder was more recent. "Swales has a heavy foot. Tell her to make it fifteen minutes. We're going to need every second."

*

Dr. Swales knelt next to the body, her gloved fingers steady, a breeze pushing her ball of hair from side to side. She eyed the gaping hole in the roof, a question making her frown. "That's different."

"We believe it occurred after the killer placed the victim. It doesn't appear to have had any impact on the victim," I said, taking hold of the sheet, waiting for her cue. Together we pulled the fabric away from the face, Tracy's camera shutter triggering in rapid succession. We folded the sheet near the victim's naval, the features faint, the skin shrunken and mummified like the others. "Female, age undetermined."

"This is also different," Swales said, brow wrinkling, her fingers prodding around the portal holes in the neck. "It's a cleaner incision. The placement of it is accurate as well."

"He's learning. This victim's death occurred after the others." I rubbed my forehead with the back of my wrist, sweat tickling my scalp as I let out a hot breath. "We have a killer who is perfecting his technique."

"Yes, we do," she agreed.

"Is it me, or is that salty smell stronger with this one?" Tracy asked.

"Definitely." I went to the other side, studying the hands, them placed one over the other. There was a note with more of the killer's words, the corner of it showing. "Could be the body hasn't been here very long. Look at the note, the paper hasn't changed much at all."

"Still, given the mummified state, it remains difficult to determine." Swales lifted the sheet to show the victim's body below the waist, skin shriveled to the bone, the texture of it like the rind of dried fruit. She sat back on her heels and took to cleaning her glasses, her mouth in a pucker while her eyes wandered from head to toe and back.

"What is it?" I searched the body, believing she'd discovered something new.

"It's the same," she said, her voice bordering annoyance. I could see she was upset, which was out of character for her. "From the first victims I've examined, this victim is identical to them, but with improvements in the mummification process made by the killer."

"We have a note to work with," Tracy said, thinking it'd suggest potential progress: a difference from the first victims.

"That you do." Swales fixed her glasses on her nose. "Still, like the others, with this mummification, it'll be almost impossible for me take any accurate measures. Let's hope the note offers something you can use."

I looked into the recessed eyes, wondering what color they'd been. "We'll know more on her identity once Nichelle gives them their face."

"What's that sound?" Swales asked, the buzz returning with a fierceness like a thousand hornets. Alarmed, we stood, Tracy putting her camera down, her arms up in front of her defensively, scared. Swales shrank back, moving toward the stairs, a light shining through the roof's opening. "Jericho, what is that!?"

"It's a drone," Jericho yelled—a white torpedo body with eight blades above it, a black cylinder in front, glass below the light. Jericho put his arms out and jumped in front of us. "There's a camera on it."

"You mean someone's watching us?" Tracy asked, shouting—the drone entering and maneuvering the space flawlessly, executing motions like an acrobat performing their routine. "It's going to the body!"

Jericho lunged for the machine, arms stretched, fingers splayed. The drone dipped and flew sideways in a white blur, it's maneuverability quick like a hummingbird darting between flowers. Jericho landed hard onto his knees and let out a grunt, his spryness falling short as the drone flew around and came back at us.

It flew close to me and I jumped at it, the drone reacting instantly and flying just out of reach. "I missed it!" I yelled, landing with a thump. The drone circled around the victim as if studying it like an animal inspecting the dead, their sniffing out a next meal. "Do those things have microphones?"

"I don't know," Jericho answered, rubbing his legs. "Could be some kids outside."

He turned to leave, Tracy shouting after him, "Wait!"

"It can't hurt us," Jericho said, assuring her as he went to the steps. "Careful of the blades."

The sound was enormous. Swales pressed her hands against her ears, yelling, "Hit it!"

"What's it doing now?!" Tracy shouted, cowering against a wall as the drone flew to her, the light beaming on her face, studying her like it studied the victim. It went lower then, easing downward, its spotlight shining on her lanyard and then on her identification badge, the picture of her new.

"Your name!" I shouted and lurched forward. I swung at the drone, backhanded, swatting it like a fly. But it wasn't a fly. It was a machine, and its blades had a sinister bite. I reeled back, a blade splitting open the skin on my hand like a chef's knife through lean meat. Blood spilled onto the clean floor, staining it as the drone tipped sideways and flew out of control toward the attic's corner. It struck a roof truss and teetered erratically before righting itself. "Put that away!"

Tracy ripped her identification from her neck, the lanyard's safety breakaway freeing it. "What if that's the killer?" she asked, understanding my reaction.

I covered my hand, blood gushing through my fingers, the feel of the injury making me brave. "I'm going to squash that thing like a bug." But as I moved closer, the drone took a defensive move and came at me, the camera's light reaching the back of my eyeballs like spikes. I had to cover my face, the sound moving about my head as it rose into the roof trusses out of reach.

"It's leaving!" Swales said as I blinked through clouds of purple and green, my sight stained by the bright spotlight.

Foot stomps told us Jericho was coming back, his heavy breathing coming next. My sight glommed by a mural of green and yellow, I could see his figure, and asked, "Anything?"

"Nah," he answered with a heave. "I ran around the house, but no idea where they are."

"That was one of the newer models," Tracy said, her voice shaking. My eyes cleared enough for me to see her hands trembling, her knuckles white with her gripping the ID badge. Tears stood in her eyes. She swiped at them, annoyed, explaining, "With the radio's reach, a high flight ceiling, the controller could have been a couple of miles from here."

"The ocean?" I suggested, thinking of the boats offshore. I went to Tracy. "Listen, we don't know who that was for sure."

She shook her head rapidly, eyes wider than I'd ever seen. "I know. Yeah! We don't know."

"That's not what I meant. It could have been some kids goofing around."

Tracy peered down at my hands, her color draining. "Casey, that looks really bad."

"Always the hero," Swales said, trying to lighten the mood. She held gauze beneath my hand and inspected the cut. "A few stitches."

An image of Jocelyn Winter's autopsy and the baseball stitching on her chest flashed in my mind. I pulled my hand back. "I've seen your work."

Swales caught on to the meaning and squeezed the wound hard to stop the bleeding. "Oh, I wouldn't use those. Some tissue glue and a few butterfly stitches is all."

"Thank you," Tracy said, her hand on my arm. Her mouth twisted to one side, lips pressing tight. "I'm sorry that I kinda froze."

"There was nothing you did wrong. It's a drone," Jericho said, peeking over my shoulder at the work Swales was doing on my hand.

"It's a drone," I repeated, the tone of my voice stirring curiosity. Tracy understood and was already typing on her phone. I looked to her, saying, "How about you explain it."

"Eight blades and a large camera," she began, typing as she spoke.

"Looked like a funky bug," Swales commented.

"An expensive bug," Jericho said, his catching on too.

"Very expensive," Tracy continued. "It's could easily be a ten-thousand-dollar rig. That's not exactly the kind someone would just pick up at a local hobby shop."

"It's also not something a bunch of kids would play around with at a beach," I said. "We have another lead."

Jericho saw it on my face. He saw what I was trying to hide. What I didn't share and I didn't say because it frightened me to my core. If it was the killer manning the drone, then he knew who we were. And with her station identification, he knew Tracy too.

CHAPTER TWENTY-SEVEN

Tissue glue, butterfly stitches, and a couple of aspirin for the pain. That's what it took to close the cut on my hand, the edges of it weepy, the touch tender, my skin puffy red and already bruising. I glanced over the cubicles toward Tracy, her monitors reflecting in her glasses. She was researching the model of drone, finding anything that could link what we witnessed to a name, someone local. It was a thin lead. Or was it?

"Tracy?" I went to her desk, the screens filled with high-end models available for purchase. None of them were like the one we'd seen.

"I wish we'd taken a picture," she said, eyes cast in blue light, her face the same. "I shouldn't have put my camera down."

"It's easy to second-guess your moves. Too easy." I grabbed my chair, rolling it between the cubicles. An officer walked around me as he dropped off paperwork, the piles of it on my desk climbing.

Tracy grimaced, looking at my hand. "Does it hurt?"

"Nothing a glass of wine won't fix."

She turned back to the screen and the pages of drones. "Who knew there'd be so many?"

"I'm sure we'll find it." While I tried to assure her, the sheer number of them had me worried. "How about we come at this from another direction?"

Tracy opened a new browser tab, asking, "What's the idea?"

"You know how there are clubs for bird watching and flying kites?"

"A club for drones. Of course!" She typed, entering terms for groups and meetings. "I've heard of competitions, racing."

"Yeah. Racing!" I liked the term and scanned the screen, club names and teams showing in the dozens, my thoughts wandering in the clouds, literally, and thinking about airspace and safety. "What about registration? Does a drone have to be registered with the FAA?"

Tracy lifted her fingers. "I never thought about it. But considering the flight ceilings, how high they are, and how far a drone can fly?" She began to type; the answer coming in the first hit. "It says here that all drones must be registered when weighing over two-hundred and fifty grams."

I felt my hand and visualized the drone, the eight blades, the glass lens big like an eyeglass. "That drone was much bigger. Easily big enough to meet registration requirements."

Tracy continued to type, opening tab after tab to show government legalese regarding regulations and registrations. She stopped. Her fingers resting on the keys. "You know, just because these pages say the drone has to be registered doesn't actually mean anything."

"That's true," I said, understanding that a killer isn't apt to abide by other laws while breaking the most serious of them all. "There's always that *what if*. And I've seen my share of them." She frowned with my explanation. "Often a killer will be fastidious in other aspects of the law, for fear of being caught out. Let's cover our bases."

"I can do that." She returned to typing. "I'll work backward, starting with the names of locals who've registered similar."

"Good," I told her, my phone buzzing with a text from Nichelle. I thought she had a breakthrough already, some newer and faster computer model. That's not what it was though. Jocelyn Winter's cell phone had been located.

The sun had gone down for the night, turning the western sky into a blaze of red and orange, edged by purple and black before reaching the sky and the first of the evening stars. I drove through a parking lot, following a green dotted path showing on my phone, the coordinates to Jocelyn Winter's phone being our destination. It was the one thing expected to be on her body, but it was missing. Every interview at the school included mention of her cell phone, the students uniformly stating they'd seen her with it at the party. When asked particulars, they'd all said they'd seen it in her hands or in her back pocket.

"Make a left here," Tracy said, joining me on the call, a bag of fast food between us, the sinful smell of burgers and fries thick like humidity. Tracy shoved a bite into her mouth, saying, "How can something that tastes this good be so bad for you?"

"I know that question," I answered, a pair of fries dangling from my fingers. "This might sound cliché, but when you're a cop, and it's late, and you're on the job, you get to eat whatever you want."

"Awesome perk." Tracy moved the phone, our arriving at the destination, a strip mall, the parking lot full, the foot traffic busy. I parked alongside the curb, taking another bite of my burger before exiting the car. Tracy followed. The air was warmer than it had been earlier in the day, a warm front taking a breath. "From Nichelle's coordinates, the victim's phone is here."

We searched the ground and around us. 'Here' wasn't anywhere. We stood outside of a Baskin-Robbins; the famous thirty-one flavors painted on the glass window; the inside of the eatery sterile white; the counter housing refrigeration units that were filled with tubs of sweet ice cream. There were attendants handing out samples on tiny, purple spoons, a line of customers to the door. I saw Tracy ogling. "About that perk. Make that just about anything."

"Funny," she said. "What about one of them?"

The line of people waiting their turn was made up of families, along with some students old enough to be in high school. None of the kids were from our interviews. "Could be?"

There was a restaurant and hardware store on each side, the sign on the hardware store door reading *Closed*. A bank was next to it, but it was also closed. I spun around, confused. Jocelyn's phone was nowhere to be found. Across the street there was an old-style drive-in stand called the Milkshake Shack, cars lined around it, and with kids from the school interviews hanging out, sitting on the trunks and hoods, and completely unaware we were there. I saw her then and asked Tracy, "How about over there. Do you recognize anyone?"

"Just a guess since I left early, but I know her from the pictures. That one in the middle. Isn't that Grace Armstrong?"

"It is." I went to the curb, stepping down. "She's not alone either. The pair next to her are the girls from the bathroom incident. The boy behind them is Michael Andros."

Tracy stood closer to me, holding up her phone, the location of Jocelyn's phone at our feet. "That's Michael Andros?"

"Sure is." I assessed the coordinates again, comparing it to where the teens were located. "This doesn't add up."

Tracy read the screen, agreeing. "Her phone should be here. If they had it, it would show on the map over there."

"How about dialing it." I had the number and placed the call. Since Jocelyn's death, her cell phone had been offline, absent, gone and nowhere to be found. Now that it was online again, calling it was a last chance to find it. And then it was there, ringing muffled, the ringtone generic. "I hear it."

"There," Tracy said, pointing to a trash can, green and white, a thick chain around the middle to secure it against a metal post.

A freckled-faced boy with strawberry-blond hair rolled to a stop on his bike, his friends skidding with him, their staring into the trash can. "Check it out!" the one said to the other.

"One minute—" I said, loud, but not loud enough to draw attention; the students from East OBX High School having no idea we were across the street from them. I couldn't reach the trash can fast enough—the boy with the freckles holding Jocelyn's phone, a look of delight on his face. When I reached him, I tried to snatch it from his hands. "I'll take that!"

"Naw!" he answered, rolling backward and out of reach. The other boy, no more than eleven, cycled with him, his arms, and legs thick, his face round, his eyes beady. "Finders keepers. Right, Jake?"

"Right!" the freckled-faced boy said. "It was in the trash."

Reluctantly, I reached for my badge. Tracy stepped closer and showed the boys her identification, the words *Law Enforcement* with her picture. "This is part of a murder investigation."

"Hundred bucks," the boy said.

I put my badge in view, Tracy's words gaining some weight, their gaze jumping from me to Tracy and then to my badge.

"We could call your parents," Tracy went on to say. She explained, "We could have them meet us at the station while we question you, ask how it is that you're holding onto a dead person's phone."

Without anymore hesitation, the boy dropped the phone back into the trash can. "Naw. It's a cheap one anyway."

As the boys rode off, I peered down, the overhead light shining on the phone, the glass like a black mirror. On it, there were smudges around the corners, and fingerprints where the passcode had been typed. There were other prints too, likely from the boys and possibly whoever had the phone. "Evidence bag?"

Tracy produced a bag and donned a pair of latex gloves. "I see the fingerprints too. Let's hope they're not just the victim's. Do you think we'll find anything on it?"

"Doubtful." The case was getting deeper. Our finding Jocelyn's phone close to Grace and her friends was too convenient.

"Why? What do you mean?"

"The only reason Jocelyn's killer would get rid of her phone is if they didn't need it anymore."

"They already erased it," Tracy said. "Which means any fingerprints are probably from the boys."

"Could be there was something on her phone the killer wanted to remove." I held the evidence bag, the phone weighing it down with a sag. I tried to find some optimism in the find. "Who knows, maybe we'll find a fingerprint or two that's questionable."

While Tracy took Jocelyn Winter's phone into custody, I tried to gauge the students across the street. If they'd had Jocelyn's phone all this time, why turn it on and ditch it in a trash can, and then wait for us to find it? By now, the group of them were staring at us, having seen the interaction with the kids on the bikes. We moved slowly, buying time to see what they'd do next. A few minutes went by before they were filing into their expensive cars and gawking at us as they exited the Milkshake Shack.

Dr. Swales had planted a seed in my head. A vicious little nagging seed that had sprouted and begun to grow and spread doubt in my believing Grace had gone back to the house and killed Jocelyn, her doing so with intent. Could it have been an accident? A fight? An argument that had gone too far?

As much as I wanted to confirm Grace Armstrong's guilt, finding Jocelyn's cell phone had also hinted at the possibility it could be someone else—someone who wanted us to find it here, find it where Grace and her friends were going to be. Or maybe Grace Armstrong thought she was smarter than all of us and this was her way of raising a challenge.

CHAPTER TWENTY-EIGHT

With the sun coming through the clouds, the temperature steady for the autumn day, it was the sixth morning after Jocelyn Winter's death, the sixth day after I'd found her lifeless body and then broke the horrible news to her mother. In front of my eyes, I'd watched the woman's world break. With the images of her crying in my mind, my chest hurt as thoughts of my own Hannah came to me, my daughter missing from my life, missing from my world. The memory of our girls was woven into our hearts and our souls, love and pain stitched together and locked forever.

There was a third mother who might feel the brutalness of tragedy soon, her daughter taken from her, her flesh and blood displaced, broken of their bond. It was Millie Armstrong, Grace's mother. Because while the autopsy showed death was a result of asphyxiation, the how and the why were still unknown and yet to be answered.

The district attorney had received all the other evidence we'd collected, including a copy of Jocelyn's account of the high school bathroom incident, along with a report from the school's janitor, his accounting of the bathroom being flooded that day. There were also the witnesses at the party, their having heard Grace's threats and witnessed her attack.

It was enough for the district attorney to decide to make a move, sending a formal request for an interview with Grace Armstrong at the station. We could have put out an APB, made an arrest, but the girl's mother was quick to comply. That meant they were bringing Grace Armstrong to the station for questioning.

Steam from my coffee rose onto my lips as I finished my drive to the station, stopping before I could reach the parking lot, a crowd picketing, this one twice the size of the one from the day before. Amongst them, I saw the same faces and read the same signs about hate crimes and injustice. I saw Jocelyn's mother at the front of the pack, her face with a stone-cold grimace, her arms interlaced with others, men and women I knew to be activists and church leaders, their seeming to show up out of nowhere, claiming a long-standing relationship with the victim.

Police were wearing their full riot gear and stood shoulder to shoulder in front of the station. They were two rows of bodies, dead-still like wooden soldiers, the sight of them unnerving. The air was thick with tension, the smallest of sparks potentially igniting a riot. I sat in my car, assessing the scene, afraid to move. A demonstrator came to the passenger window, a man in his early forties, his hair receding, long dreadlocks draped from the side of his head. He showed me a rainbow tie-dyed shirt with Jocelyn's face in the middle of it, and pressed his sign against the glass, the words reading *Justice Begins with One*. I grabbed my phone and called the district attorney. There was no way we could bring Grace Armstrong to the station. If we did, someone was going to get hurt.

Less than ideal, but for the safety of all, we moved the interview to Grace Armstrong's house. With my instruction, we each left the station at different times so as not to tip the demonstrators or reporters. As of this morning, the only conversations had about the interview were between a few of us.

The Armstrong property was beautiful. It was one of the grandest of estates I'd passed on occasion, admiring it from afar, and having no idea who lived there. There was a fountain at the center of a circular drive, the main house standing three stories high, red-bricked and with traditional white framing. The roof was steepled with slate tiling, a large steel and glass chandelier hanging between tall pillars above the front door. I nudged Nichelle's arm as we approached, showing her the security cameras perched at every corner. A pair of red and gold cardinals flitted along the evergreens, one landing on a larger security camera with a dome shape. She saw it and was already at work on her laptop, cradling it with one arm while typing.

"Detectives," a stout man said, greeting us at the door. He wore a silver-gray suit with gold cufflinks and a watch to match. He took my hand, his skin supple, his touch gentle, his age deceiving, but I guessed him to be older while he tried to look younger. "My name is Francis Martin. I am representing Grace Armstrong this morning."

"Detective Casey White," I said, handing him my card. "This is my colleague, Nichelle Wilkinson."

"The Armstrongs appreciate your changing the location," he said, putting his hand to his chest. He shook his head saying, "The news coverage of the demonstration is just awful."

"You're criminal law?" I asked, curious.

"I'm the family's general counsel," he answered, eyes shifting to the card in my hand. "But I've also had experience with criminal law. If you'll follow me."

We walked through a stone and slate covered foyer, passing a great room with a table at the center that was twice the length of the one in our conference room, and then to the back, a sunroom, the south side open to a patio and a deck with a pool that faced the ocean, the edge of it seeming to disappear like the edge of a cliff.

The Crying House

I found myself staring at the ocean—the rear of the house more elegant and elaborate than any resort I'd ever been to. "It's called an infinity edge pool," a woman said, her hand extended, a bangle with white stones, possibly ivory, dangling from her wrist. "My name is Millie Armstrong."

"Ma'am," I said as she took to a seat across from us, the brim of a broad red sunhat covering much of her face. She removed it and fluffed her hair, pressing and pulling, her scalp moving strangely, a wig sliding into place. That's when I noticed the disc-shaped plastic on the woman's chest beneath her collarbone, a tube at the center, her blouse opened enough to reveal the medical apparatus. It was a chemo port—the woman's pallid complexion, her sunken eyes, and her hair loss telling me that she was very ill.

"Detective," Millie Armstrong answered. I felt an unexpected touch of emotion for the woman, my not knowing she was ill. From Nichelle's background check on the family, we'd learned of Grace's father having been tragically killed in a car accident earlier in the year. I hadn't expected to feel anything with the interview, but I did. It wasn't just for Millie, but surprisingly it was pity for Grace. She'd already lost one parent and might lose another. Maybe this could explain her behavior and insecurities, and the violence at the school?

"Ma'am, my sincerest condolences for your late husband."

The lawyer cleared his throat, a frown forming as he pushed Mrs. Armstrong's chair into place. Speaking for the family, he answered, "Thank you kindly." He waved toward the house, Grace Armstrong appearing from inside.

"Will anyone else be joining us?" And though I asked, from the looks of it, there was no family lineage, no generations of relatives, and there was no team of lawyers as the high school principal had warned.

"We're complete," their lawyer answered. "Before we get started, can we offer coffee or tea, water perhaps?"

"Water is fine," I said, but didn't wait to begin as Grace sat across from us, her demeanor different to who I'd met in the school library. Her face was soft, the hard lines, the meanness she'd worn was gone. Her eyes were doting as her mother reached over the table and took her hand. Regardless of the circumstance, I could see I was working with someone who wore many faces. Who we spoke with today may depend on whose company we were in.

"Ma'am. Some of the questions, the subject matter, the pictures, they are difficult."

"My daughter is underage," Millie Armstrong said, her voice raspy and strained. Her eyelids moved slowly, her focus easing toward the lawyer. "I've conferred and understand my right as a parent to be here while my daughter is questioned."

"You're correct, ma'am." I couldn't make the woman leave, but I also wouldn't soften the questioning given hers, or anyone's, condition. From my bag, I put pictures of the girl's lavatory on the table; the report filed by the janitor included photographs, the school's intent of filing an insurance claim for the water damage. "Grace, can you tell us what happened here?"

Grace let go of her mother's hand to take one of the photographs. She put on a childlike expression, her mouth pursed to the side. She shook her head. "I don't know."

"We have an account of an altercation between you and Jocelyn Winter." With the mention of her name, anger appeared with a flash. It wasn't just anger though. It was hate.

"Yeah. So!"

There she is! The girl I'd met in the library was back. "You fought with Jocelyn Winter?" Before she answered, I placed a picture of

Jocelyn's body on the table, taken at the abandoned house and showing her as I'd found her. "And you fought again?"

Grace scanned the photograph, her expression unchanged, unmoved by the sight of the dead girl. "Yeah, we did," she said, nostrils flaring. "But you already know that."

"Detective?" the lawyer asked.

I raised my hand and produced a picture from the morgue: Jocelyn's face and chest, the sheet covering just enough to cover the autopsy work. "After the fight, did you return to the beach house?"

Grace shook her head. "Nuh-uh. I was home."

"You didn't return to the abandoned house? You didn't want to go back and confront Jocelyn again?"

She cocked her head, lips pressing tight. Her mother gave her a look, and the girl's expression relaxed. "Like I said, I was home with my mother. Jocelyn was alive when I left." She was sticking to the story she'd told us.

Grace's mother leaned in. "The news reports said the girl might have died from a head injury."

"Mrs. Armstrong, the cause of death hasn't been made public. I can share that it wasn't a brain injury. We need to investigate every avenue, including the possibility that Jocelyn Winter was murdered."

Grace continued to shake her head, the word *murder* jarring an emotion. "I was home," she said again. "Everyone saw me leave the party."

"Can you corroborate her being here the entire evening?" I asked.

Fear swept over her mother's face as she shook her head. "I... I saw her come inside, but I was so tired." She touched the outline of her chemo port showing through her blouse. "I could barely stay awake."

"Mom, you have to believe me!" Grace snapped. "I was here. I was here all night long."

"Detective, do you have a time of death?" the lawyer asked.

"We have an approximate time," I answered him.

"We can furnish ample security footage." He pointed toward the roofline. Though we'd tried, Nichelle was unable to access their security, leaving it until now to get access. I felt a small gush of disappointment—Grace's alibi possibly being secured. "I personally oversaw the installation of the security system and can tell you nobody can enter or leave the property without footage."

"What's your retention period?" Nichelle asked and began typing. He tilted his head toward Nichelle. "I noticed the brand used. I'm familiar with the system and its cloud access."

"Thirty days," he answered, moving between us, the smell of his aftershave strong, the scent like peaches. "May I?"

Nichelle turned the laptop toward the Armstrongs' lawyer—his fingers gliding over the keys; his fingernails manicured; his skin clear and without blemishes. Nichelle watched intently, ensuring all activity was on the up and up. "You're making me a guest account?"

"Yes, with limited permissions to view?" he said, asking Grace's mother.

"Of course." She sat up; a pitcher of water was delivered with four glasses. Her hands shaking as she struggled with a glass. Without hesitation, Grace attended to her mother's needs, pouring the water, and then fixing a shawl around the woman's shoulders. The moment was endearing—the sight of a daughter tending to her mother's needs tugging on a heartstring. Had I judged the girl too harshly? "Thank you, dear."

"There you are," their lawyer said, taking his seat. "You have full guest access and privileges."

"Thank you." Nichelle went to work, adding, "I am putting in the date and times surrounding Jocelyn Winter's death."

There was silence as Nichelle viewed footage. She sped through the timeline, video frames playing in a fast-forward motion, trees swaying and spitting leaves into the pool, the water rippling, the spent leaves disappearing abruptly, the footage ending, dashing my hopes we'd finish this investigation with an arrest today.

Grace must have noticed the look on my face. She began nodding her head. "You see that I'm home! You see that I was home all night!"

"One second," I said, swallowing a sigh.

Nichelle peered over her laptop without offering an answer. Her eyes said what Grace Armstrong had exclaimed. Nichelle's posture was hunched, her eyes downcast. She'd come up short this time, but she had warned me about their security system. As much as I hated to admit it, not all cases were cut and dry. Even our best theories weren't always going to support the evidence just because we wanted them to. Grace had arrived home at a time that was supported by the witness statements, their accounting for when Grace had left the party. From then on, she'd stayed on the property. There was no evidence of anyone coming or going during the time we believed Jocelyn Winter was murdered. Resignation sat cold in my gut, knowing I didn't have the evidence to move forward.

"I want to thank you for your time this morning."

Nichelle eased her laptop closed, adding, "We'll require time to review all of the video footage and to confirm."

"I told you!" Grace said, barking the words at us. "Get out of my house!"

"Grace!" Her mother said with a cough, gasping, chest rattling horribly. For a moment, I thought the woman was going to drown in her own fluids. Grace jumped up and patted her mother's back until color returned and she regained her voice. "Grace. Manners. Your temper."

The Armstrongs' lawyer raised his hand, his voice unheard, but the look on his face speaking for him with full understanding of the Armstrongs. When they were quiet again, he said, "You'll continue to have access to all surveillance footage during the course of your investigation."

"Thank you," I said, repeating myself, eager to leave the property and get back to the station.

Although Grace Armstrong might have been guilty of many things, she was innocent of Jocelyn Winter's murder.

CHAPTER TWENTY-NINE

We left the Armstrong house, an estate really. And we left it empty-handed. Nichelle was quiet on most of the drive back to the station, her brown eyes glowing with the security footage playing on her laptop. She reviewed footage from the closed-circuit cameras we'd seen in every corner of the house—inside and outside. That included the spacious grounds, the pool house, the sheds used for yard management, the inside foyer, rear exits, and the three-car garage. If Grace Armstrong went back to the party that night, she did so with a black magic that hadn't been called up since before the witch trials. Grace Armstrong had an alibi.

"Tampering?" I asked, offering a suggestion as I parked at the station. The demonstration was gone—the police breaking it up, the people disbanded. "Is it possible you're watching footage from another day?" Nichelle slumped over her laptop, her answering without saying anything. "The timestamp can't be altered at all?"

Her palms up with defeat. "I'm familiar with the system. The cameras terminate at the house on a secured computer. Everything else, all the data, it gets sent to a cloud server. I don't know how they'd change it."

"You're talking about a tenant system. It's shared. The system is hosted and managed by a company. The Armstrongs subscribing to the service."

A smile eased onto Nichelle's face. "You've been reading the IT books I gave you."

"I have." The truth was, I'd been reading everything I could. Learning was necessary if I was going to keep up with the technology. "Without tampering as a possibility, it means that Grace Armstrong has an alibi."

Tracy knocked on the window, waiting to trade places with Nichelle. "Give me a few more hours with the videos before we finalize on calling it an alibi."

"Do you think there's someone at the security company working with the Armstrongs?" I waved Tracy in as Nichelle opened the car door.

"That, or there could have been a breach from the outside." She wrinkled her nose, unconvinced. "Both are not probable but should be ruled out."

"Thanks, Nichelle," I said as she traded placed with Tracy. "Ready?"

"So where are we headed?"

"North Carolina Correctional Institute for Men. NCCIM."

"Got it. Gerald Jamison," she said, opening the Jamison case, flipping the first page to show his mugshot. "It's been a lot of years. Are you sure he's still alive?"

"He's alive, but he's no longer in the general population. The prison has its own nursing home."

We drove an hour west, picking up lunch on the way, my penchant for fast food becoming a dangerously attractive staple on the drives. We reviewed the Jamison case—Tracy reading as I devoured a cheeseburger, chasing it with a strawberry milkshake. It was in her reading I heard the gap, the estimated timing of Connie Jamison's death not matching with the original account. Not by a little either, but days.

"Let me see that?" I asked, Tracy holding an unfolded paper we'd overlooked. On office stationery as old as the case there were dates and times listed by the interviewing detective, just visible under a coffee stain. "Look at this, Gerald Jamison was in the interrogation room for fifty-six hours."

"I bet he'd say just about anything by the end of that interview," Tracy commented sarcastically. "Wait, do you think his confession was coerced?"

I shook my head, but then nodded, uncertain. "I mentioned to Nichelle this one seemed off. Look at the other sheet in the back."

Tracy dug our part of the court transcript and began to read. "The last reported sight of the mother was by a neighbor on the evening of April fifth, which was a Wednesday."

"Are you catching on to where I'm going with this?" I said, finishing my milkshake.

"Maybe?" Tracy asked, searching the pages, but not sounding sure. "There's a statement from a neighbor testifying that his truck wasn't in the driveway… oh, okay. I see it now." Tracy closed the file, her questioning the timeline.

"That's right. If the account from the neighbor is accurate, then Gerald Jamison wasn't home at the time of his wife's death."

Tracy waved toward the prison as we turned into the parking lot. "Then how is it he was convicted?"

"Connie Jamison's time of death was an estimate only. The woman was placed in salt, her body discovered later. And then there's the last page." She opened the folder to the last page. Her lips moving as she read.

"There was no trial? And the neighbor's statement about Gerald's truck was disregarded. Why?"

"There's an additional comment about the neighbor having worked two shifts at a local diner, and then being cited later for driving while intoxicated."

"That seems thin to disregard. And then there's the signed confession?"

"Signed confession, and because Gerald tried to hide his wife's body, the DA went for second-degree murder."

"He got it too."

"With the fifty-plus hours of interrogation, I doubt Jamison knew what he was signing." I stopped the car in front of the guard post, an attendant waiting, a man no more than twenty. He tipped his hat as I showed my badge, the afternoon sun catching it sharply. "The hospital ward?"

"To the left, ma'am; park all at the end." He shielded his eyes from the light as I tucked my badge away. "It'll be the last door. From there, you'll follow the smell."

Puzzled at his words, we headed in the direction he explained.

"Did he say follow the smell?"

"He did." I found a parking space and exited. Tracy followed while continuing to read the pages. "His lawyer was court appointed. Is there a name?"

"Umm," she began, brow lifting when she found it. "Yeah. Court appointed but waived by Jamison."

I opened the outer metal doors and glanced at the prison walls, the stone facade, the spiraling razor wire, and the guards in the roof and perched in towers. "Waiving it wasn't a good idea."

"Whoa." Tracy stepped back, the smell hitting us immediately—a heavy mix of cleaning solvents and waste. I motioned for her to follow, the door closing behind us.

"Let's keep moving." There was a laundry facility just beyond the first guard's station, bordered by heavy iron doors separating the outside world from the prisoners. Beyond the guards, men with walkers roamed the hallway, their heads shaven, their faces in silhouette, their long shadows like roaming giants. The men moved at a snail's pace, any hurry in their step left in the past when they were free men.

Tracy held her nose, letting it go reluctantly to sign the paperwork which gave us access to visit with Gerald Jamison. We turned the corner and entered a room where a television hung from the ceiling and green vinyl couches lined the walls, the covering torn and taped in patches. I glanced at Gerald Jamison's mugshot and then to the men in the room, finding just one who might have been the same person. Alone, sitting in a wheelchair and facing a window, a steel grate casting diamond-shaped shadows onto his face, his eyes half-lidded.

"Is that him?" Tracy asked.

"Mr. Jamison?" I asked, snagging the back of a plastic chair and placing it next to him. Tracy did the same. The old man's eyes were yellow and weepy, his looking as though he hadn't slept a night since the first day of his incarceration. "Mr. Gerald Jamison?"

"Who's asking," he said gruffly, glancing up while pushing his fingers lazily across his chin.

I showed him my badge, and said, "I'm here to ask you about your wife."

"She's dead." Gerald Jamison turned back to the window and closed his eyes, his interest gone.

"Mr. Jamison, have you received any visitors recently who have wanted to discuss your wife's death?" My question was specific to determine if there was a copycat, a killer who had read about Jamison.

The old man let out a groan as he shifted to see Tracy. "She's a pretty one." He sat back, looking at my face. "Not so bad either. Lovely eyes."

"Sir?" I asked, his attention wandering. "Has anyone come asking about Connie? Or anything about salt?"

"I delivered the salt," he answered as he patted his chest, fingers thick, nails dirtied and yellow like the whites of his eyes. "You got a smoke?"

I looked at the pair of green canisters slung from the back of his wheelchair, a tube leading to an oxygen mask—the hoarse rasp in his breathing explained. "I'm sorry, sir. I don't smoke."

"Nobody smokes anymore," he said and then looked to Tracy, holding two fingers up, twiddling them. She shook her head. "Damn young ones. Man, I miss them sticks."

"Sir, about your wife?"

Slowly, he answered, "Nobody come and see me about Connie."

I thought of who I knew to be home at the time of his wife's death and bit my lip, unsure of how the old man might react to what I was going to ask. There was only one reason I could think of that would make Jamison sign a confession.

The moment of silence stretched on. As his gaze wandered toward me, I asked, "Did your son kill your wife?"

The man's eyes sprang open, the years seeming to disappear from his face. The shock of the question lasted briefly as a look of solace, of relief came to it. "I did the time. I paid the debt."

"I know you did." I agreed with him. I believed he'd been on the road, and he had come home to find his wife dead. "You were delivering the salt when it happened?"

"The love of my life," he answered. His eyes were wet, unblinking. "Karl... Karl was troubled, but he loved his mother so much. He didn't hurt her. What happened to her was an accident."

"What kind of trouble?" Tracy asked. There'd been nothing in the file about the son, but Nichelle had sent us the old police reports, the boy going into neighbor's homes. There had also been arguments between Gerald and his wife, the fights reported. "What did Karl do?"

Jamison lifted his head higher. "The teachers said Karl had issues, that he was hard to handle. Me and Connie argued about it, but it was all a misunderstanding."

"What was a misunderstanding?" I asked, my hand on his arm, keeping his attention with us.

"Those times the police came to the house. It was our neighbors that reported him. Said he'd been in their girl's bedroom again." The old man shook his head, jowls shaking as he waved it off. "Connie was good at explaining the boy's issues. Said he was just curious."

"Did your son push his mother?" I asked quietly.

He leaned up, a fist clenching the arm of his chair, color rising on his neck and face. "Karl had nothing to do with that. He loved his mother!"

"Sir, you were accused of your wife's murder, and you signed a confession." Gerald's eyes were the most tired I'd ever seen. I didn't think it was from the guilt for his wife's murder that he'd been carrying all these years. Or from the sickness that'd take his life before the prison sentence did. It was the truth he'd been holding inside. "Your logbooks from your job. With your court appointed attorney, you could have cleared yourself if you'd offered them and had them entered as evidence."

He raised his hand, knuckles round, skin creased and gnarled. Jamison tapped the side of his head before pointing a shaky finger toward me. And then the moment came where he admitted it. "Pretty and smart you are."

"Why sir?" Tracy asked.

Though he knew we knew the truth, it was as if Gerald could finally put his guard down. He began speaking more quickly, more coherently. "I found her. I found her when I got home, and I was so scared. I knew how it'd look. They would take my boy and put him in one of those homes." Jamison wept silently, breath shuddering. "Connie always said he was special, that he just needed more time."

"Do you think your son pushed her?" I asked, digging deeper, pushing to hear the truth.

"No!" Jamison answered, his voice powerful. "I know it could never be proved, and any jury could be persuaded. My son loved his mother."

"Why the salt?"

He shrugged, confounded, answering, "I didn't know what else to do!"

"You hid your wife's body to protect your son," I said, assessing why he'd signed the confession.

"Did the time," he repeated, his gaze drifting. "It was an accident. He'd never hurt his mother."

"Yes, sir. I understand. Can I ask what ever happened to your son?"

"Karl?" The old man leaned closer to me, the smell of body odor strong. He cupped his mouth so only I could hear him. "Ya know, he sneaks me the sticks sometimes."

"Karl visits?" I asked.

"When the weather is good, and we can go for a walk outside." The man fell back into his chair with a grunt, the motion exhausting him. "He's a good boy. My sister tended to him when I got sent away. She died though."

"She died too?" Tracy asked, her voice lilting with surprise.

"It was a heart attack," Gerald scolded, hearing the implication. "But she done good with my boy. Raised him right."

"I'm sorry for your loss," I said. "What else can you tell us about your wife?"

"Connie?" he asked, shutting his eyes. He took a deep breath, his chest rattling. The old man stayed like that a long time. Long enough for Tracy and I to exchange a concerned look. When he was ready, he answered, "I think it was that damn step. Third from the top of the landing. It was loose from the day we bought that place. I must've told Connie I'd fix the thing so many times, but… but

I never got around to it. And that newel post! It would have been right there waiting for her. My Connie." His voice trailed off. It was a heartbreaking scene to imagine.

"Can you tell us about your son's relationship with his mother?" I wanted to hear more, making sure his earlier statements remained consistent. "I'm sorry to ask, sir, but was your wife ever abusive toward your son?"

An even more sorrowful look fell over him now, his lips quivering. He sighed heavily, managing to answer, "Connie was a beautiful mother to Karl. But… but I wasn't there, and that damn step."

"And Karl?"

"Already told you! He loved his mother! He was a good boy, did as he was told," Gerald said, continuing to defend his son. After decades in prison, decades behind bars, and with his possibly dying inside here, Gerald Jamison would continue to protect the truth. The old man's attention drifted, his gaze turning back to the window, his words slurring, "he's always been a good boy."

The sticks, I thought, Jamison mentioning his son visiting. "Sir, what is it your son does for a living?"

"Karl?" His focus sharper with his thin gray lips forming a grin. "He delivers the salt."

"Delivers salt?" Tracy asked.

"Did the time." Gerald's expression emptied then, his voice weakened as he mouthed, "Paid the debt."

Gerald seemed stuck in a repetitive conversation with himself. We'd gleaned all we could. After gently saying a goodbye, I motioned to Tracy and we left the room, my pace increasing until we got to the guard's station, where we exchanged the temporary IDs for our phones and my car keys. Gerald Jamison did the time like he said. But did the man pay a debt that wasn't his to pay? Although Gerald

Jamison was certain of his son's innocence, he must have had some doubt. After all, if he'd been sure, why would he have gone to prison to protect his son? I texted Emanuel and Cheryl.

Gerald Jamison's son Karl. There is a possibility he may have killed his mother.

Emanuel texted back.

His name came up as an employee of Salt Mineral Inc.

We just learned about him. Karl delivers the salt.

CHAPTER THIRTY

I'd found myself in the morgue again, the morning already with a chill, the islands deeper into the autumn season, leaves falling steadily, sunlight dimming, and a cloudy breath on my lips. There weren't enough clothes or lab coats to stave the chill in my bones. But it might not have only been the colder days and even colder temperatures in the morgue. It was what we found. We had faces.

Nichelle and Dr. Swales had been successful. They'd used the techniques Nichelle had come up with, computer modeling and artificial intelligence, beginning with the morgue photographs as a base. With the hair color, the length, and development of a tissue replenishment technique applied around the eyes and the cheeks, we had faces to go with each victim. With the computer-generated pictures, we'd also scoured through the area's missing persons cases and enlisted help from the FBI, as well as posted an online campaign and begun a run of television spots, the faces shown with phone numbers and social media handles—our seeking help from anyone who might recognize them. But I was here for a more personal reason. I was here for my daughter, Hannah.

It was the last victim that I came to the morgue to see—the one we'd discovered as a drone attacked. Nichelle had forwarded me the generated photographs, the image resembling a picture of my own Hannah, missing since she was three years old.

For years, a forensic artist, a close friend, used pictures of my daughter's relatives to age progress her face and give me a glimpse of what my daughter would look like today. It was the last picture of my daughter that resembled the victim. In my heart, I knew Hannah was alive. I sensed it. But the cop in me had to check too. It was like a reflex, like a flinch when brushing a hand close to a flame. I couldn't help myself and had to know for sure.

"Casey?" Dr. Swales said, her greeting with a question. She knew why I was there before I could say a word. Swales jerked the collar of her lab coat, a puff of wool fabric bulging beneath it. When she noticed my staring, she added, "I can get cold too."

"I brought you a cup," I said, offering her a tall coffee, a dark roasted blend and two Splenda with a splash of half and half. I put the coffee down to help her with the lab coat, stretching it, the fabric without any give. "It's too small."

"Nonsense!" she said with a bark. "I've been wearing the same one for ten years."

"You know why I'm here?"

Swales gave me a consoling look. She knew me, and she knew Hannah's case too. "It's sad to say, and it breaks my heart every time, but you're not the only visitor I get on a regular basis."

I hadn't considered it until now, but surely there were others like me. That is, mothers and fathers who were still looking for their missing children. My stomach flipped with the thought of those coming before me. "How many?"

"Let's see." Swales nudged her chin, thanking me for the coffee. She took the top off and drank, a look of fulfillment showing. "I think you're the fourth already this morning."

"They came to see you even though the faces aren't recognizable."

"Well, we do have the blood types and DNA now, but that's not it," Swales said, her complexion clammy, the morning growing long already. "They're here whenever a body arrives. Persistent to check if it is their child."

"Fourth?" A chill fell over me that was nothing to do with the morgue temperature. What if the killer had seen one of the news reports? "Doctor, was any of the visitors suspicious in any way? Anyone you haven't seen here before?"

"Suspicious?" Swales asked, her glasses fogging as she breathed in the steam from the coffee. "What do you mean?"

"You knew why I was coming." Swales gave me a nod but fixed a hard look. She was catching on to where I was going. "Of the three others that visited, did you know them all?"

She pondered over who'd come to the morgue. "The first were the McMillians, their daughter went missing… I guess it's ten years ago now. Poor girl. She was just eight when she vanished from the beach." I followed the doctor to the refrigerated units, cold spilling from the steel face. She opened a drawer, a toe-tag swinging against the rush of air.

"Who else?" I asked, unable to break my stare of the mummified feet, the skin ghostly with a faint color of orange and brown, aged, and wrinkled. She jerked on the drawer, the ball bearings screeching as the body was placed in front of me.

"Then there was Mrs. Clifford, her son had disappeared eight years ago." The news reports had refrained from divulging the victims' genders, our withholding some of the details. "Mrs. Clifford didn't know that all the victims were female."

"And the last?"

Swales tapped her finger against the side of her glasses, pushing on them as they began to slide. "Him? I can't say I'd ever seen him before."

"Did he have a name?"

"You know, I don't recall him saying." Concern reached her then, the doctor clutching her lab coat, closing it. "He didn't say who he was looking for either."

With her words, I glanced at the camera in the corner of the room, its red eye glowing, the building municipal, the security system recording every activity paid for by the taxpayers. "He didn't say who it was he was looking for?"

Her hands trembled—the thought of the killer having been there coming as a shock. "He said it was his sister... Casey, do you think?" She couldn't finish what she wanted to ask and took a heavy gulp of her coffee. "Oh, my stars!"

There was dark fright on her face. "It's okay, Terri." I went to her side.

"Casey, he wanted to see them all." The doctor went to a stool, her coffee set aside so she could sit. She braced her head in her hands. "He insisted on seeing them all."

"Did you show him the pictures you and Nichelle made?" I asked. "Maybe he was looking for his sister—"

Her eyes bugging wide, Dr. Swales took her glasses off. "That's what I'm trying to say. He didn't want to see the pictures. He only wanted to see the bodies."

"Nichelle," I said, calling her directly.

"I'm on?" she answered, her voice groggy. "What's up?"

"Surveillance system, the morgue." I cupped the phone a moment and braced the doctor's arm. "Terri, it'll be okay."

"What about it?" Nichelle asked, alarm rising in her voice. "Is everything okay? Dr. Swales?"

"She's fine," I said, assuring her. "There was a visitor this morning, an unexpected visitor. He said that he was looking for his sister. He thought she might be one of the victims."

"The victims? Didn't she show him our pictures?"

"That's why I'm calling. He only wanted to see the bodies." As I relayed what I knew, I went to the body of the victim whose picture resembled Hannah. Atop the sheet on the body was a folder, the contents carrying every detail the lab could drum up. There was only one thing I needed to look at. "Nichelle, could you still images from the lobby and the stairwell, maybe the elevator."

"And the morgue," she said, finishing for me. "I'll get on it as soon as I'm back in front of my computer."

"Good," I said, opening the folder. I ran my finger down the left side of the chart which listed the details of the blood work. "I'll be back at the station soon."

The place on the form where the blood type was located had remained blank, the space empty. I looked to Dr. Swales, her frame a tiny lump atop the lab's stool, the sudden shock of her visitor taking its toll. She caught me staring, caught the concern. She was quick to wave it off, saying, "I'm tougher than I look."

"Maybe you should come back to the station with me." My suggestion wasn't a bad one. "I'd like you to meet with a forensic artist."

"I could do that," she answered, perking up. She glanced around the room as though seeing it for the first time in a different light. "Yeah. I'll do that."

I held up the folder. "The blood type is missing."

"There was no blood," she said with a shrug, joining me. "Mummified."

"Of course." I felt stupid for the oversight.

"But there's DNA." Swales took the folder and flipped to the next page. "Genomics is the most precise blood typing method there is."

"What's her type?" The butterflies were gnawing, demanding an answer. I had a blood type of O negative. Hannah's father was also O negative. And our daughter's blood was the same. Having been here before, the circumstance similar, Dr. Swales knew this, and knew it was what I'd come here to find out. "Same as mine?"

Her mouth twisted, lips firming. "B positive."

And with her words, the butterflies rested, the purpose of their visit over. I gazed at the documents and the outline of the victim beneath the sheet. "She's somebody's daughter though."

"She is," Swales said as she put the folder back in place and closed the drawer, the bearing screeching raucously again. Referring to the new visitor, she added with fright in her voice, "Or someone's sister?"

"Come on," I said, encouraging her to follow, my arm around her. I didn't like seeing Dr. Swales scared and wished I had kept my mouth shut, wished I hadn't planted the idea of the killer visiting the morgue. "Let's get to the station."

CHAPTER THIRTY-ONE

After the interview with Gerald Jamison, his son Karl had become a person of interest. A search was on to determine his location. A patrol was dispatched to Karl's listed address, and found the house locked, the driveway empty. With Jamison being an interstate truck driver, and with his rig gone from the residence, we had no confirmation of the man's whereabouts. Was Karl the doctor's mysterious visitor?

Whoever it was that had visited the morgue, they were smart enough to hide their face from the security cameras. Lean and approximately six feet tall and one-hundred and sixty pounds, the man wore a bright red baseball cap which kept his face shielded. What he didn't hide was the stringy locks of black hair sprouting from the back of his hat and over the ears. From the video surveillance and Nichelle's analysis, we didn't find any graying hairs or identifiable marks. The morgue visitor wore a flannel shirt, thick material with patchy black and dark blue. He also wore faded denim, a hole in the knee with the jeans frayed, threadbare, the fabric ragged. I couldn't tell if the hole was by design, or his jeans were worn through.

We were already working to acquire pictures of Karl Jamison, the department of motor vehicles becoming a blocker in releasing vehicle and license records. Once we had his picture, we could compare it to the morgue visitor. The missing piece we needed was a sketch of the man. I had Dr. Swales meeting with our station sketch artist.

Within the half hour, we'd have a picture of him, and we'd have an APB issued. By tonight, we might have him seated in an interview room to answer our questions.

Cheryl countered us, questioning the APB, suggesting that the man at the morgue had in fact been there to search for his missing sister. She might be right, which only made finding him even more necessary. Worst case, issuing the APB would bring an innocent man in for questioning and we'd clear him immediately, the embarrassment of having egg on our faces brief. Best case, he was the killer, and he was visiting the morgue to claim his prizes in what might have been his farewell to his victims. What if it was just the first of his visits? What if he returned? Without knowing the answer, I'd also suggested a guard to remain stationed around the clock, giving Swales and her team some security.

Dr. Swales stood behind the station's forensic artist, his large sketch pad in hand, waiting for me as I finished the details of the APB. I held out my hand, fingers clutching the air, eager to see what the doctor and the artist had come up with. The artist flipped his work around, the page blank. He leaned forward for me to hear him. "She couldn't remember." I gave him a *what gives* look, confused, Swales seeming fine in the car ride.

"What do you mean?" I glanced around him. Dr. Swales stood quietly, her posture sagging. "Surely she saw his face. The video shows he was there for fifteen minutes."

He grimaced and scratched the side of his head. "I don't think she's aware of where we are." He closed his sketch pad and stepped aside, presenting Swales as though I was receiving her into custody. "I've got another case. But if she remembers, bring her back and I'll get a sketch made up for you."

"Thank you," Dr. Swales said unexpectedly, her face upturned to meet his voice, her southern accent stronger than usual.

The artist looked confused, answering, "Yes, ma'am."

Swales came to my desk, her step wobbly as she peered around as though seeing my desk for the first time. I offered her a chair. "How are you feeling?" I must have drastically underestimated how shaken she was. The skin beneath her eyes was moist, her upper lip damp and her face flush.

Unfocused, Swales leaned forward, close to me. "Is it time to go?"

I called to Nichelle, "Get some water." I held the doctor's hand, her stare vacant. There was something wrong. "Terri? Do you feel okay?"

"Feel okay? Am I at the hospital?" she asked, pinching her lips between her finger and thumb. "No. No, that was before. I work at the morgue now."

"Terri?" Jericho asked, entering my cubical, his coming to the station when I texted about the morgue's unexpected visitor. His relationship with Dr. Swales was years deep and close like family. He knelt, her thick glasses sitting askew, the look of her strikingly sad, the might of her suddenly small compared to who I knew. Jericho offered the water from Nichelle. "Terri, take a sip of this."

She did, as asked, seeing Jericho, recognizing him. "Oh, Jericho dear," she said, eyes weepy, her palm cradling his face. "I am sorry about Jessie."

"Jessie Flynn?" Cheryl asked, standing tall onto her toes to see over the group gathering. "Why is she—"

"She's confused," Jericho said, upset and angry at the mention of his ex-wife. "Terri, do you know where you are?"

"The morgue," she said, the corner of her mouth drooping, her words slurring.

Jericho stood abruptly and put his arm beneath the doctor. "Terri, we're going to go for a ride."

"Emergency room?" I asked, his eyes fixed on Swales while he held her. "I'll go—"

He shook his head, answering, "I'll take her. Might be nothing. Dehydration, maybe."

"Call as soon as you see a doctor," I said, scared for her, dread aching.

As Jericho and Dr. Swales left the station, I had to focus on the work at hand: the victim's faces Nichelle was able to generate, and a flurry of emails and text messages waiting for me from the FBI. I held up my phone, Nichelle seeing it, her receiving the notices as well. She saw the worry on my face. "We have names!" she said, hinting at her excitement as she tried to lift my spirits. "I'm sure Dr. Swales will be fine."

"I hope so," I said, thinking of her dancing to Helen Reddy's "I Am Woman." "I really hope it's nothing at all."

"Conference room?"

"Emanuel?" I asked, getting his attention. When I had it, I said, "Conference room, and bring up the map with the salt mining company."

"There's more than one," he said.

"Bring whatever you have." I grabbed my things, looking at my phone briefly to see if any of the names were familiar to me. They weren't. The FBI agent who'd sent the email commented on Nichelle's work, the agency being greatly impressed with the facial reconstruction. Along with the email, the agent provided every case detail, including the victim's last whereabouts. "We've got last known locations. Let's get them on the map and see what's what."

"X marks the spot?" Emanuel asked, his hand out, offering to take some of my stuff for me.

"Yeah. Something like that." I handed him my laptop, the power cord dragging behind him as the rest of the team joined us and we made our way to the conference room. "Only these kids didn't find buried treasure. The killer did."

*

We already knew Tina Sommers. She was the first mummified victim discovered. Today, we'd received the FBI case file, and the last known pictures of her alive—a grainy surveillance video taken at a truck stop. Nichelle played the video clip, putting it on replay as we settled into the conference room, chair wheels rattling, seat backs creaking.

"The map from the last meeting," Emanuel said, showing it on a second monitor. "I've put a pin on the truck stop for Tina Sommers."

"Sticking to the routes from the salt mining company, highlight the most probable path to Karl Jamison's home." I stood between the two displays.

"Look at her shoes," Tracy commented, Nichelle freezing the video. The girl's shoes were tattered and worn, her clothes appearing wet. Tina Sommers came into the camera's view to take a seat where food had been left behind. She picked at the leftovers, my thinking sadly that this might have been her last meal. "The timestamp shows January twenty-second last year. I reviewed weather sites and there was a storm that day. Actually, for two days the temperatures dipped into the teens."

"We have a truck stop, late evening, poor weather, the victim in danger of the elements," Cheryl said, summarizing.

"Wait for it," Emanuel said. After a moment he snapped his fingers, a burly man stepping into the picture and taking a seat across from Tina. He carried a tray with two of everything, including a soda for the victim and a tall coffee for himself. "And freeze now."

On Emanuel's cue, Nichelle froze the video playback, the truck driver looking directly into the security camera, unencumbered with any need to hide his identity. "I give you Karl Jamison. We've also received a report of the FBI interviewing Jamison. DMV records should be released soon too."

This was a massive break in the case, but he looked nothing like the man who'd visited the morgue. "Bring up the latest picture we have of Karl Jamison." Nichelle opened a folder marked DMV for the department of motor vehicles. Karl Jamison's round face appeared. He wore a thick white beard, his head bald, eyes a greenish brown, his cheeks rosy and plump. "Hmm?"

"What is it?" I heard Emanuel's low baritone voice.

"No stringy hair. He's not skinny. He doesn't look at all like I was expecting," I answered.

"The guy looks like a model for a holiday greeting card," Emanuel said.

"That he does." I then warned, "Can't judge a book by its cover. He's already been interviewed?"

"He has." Emanuel showed us the interview. "The FBI had questioned him at the time of her disappearance. He stated he'd only driven her to the truck stop."

"With a body, we can question him again." Cheryl stood up, her phone in hand, texting. "I'm getting a search warrant for Jamison's property."

"Any additional interviews?" I asked, thinking of the FBI, the materials received from them.

"Hold on a minute," Tracy said, hand raised. The files from the FBI were many. "Karl Jamison. He was interviewed twice."

"And let go both times?" Cheryl asked, jamming her thumb on her phone. "We'll question him again."

"Agreed. The difference between then and now is we have the salt used in his mother's death linking him to the victim." It was enough to justify the search warrant. "We only need to find one piece of physical evidence that links back to Jamison."

Cheryl resumed her call. "There's word Swales recovered salt from the most recent victim."

"That's huge news!" I said. Until now, the mummification process had lacked any evidence of salt, there being only residue and stains on the sheets, the body expelling it. But this find was actual salt, constituted in a form we could analyze. "The killer must have missed it."

Emanuel put a pin on the map of the last victim. Cheryl saying, "It is, but what do we do with it?"

"Without Swales?" I asked, thinking of her assistant Derek and the others working for her. "I'll follow up with her assistant, tell him we want the evidence analyzed."

"What does that even mean?" Cheryl asked, her face fixed with a confounded look.

"Chemical analysis. The team will know what to do," I replied. As detectives in the field, neither Cheryl nor I could know the specifics of the analysis or what to search for, but we had to trust the team at the lab to do their job, even without Swales. This was a vital piece of evidence.

"Let's hope so," Cheryl said, rolling her eyes, the look edging on unprofessional.

"What about the other victims?" I asked, shifting gears as I moved to the map, the highlight roads showing Karl Jamison's delivery route along with his route between home and the salt mine.

"This is Beth Fremont, who we believe to be the second victim. She was missing for more than a year." Emanuel flicked his keyboard, a school picture of the victim showing alongside her mummified face, the contrast between them devastating. "She was reported missing by her parents. She also had a history of running away, and we have a witness account of her being picked up, hitching a ride on route I-64."

"From I-64, her route connects to 168 and then 158 and then across the bridge," I said my finger on the intersection. "Tracy, who was next?"

Tracy straightened. "The third victim is Jennifer Wilcox, a runaway. She'd also been in and out of juvenile detention. She has an extensive record dating back to her early teens." Tracy motioned to Emanuel, his placing Jennifer Wilcox's pictures on the screen and pinning her last known locations on the map.

"None of the girls look anything alike?" he said. "Even the fourth victim, Heather Jones. All different."

"That's not what the killer wanted," I said, scanning the pictures, the range of hair and skin colors vastly different. Even their heights and weights lacked commonality.

"What do we know about the fourth victim?" Cheryl asked.

"A runaway too," Emanuel answered. "From New Jersey."

Tracy held up her hand, but kept it reserved. "Was it random selection?"

Randomness was possible. But what I saw were girls who were alone and broken and vulnerable. These girls were similar after all. They were in a class together. A common one. The most victimized of any I'd ever seen. "I believe the killer seized on their isolation. He targeted their loneliness and vulnerability."

"How?" Tracy seemed bothered. The girls were closest to her age. "Did he search for them?"

"He hunted for them," I answered, the coldness in my voice making Tracy cringe. "And when there was opportunity, he took it."

"All the more reason to visit Jamison, regardless of the previous interviews," Cheryl said. "Search warrant will be submitted by the end of this meeting."

"Make sure that warrant includes his truck," I said, fixing my gaze on Tina Sommers and her meal with Jamison. "His routes are along the interstate. There will be GPS tracking in his truck, along with a logbook."

"I'll add a property search to it?" Cheryl said, working her phone.

There was one more victim, the last one we'd found; the cut on the back of my hand healing slowly, its sting a constant reminder. "Who was the last victim?"

"The fifth victim, that last identified is… Angela Murphy." Emanuel's words came out in a stammer. "The victim disappeared shortly after her graduation, over two years ago."

He updated the screens to show her face. It was a recent graduation picture—the girl wearing a gown, a tassel made of silver and indigo blue draping from her cap, a sign in the background blurred, but showing the girl's high school. She was white with a tan, green eyes and dark brown hair. "Local girl?" Cheryl asked.

"We did investigate her disappearance at the time," Emanuel answered.

"Outer Banks?" I went to the screen, focusing on the sign behind the girl, the name of the school. "Does that say West OBX High School?"

"It does." I searched my memory, searched every name, every missing person case I'd reviewed. I'd seen so many names, a pang of shame for not recalling Angela Murphy burning my cheeks. Emanuel must have noticed. "Her disappearance was investigated before you arrived."

"Till now that is. She's been found," I commented, feeling restless with where this was going. "But the school—"

"Yeah, I know." Emanuel opened Jocelyn Winter's case, adding her picture to the monitor.

"West OBX High School." The recent demonstrations echoed in my head. The shrill voice of Jocelyn Winter's mother. I'd hear it forever. "Angela Murphy was mudborn."

CHAPTER THIRTY-TWO

I had a moment of quiet in my cubical before we teamed up and traveled to Karl Jamison's property to execute a search warrant. I couldn't get the notes out of my head, the words the killer had left behind. The killer had a message he was hiding, and I desperately needed to find it. Across my desk, I placed copies of the five notes recovered, attaching a victim's name and disappearance date on a tangerine-colored Post-it note. With the dates, I had the order—not that I knew if order made a difference. But with the meticulous nature of the bodies preparation, I believed order mattered.

I erased everything on my whiteboard and wrote down the first note's words, retaining the sequence as they appeared. The marker's fruity chemical smell filled my cubical, and its tip squelching against the board called to Tracy and Nichelle, their faces appearing. When I was done writing, I stepped back from the board, finding Emanuel had joined us, his lips moving as he read the words to himself.

With a shake of my head, I said, "I know we've all been staring at these words, but we have got to come up with something."

One by one, the team sounded out the words, saying, *"Distressing calumnies I am toward affect."*

Nichelle shoved her fingertips into her hair, pulling and pushing as though it'd help jar her thoughts. "I don't like to say I'm beat, but I've entered every word from those notes and searched every bit and byte of the internet universe."

"Nothing?" Tracy asked, her jaw slack. "No references to anything?"

"Literally, nothing!" Nichelle answered, hands dropping to her sides with a slap.

"Let me throw the second note on here," I said, taking to the whiteboard and writing.

An affect I am toward abide.

"We're assuming the notes are in order?" Emanuel asked.

I let out a sigh and shrugged while writing the words. "We can't assume anything really. Which only means we have to keep trying every order, maybe even mix the words up."

"The words again?" Cheryl asked, voice gruff, disdain on her face. She elbowed past the team, her hands filled with paperwork and dropped two files on my desk. "Has a team ever spent this much time staring at the same words."

"I don't think we have," I answered, hating that we hadn't gotten anywhere with them. And hating that Cheryl noticed. "With the dates and names, we're giving the words a fresh look."

As Cheryl made her way back to her office, Tracy entered my cube, sitting in a lean against the table. She read the second sentence. "*An affect I am toward abide.*"

"The second note almost makes sense," Emanuel said, my cubical wall groaning as he perched his arms atop it. "It sounds like there was a burden?"

"Or something he has to endure?" I suggested. Nichelle raised her brow, Tracy turning to the idea too. Questioning myself, I added, "Would that be too literal?"

"Not so much," Tracy answered.

The team began to debate the sentence when I saw an idea and took to the first sentence with a red marker. "What if the words are encoded?"

"Nuh-uh," Nichelle said, her voice raised. She entered my cube, the space getting crowded. "I've been through every known code imaginable. There's nothing here. If there was an encrypted cipher, a word or letter substitution, I would have found the key."

"Maybe it isn't substitution at all. Maybe there isn't any key for us to find." On the first sentence I underlined the words, *I* and *am*. "These words are alone. I think the killer did that on purpose."

The team wore a confused look, uncertain of the idea, Tracy suggesting, "Like he was leaving a clue, a challenge."

"How does that help?" Cheryl asked, returning—the mystery of the words more an interest than she'd let on.

"What if the message is hidden inside the words," I proposed. On the word *distressing*, I underlined the word buried inside it, *stress*. "See it? There are words inside the words." I went to the word *toward*, underlining the word *to*. When I saw understanding, I double underlined ward. "See what I mean, words within—"

"They're called kangaroo words!" Tracy said abruptly, her voice a near shout. Heads turning to face her, she held up her phone. "It's a puzzle thing. The words that are carried inside the kangaroo words are called joeys. And there are certain rules they follow."

"Damn. It is encoded," Nichelle said, her head shaking. "I should have figured—"

"Nonsense," I told her, seeing she felt bad. "We don't even know what we have yet. Let's keep going."

"Kangaroos and joeys? Is that a joke?" Cheryl crossed her arms and squinted. "That can't be real."

"Serious," Tracy said. She stood and showed her phone's screen. "Look. There are words called kangaroo and joeys—"

I raised my voice, hands raised, saying, "Guys. Let's run with it. Words inside words."

"Okay, but not all words found inside other words are considered joeys and kangaroos," Tracy went on to explain as she held up her computer and showed her screen. "According to this website, there are rules."

"Rules?" Emanuel glanced at Tracy's screen.

"Yes, rules. First, the joeys have to be a synonym of their kangaroo word," she began.

Cheryl punched her hips with her balled hands. "You mean words that mean the same thing?"

"Correct!" Tracy answered, putting her finger to her nose. "We could use a thesaurus to help with those."

"What's the second rule?" Emanuel asked.

"The second rule is that the letters need to be the correct sequence."

"Which means we can't juggle the letters and pick whatever we want." On the board, I saw more words to use. But were they the ones the killer had put in the note?

"Stress?" Cheryl asked, her face in her phone. "That's not a synonym for distressing."

"You're right. It isn't." I wiped the whiteboard with the heel of my palm, erasing the underlined word. "But the word *dire* is a synonym." I underlined the letters, saying, "dire calumnies? What is the joey for the word calumnies? What are the synonyms?"

"Calum?" Someone said while someone else mumbled, "lumis?"

"Got it," Emanuel announced, rapping his knuckles on the table as though this were a quiz show. From his phone he read the words, "*Slanderous, libel, defamations, lies—*"

"Lies," I interrupted. I underlined the letters l, i, e and s. "It's got to be the word lies!"

"You're right. Lies is a synonym for calumnies," Nichelle said, returning with a tablet in hand. "Dire lies?"

"Does that make sense to anyone?" Cheryl asked.

"Lies works as a synonym. That gives us the first six words. *A dire act I am to—*"

"What about *I* and *am*?" Cheryl asked, hand on her chin. "And what's a synonym… sorry, a joey, for affect?"

"Maybe the killer only used joeys where kangaroo words fit." I underlined the first word I saw in affect. The letters a, c and t. "An act is a synonym for affect."

"Dire lies I am to act." I turned to the group, a weight lifting from my shoulders. "I think we have a first sentence."

"I think we do," Cheryl muttered, picking up the second note, reading it aloud. "*An affect I am toward abide.*"

I underlined the joeys, having already found joeys *act* and *to*, and adding *bide* for abide. "We have two now: *Dire lies I am to act. An act I am to bide.*"

"Is it a poem?" Cheryl asked.

I stepped back from the whiteboard, reading to myself what we'd come up with. "Let's try the next one." With the third victim's note in hand, I wrote the words on the whiteboard.

Situation exists for myself toward cleanse.

Nichelle asked, "May I?"

I handed her the marker, seeing the joeys, hearing the team behind us speaking them softly. "By all means."

"Let's start with *it* in situation. How about *is* in exists?"

"*For*? Synonym for the word *or*?" Tracy asked, Nichelle underlining the word.

"It's not a synonym?" Emanuel asked.

"Right, it's not," I said, uncertain myself. "Go ahead and leave the word *for*, no joeys. I want to see what we get. And for the word *cleanse*, we could use *clean*, let's leave it."

"For the word *myself*, the joey could be *me*," Tracy added.

"I like it."

Nichelle read what we had. "That gives us. *It is for me to clean.*"

"Next note," Cheryl said, getting into the swing of it, picking up a note and marker, writing on the whiteboard as she recited. "We've got, *an devilish apposite toward arise.*"

Without waiting for feedback, Cheryl pulled the joeys, rewriting the sentence as I read the results. "*An evil apt to rise.*" I went to my desk feeling bothered, a dark notion rearing its ugliness. The killer had written a poem, but did we have all of it? I said nothing yet, taking the fifth note and writing it on the whiteboard.

Tracy read the killer's words. "*A clue toward allure the postured.*" She clapped her hands excitedly. "Oh I see it."

"Go ahead," I told her.

"The last note is, *a cue to lure the posed.*"

With the killer's words decoded, the team seeing them complete and together for the first time, we stepped back to read the whiteboard.

Dire lies I am to act. An act I am to bide.
It is for me to cleanse. An evil apt to rise.
A cue to lure the posed.

I asked, "Does anyone see it?"

"Other than it doesn't really make sense?" Cheryl asked.

There were head nods, faces in their phones, the team reading and re-reading.

"It's not complete," I said, a chill racing over me with goosebumps on my arms. "We're missing the last sentence."

"Not complete?" Cheryl asked, annoyance in her voice.

I picked up the notes, the five groups of words decoded—five sentences for five bodies. "If I'm right, we need one more sentence. There should be a sixth." The team shifted uncomfortably, understanding what it was I was implying. "There's a sixth victim."

CHAPTER THIRTY-THREE

An opportunity. That's what this was. Tracy Fields stomped on her gas pedal, glee rising inside her, delighted to play a bigger part. She'd show them what she could do. Casey had given her a chance to work side by side with the team on the details of a search warrant.

She felt giddy. Glimpsing her work bag, she listed everything in her head that needed to be in there. She let out a groan, hoping that she hadn't forgotten anything. This afternoon wasn't just about a crime scene. It was about a suspect, Karl Jamison, whose face they saw on a video with one of the victims. This was about searching him, and his property, and catching a killer.

That nagging feeling came again, of being less than them, inferior. She could have taken a ride with one of them, but with a new car, she wanted to show she could arrive on her own, meet them there, be a reliable and self-sufficient member of the team. She tugged on her hair, a nervous habit she hated. Still, reliable, or not, they were all detectives, and she was only a crime-scene investigator. If Cheryl had her way, she'd never get the chance to do more.

Maybe the academy? Tracy thought to herself, spinning the dial on the radio until it landed on the only decent local station playing the top hits. The car speakers blared with Post Malone's "Circles". She hummed along with the song, considered what it'd take to become a detective. *Maybe that'll be my next step.*

Tracy pushed the heater button next, turning it up, the car still cold, a shiver running through her. She made a right turn and drove onto Wrights Bridge, entering the light flow of traffic. The wind and the whitecaps on the bay were dying, a snow squall dropping fat flakes that drifted like lost butterflies. The short wintry blast was early for the season, and she took her eyes off the traffic a moment to see the season's first, the flakes landing on her windshield where they melted instantly.

Her phone showed an exit to take, the navigator's voice tinny, telling her to turn right onto a road marked *unnamed* after exiting the bridge.

"Unnamed?" Tracy asked, doubting the app's reliability. "You better be right."

The Jamison house was fifteen minutes inland from the bay. If the right turn was a bust, she'd turn around and try the other navigation app. She searched behind her and to the sides, looking to see if anyone from the team was close to her. She didn't want to be the first to arrive on scene. Not officially. If needed, she could pull back and wait for them. As her tires rolled onto the road's gravel and dirt, her doubt about the app's accuracy grew. This wasn't the road she wanted.

The engine sputtered and kicked then, the lights on the dashboard winking alarmingly. Tracy flinched, an unease replacing the earlier glee. Annoyed, she hammered the gas pedal, feeding the engine, the motor rearing and revving briefly. But it was the last of it, the engine's pistons churning without fire, slowing until they stopped, the motor gasping with a ticking sound. The power in the tires slipped, the car stalling, the quiet coming as the momentum carried her forward.

"You have got to be kidding me?" Tracy said, thinking this wasn't possible. Her gaze swept over the rearview mirror, finding the dirt road behind her was empty. She scanned ahead, seeing the front was vacant too. Alone, trees lined one side with leaves that were nearly gone for the year. And on the passenger side, there were high reedy grasses like cattails, only these were a light brown, the lush green exiting with the summer heat. Beyond their tipped fronds, she could see the edge of grounds turning to marsh, the bay beyond it.

The search warrant came to mind, along with her not making it to the Jamison house. Tracy shook her head, thinking of Cheryl and how much she was going to love this. She'd use it as an excuse to cut her from the team. But Casey? Tracy hated the idea of disappointing her. "Shit!"

For a moment, Tracy didn't move. She didn't speak. She sat in her dead car and watched the snow squall move east, the flurries a distant thought. She was breathing heavy, clouds in her breath, her insides quivering as she fought the need to cry.

"It's just a breakdown," she said to herself, turning the key, the motor whirring with a sputter. Again, there was no fire, no kick. Tracy sat back and tried to reassure herself, telling herself this wasn't her fault. She had much to prove though. "Surely they'll understand."

The sun peered through patches of gray sky, the rays shining into her car window, its heading west while her destination was due north another five miles. And though it was cold, she felt the heat of embarrassment. Cheryl was apt to be the first to drive past and see her abandoned on the side of the road. What a laugh she'd have. "Please let it be Emanuel or Casey," she mumbled, her face stinging with a tear.

A car horn jolted her, its approaching from behind, tires crunching stone as Tracy realized she was blocking the road. Tracy lowered her window, grateful the problem with her car wasn't electrical. She waved the car by, the road narrow, but wide enough to fit them both. There was no shoulder for her to park.

Another honk, the car parking behind her, hazard lights blinking. It was a white truck, the front of it like an SUV, but the back opened with a bay like a work truck.

"Go around me!" Tracy yelled out her window, waving her arm. But the truck remained, the driver's door opening.

"Troubles?" a voice called to her, the wind stealing it.

"It died," she yelled back.

"Did you call for a tow yet?"

"Not yet. It just happened." She dipped her face to see through the mirror, the man's height keeping his head out of view. "It literally died a few minutes ago."

"Shame. It looks like a newer car too," he said, his hands on his hips as he assessed her status. He wore light-colored khaki pants and a thin jacket that reminded her of the kind pilots wore: the leather soft and smooth and tanned; the inside lined with a fluffy cream-colored sheep's wool. "How many miles?"

"Not even three thousand," Tracy answered. "The engine kinda stopped. But the battery is still working. I have electricity."

"Might be a problem with the gas then?" he asked, offering an idea.

Tracy decided that his interest in helping her was genuine, her reservations set aside. She opened her car door, exiting, the man eyeing her over the roof of her car, the sun behind him.

"Is it possible you're out of gas?"

She shook her head as his face emerged from shadow. He was attractive. A lump in her throat formed. She felt self-conscious. He wasn't her age, but he wasn't old either. And though his hairline was receding, he wore it well. His face was boyish and unshaven with a thin beard.

"I filled the tank two days ago."

He went to the side of the car with the gas cap, his focus on the car's fuel as being the problem. He pawed at his chin and then signaled for her to join him. "I hate to say it, but I think you've been robbed."

"What?" Tracy said, raising her voice. She rubbed her arms absently, the motion guarding, his words unsettling. He waved her around the car to show what he was referring to. Instinctively, Tracy sided with caution, and she went around the front, heat from the engine brushing her body as she stepped onto the grassy shoulder, the stalky plants cracking while she made room for herself.

"Do you see the gas stain? It runs down the length of the quarter panel. Look at the latch on the door too. It's broken."

"Where?" Tracy asked, moving close enough to see the door covering the gas cap. She made a fist when she saw it—the damage, the bent corner, the paint creased. There was the stain too, coating the paint, her new car damaged. "They siphoned my gas?"

"How else was I going to get to you?" he asked, suddenly spreading his arms wide, his height and weight overpowering her and swallowing her whole.

Tracy's body was suddenly in darkness as the man tackled her. She felt the first strike, a knee perhaps, solid like a tree branch driven into her middle, her lungs collapsing in a violent wheeze. Tracy doubled over, tumbling backward, her head striking the side of her car. She peered up with watery eyes to see the man's figure doubled over, his hands balled together and coming toward her. The second strike was punishing and made her head spin. A second later, her mind shut down like her car, entering a world that was gray and hazy. There was emptiness, a sense of nothing.

She felt a breeze on her lips. Her cheek was pressed against the road's dust and rocks. Branches clacked, rustling with leaves from a stiff wind. "Wha—?" Tracy tried to say. Her eyelids fluttered, her sight blurred, the view like a mix of watercolors running wildly across a painter's canvas. She saw him then. Panic gripped her heart with its cold fingers, his sitting squat and hovering above her while she struggled. "Who are you?"

"Who indeed?" he asked, returning her question. He ran his fingers along her bare neck and then beneath her shirt, pressing against that place above her collarbone, digging his finger into her soft flesh. Tracy reared back, but her movement was slowed, his hand like a tool, holding her in place with little effort. He took hold of her station identification badge, his lips moving in silence. "I knew I'd have you the moment I saw you."

Tracy eyed the road leading away from the bridge, the traffic speeding back and forth. "They'll be here."

"Nah," he said. "Well, possibly. That is if they don't realize this is a service road."

"Service road?" she asked, realizing her navigation app declaring the road *unnamed*, the access meant for workers. "'For the bridge?"

"Imagine my fortune," he said, sunlight bright on his face. "I mean the timing of it. I thought you'd get another mile down the road before hitting that last drop of gas. This is fate. Our fate."

"Why are you doing this?" she asked, struggling to get up.

"Because you took them!" he yelled, striking suddenly, the force driving her into the hard ground. The man snatched her legs like a sack, dragging her to his truck; the road scraped beneath her, the back of her head grating on grit and rock. "You're payment. You'll do well to cleanse."

With a grim horror she understood what was happening, what he planned to do. Tears welled in her eyes as she clutched a handful of the tall grass, the vegetation snapping in half like candle sticks. She grabbed the rear tire of her car and glimpsed the gas stain, touching it, running her finger along it as she struggled against his grip on her leg, screaming the whole time. But there was nobody to hear her.

"Please! Please let me go!"

He spun around to face her, his grip on her ankles vicious, crushingly strong, pain rising, screams louder. In his wet blue eyes, she saw hatred and rage. His voice was deranged, "You took them!"

Kick, she heard in her head, fighting the dizziness and jerking her knees. She struck him in the hip and his thigh, her heels landing squarely and causing him to lose hold. But as she rolled toward the grass and tried to scurry away, his shoe landed on her middle, stomping on her like a bug, stealing her air again and taking the daylight with it.

She floated in and out again, stirring at the sound of metal clicking, a bright orange strap near her face, tightening, his ratcheting it to lock her into place. He'd managed to tie her body to the bed of his truck. Tracy peered up, the sky growing dark with another passing snow cloud, flakes wandering, the sting of cold brief as they landed and melted on her face. "Casey," she mumbled, thinking of her phone and keys, how she'd left them in her car.

"It'll be over soon," he said, covering her body with burlap, and tying it down. The material was scratchy and rough on her skin and smelled like salt, causing her to turn her head away from it. She saw the round gas can, the tip of the yellow nozzle, a plastic hose for siphoning which laid coiled like a snake next to the billowing red jug. The size of the jug wasn't enough to suck every drop. But of course, he filled his truck with what he stole. The irony of it made her want to laugh, but a cry came instead. A scream roiled from deep inside her, from a place she didn't know existed as she saw the bags of salt nearby—the sight of them firing every nerve in her body.

"Shut it!"

And with his words there came a strike so dense, the impact of it so hard that it flashed like lightning behind her eyes. Only there was no sharp crack or air sizzling or rolling thunder that went on and on. There was nothing.

CHAPTER THIRTY-FOUR

Failing light. It was four o'clock by the time we reached Karl Jamison's place, the daylight already fading, the sun poking its head in and out of the clouds while we drove west. On first appearance, it was quite homey. A craftsman-styled house, the front yard littered with spent acorns, a giant oak tree shading most of the property. Stout, round gardens edged the front porch with perennials and garden gnomes, one pushing a wheelbarrow around colorful ceramic mushrooms. I held the search warrant in hand as Cheryl and Emanuel joined in the yard, a clothed police officer standing by his patrol car with the lights off, a neighbor nearby taking notice.

"Not at all what I expected to find," I said, admiring the well-kept home. "Is Tracy with you?"

"I think she's driving herself," Emanuel answered. I glanced at my phone, its face empty of any messages. He saw the worry, adding, "There's a dozen different ways to get here."

"Yeah. You're probably right." I still felt a nagging worry, wanting her to experience this.

"Fucking shit!" Cheryl snapped, catching her balance after rolling an ankle, her heel snagging a protruding root. She stopped in the middle of the yard and looked up at the house.

"Are you okay?" I asked as a courtesy.

"I'm good." She gazed at the house, turning back. "Like you said, Casey. We can't judge a book by its cover."

The Crying House

"This is true," Emanuel agreed. He held out his arms, the span of them seven feet. "I mean look at me. You'd never know I just finished crocheting my first pair of booties for my baby."

"You knit?" I asked, having no idea.

He held up a finger, brow raised, and corrected me. "I crochet."

"Pardon me. Crochet," I said with a laugh. "I'm impressed."

"There's a difference?" Cheryl asked in a snarky tone. I expected no less.

"Let's get moving guys." I went to the side of the house, a blacktop driveway leading from the road. "Would you go see what's in the back?"

Emanuel went to the rear as Cheryl and I made our way onto the open porch, the wood flooring clean and well taken care of, a pair of rocking chairs and a bench seat on a swing. "Who is this guy?" she asked. "Wonder if he'd manage my place."

"This is the same house his mother died in."

"Or was killed in," Cheryl said. "His father's sister lived here afterward, took care of our suspect. She passed ten years ago."

"Good, you've got the background."

"Of course I do," she said. She paused before knocking, reading my face, seeing my opinions might differ. "You don't think he did it."

"The father?" She nodded. "If I was a juror at the time, given what was presented, I'd vote guilty. But after interviewing him, learning about the testimony from the neighbor, I wouldn't have been able to find him guilty." I rapped my knuckles against the door, the red paint warmed by the sunlight breaking through the trees.

"Who's there?" a voice shouted from inside, the pitch high, the sound scratchy like an old record.

"Karl Jamison!" I said loud enough so he could hear me. "This is the police. We have a search warrant."

"Truck is parked back there." Emanuel returned. He surveyed the road and the driveway. "It's a big thing, one of those Mac trucks. Surprised he can get it back there."

"Who's there!?" the voice shouted again.

"Sir!" Cheryl shouted. "We're executing a search warrant of your property and expect your cooperation."

Emanuel struck the door, his fist closed, his knock rattling the windows. "Karl Jamison!"

"Who's there!?" the voice repeated as a white-colored pickup truck entered the driveway.

"Guys!" We turned around. The man behind the wheel was Karl Jamison.

The patrol officer followed the vehicle as it parked, and went to the driver side as Karl Jamison exited, his saying, "Mr. Jamison?"

"I am," Karl answered, his height over six feet and his weight close to two-forty. He was bald and wore a long, graying beard, his head round and his face plump. "What's this about?"

"Sir, we're here to execute a search warrant—"

"Is this about Tina Sommers again?" he asked, annoyed.

"Yes, sir," Cheryl replied as a second patrol car pulled into the driveway, blocking Karl's truck. "Her remains were recently identified."

"Yeah. I know. I seen it on the news."

"Who's there!?" I heard again from inside the house.

Karl reached back into his truck, ducking his head beneath the window. Alarms rang, our training defensive, each of us lowering our center of gravity with hands on our gun holsters. The patrol officer was closest and had pulled his weapon, yelling, "Halt!" He was newer in his career in law enforcement, his voice breaking, his gun wavering.

"Hold on!" Karl yelled, his voice hollow inside the truck. "I'm getting my bags!"

"Officer!" I caught the officer's eyes, his glancing briefly before returning his gaze on Karl. "Mr. Jamison, I need you to raise your hands and back away from the vehicle."

"I'm doing it," he shouted, his arms in the air, his body hunched forward as he slowly backed out of the truck. Emanuel had taken a position facing the house. If there was a second person inside, and they had a weapon trained on us, then we were in danger, our positions like fish in a barrel.

"Who's inside!" Emanuel asked. "A roommate?"

"So to speak. His name is Pauly," Karl answered, putting his hands behind his head, and lacing his fingers. He'd done this without us asking and must have been familiar with the position. The officer holstered his weapon and raced around the truck, cuffing Karl Jamison's wrists for his safety and ours.

"Why won't he answer the door?" Emanuel asked.

"He's my parrot." Karl lowered his head and followed the officer's direction.

"Your what?" Emanuel's expression shifted to a perplexed look.

"He's an African gray." The officer brought Jamison around to the front of the truck and helped the man sit back in a lean on the front bumper. "I've had him since I was a kid. He's harmless."

"Who's there!?" the bird squawked.

"You almost got yourself shot," I said to Jamison, feeling vexed.

"I'm sorry," he said. "I wasn't thinking. I mean, I've had so many of you guys around that I'm used to it by now."

"FBI?" Cheryl asked. "Recently?"

"Not since before the news." I waved the man to lean forward so I could remove the cuffs. I saw that he wasn't a threat and knew his pet bird wasn't a threat either. "When that video from the truck stop with Tina Sommers first showed up, I had the FBI here for a week. At least once a week since then."

"Then you know what to expect?" Cheryl asked.

"Sure thing," he answered. "Under the garden gnome with the fishing rod is the key to my house."

"This one?" Cheryl asked, an officer joining her.

"That's it," Karl answered, his demeanor soft. Cheryl tapped the gnome, kicking it hard enough to knock over, its head striking an ornamental rock and snapping its neck. The officer picked up the key, Karl muttering, "She didn't have to do that."

"Keys to the rig?" Emanuel asked. Karl tossed him a keyring. "I'll get started on the rig." Emanuel slipped to the rear, an officer joining him, the two sleeving their hands with latex gloves as they walked.

"You were driving the interstate earlier?" I asked, his rig missing when we had patrol checking on it earlier.

"Overnight," Karl answered with a nod. "I got back this morning. I'm finishing up the deliveries with my pickup."

"Take a look here," I said, opening a folder, using the hood of his tuck as a table. I showed him a picture of Jocelyn Winter, and searched his face for any flicker of recognition. A sign that he knew her came then, turning on like a lightbulb. "You recognize her?"

"Sure, she's been all over the news," he answered, eager to share, his hazel eyes narrowing. "I haven't seen that picture before."

"You watch the news often?"

"All the time." Karl stood up onto his toes, his interest in the work Emanuel was doing. "And I listen to it too when I'm on the road."

"What's in the truck?" I asked. Karl was anxious and annoyed, scratching at his beard, his gaze locked on the rear, the top of his rig showing through the tree branches. "What are you afraid they'll find?"

"Not find," he answered, folding his arms across his chest. "It's my livelihood, and the last time you guys ran through here you broke the navigation system."

I took a step back to see Emanuel at work. "*You guys.* That wasn't us."

"Please," he scoffed.

"Tell me about Tina Sommers, and why the FBI is still interested in you."

Jamison held his chin high, his breathing heavy, his face red. "It's that video."

"You were the last person seen with her?"

He flexed his arms at the question and took a moment, his jaw clenching. "I've been over this a hundred times."

"Not with me you haven't."

"She was walking in the snow, a bad storm. All I did was offer her a ride. When we got to the truck stop, she got another ride." Jamison paced, his focus staying fixed on his rig, Emanuel's hulking body behind the windshield. The officer on the other side. "Oh jeez! They're gonna break something and I got to work tonight."

"You work for Salt Mineral Incorporated?"

With that name, Karl's attention shifted. "Yeah. I deliver the salt for them."

"Have you ever visited the abandoned homes on the beach?"

He knocked on the hood of his pickup truck. "No, none of the residential homes. But I drive the area with my pickup truck to do deliveries for restaurants. I can't get my rig down there since the roads are too narrow."

Cheryl exited the house, the African gray calling after her, "Y'all come back now ya hear."

"That bird has got a mouth on him!" she declared, her hands and arms full of evidence bags.

"Yeah. I taught her a few choice words." Karl watched Cheryl, trying to see what was bagged and tagged.

"Mr. Jamison, we'll need to search this pickup truck as well," I informed him.

Cheryl went to the pickup's bed and lifted a blue tarp, her head disappearing beneath it briefly. "Casey!" I heard—the tone in her voice standing the hairs up on the back of my neck.

I fixed my gaze on Jamison, watching him watch Cheryl. "What is it?"

"Salt," she answered. "It's a lot of salt."

"Yeah! Like I said. I deliver the stuff." His voice was subdued with a flash of worry, his brow creasing. "Listen, I know how it looks. It's just bags of salt for the restaurants. I can't fit the rig on those narrow streets."

Cheryl held up an evidence bag, having filled a quarter of it with salt. With her back turned to Karl, she mouthed the word, *arrest*.

I gave a nod, uncertainty needling, but this was her case and I stepped back to make room. My phone rang then, the suddenness of the ringtone alarming Karl. It was Jericho, but I didn't answer. When handcuffs were shown, there was no knowing how a person was going to react. This moment was sensitive, and I needed to have Cheryl's back.

"Mr. Jamison, you are under arrest," Cheryl said, taking Jamison's hands in hers, and bringing them around to his back. The salt in the truck's bed gave her what she believed was enough to take him into custody for murder and to satisfy a jury's requirements to assign guilt. It felt like a stretch, but I didn't question it. "You are under arrest for the murder of Tina Sommers."

"You guys!" he said, stomping a foot as the bracelets clicked into place. "I just deliver the salt."

"You have the right to remain silent," she went on to say, my phone ringing again.

Emanuel joined us, the truck driver's logbook in hand.

"That's my livelihood," Jamison protested.

When Cheryl finished mirandizing, a patrol officer took custody of Karl Jamison and led him to the rear of her patrol car, where she patted him down. Karl's gaze wandered aimlessly, his lips moving in silence until he saw a neighbor arriving home across the street. A slender man exited his pickup and meandered around the back of it, making himself look busy while he watched the activities.

"Hey Arnold!" Karl shouted, startling us. The man stopped to listen. "I gotta go do this thing again. Watch my bird, will ya!"

Tensions eased with Karl Jamison secured in the patrol car, and I searched my phone's screen to see that it was Jericho calling. "Hey. What's up?" I asked.

"Casey, is Tracy Fields with you?" There was panic in his voice.

"She never made it here," I told him. "Why? She might be at the station."

"I was afraid you were going to say that."

"What? Why?" I heard Jericho cover his phone, his talking to someone. "Jericho? What happened!?"

"Listen, Casey," he said "it might be nothing."

"Or it might be something!" I answered, raising my voice with worry.

"I got a call from a guy from the bridge authority, an acquaintance. He and his crew found Tracy's car."

Bridge, I thought. *The bay*. And then I imagined the worst, my legs turning wobbly and weak. "Jericho, is Tracy's car in the water?"

"No, nothing like that, but they found her car abandoned on a service access road." Wildly frantic thoughts ran through my head. "Their best guess is that it broke down."

"Okay, okay! It broke down. It's a new car. They can break down," I said, trying to find reason, my words slamming together rapidly.

"I had them leave it as is and told them to block off the area and not allow anyone near it."

What Jericho described was a crime scene being protected. "What else did they find?"

A pause. Jericho was silent as Cheryl and Emanuel traded looks and gave me a *what's up* look. "Casey, it's her station identification," Jericho answered, and then spoke to someone else, coordinating with the bridge authority. "It was on the driver seat, along with her phone and the car keys."

"It's Tracy's car," I told Emanuel and Cheryl.

"Is she okay?" Emanuel asked, his eyelids blinking fast.

Tracy would have never left her stuff like that. "Are there any signs of a struggle?" I asked, my nerves firing as my breathing turned short and fast.

"They think so. They found something along the side of her car. But Casey, they're not cops." I couldn't stand still and waved to Emanuel and Cheryl for us to leave. "I think it best to take a look."

"We're on our way."

Jericho hung up, Cheryl's eyes huge as she asked, "What happened?"

"I don't know yet," I said, and went to the rear of the patrol car, the officer making room for me to see Karl.

He was hunched over in the back seat, his head still shaking with disbelief. He peered up at me, saying "You guys—"

"Sir, when you went on your deliveries to the restaurants today, what bridge did you take?" Karl ignored me, his gaze returning to his feet. Concerns for Tracy bloomed. My question going unanswered, I thumped the top of the patrol car, demanding, "Mr. Jamison!"

"Wrights Bridge," he answered me, his voice quieted as he bowed his head again. He shook it slowly, muttering, "You guys."

I led us away from the patrol car, Emanuel asking, "Casey? What happened?"

"It's Tracy's car!" I felt a tearful shudder rise in my chest. I swallowed it, took control of it. The thought of any harm coming to her was overwhelming.

"What did Jericho tell you?" Cheryl asked, her voice turning soft.

"He said the bridge authority found her car on a service road, her belongings inside—"

I had to stop a second or I'd lose my composure. "And?" Emanuel demanded.

"Jericho said that they found signs of a struggle."

CHAPTER THIRTY-FIVE

The sun was gone, the evening marching from the east, the day dimming to a dusky light that would turn blue-black soon and put us into nightfall. It took me two passes over the bridge before I could find the entrance to the service road. It was the first right immediately after the bridge's pavement changed. It was also just before the road we had turned onto when we went to Karl Jamison's house. That is, all of us except Tracy.

Service vehicles lined one side, the white trucks with their logos painted on the side and their yellow caution lights flashing. Trees next to them swayed to a slight breeze coming off the bay as jays squawked from the branches, acting as if they'd witnessed a crime and wanted to give their statements. Patrol vehicles were parked, flashing red and blue across the scene; the officers perched nearby, thumbs hooked in their utility belts as they waited to received direction. In front of them, I saw Cheryl's and Emanuel's cars. I took a spot, parking opposite of where Tracy's car had been discovered. Seeing it in this state of inspection turned my body raw with a foreboding concern.

Three tripods stood eight feet tall and carried square LED lights as bright as the stars. Orange electrical wires wound around the poles and snaked across the road, where they sucked on the juice from a generator. The sight had all the earmarks of a crime scene, which only made it that much harder to work.

I hoped it was nothing at all, hoped it was a terrible mistake, a misunderstanding. Cars do break down and if that's what this was, maybe Tracy had been picked up. But why leave her things? I kept my hand on my phone, waiting for it to buzz with a message from her. But since leaving the Jamison place, there'd been no messages or sightings of Tracy anywhere. By now, a consensus amongst the team was growing with a notion of what had happened here. Tracy had been taken. When I shut my eyes, I saw the drone in my mind and let the worst of the ideas come forward—the most terrible kind we can imagine for the ones we care deepest about. If it was the killer's drone, then he knew who Tracy was and he'd targeted her.

"It's over here," Jericho mouthed, his face appearing on the other side of my car window, my hand on the door, but my legs stuck. "Casey?"

I couldn't move. I was frozen in my seat and staring up at him, a chopper flying overhead, a round spotlight streaming down on us, waving back and forth, searching for Tracy near the edge of the bay. I gripped my steering wheel, trying to muster the courage. But getting out of the car would make this real.

It is real, I told myself, swinging the door open, dressing my belt with my gun, and throwing my badge around my neck. Jericho led me to Tracy's car, talking without words, the helicopter batting the air violently and stealing every possible sound. When it drifted over the bay, I could hear again, asking, "Anyone else been here?"

Jericho shook his head, Nichelle pulling up and parking behind our cars. The helicopter tilted forward, its beaming light touching open water. The knowledge that they were searching for a body was almost more than I could bear.

I shook it off as Nichelle tugged on my arm, asking, "What can I do to help?"

"Listen up!" I shouted to the team. "I know we are searching for one of our own here, but treat this like it was any other crime scene.

Investigate with the assumption of an abduction. Leave nothing unturned."

"I'll start with pictures," said Nichelle.

"We'll need pictures, but first I want you to review her phone."

Nichelle's eyelids flipped open wide. "Her phone is here?"

"Driver's seat," Jericho answered. "Along with her station identification and the car keys."

The driver's side car door was open wide, Cheryl and Emanuel working the inside and outside, their fingerprint kits opened beside them. All our prints were on file, including Tracy's, allowing us to exclude them during an investigation. They'd coated the door panels with latent powder around the handle and lock, Cheryl spinning the fine-haired brush, revealing prints. It helped that Tracy bought a white car, the cost of it cheaper than other colors. The fingerprints were bold against the white paint, leaving nothing to the imagination.

I knelt next to her. "What do you guys have?"

Cheryl held up her fingers, comparing the tips of hers to the fingerprints she'd found. "Tracy is a small girl. She's petite."

"And these prints are small. They're probably hers." Nichelle flashed her camera, the ring light casting the car in shadow against tall vegetation that edged the roadside. "Keep at it. Let me know if you find any suspicious prints."

"Over here," Jericho said, motioning to where the service workers had reported signs of a struggle. I walked around the front of the car, my hand hovering a quarter inch above the engine, careful not to touch the hood. It was dead cold. There was no heat. There was nothing to indicate the car had been running recently. On the passenger side, adjacent to the bridge, reedy cattails stood over me, a collection of them broken, their shoots snapped in two. "This is what they were talking about."

"I see it," I said, acknowledging—the sight of the disturbed area fitting for a body, a person falling perhaps, someone Tracy's height and weight. The idea of what had happened was difficult to bear. "There too." I shined a flashlight onto the road's edge where the gravel met the ground, the grass pressed flat while the gravel was rutted, earmarks of a body having been dragged.

"Is there any blood?" Nichelle asked, voice quivering.

My throat tightened, seeking out any evidence of blood. I beamed my light on the ground, putting it on the pebbles and stones, covering the ridge of the drag marks. I found none. "There doesn't appear to be." I shined my light around, trying to understand what would have brought Tracy to this side of her car. That's when I saw the gas cap. I saw the one corner of it bent, along with a gas stain beneath it. "Her car's gas was siphoned."

"Gas tank emptied, her car dying—" Cheryl began to say.

I knelt next to the stain, yelling, "Jer—" but had to cover my mouth; the surprise of what it was stole my words. In the gas stain, the road's dust clinging in a thin layer, there was a dot and dash and a dot. "Guys!"

Emanuel's head popped up from the other side, Cheryl going around the rear where she joined me and Jericho, our concentrating on the one spot behind the rear tire and closest to the ground. "It's like the houses," Jericho said.

"Dot, dash and she added an extra dot. It's Tracy telling us it was from her." I made room for Nichelle, her camera flashing repeatedly. "Tracy is telling us he took her."

CHAPTER THIRTY-SIX

He had her. But we had him. Or so I thought. Karl Jamison remained adamant about his delivery schedule, about Wright Memorial Bridge and using it only twice yesterday. He used it once to go to the restaurants on the islands, and then again to return to his home. It was soon after that second trek over the bay we met with him at his house. He'd stay in our holding cell for a couple of hours while Cheryl worked with the district attorney to make their case against him for the murder of Tina Sommers. That left the rest of the mummified victims to account for. And it left Tracy too, unless Karl Jamison suddenly grew a conscience and told us everything.

What if he hadn't murdered anyone? His father was adamant about his wife's death being an accident. If I were on a jury today, and a defense attorney entered testimony about the third step above the staircase landing being dangerously loose, any sense of reasonable doubt would have been compromised. Even if it was the possibility Connie Jamison fell and struck her head on the newel post. It was an inkling of doubt and that'd be all I'd need to vote Karl innocent of pushing his mother to her death.

What was more convincing was Karl's father sitting in prison for a crime he didn't commit, his protecting his only child. What if Karl Jamison had nothing to do with Tina Sommers, other than what he'd told us and the FBI and what was recorded on the surveillance video?

I shook with annoyance, hating the way doubt could turn its ugly head and creep into your thoughts like poison seeping into your skin. I suppose it was a tool too, our capability of using it to apply reasoning of what might and might not have happened. If what Karl had said was true, he'd saved Tina Sommers's life when he picked her up out of the snow and took her to the truck stop. He'd put her in a warm place that was safe from the dangerous weather. Then again, if Karl had never picked Tina up, we didn't know if she could have survived the ice and snow. She might have never run into the killer at the truck stop. She'd still be alive. Of course, that's only if Karl wasn't the killer at all. This is where reasoning and doubt clash like hot and cold, brewing a thunderstorm of thoughts ahead of any calm needed for the hard decisions to be made.

My head was spinning with questions and emotions about Tracy, which made it impossible for me to think straight. I sat alone, hiding in the darkness behind my own closed eyes. This early in the morning, the station was silent. In my mind I saw every inch of Tracy's car and saw the surrounding road, the area of her struggle and the gas cap cover and stain with her cryptic message to us. I saw these with detail, scrutinizing each, making certain I hadn't overlooked something that could be vital to finding her, to saving her life.

My eyelids flipped open with a cold understanding. I did see it all. I hadn't missed a thing. Tracy's car was taken to a police impoundment yard for further investigation. There, a forensic review was scheduled. They'd use a blacklight and remove the seats and dash and center console in search of a hair or speck of blood. They wouldn't find any though. He was smarter than that. It pained me to think it, but for the moment, he was smarter than all of us.

Nichelle slowed and glanced toward me, handing me a cup of my favorite coffee, her arriving this morning alone. "I knew you'd be here."

"I think we'll all be in early today," I said, raising the cup up with a welcome gesture. "Thanks. Any word from the bridge authority?"

Her brown eyes were puffy, and her hair disheveled which was enough for me to see she'd been working through the night too, studying the bridge's surveillance footage.

"I have Tracy's car turning onto the service road."

I sat up. "And Jamison's truck? Any signs of it?"

She tilted her head and made that *I'm not sure* face I'd come to recognize. "It's another pickup truck, and they're really similar."

"Get your laptop ready so we can review the video with Cheryl and Emanuel." From my desk, I gathered my things.

"Dr. Swales?"

While the evening had been devastating for the team, there was a flick of good news, Jericho keeping me informed on the doctor's status. "She had a mini-stroke."

"A stroke?" Nichelle said with a look of shock. Her backpack slid from her shoulder, dropping onto her chair so she could fish out her things. "How bad?"

I held up a hand and tried to comfort with a grin. "She's good." I got up and followed her, eager to get to the conference room. "From what I was told, if you're going to have a stroke, then that's the one to have."

"Good news, I guess?"

"It is. In fact, Jericho took her home last night and had to insist she get rested. She argued she'd rested enough for one day and wanted to get back here."

"She heard?" Nichelle asked, and then eyed the reporters at the front of the station, Tracy's disappearance making the headlines.

"Yeah. By now, the news is everywhere." Across from me was Tracy's seat. Empty. I couldn't stand the sight of it. "Conference room."

Emanuel and Cheryl were already at work—Karl Jamison's logbook on the table, pins on the map to show his routes and stops. Cheryl rested her head in her hand, tapping the end of a pen against the table's glass top, and looked every bit as weary as I felt. She peered up at us, bleary-eyed and pale, her freckles blank. That's when I noticed she was wearing the same clothes from the day before.

"Up all night?" I asked.

Emanuel turned, answering, "I've been here a few hours, but Cheryl—"

"Yeah." Her voice was flat. From the look of her, the logbook and the map, Cheryl had hit on some bad news.

"What is it?" I asked, putting my things down as Nichelle followed and readied her laptop.

"Jamison."

"He's keeping to his story?" I asked, expecting nothing less.

"Pretty much." Cheryl stood and arched her back to stretch as she yawned. With a shake of her head, she went to the screen, colorful markers sitting on top of one another and making a line between the suspect's house and the salt mining company. Along the way, there were branches jutting to the left and right, equally populated by markers.

"From his logbook." Emanuel added another pin, a magenta color, its landing on a location two blocks from the station. "Another restaurant, another location he delivered to."

Cheryl pointed to a handful of white markers: the only white markers on the map. "And these. They're the victims, and their last known whereabouts as identified in the FBI files."

I saw it immediately, saw that Jamison had never once been in their vicinity—his logbook tracking every pickup and delivery to the date and minute. While Jamison might have had contact with Tina Sommers, he'd never crossed paths with any of the others. "Navigation system on his truck?"

"I've got a copy of his memory card," Emanuel answered. He flicked his keyboard, an overlay appearing on the screen, the truck's route highlighted in bright yellow. "It's a perfect match. Jamison kept a clean logbook."

"We don't have a case," I heard myself blurt, any case against Jamison in question. "Has the district attorney been told?"

Cheryl's lips were pinched white, exhaustion and stress aging her. "We're the only ones that know any of this."

"Casey?" Jericho asked, his arriving a surprise. He was fully dressed, his schedule for an offshore patrol this morning. He held up a manilla envelope, a Post-it on the front. "I've got something from Swales and her team."

"Swales?" Emanuel's face lit up.

"Yeah, would you believe she's already back at it," Jericho said and handed me the envelope. "But only a few hours at a time."

The Post-it was written in her handwriting, tall letters with a sharp left-handed slant. "Call Me!" I read and dialed her number on the conference room phone.

"It's the samples!" I heard, her voice scratchy.

"Hello to you too. You're feeling better?"

"Sure, sure," the phone speaker bellowed. "Casey, open the envelope."

I did as Swales instructed, her voice with urgency. Inside, I pulled out a handful of eight-by-ten photographs with pictures. I put them on the table, the team gathering around, their sharing in my confusion. Maybe she needed more rest. Maybe the mini-stroke was more damaging? Nobody knew what these were pictures of.

"What is that?" Emanuel asked.

I shook my head, looking at one with white around the edges and a pronounced chameleon color at the center that had green and gray undertones. "Doctor. We're looking at your pictures," I said, speaking into the phone, passing the photographs back and forth. "Help us out. What are we looking at?"

"Casey, those are the salt crystals we recovered from Angela Murphy's body. These are the only sizable samples we found, making them usable for our analysis." Swales juggled the phone, the speaker relaying the noise.

"Doctor, these samples." I went closer to the phone. "These pictures don't look like your everyday table salt."

"They're magnified. What you're seeing are the crystals." Her voice was louder, clearer. "Derek did a fabulous job."

I motioned to Emanuel, his bringing up pictures from yesterday's search, the bed of Jamison's truck, a forty-pound sack sliced open and spilling the salt. "Doctor. About the color. The greenish center in the middle?" I asked, the image on the screen showing salt that was white like snow. "If the sample you recovered was in large quantity, what color would it appear to us?"

"Fascinating stuff. The colors are from the microscopic life in the ocean waters where the salt was harvested and dried."

Swales was feeling better. A lot better. But I needed an answer. "So it's sea salt." Jamison and his father worked for a salt mining company. That wasn't the same as salt from the ocean. I'd think that salt from a deep mine couldn't have the types of colors seen with ocean life, the microscopic organisms trapped inside the crystals.

"Emanuel, Salt Mineral Incorporated, do they harvest any of the salt from the ocean? Or is it all from mining?"

He flipped through screen after screen, my suspicion of the salt's source growing. "Nothing from the ocean. Their products are all interior. That is, they're land based mining only."

Nichelle snapped her fingers for my attention and showed her laptop. "This is what that salt sample looks like without magnification."

On her screen, I saw a cloud. I saw a beautiful pile of salt with the same tones of green colors throughout.

And suddenly I knew where I'd seen ocean harvested salt before. Specifically, from the Atlantic.

"Doctor, the microscopic lifeforms, their color. Does that change depending on area or region?" I asked in a near shout as I tore through my bag and dug out the gift Jericho and I had bought for the doctor's retirement.

"Sure. I mean there's amber and gold and green and blue. All different colors. Why?"

"It's your gift," I shouted while tearing into the wrapping paper and cursing that I'd used too much tape.

"You didn't have to do that—"

"She's opening it," Jericho said, speaking for me while I worked.

"Oh, okay. I suppose that's fine."

"Terri, I'm sorry for the confusion." I held the jar of bath salts, taking it to the closest window, the daylight bleeding through it, the crystals offering a show of colors that were green and gray like the ones found on the victims. "Guys? Take a look at this!"

"Doctor, how unique are the colors?" Emanuel asked, joining me, his gaze locked on the jar.

"I suppose they would be quite unique, probably changing over time as temperatures fluctuate with the seasons, and—"

"Oh man. That is a freaking beautiful match!" Cheryl's comments loud enough to talk over Swales, the doctor having no idea what was happening in the room. Cheryl joined us at the window and held the picture of the magnified crystals, the colors the same as the salt in the jar. "Casey, where? Where did you get that!?"

"It's from an artisan shop on the boardwalk," Jericho answered, taking a picture with his phone. "The owner told us he sourced all the goods locally, even made some of it himself."

In my head I saw a stack of books at the counter next to the cash register, remembering them from when Jericho and I had been at the boardwalk store to purchase the bath salts. We'd been discussing the word bourgeois. The attendant had told us he liked crosswords, and I remembered seeing books—a dictionary and a thesaurus.

He'd used them to write his poem. And then he used them to find the joeys, the synonyms inside the kangaroo words, and to write the notes. My chest was pounding and my blood rushing. "I know who took Tracy!"

CHAPTER THIRTY-SEVEN

Tracy Fields didn't have the time. She didn't know the day. And she didn't know where she was. Her head was clouded, congested and groggy. She was alive, though, and that was everything. Her eyelids fluttered, but just a sliver, the room dimly lit, the sound of waves breaking far away. There was smell in the place. It was musty and overpowered with heavy salt. There was a mix of another odor too, metal maybe, like copper. It reminded her of the pennies she used to collect with her uncle, the two of them spending hours staring through a magnifying glass to date and sort them, her mother insisting they wash their hands afterward.

The taste of mold. The taste of damp sand and stone. Her eyes sprang open when she recognized the taste of death—the stench she'd learned while working at the morgue with Dr. Swales and Derek. Tracy gagged and sipped at the air, her lungs aching, her head swollen and feeling lopsided and strangely heavy. She whimpered, letting out a cry as the first of the restraints fought her. This was really happening. It wasn't a dream after all. It was a nightmare.

Her arms and legs weighed heavy, and there was the touch of something skinny across her middle, and another one across her legs too. Her mind was heavy, though, like her arms and legs, whatever drug he'd used scattering her thoughts. A breeze brushed over her, soft and tempered like the kind from a ceiling vent, its coming with a bit of warmth and raising bumps across her skin. With the forced air's warm touch, the truth of her predicament was revealed. She was naked. Every stitch of her clothing gone. Her mind filled with shame, forcing her to cover herself. She had to bring her arms over her breasts and had to cross her legs, the degrading embarrassment petrifying. But she stayed still, unable to move, her nakedness remaining on display.

Her gaze was still clouded, the colors washed out, but there was more she could see. She could breathe as well, her body getting used to the air. It was a start. She shut her eyelids and licked her lips, the touch of her tongue swollen, the feel of her lips dry, like paper. How long had she been unconscious? She'd need water. She'd need it soon. And she'd need to escape this place, wherever it was that he'd brought her.

A boat, she thought, recalling the sound of it. *Was it far from shore? Was she at an abandoned house?*

Fright tugged on her heart, jerking a tear from her eye with images of becoming one of his mummified victims.

"Stop it," she mumbled, her voice a crackly puff of air.

Tracy forced herself to see past the grogginess, feeding on the danger and the urgency. In the dimness, she saw a computer, the screens faint. On one monitor, there was a video playing of her standing in the abandoned house, the team recovering a mummified victim—the drone's footage leveling with her station identification. The other monitor showed her picture, the details listed beneath it. There were shelves next to the desk and computer, the drone that sliced into Casey's hand sitting on its belly, the blades motionless, its controller sitting silently with a wire connected to the computer.

On a hook on the wall hung a red hat, black scraggly hair dangling from it. A fake mullet. The hat was a joke, a gag prize. The kind she'd seen on the boardwalk. He'd worn it as a disguise to visit the morgue. It had worked.

The walls. She searched the stud with the hat, seeing it was clean of rot and of mildew. The sheets of plasterboard were clear of any staining also. If this was an abandoned house, it was cleaner than the others, in better shape. There was the electricity. There was power. But there was no generator, no smell of fumes or the familiar mechanical sounds reaching her ears. Wherever this place was, it was on the grid—it was a place Casey and Nichelle could find. *An oceanside house? Or maybe the bay?*

Get up! she demanded, and tried again, her skin sliding beneath straps, nylon squeezing and pressing against her chest and middle, their definition coming to her more clearly, the drugs wearing off. Her legs were stuck in place too, another pair of restraints securing her. She squirmed and wriggled her middle, thinking she could slip through them, but tubes entering her body fired a warning shot with pain knifing where they were buried. White tape covered the first tube in her left arm, a clear liquid inside it, the tube draped from a small square bag. It wasn't fluids though. Her lips and the papery dryness in the pit of her throat told her that. Was it a sedative maybe? A preservative? She shuttered at the idea, and then found a second tube. This one was wider and closer to her chin, a sharp twinge when she moved, the area throbbing, the tube filled with black fluid like ink, the end of it sewn to her neck just above the collarbone, the stitches enormous like laces.

"Oh no," she said with a gasp and a stabbing pain rocking her insides, the fear of what was happening stealing her ability to think.

He's draining me.

Motion. A slight movement to her left freezing Tracy. She dared a look to see what'd been waiting in the shadows. Another gurney. Another girl.

She was no older than Tracy; the color of her skin as white as a ghost. She was naked from head to toe, the straps cinched tight, her flesh bulging beneath, a tube stuck in her arm, and another sewn into her skin above her collarbone. She was awake; her eyes ghastly wide and staring at the ceiling.

When the girl's head fell to the side, the suddenness of seeing her skeletal face gave Tracy a start. Rage and the want to cry out were powerful, the sight showing Tracy what was coming for her. The deterioration. The wasting. The girl opened her mouth, her lips moving, her voice like a child's, "Mm. My... my name is Amelia Branson."

"I'm Tracy." Amelia's naked form was bony, the straps showing cinch marks, the killer tightening them as the girl had become thinner. "How long have you been here?"

Amelia's eyelids slowly closed. The moment grew long, Tracy thinking the girl had gone unconscious, or had died right then. When she opened them again, she answered, "Days? A week maybe. No food and barely any water."

"Amelia, listen to me," Tracy said, raising her brow and pressing against the straps, the nylon straining. "You stay awake. Understand me! I'm going to get us out of here!"

Amelia began to gag, her mouth puckered perfectly round, her breath whistling in and out. Tracy froze. She stopped moving, and then realized the girl wasn't choking. She was laughing. "You sound like me."

"What? What do you mean?"

Amelia nudged her chin beyond Tracy. "I told her the same thing."

Tracy looked in the darkness, seeing nothing, and believed Amelia's mind was slipping. "There's nothing."

"Any second now. It comes on every thirty minutes."

Tracy waited, but only a minute more, a sharp, static charge snapped, a red light glowing warm in the dark. There was a motor whirring somewhere near her feet, hot air brushing lightly against her arm. She saw that it was a heat lamp strung from the ceiling, a fan at the end of a third gurney which blew hot air onto a girl their age. The tube in her arm was gone. The tube in her neck was gone too. Her body had wasted to nothing. At the foot of the gurney were slats of pinewood, a hammer and nails, and the burlap sacks she recognized from the truck. The heat lamp got bright enough for her to see what was piled around the girl. It was white and green and gray, pebbly stones, gallons of it covering every part of her, coating her skin.

It was salt.

That was when she screamed.

CHAPTER THIRTY-EIGHT

The *Clean Living* store was empty, the boardwalk nearly the same. An old couple walking two dogs saw my team approach, along with a parade of patrol officers fanning to the left and right of us. Without a word, they turned around and hastened their pace in the other direction. I led the team with Cheryl, crossing the boards to the storefront, our foot traffic light, the police taking positions on each side of the door beneath the sign *All Products Locally Sourced*, another reading *seventy percent off*.

A few of us entered the store, one at a time. The plan was to act like patrons, taking it easy and careful so we wouldn't tip off the owner. Emanuel took to the first aisle on our left while Cheryl went around the back to approach the counter from the other side. I moved toward the counter, an overpowering smell of soaps and scented candles making my nose wrinkle. When I reached the cash register, I saw the stack of books I'd remembered—the crosswords, the dictionary and a thesaurus.

We kept our guns holstered, but at the ready without knowing what to expect. I wanted to question him first and assess. If needed, we could take the owner into custody and search the property, not needing a warrant as we believed there was immediate threat to life. From the store counter, I searched the opening that led to storage, a light inside the room, shelves lined with product. Cheryl came to my side, shaking her head, finding nothing in the rear. The store owner appeared behind the doorway, catching us exchanging a look.

"Can I help you, ladies?" he said with caution, looking beyond us, seeing Emanuel whose head and shoulders were above the shelves. I recognized him as the man who'd sold us the bath salt. I recognized the square glasses which were too big for his narrow face. But it was the eyelids that I remembered most, their droopy corners unmistakable. His hair was jet black, slicked back, a peak like an arrow on the bridge of his forehead. If not for the hairline, I would have pegged him for Dr. Swales's mystery visitor, his build the same. "I'll be closing today. My season is over."

"I know, I saw the sign. Where did the summer go?" Small talk. I'd start with small talk. From my bag, I brought out the jar of bath salts and asked, "Not sure if you remember me? I purchased this from you?"

With the sight of the jar, he relaxed, his shoulders eased as he stepped forward, his reluctance waning. "Yes! It's one of my better selling items." He peered at Cheryl and then back to me, leaning forward as though telling us a secret. "You know, salt is a gift from the earth. It's invigorating. Cleansing."

"The sign out front mentions you source it locally?" Cheryl asked, tipping her head toward front.

The attendant picked up his phone, typing, his focus locked on the screen, the moment growing long. When he finished, he tucked the phone away and looked to the door. The sun was high in the sky, nearing the afternoon. And though the shadows it cast were short, he saw the shapes of the patrol officers standing guard, the sight of them registering. He said nothing and acted casual as if he'd seen nothing, his left foot raised to take a step back.

"Whereabouts do you get it from?" I asked, raising my voice but keeping it chatty, Emanuel moving toward us.

"I have more," he answered, his thumb hanging over his shoulder.

"I'd love to buy some more. Could you tell us about it?" I wanted him still and in sight, the counter between us leaving him out of my reach.

He took another step, returning to the storage room's doorway. A blackness crept into his eyes. "It's not a problem. I'll go get—"

He was gone then, disappearing as we drew our weapons and ran around the counter. Cheryl was ahead of me, her footing spry, cutting the corners at tight angles, and entering the space behind the store. The storage room was dim, the space unfinished, the walls lined with shelves that were stocked with boxes of goods. But the room was deceivingly small, leaving no room to hide, no exit to withdraw to.

"Where did he go?" Cheryl asked, words tumbling in a yell. At the far end, a wall with shelves and a pile of boxes. "He couldn't have gone in that direction!"

"Cheryl!" I shouted, finding an opening in the floor behind the stack of cardboard boxes. All the boardwalk stores were raised above the beach. "He's beneath us."

I turned to face the store and saw Emanuel leading the patrol officers around the back to the rear alley, where the recyclables and trashcans were picked up. "Emanuel is taking the back; we have to go below."

Cheryl went to the opening, the square hole with its trap door like something out of a movie. She held her gun, trained it on the darkness. I followed, the two of us poised to shoot anything that moved. She cupped her ear. "Listen?"

It was shuffling sand and hands slapping against wood—the killer bracing the pilings as he ran away, his height forcing him in a crouch.

"I hear it!" I said, and didn't wait another moment, jumping into the pit, my feet swallowed by cold loose sand, the color of it stained. I was beneath the boardwalk, the space shallow, my sight blind while I adjusted to the lack of daylight. I got out of the way, Cheryl landing next to me. I held my ear, spinning around until I honed onto the killer's escape route. "This way."

"Good ears," she said as we moved swiftly from piling to piling, our height working to our advantage: the store owner being tall slowed him, his figure moving swiftly in a four-legged crawl. "There he is!"

"Hold it!" I shouted, my gun pointed, his shoulders hunched, his back curved in a lump. "Don't you dare move!"

"You took them from me!" he shouted in a cry, and began mumbling and whimpering, his words leaving no surprise to who it was we were apprehending.

Fire exploded from his middle, the sound deafening, a gunshot sending a bullet whistling by my head and chipping the piling behind me.

"He's armed!" Cheryl shouted, dropping to her chest while I knelt behind a piling, my back against the wood as I dug my feet in firmly.

Sand clung to Cheryl's sweaty face, her eyes glazed with fright as I motioned silently for her to flank him, shifting perpendicular toward the ocean, and then advancing forward. I'd do the same, but from the opposite side. I held my fingers, counting to three, and then we split, taking to our paths; the store owner continuing his fast crawl toward freedom, his shadow looking like a giant crab.

My sight adjusted well enough to see him, and to see Cheryl's movements. She was dangerously close; her motions giving away her position. I tried waving her away, but he saw me then, another explosion coming from his middle—the bullet careening past me and striking the sand at my feet.

"Hold it there!" Cheryl shouted, running at him, shoulders hunched, catching him while he'd aimed and shot at me. "Throw down your gun!"

"Do as she said!" I shouted, advancing as fast as I could, knocking the top of my head on one of the beams. I didn't slow, ignoring the injury, driving forward, the two of us trapping him. "Raise your arms!"

The store owner dropped to his knees, stretching his shoulders and back, his face shiny. As he raised his arms, his wrists went limp, the gun tilting in a lean toward Cheryl, her screaming, "Don't you—" but he fired his weapon, the gunpowder's charge erupting the scene in a ball of light. Cheryl dropped instantly. Without notice, I returned fire, squeezing my trigger. The first bullet struck him and spun him around like a top.

"You took them!" he shouted and raised his arm, firing again as I returned a shot, striking his front, my reacting as trained. He fell backward, feet kicking out from under him, sand spraying, his body unfolding and then becoming still, groaning and crying. He was still alive. My gun was smokey and my nostrils filled with the acrid stench of gunpowder. Far behind the killer, a line of patrol officers were advancing in a crab-crawl, their figures faint as the shine of flashlights bounced in our direction.

"Over here!" I shouted with a wave as I approached and pried the gun from the killer's hand. There was blood on his shoulder, his neck and face covered with it, his eyes wet. I rolled him over, his shouting in pain as I slapped a pair of handcuffs onto his wrists, an officer dropping to his knees to help secure the killer. "You're under arrest!"

"You okay?" the patrol officer asked. My heart was bouncing hard, my ears ringing, but I gave him the okay sign. Another officer carefully applied pressure to the killer's wound as he rolled him onto his back to face us. The killer's body went limp like a rag doll, resignation reigning on his face, his stare emptying. He'd been beat and he knew it.

"You got this?"

"We do!" he answered, joined by three more. "Your partner?"

"Cheryl!" I shouted and scurried to her. She was motionless but moaning. "Call for an ambulance!"

"Did you get him?" Cheryl asked and tried moving. She let out a scream, her face sweaty and covered with sand, a terrifying grimace fixed on it. I searched her body for the injury. And even in the faded light, I saw a bright pool of blood coming from her side. She let out another scream and bit her upper lip, tears springing from her eyes, streaking through the grit. "Oh my God, Casey! That fucking hurts so bad!"

"Yeah, I bet it does." I dared to offer a smile, hoping it'd help, feeling relieved to hear her talking. "Where does it hurt?"

"Everywhere!" She rocked her head with a look of dismay as she fought another scream. "I think it's my hip! It feels like my middle is shattered!"

"Stay still," I told her. I stripped my jacket and tucked it beneath, padding where I saw the most blood.

"Oh man! What the fuck!" she shouted, her cries bouncing, her choice of words bringing me another smile, telling me she might not be in immediate danger. She lifted her head enough to dare a look at where she'd been shot. "Shit! There goes my bikini season."

"Press this." I gave her instructions to slow the bleeding, my gaze toward the trap door, the opening bright.

Cheryl followed. "You go!"

I squeezed her hand. "Are you sure?"

"Yeah." She peered toward the body. Three more officers nearby. "Go find Tracy!"

"I will!" I said, kicking sand as I jumped up and ran. I dove into a squat over to the killer, thinking for a moment that he'd died, his having not moved since I'd put the cuffs on him. He was breathing, though, and as the officer held him, I searched his khaki pants and found the outline of keys buried in his front pocket. There were no less than a dozen and I had no idea if any of them would lead me to Tracy. I was working a hunch, driving on instinct, every part of me saying this man had Tracy locked away.

"They were mine!" the killer shouted into my ear. I looked up, his face inches from mine, his eyes wide with a craze that frightened me to the bone. I scurried backward, sand flying, believing he was looking deep inside me, probing me like a thief in the dark, prodding my soul for a keepsake. Isn't that what he was? A thief. Stealing life.

"No," I told him, getting up and standing over him. "Nobody was yours to take."

A devious smile crept onto his mouth, blood glazing his teeth, his gaze shifting to the keyring clutched between my fingers. "They're still mine," he said, spitting a wad of blood and phlegm near my shoes. "For now."

"I got this," I told the officer, motioning to Cheryl. Without questioning, the officer lifted his foot, making room for me. When the officer was gone, I dug my heel into the killer's shoulder, using the bullet hole I'd made as a bullseye. He let out a shout, his voice raw with pain. "Where?"

"She's almost ready," he answered with mixture of laughs and cries. "Tracy. So young and beautiful."

My expression turned stone cold, my voice empty of emotion. I put my weight into my foot, the killer squirming like a bug trying to burrow into the sands. "Where?"

"Never gonna happen," he answered with a look that told me he could keep this up forever. "I've survived far worse."

One of the officers came to my side, his flashlight beaming onto the killer's face. I leaned over, looking into his vacant eyes. That's when the recognition hit me. I'd seen him elsewhere, and it wasn't just from his being the store's attendant.

"African gray!" A flash of disappointment appeared on the killer's face. "You're Karl Jamison's neighbor!"

I gave the officer the address of Jamison's home, telling him to get a dispatch and ambulance to the residence across the street. He acknowledged, my blood rushing into my head.

"I know where Tracy is," I yelled to Cheryl, her face in her phone while an officer treated her. "Neighbor's house across from Jamison's. Tell Emanuel!"

I didn't wait for her reply and sprinted beneath the boards, shoes pounding the damp sand, my heart racing fast and hard enough I thought it'd burst before I saw daylight again. Tracy was miles away. Two officers offered me their hands and lifted me from beneath the store effortlessly, my clothes covered in sand which sprinkled across the floor like a hail storm. I ran through the store, begging to whatever spirits might be listening that there'd be no traffic, that I'd have a clear shot through the streets leading away from the boardwalk and across the bay to Karl Jamison's house.

The salt, I thought earnestly as I dropped in behind the wheel of my car, tires peeling against the slick blacktop, a steady rain with fat drops smacking my windshield. How long had the killer lived across from Karl Jamison's house? Were they childhood friends? If so, the killer must have known about Karl's mother, Connie Jamison. He would have known about the salt too, and how it was used by Karl's father. I thumped the steering wheel, red taillights beaming into my eyes as traffic came to a crawl leading onto the bridge. *Connie Jamison.* That's where the killer's idea for mummification must have been born. If that was half the puzzle, what had made him a killer?

CHAPTER THIRTY-NINE

What started as a sprinkle turned into a rainfall, turning heavy as I wove through traffic, changing lanes, driving as fast as I could without crashing into oncoming traffic. When I made the final turn, entering the street with the Jamisons's house, there were patrol cars already blocking the road, officers in dingy rain parkas, their positioning themselves on the lawn and around the property of the killer's house.

I jumped out and gripped my gun, holding my badge high enough for them to see, clearing a path to the patio. One of the officers held his closed fist above his head, a line of officers around him, their concentration on breaking down the front door, a heavy black ram gripped in their hands, the man in the lead swinging it like a pendulum, its weight slamming the door with a thunderous boom.

The front door exploded inward, its frame splintering into a confetti bomb of wood shrapnel. I followed the patrols inside, sweat mixing with rainwater and falling into my eyes, my wet shoes squelching against a wood floor. The house was small, and we piled tightly into a foyer, cramping around a staircase at the center and a dining room to the left, a living room on the right. Both rooms were immaculate, pristine, but set in a time that was decades before. There were plastic covers on the furniture, doilies and ashtrays on the end tables, a burgundy shag carpet and television trays stowed against a wall that was papered with an art deco design. I saw it all in a blink, but I didn't see what I came for. I didn't see Tracy anywhere.

I raced through the room into the kitchen, shoes slipping on black and white checkerboard linoleum, my hip crashing into a kitchenette dining set, the appliances aged like the rest of the house. Next to the range, I came upon a narrow door with a string of padlocks racing down the front like buttons on a coat. It was another room, a bump out extension behind the kitchen, the officers crowding in front of it, their battering ram at the ready.

"Make way!" I jangled the killer's keyring, hoping six of the twelve or more would fit into the padlocks. When they saw the keys, I told them, "Get ready to use that thing just in case."

But I was in luck: the first key fit snugly and turned effortlessly, the padlock dropping onto the linoleum like a rock. And then the second fell, followed by the others, the locks falling as I shed the door of each. I no longer felt my heart beating, the massive earthquake in my chest a constant tumultuous rumble. Rain had been replaced with sweat covering me, my mind screaming for my hands and fingers to move faster. I fumbled the last lock as it slipped between my wet fingers. An officer took a firm hold of it and held it for me as we opened it, my stripping the door of the killer's barricade and turning the handle, squeezing hard enough to make my fingers cramp. Other officers were yelling *clear* from the vacant rooms, but we still had no idea if the killer was working alone or if this room held danger, a booby trap that was intended to be more than a deterrent.

"Easy," the officer next to me said as a sliver of black expanded, the door swinging until it was completely open.

I searched the floorboards for any dashes and notched dots, seeing nothing. "Light," I demanded. He shined his flashlight to show another wall directly in front of us, our entering into a hallway.

The officer moved ahead of me, my staying one step behind him. "Do you smell that?"

"It's salt. A lot of it too." The taste of metal filled my mouth, adrenaline spiking in my veins. Any more of it and I think it'd turn me toxic. We turned right, following the opening, a whirring sound growing loud. It was mechanical, a machine at work in the darkness. "I don't see anything." My ankle pitched with a roll of my foot when I stepped onto a run of thick cords.

I grabbed the officer's shoulder. He shined his light down, his shoe catching onto the same. Beneath us there were power lines. I took the officer's hand in mine, felt it trembling, our breathing heavy as I moved his flashlight to follow them. It raced upward toward the ceiling and to a single lightbulb with a pull string dangling from it. I yanked on it, the bulb's filament warming red and turning orange, the coil heating until it was shining bright enough that I had to look away.

"Jesus!" the officer said, his mouth gaping. "What is that?"

"Tracy!" I shouted, seeing only her face, ignoring everything else.

"Casey?" Her voice was scratchy, mostly air, her fingers moving frailly.

"Get help!" I holstered my weapon as the officer ran from my side, jumping clear of the power cords and knocking over a tray of medical equipment, metal clacking and jangling as instruments bounced onto the floor. I took her fingers, the feel of them like ice. "Call for an ambulance!"

"Casey," Tracy said again. The sight of her was overwhelming. I tried to understand what I was looking at, tried to understand what I should do first to help her.

Tracy's face had a haunted look that made my heart skip, her eyes recessed in a pool of dark flesh, her cheeks sunken, her lips thin and without color. She was naked, her chest and middle covered with nothing but leather straps that were tightened against an ancient hospital gurney. Her skin was like ash, faded and sickening gray that bulged against the straps which had sliced into her, a fight she'd lost when struggling against them. From above her collarbone, there was a narrow tube no more than a quarter-inch wide that was stitched into her flesh, the inside of it filled with blood. When she tried to move, I touched her carefully, saying, "Tracy! Wait."

My stomach flipped as I followed the tube to a bucket, one gallon deep, the bottom of it covered. She continued to fight the straps, the tube shifting, her arms and legs cramping, a low groan coming with a cry as her muscles went rigid, showing like sinew, her body dangerously dehydrated. The killer's choice in the tube's diameter was by design, his wanting to slow the draining, finding it must have benefited his mummification process.

"Casey! Undo the straps. I want to go home."

I froze, a look of shock on her face. "Listen to me. You have to stay still." The hurt in her eyes worsened, her struggle gaining, the tube slipping. I pleaded with her, placing my hands on her belly. "Please, Tracy! Please, don't move. The paramedics will be here soon."

"Why!?" she asked, her eyes weary but glaring fiercely with a look of anguish that pained me.

"I don't know what to do if that tube comes loose," I said, insisting.

Tracy eyed the tube, blood appearing around the sutures like a tiny flower; the blossom growing to full bloom as drops rolled and pooled in the pit of her neck. She looked to her left. "Help her!"

"Okay, Tracy, hold on." I went to her side, to a second girl, another gurney, another tube draining into the same bucket. I stopped though, the look of the victim frightening, fearing she was already dead. "Did she talk to you?"

"Her name is Amelia," Tracy answered, the strength in her voice weakening. "She hasn't talked in a while."

I gauged the amount of blood in the bucket, thinking Amelia had lost too much blood already. She was sickly gaunt, her body emaciated. The killer had been withholding fluids while slowly bleeding the girls dry—the process probably taking days; the torture of it more than I could comprehend. "I feel a pulse."

"You have something?"

"A heartbeat. But it's really faint. I have to stop the bleeding!"

"He pinched the tube sometimes," Tracy said, her eyes swimming. When her focus settled, I followed where she was staring—the bloody tube running from Amelia's neck. "I heard him talking to himself, telling himself the steps to follow."

"Tell me what he did." I raised my hands like a surgeon, ready to follow Tracy's instruction.

"He didn't want us dead until we lost weight and… and dried out." She began to cry then, bringing the sting of tears to my eyes. "That's what he called it. Dried out."

"You said, he pinched the tubes?" I wiped my face and searched around, looking for something I could use.

"Right," Tracy answered. "A tool, like scissors, only they'd crimp the line."

Desperate, I went to the cart of medical equipment, dropping to my hands and knees, feeling where the instruments had fallen. I found what I needed and picked up two, having no idea what it was called. "Got it! I'm clamping the tube." I pinched the line, the instrument clicking and keeping hold, the blood loss stopped. I did the same for Tracy, her eyelids fluttering, her consciousness failing.

"Thank you, Casey." Her head fell to the side as she slipped away, sirens telling me an ambulance was on the way. I put my ear to Tracy's chest, her heart beating strong.

"You'll be okay," I said as I ran my fingers through her hair.

A lamp ticked on with a sharp spark, a third gurney appearing out of the darkness on the other side of Tracy's. At once I felt heat coming from it, the lamp powered by gas, a stout propane bottle on the floor. I went to the gurney, finding wood boards propped around it to make a box like a coffin. Inside, there was salt piled, a body at the center, toes and fingers and a face breaking the surface. The heat lamp hung above it, a fan blowing the air. The arrangement was as Tracy had described in the team meeting. It was how the Egyptians used arid desert winds to mummify their dead, the killer doing the same. While I could save Amelia, and I could save Tracy, it was too late for this girl. She was the killer's last victim.

CHAPTER FORTY

His name was Arnold Lidder. He was in his early forties, and he was the sole owner of the boardwalk gift shop where Jericho and I had purchased a gift for Dr. Swales. I think back to that moment, to when we stood at the store's counter, facing the killer, his explaining to us the origins of the word, *bourgeoise*—key to the Jocelyn Winter case. If only we'd known that in his home across the street from Karl Jamison's house, there were women being held prisoner, their life draining into a bucket.

I remembered the moment Karl asked Arnold to watch his pet bird. Lidder had pulled into his driveway, the bed of his pickup truck covered. Was Tracy in there? Was she already his prisoner? Those thoughts will haunt me the rest of my life. The woman found next to Tracy remained unidentified, her body already encased in salt, the process of mummification under way. Unlike the other five victims, there was no note, no line of poetry to complete the poem we'd discovered.

Both Amelia Branson and Tracy would survive their ordeals, both taken to the hospital with life-threatening blood loss and dehydration. I kept my phone in hand as we surveyed the killer's dungeon, Nichelle updating me whenever the doctors had news for her. Along with Emanuel, the FBI joined our team; the missing person cases for the victims helped give us the identifications, and they could finally close the files. With the victims removed, the gurneys remained, and the room was made ready for forensic analysis, our standing sun-bright halogens on tripods, ensuring nothing in the room escaped scrutiny.

I passed a wall of shelves with books on Egyptians and mummification. There was a second shelf containing chemistry books and medical journals, including a lengthy volume on autopsy practices. Above the shelves, a giant star chart and the sun's position to each day of the year. Marked in bold red lettering, the killer circled the days of the year, a schedule he'd come up with, perhaps, his making a calendar of when to place his victims. Or maybe it was when to visit? Some of my questions could only be answered by the killer. It was the wall adjacent to the kitchen that had grabbed the most attention—Emanuel standing in front of it like a statue, unmoving, fixed in place with a firm look. I joined him and shared in the sentiment, staying quiet as I tried to digest the extent of what the killer had done.

The wall was filled with polaroid pictures that stretched from floor to ceiling, the killer keeping a chronological log of his mummification process. Every day of captivity included his taking pictures of the victims' faces and their bodies. And in the pictures, we saw the progression of what he was doing. We saw the deterioration, the healthy and lively look on their faces turning sallow and morbid. It was their eyes that would haunt our thoughts, a living nightmare in them, the killer holding his camera close and forcing them to look at him. The picture taking continued after death as well, the killer recording the effects of his work, the impact when applying salt and hot air. It was as terrible to see now as it was on the day we found the first victim.

"This is all of them?" Emanuel asked, fingers on his mouth.

"I think it is." I focused my phone's camera on the unidentified victim, framing the view on her first picture, her face stark with terror. "Let's get this one distributed."

"Sound proofing." Emanuel plucked at the walls, a thick layer of pillowy material stapled into place. "He used a couple layers."

"This explains why nobody heard them screaming." I scanned the dates on the polaroids, some of the pictures faded, the earliest going back years. "He's been at this a while. Five victims plus the girl next to Tracy. We're still missing one."

Emanuel looked puzzled. "But the deceased girl with Tracy and Amelia? That's six."

"There was no note found with her. The victim wasn't ready," I explained. "I think he only places the note once his process is complete, when it is done. That means there is still one more."

Emanuel continued to pick at the insulation, his expression turning weary, the case trying. "Note or no note, it's crazy to think it was here and the neighbors never saw anything."

"Maybe they did?" I said, suggesting Karl Jamison could have. "But just didn't know what they were seeing?"

My gaze fell to the bottom row, the killer's most recent attempt: Tracy. The sight of her face in the picture turning my heart cold. I grabbed my chest. "Tracy."

"She's strong." There was the warm touch of Emanuel's hand on my shoulder. I leaned against him, stifling a cry. "Casey, she'll bounce back. You'll see."

"I hope so," I said, and dried my face. "Let me show you something."

I led Emanuel to a storage bin which had been constructed with plywood, elevated off the floor, approximately two-hundred gallons in size. Inside it, chunky salt, the same green and gray colors. "From the ocean?"

"He made it himself. Years of collecting seawater, evaporating it, harvesting the sea salt."

"Looks like he was going to run out," Emanuel said, picking at the bottom of the storage bin.

I moved to the gurney where Tracy had been, and where the mummification took place. "He reused what he had. Reclaiming and replenishing as needed. But he got sloppy with the last victim, leaving some of the salt behind while he prepared the body."

"Ma'am?" an FBI agent said, requesting my help. He motioned behind him. "I have someone here who claims to be the store owner's doctor. She said that she is his psychiatrist."

"This could be helpful," I muttered to Emanuel. Although it was general practice not to allow anyone outside of law enforcement onto a crime scene, I could choose to do so with discretion. I allowed the access. I was also curious why the killer's doctor was here—and to see her reaction to what she would find here.

In the door, a middle-aged woman entered, her face narrowing to a pointed chin. She had blonde and silver hair that was tied back in a bun. She wore a pantsuit with expensive shoes which she guarded as she walked, looking where she stepped. In her hands, she carried an ivory clutch bag with a gold chain slung from her shoulder. She squinted against the bright lights and raised a hand to shield her eyes. When she saw the wall with the polaroids, she stopped as though the dead had just appeared to her. She cupped her mouth, gaze fixed on the wall. Maybe the dead were speaking to her. If so, I hoped she could help answer some of our questions.

"Ma'am," I said, greeting her, trying to be cordial. She wasn't the murderer, but as a psychiatrist she'd probably known the killer well—an inherent bias seeded in the back of my mind. She saw that our hands were gloved and kept hold of her bag, gripping it tight against her middle. "Do you often make house calls?"

She shook her head. "Arnold missed his last two appointments."

Emanuel handed the doctor a tissue, her eyes rising to meet his. "Does he often miss appointments?"

"Never," she said, wiping her cheeks and nose. She narrowed her brow with a pensive look.

"Is that what brought you here?" I asked.

The doctor held up her phone, answering, "It was a text message that I got earlier."

I thought of the store, the owner with his phone in hand before he took off on us. "What did it say?"

"He told me it was an emergency, and was coming to my office," she answered, her eyelids peeling open at the room behind me. "If he didn't show up, then I was to come here."

"Save that text; we'll want to make a record of it," I told her.

"Yes, of course." Her focus darted from corner to corner, her nose wrinkling at the smell. There was shock growing in her round blue eyes, her fingers trembling slightly. Her mouth dry, voice a puff of air, she mouthed, "I didn't know he did this."

"It's okay," I said, seeing her state worsen, and thinking the guilt was heavy. I'd cut her some slack, any prejudices held.

"Arnold. He... he had problems. But... what he did to these poor women."

Tears stood in the doctor's eyes. Her chin quivering.

"Did he say anything that would make you suspect his being involved?" I questioned, seeing the look on her face.

With the accusation, the doctor pinched her eyelids shut, confirming.

"Is that why you are here?"

"I couldn't be sure though. He'd never been violent. Never."

"What then?" Emanuel asked, his tone lower, tougher, our roles in questioning her decided. "What was it?"

"It was the girl on the television," the doctor said, searching Emanuel's face, looking for him to fill in the blanks. She searched mine next, saying, "The one from the school."

Emanuel side-eyed me. The mummified victims had only made the news once we'd established their identities. But that wasn't who she was referring to. I showed her my phone, showed her the school picture I'd snagged at Jocelyn's home. "Is this the girl you're talking about?"

Her eyes grew wide and wet with angst. "Jocelyn Winter. Yes. That's the girl."

"How did your patient come to know Jocelyn?" Emanuel asked.

The doctor waved her hand. "Arnold didn't know her. But he watched them. He talked about watching all of the kids."

"On the beach?" I looked over at the shelf with the drone and the red hat with the fake hair. "He watched the abandoned houses?"

She offered a quick nod. "A lot too. When I saw her story on the news, and heard where her body had been found, I got suspicious."

"That's when he stopped showing up for his appointments?" I asked, understanding her concern as I texted the new information to the team, including Cheryl, though she was out of commission for the time being. "It was the last two appointments?"

"The last two. He was usually so good with our meeting. Twice a week, going five years." The doctor grabbed her chest, asking, "Is that salt I smell?"

"It is. He used it extensively with his victims." A thought flashed, my showing her the storage bin, thinking it'd jog something from one of their sessions. I opted to forgo, asking instead, "Would there have been any significance with salt?"

Her face blanked, her expression like stone. The answer was on her tongue, but she struggled. She nodded briefly, adding, "It... it was his mother's doing."

I grabbed a water bottle for her, Emanuel having sacrificed a case from his car for me and the FBI agents to use. The doctor drank, her nerves rattled, leaving her to only sip enough to wet her mouth. "What was behind the salt?"

"She was abusive—" the doctor began, cupping her mouth again, eyes drifting from the polaroids to the hospital gurneys, and then to the bucket of blood on the floor with the half-filled tubes. "His mother believed salt was a tool to use."

"What kind of tool?" Emanuel asked, shifting so his large frame blocked some of the room.

"She wanted to… to cleanse him of sin."

I thought of Tracy's research, the shelf of books behind the doctor, a stack of them on ancient Egyptians. The doctor shook again, her shoulders and hips moving, the death of women at the hands of her patient too much to grasp. We were losing her. I rushed my words, "Anything you can tell us will help!"

"She used to put it in his eyes, thinking it cleansed the sins of sight. And the kneeling. Oh it was terrible what she did."

"Kneeling," Emanuel repeated, his also sensing we'd lose her soon. "Please, ma'am, go on."

"Rock salt. She forced him to kneel on it for hours at a time while he prayed." Her stare fell to the floor then. "I… I've already said too much."

"Doctor's disclosure of confidential information is permissible under these circumstances," I said, trying to assure her. The FBI would be questioning her soon too. "This is a murder investigation and Arnold Lidder will stand trial to be judged by his peers."

"I suppose you're right." The doctor spun around to leave, shielding her eyes again. This time it wasn't the bright work lights getting to her. It was the room. She couldn't stand to be inside it anymore. "I am sorry. I think I've said enough for now."

"We'll want to ask more questions," I said, offering my card. "We'll be in touch."

Reluctantly, the doctor accepted, pinching the edge of it and tucking it into her bag. She lowered her head to leave, her pace quick as though being chased by the ghosts her patient left behind. Sadly, I knew it wouldn't end when she reached her car. She'd be chased in her dreams, in her thoughts, and in those moments of calm when all seemed right in her world. That's when the questions would surface again, asking her if she'd done enough, asking if she could have done more. Her burden was a mountain to bear.

"Jocelyn Winter?" Emanuel asked, the doctor's comments placing the killer in proximity to the girl.

"I'm not sure." He looked at me as though I'd made a joke. "Think about it. Even if they'd crossed paths, the killer would have brought her back here."

"Yes, if she were alive. What if he killed her prematurely? She fought back, and he killed her to keep her quiet?"

"The autopsy is lacking defensive wounds to support it." Kneeling to take a closer look at the latest polaroids showing Tracy's face, I thought about how Arnold Lidder desired control. He wanted it because his mother stole it from his childhood.

"Jocelyn Winter's murder isn't a good fit. If she was a target, Arnold Lidder would have overpowered Jocelyn Winter, and then he would have brought her here. He wanted full control of his victims. And he especially wanted to control their death."

"You know what the press is going to think," Emanuel said, his phone in hand as he swiped through the latest headlines.

"I know. So let them make their assumptions." I stood to leave. "I'm not ready to close Jocelyn Winter's case just yet."

I turned toward the exit, the FBI busily capturing every inch of Arnold Lidder's house of horrors. There wasn't more we could do here, and there was someplace else I wanted to be.

Emanuel saw the same, his hand digging through a front pocket to find his car keys. He held them up to show me. "The hospital?"

"Detective!" someone screamed, my body instantly descending into a crouched position, guarding with my hand on my gun. Emanuel did the same, his eyes huge and bulging. Footfalls came like rolling thunder, patrol officers securing the second floor. There were footsteps crashing each step as they took to the staircase. Our focus was fixed hard on the entrance to the kitchen, listening to someone approaching. An officer appeared in the doorway, his face gleaming. He swiped at the spittle on his lips and said, "You gotta come see this!"

CHAPTER FORTY-ONE

Before we could leave for the hospital, the search of Arnold Lidder's house had turned up something that'd require our attention. I held my gun at my hip, and at the ready to use. Emanuel followed my lead, until the officer ahead of us noticed. He motioned it was okay, that we were safe. It didn't help, though, the both of us staying on edge. The stairway was open at the bottom, the left and right sides without walls, but as we climbed, the papered walls closed around us, leading us to a landing and a narrow hall.

"The bedroom at the back of the house toward the bay appears to be the owner's," the officer said. The hallway was drab with a single bulb lighting the ceiling, the walls in a faded gray floral pattern that might have been hung when the house was built. I peered inside the small bedroom above the kitchen. It looked like a child's: the bed made tight and square without a single wrinkle; the window showing a view of the bay, the sun dipping in the west with light sparkling atop the water. There was a small bureau with men's deodorant, a hairbrush and comb, along with other personals. Instinctively, I covered my hands with gloves and slid open the top drawer, a box appearing, the kind I'd seen used to hold recipe cards.

"Let's see what's inside," Emanuel said, sleeving his hands with latex. He flipped the lid open, showing what could have been recipe cards, a hundred or more index cards, the writing on them the same as the writing on the notes.

"These are his," I said, voice curt, my throat closing with disgust. I picked up the first of the cards, three sentences on it, the style macabre and ugly, a fourth line with words of half-written sentences, half attempts at a new poem that had one intention—to be encoded and tucked in the hands of his victims. "These were for the victims we found, including Tracy."

"I wonder if there aren't more already?" Emanuel asked.

I gave him a shrug, fanning the index cards, showing most were blank. "None of these are finished."

"But the poem on the whiteboard?"

"I thought we would have found another note on the body next to Tracy," I said, knowing there was one note we hadn't recovered, one line to complete the killer's poem. "She was still in the salt though. I think Lidder places the note after he has placed the body."

"Or there's still one victim out there somewhere."

"Officer, we're going to need to secure the room for a broader search," I said, my mind wandering with why Lidder slept in the back bedroom. Pointing to the bedroom at the top of the stairs. "I would have thought Lidder would have used the master bedroom?"

"That's what we wanted to show you," the officer answered. He led us back down the hall and opened the bedroom door. I let out a gasp when I saw the bed, the blood in my veins running cold. Every serial killer has their first and I thought we may have found Lidder's.

The bedroom walls were bright white, no retro paper used, the paint clean, an accent wall painted a deep blue that had faded, possibly indigo at one time. Across from the entrance was a large tallboy bureau, the top of it covered with a sheet of glass, dressed with picture frames showing black and white photographs, my guessing them to be pictures of grandparents and great grandparents. There was a long dresser on the wall perpendicular to it, a large mirror with rosary beads draped at the center. A queen-sized bed sat at the center of the wall closest to me with the subject of my shock. In the bed, a mummified corpse positioned with what I had to guess was in perfect orientation to the setting sun, head to toe, an east to west direction like the bodies we'd discovered in the abandoned houses.

"I believe we have the missing victim," I said, the sight of it taking my breath. Next to the bed was a traditional wood chair with a waitressing outfit neatly placed over the back, a pair of shoes polished and sitting beneath, ready to be worn for work. "And I believe this must be Arnold Lidder's mother."

"First or last?" Emanuel asked, referring to when she'd become a victim. We closed the distance around the bed, the woman's skin gnarled and taut, and her bones protruding and poking through like edges of a sharp rock. She had no eyes, and her hair was wispy thin, nearly gone from most of her scalp.

"She's more skeletal than she is mummy. I think she died a long time ago," I said, carefully touching a rib, wiping a layer of dust from the corpse. The bedsheet around the body was soiled with whatever decomposition occurred after the mummification. "There's no sheet draped over her either." I pointed toward the head where it was crooked. "And death appears to have resulted from a broken neck."

"A fall down the stairs?" Emanuel asked.

"I'd suggest a push down the stairs." I went to the end of the bed and faced Arnold Lidder's first victim. "Those polaroid pictures downstairs, the top row was of an older woman. She was the only victim her age. He started with her. He started with his mother."

Emanuel touched the residue on the bedsheet, smelling it. "It's faint, but I can still smell the salt."

I lifted my chin toward the bedroom window, motioning to the Jamison house. "Now we know where Lidder got the idea to use salt. He was here. He was living here with his mother when Gerald Jamison's wife died, and he put her in that box of salt."

"Lidder saw it all." Emanuel went around the other side of the bed to search the work clothes—finding a woman's bag and identification. "Theresa Lidder."

"Look," I said, returning to the woman's bedside. I took care as I lifted a mummified finger, the corner of a note showing. "We've got a note."

"That would be number six." While I held the bony fingers, their cracking as I maneuvered them, Emanuel fished the aged paper from beneath, and handed it to me. "You open it."

I unfolded the sheet, expecting to find more kangaroo words, more joeys for us to hunt down and make sense of. But I didn't. Instead, the words were left naked like Lidder's mother, a single phrase written without obfuscation, and it was the last sentence of the poem we'd assembled from the notes discovered with the first five victims. "It says, *And a tomb to save the dead.*"

Dire lies I am to act. An act I am to bide.
It is for me to cleanse. An evil apt to rise.
A cue to lure the posed. And a tomb to save the dead.

CHAPTER FORTY-TWO

East OBX High School's football stadium seats were filled, the varsity football team on the field, wearing their football jerseys, standing alongside the cheerleading squad. The school mascot, a hawk, ran into a tumble of cartwheels and somersaults, one after the next, ending the series with a backflip. The people in the stands cheered as the marching band seated nearby played loud enough to hear across town.

It was a pep rally for the varsity team, the turnout high, the weather a perfect autumn evening—football weather. Blaring horns and bass drums were beating. There was the smell of popcorn and hotdogs and hot chocolate. But this evening had another purpose also. It was a memorial.

The school administration, the mayor and the church leaders wanted to honor Jocelyn and to bring rest to the rising tensions that had plagued the student body and had led to demonstrations and altercations.

With Arnold Lidder securely in custody, his surviving surgery and recovering in the hospital, the evidence pointed to him as being the sole person responsible for the crimes. Based on the comments from Lidder's doctor, Arnold's proclivity toward watching the students, his having used the abandoned house, the team also suspected he was the one who'd killed Jocelyn Winter.

On paper, sure, the story seemed right. Try as I may, I wasn't convinced. And though I'd been pressed by the sheriff and the mayor to close the case, I asked for another week. I needed more time.

"Take a bite," Jericho said, nudging my arm, a chewy soft pretzel in his hand. "You look like you're thinking too much."

"I'm always thinking too much." Jericho joined me for the evening. He was in full dress, as were the police patrol, along with a squad from the firehouse. He chomped onto the end of the soft pretzel, yellow mustard dancing on his upper lip. I wiped it for him and stood closer. I loved that he was with me, that he was here, our being able to work together. He also made me feel grounded, something I needed in my life. "This place hasn't changed in twenty years."

"No. I suppose there's not much reason to change when something works." Nichelle bumped my arm, her arriving a surprise. "Here for the rally?"

Nichelle had that look on her face. The one when there was news to share. "You gotta see this."

"What is it?"

She shoved a photocopied sheet into my hand, a breeze curling the edges. I pinched the corners, bringing it closer and seeing it was a copy of a page from Jocelyn's diary. Jericho leaned over my shoulder, the mustard strong on his breath. I scanned the words, an entry made in the diary a week before her murder.

"Another fight? And look who it was with," I said, shock in my voice, seeing it wasn't with Grace Armstrong or any of Grace's friends.

"I know, right!?" Nichelle yelled over the band, Jericho covering his ear.

"Was there another fight or is this the only one?" I held the page straight for Jericho to see, adding, "Did they settle their argument?"

She shook her head, "Not that I could find. I don't think they made up at all." She reached between us and snagged a pretzel chunk.

"By all means," Jericho said as he read the page.

I searched the bleachers, searched for the face of the person Jocelyn had fought with. Grace Armstrong's voice boomed then; her voice was godlike, the volume of it enormous. I found her at the podium, the school officials standing behind her. The marching band quieted as a hush fell over the crowd when Rose Winter entered onto the field and then stood next to Grace.

"What's going on here?"

Grace cleared her throat and held up a paper to read. "This poem is titled, 'I Am Mudborn'," she said, slowing her voice, timing it to the fading echo. "By Jocelyn Winter."

"That's from Jocelyn's diary," Nichelle said, a bemused look appearing. "How—"

"I think Jocelyn had more than one draft." I held the photocopied page, continuing my search of the bleachers. "Nichelle, guess who isn't here?"

"Based on that page. I'm not surprised."

"The funeral," I began, the idea of a motive in mind and where the suspect would be. "I was told this person wasn't there either."

"You onto something?" Jericho asked.

"I think I am. Let's go," I said, tucking the photocopied page into my jacket, Jocelyn Winter's words booming in my ears, from the mouth of a girl who'd made her life hell.

"Where we going?" Nichelle asked, following us.

"We're going to catch Jocelyn's killer."

CHAPTER FORTY-THREE

I went back to where it all started. We found Jocelyn's killer at the scene of the crime—the abandoned house. It was evening by now, the moon in its last day of being full, bathing the beach in a silver light that was bright enough for us to see the house. The tide was high, fast-moving seawater running between the pilings, and in one of the windows was a faint yellow glimmer, flickering like a candle's flame.

"It's safe," Jericho assured me, his hands cupped, my foot on top of his laced fingers. He whispered, "One, two, three." And hoisted me inside the house.

I climbed the remainder of the way, dipping my head beneath the black and yellow crime-scene tape, my chest pressing flat against the soggy plywood floor. A flash of blue and red skipped across the water beneath me, a beach patrol car arriving—the township tripling the force since the troubles in the desolate houses began. "You take care of that?" I asked, and added, "I've already called in a patrol."

"I'll join you in a second," Jericho said, holding up his hand, Nichelle staring up at me wide-eyed. "Don't move."

He left the house then to let the patrol know who we were. Nichelle gauged the jump, finding it no match for her build. "Want me to come up?"

I shook my head. "Not until it's secure—"

"Who's there!" a voice yelled from inside the house.

"Casey, wait for Jericho." Nichelle paced, feet sloshing in the moving water. "Casey—"

But I was already on the move, my gun drawn, a flashlight held above it, beaming light and painting circles on the walls and floors as I made my way deeper. The floor creaked, warning me. It was only the rot, none of the booby traps had been found in this one.

"Detective?" the voice shouted, shock in her voice, knowing who I was.

"Laura Sumter," I answered.

My idea had been correct. When my beam of light shined on her face, she shielded her eyes. The fireplace candles were lit—a hundred of them, if not more—amber light flickering, tall shadows thrown onto the ceilings and walls. I put my flashlight away, but kept my gun drawn, uncertain of what the girl was going to do.

"I didn't see you at the stadium."

Laura sat on her feet, kneeling inside the chalk outline where Jocelyn's body had been. Her hands were tucked in her lap, a purple windbreaker covering them. She wore denim jeans which I could see were wet, her shoes hidden from me, tucked underneath her legs. The girl's cheeks were sunken, and her hair was greasy and flat. There were dark shadows beneath her eyes and a rash of acne on her cheeks and chin. She didn't look like she'd slept in days. Perhaps she hadn't. Perhaps the guilt for killing her best friend robbed her of the necessities such as eating and sleeping.

"I couldn't."

"It was your pink jacket that got left behind the night of the party?" I asked, the first of blue and red lights flashing from the outside, the patrols keeping their sirens silent.

"Uh-huh. I went back to get it." She shrugged, the windbreaker on her swishing. "I took this one from my little sister."

"That's when you saw Michael and Jocelyn?"

"Yeah, that's when I saw them." Her eyes flickered with candlelight. "That's when I saw them together."

Carefully, I moved toward the hearth, the fireplace, the air warmed by the hundred burning candles. Laura didn't move, didn't alarm at my taking a seat on the brick and stone. A salt-laden wind came, breathing through the fireplace as if it were a mouth, the flames twitching, throwing the light, my glimpsing a shine of metal hidden in Laura's hands. She saw that I noticed and closed her fingers around it.

"Why did you come back here?"

She shrugged again, eyelids heavy with a look I was familiar with, her teetering on life or death. "I have to end it. A life for a life. I mean, I can't keep living with this."

What happened between Laura and Jocelyn was clear. Dr. Swales's assessment, her opinion over medical fact. She was right. "I know it was an accident," I said, citing what Dr. Swales had said. "We have the medical examiner report that proves it."

The words caught Laura's attention, her head lifting. She shook it then, stringy hair whipping. "I killed Jocelyn. I didn't mean to, but it *was* me."

"Tell me what happened. It's okay."

Her eyes sprang open to my voice. I was trying to keep it low and calm, make her feel comfortable.

A question formed on her face. "How did you know?"

Relief. She was willing to talk.

"Jocelyn kept a diary." I pulled the page from Nichelle, holding it up for Laura to see. "She wrote about the awful fight the two of you had." I didn't say more. The fight had been serious. Jocelyn mentioned the darkness in Laura's eyes, her jealousy, and that she wasn't sure they could stay friends.

"He liked me first," Laura said, her gaze falling, eyes half-lidded again.

"You loved Michael Andros?" I asked.

A grin appeared, "Yeah. Since we were kids." Her grin faded, a sad look returning.

I dared to show her a picture on my phone: the inside of a locker; the heart shape with the initials. "Is this your locker?"

Recognition flashed and turned into a scowl. "You went in my locker?"

"Well, to be honest, we thought it was Jocelyn's"

"Her locker is two-fifty-nine. Mine is two-fifty-seven, next to hers."

"Can I ask what you did with Jocelyn's cell phone?" I knew what she did with it, but wanted to hear it, to better understand what it was she'd had in mind.

Her mouth twisted, pinching to the side as she considered how much she wanted to share. "I thought I could make it look like Grace had it."

"You wanted Grace to take the blame?"

"Uh-huh. She hated Jocelyn."

"Did you hate Jocelyn too?" I asked.

Laura reeled back, the question painful. "She was my best friend," she answered me with tears returning. "I hated that she loved him!"

"You and Jocelyn fought. Was it here?" A rabble of voices gathered outside, alerting Laura, her attention snapping. "Tell me what happened?"

"It was when I saw them together. I mean they were *really* together! You know!" she yelled, a look of disgust on her face.

Slow realization dawned. Laura had lied to us. "You told us you saw them kissing, but that wasn't all. Was it?"

The look of disgust faded, tears streaming as she shook her head. "I saw Jocelyn and Michael having sex."

"That must have been a shock for you? Did you interrupt them?"

"Nuh-uh. I waited until he left." Her voice changed, filled with righteousness and justice, saying, "That's when I confronted her and told her it wasn't fair. I told Jocelyn that he liked me first, but she didn't care!"

"You hit her then?"

"I think so." She searched the ceiling, trying to find the words, tears rolling down her face. "She fell to the floor saying she was dizzy, but then she started screaming at me and… and, I hit her again."

"How many times?"

She shook her head wildly in a fit of cries, her eyes like fire. "I just wanted her to stop screaming!"

"Is that when you held her mouth?"

There was calm then, Laura's face draining as though in shock. "I was on top of her. I don't know how, but I was. And her feet were shoved into my gut. I tried to shut her up, but she just kept screaming. That's when I put my hand on her mouth."

Tears flowed in the calmness, the purge endless, the confession being her first time telling it. "We can go somewhere. We can talk about this. We can talk to your family." From the corner of my eye, Jericho stood with one of the patrol officers, their hands trained on their weapons.

"What?! I can't tell them." Laura saw the officer with Jericho and then held up a gun. "I got this from my dad's gun locker. He didn't think I knew the combination. But I did."

Without hesitation, guns were drawn, the steel revolver in Laura's hand glinting in the candlelight. "Laura!"

"Tell Ms. Winter that I'm sorry." She pulled the gun's hammer back, knowing how to use it, making the trigger hair sensitive. Laura said nothing else, her focus fixed on the weapon in her hand, the guilt urging her to bring the barrel to the side of her head.

I had one chance and jumped; my sight tunneled. I took a leap, muscles straining in my legs as I threw myself toward Laura's arm, my hands aiming for the gun.

Laura pulled the trigger, the hammer clapping metal on metal as my fingers wrapped around her arm, jerking her backward, my weight carrying us into a tumbling ball. There was no explosion, no white flash, no smell of gunpowder. There was no bullet.

"No!" Laura screamed and jumped to her feet. "That's not right—"

She never finished, the patrol officer tackling her from behind, flattening her body against the floor in a heavy thud. He moved fast, spreading her arms and legs; her face twisted in a torture of rage and grief. When the handcuffs were on, he called out to the room. "Secured!"

"Are you okay?" Jericho asked, helping me back to my feet.

I was breathing fast, the moment making my blood rush like thunder in my head. "I'm fine," I said, Laura's gun secured in my hand as I patted my front and sides. "It didn't fire."

"Let me see that." My hands were shaking as I handed him the revolver. Jericho carefully opened the cylinder, and showed it to me, the chambers empty.

"It's a good thing her father kept the bullets elsewhere."

"It is," he said, agreeing, blinking fast, trying to hide a show of emotion.

"I'm fine," I assured him. "I need to—"

"Go ahead," Jericho said, turning toward Laura.

Laura was put into a seated position, the officer standing guard over her. Her head was down, and the tears were gone. I knelt next to her.

"We're going to take you to the station."

"I didn't mean to kill her," she sobbed, trying to move the hair from in front of her face. "Really, I didn't. She just made me so mad."

"I know. We'll figure it out."

"What now?"

I had to say it. "Laura Sumter. You have the right to remain silent. Anything you say can and will be used against you in a court of law. You have the right to an attorney. If you cannot afford an attorney, one will be provided for you. Do you understand the rights I have just read to you?"

Laura lifted her chin, eyes glassy, candle flames dancing in them. "I do."

"With these rights in mind, do you wish to speak to me?"

"No, ma'am." She put her head back down and brought her knees close to her chest. "I've said enough."

CHAPTER FORTY-FOUR

With my help, and some insistence, the Connie Jamison case was reopened. After interviewing Gerald and Karl Jamison, I believed Gerald was correct, that his wife's death was an accident. With Arnold Lidder in custody, Karl Jamison was never guilty of anything, except for being nice and helping a young woman out of the cold. In talking with him about his mother, I heard nothing but love and an everlasting guilt for not being there when she'd fallen.

Dr. Swales was back to work, one-hundred percent recovered. The idea of retiring was deferred for the time being. In her words, she wasn't tired enough yet, and there'd be plenty of time to rest later. Just not today.

To support the reopening of Connie Jamison's case, Karl walked us through the events that took place the evening his mother died. He didn't see it, didn't hear it even. He'd been busy cleaning his bird's cage and found her body later, after she'd already died. While not a witness, he corroborated the story of a loose step at the top of the stairs, the same as his father had claimed.

Swales was able to establish that Connie Jamison had struck her head on the edge of the staircase newel post. The corner of the post distinct enough to identify what had happened. Swales used a new imaging technology to confirm that the shape of the post was a perfect match to the injury sustained in the woman's skull. With Nichelle's technical help, they employed a scanner that projected the case's original X-ray pictures of Connie Jamison's skull in multiple dimensions. Swales also scanned the newel post and presented the findings to the district attorney. In a presentation we were all invited to, Swales rotated the projected images to show the woman's fall, and the most likely scenario that could inflict a mortal wound. She used the woman's height and weight, and a computer model to demonstrate the fall, proving the depth of the injury could occur without force, making the finding conclusive. Connie Jamison's case was ruled an accident and, soon after, Gerald Jamison was released from prison hospice. He returned to his home, where he could spend his final days with his son.

Laura Sumter was taken into custody, the DA facing a difficult decision on the charges the teenager would face. Given the attempt on her own life, Laura was placed into protective custody—a mental hospital with the type of care she'd require. I met with Laura's mother and father soon afterward, their having no idea of the trouble with Jocelyn. They invited me into their home, a quaint house across the street from Jocelyn's where I saw a half dozen cars parked, a dozen people on Rose Winter's lawn and porch. Word about Laura having killed Jocelyn was quick to get around—the Winter family and friends staring into the Sumter home. Jocelyn Winter's case was officially closed, but that didn't mean the families would heal. For them, the wounds were new and raw.

The case of the mummified bodies was also closed, Arnold Lidder being named as having worked exclusively alone, his house inspected through and through. Though I'd found the recipe box in his room with the index cards, a few of them having new poems, none were completed. When asked, Lidder only spoke of the victims we had recovered, including his mother's body, his speaking of an abuse that had gone too far. In our short conversations, I found out I was right about the salt as well. Lidder had first learned of it from the Jamison case. He'd murdered his mother soon after Gerald Jamison was convicted, and then used salt his mother had in store, along with bags he'd taken from the Jamison property. With the salt used to hide the smell of decomposition, his study of ancient Egypt and their tombs and mummification had become his modus operandi, his process to cleanse the world of its evils the way his mother had tried to do with him. Committing himself to the task, he began to harvest salt, and improve his skills, leading him to his next victims.

Arnold Lidder's doctor became the focus of the reporters, and they drifted away from the station and from my sight. They'd found a new star, her mannerism and good looks making for a likable face to interview. As part of Lidder's cooperation, his request to continue sessions with her were approved. With every visit, the reporters followed, waiting on her words, a news story arriving that evening about the serial killer and his mummies. I could smell a book deal coming. Maybe a podcast, or one of those true-crime mega-episode documentaries everyone would binge-watch over the course of a weekend.

I had big plans. A big move. A folded stack of cardboard boxes waited in my apartment, along with bags clumped in heaps. It was finally time for me to move to Jericho's house, time for us to make a home together.

With the move, I'd also made one of the most difficult decisions of my life. Jocelyn's case, and the case of the poor mummified girls had taught me that life must be for living. A few months ago I almost found my own missing daughter, Hannah. But now, I needed to rest my search for her, or at least pull back and live. That included staving the nightly rituals of studying surveillance videos and working with my online sleuthing team—something I'd been too busy to do anyway as we worked Jocelyn's case, and the cases in the abandoned homes. It meant no more last-minute treks to county morgues where I'd lay my eyes on a decedent, trying to identify if they could be Hannah.

I broke the news to my online team, assuring them that I would never stop looking altogether, but that I had to take care of myself, for my own health and sanity. I needed this if I was going to grow.

As I turned off each of the monitors that made up the wall Nichelle helped build with me, one of our online *sleuths* sent me a video. He said it was a new clue. By now, I knew to look at it for what it was—another tease. Another hint. And like all the others, the clue would take me to yet another clue, which would grow like a weed and inevitably lead me to finding more and more clues, my connecting an endless count, and spinning them around with new theories. I had to face the sad truth. All clues, all the leads to finding my daughter, they led to nowhere.

I cursed under my breath before flipping that last switch, knowing I'd have to look or it'd follow me into the day, a bothersome nag making me wonder. On the screen I watched a black and white grainy video, a swaddled child, unconscious and lying on a wet pavement. I raised my fist to punch the screen. I'd seen this video before. My online team was regurgitating an old lead, probably sending it out of desperation to keep me involved.

A message popped up from the corner of the screen. It was from the sleuther who'd posted the video. They had information and a promise that it was new. Unlike the time before, they were finally able to identify the hospital, and Hannah's last known location. The raging disappointment simmered and was replaced by a new thread of hope. Until now, we'd never been able to identify the hospital. This wasn't just new. This was huge. Before turning everything off, I added the hospital address to my phone, where it would get pushed to the cloud, and where it would live forever. It didn't matter if I turned off all my computers. Unsolved cases never close.

*

In traditional style, when one of us has fallen, we all go to the hospital. We do so each and every day until the day of their release. It's a show of unity, of family, of no one ever being left behind. The team had once done this for me, just as I was doing now for Tracy and for Cheryl.

We all donate blood too, continuing within safety guidelines, our arms like pincushions with needle marks and veiny bruises. For me, they had to resort to the top of my hand and use the smallest of needles. It was my recent stay in the hospital that caused the veins in my arms to collapse. But that didn't stop me. It wouldn't stop any of us. Jericho and his teams did the same, the total number of us keeping our small hospital staff busy. As a thank you, we brought them donuts and coffee.

Cheryl would be out of commission for months, possibly half the year or more. The bullet that found her beneath the boardwalk had shattered her right hip. While she'd cried and cursed about her bikini line, Cheryl had more to worry about than the coming summer months. For her, it was a replacement hip and many months of grueling physical therapy. She had an arduous climb ahead, but something told me she'd fully recover, beating all expectations to be back soon enough. And I think I might want to see her back too. She was better than I'd given her credit. If we happened upon another case of a serial killer, I'd want her to be at my side.

It was Tracy I worried about the most. It was her psyche, what happened to her and what it was going to do to her. I'd been a victim before and knew first-hand what she was feeling. She was much younger than me, and where I had years of being on the force, she was only getting started in her career. What was this going to do to her?

I was done giving blood for the day, and had a fresh, gauzy bandage on the top of my hand. I'd leave it for an hour, ripping off medical tape later, the adhesive making my skin itch. I took a seat on Tracy's hospital bed, her eyelids heavy, but saw a faint spark of recognition when I held up her identification badge. She was already starting to look a lot better, the blood transfusions helping to replace what the killer stole. He'd stolen a lot more though, and none of it could ever be replaced. There was the faintest pink in her face too, a shade of it around the dimples when she saw me.

"Would you like this back?" I showed Tracy her identification, afraid of what she'd say or how she'd react. While I could understand if she said no, I think it was her saying yes that scared me more.

"You look tired," Tracy said as she tried sitting up.

"Worrying about someone is apt to do that to a person." I moved closer and brushed hair from the front of her face while propping the pillows behind her back. She put her hand on my arm as I retied the laces of her hospital gown. When our gaze met, I stopped. "Tracy, I am sorry for what happened to you."

"I'm fine," she said, trying to smile. I could see she was bothered. "It's part of the job. Right?"

I shook my head, choking back a cry. "This was too close, and—" I couldn't finish. I'd worked with a lot of cops and detectives over the years but had never felt emotional like this.

"Casey? I am okay. It's a dangerous job, but I want to do this. We saved a girl. She's alive because of us, because of you! I want that in my life."

I cradled her hand in mine, and reluctantly placed her identification badge in it. My lips pressing tight to fight what I wanted to say. I tried to add some humor instead. "Well, you better let this be the last time I ever find you in the hospital, or we'll have to dock your pay for missed days."

Tracy closed her fingers around the badge, a look of gratitude and pride telling me she *was* meant to do this.

"I'm serious, once more and you're off the team."

She laughed at me, her nose snotty and wet, which made her laugh harder. It was a good laugh. "By the way, guess what I learned?"

"Oh, I don't know," I said, mocking her sponge-like brain. "The cure for some mysterious disease?"

"My blood type. There must have been a mistake in my records. I always thought I was A positive."

"You're not?" I asked and thought of all the recent trouble I'd had with my own blood type. "You definitely don't want mine. We make great donors, but when it comes to getting some, forget about it!"

"I remember. I remember what happened." She nudged her face toward the bag over her shoulder. On the label, I read, "O negative." A jab of disbelief made me read it again. "I'm the same. From now on if we ever need blood—"

"—then we'll know where to go," I said, finishing for her, the moment's humor replaced by dense shock.

I only knew two other people in my life with a blood type the same as mine. The first was my ex-husband. And the other was my daughter, Hannah. I looked at Tracy's face long and hard, my heart jumping out of my chest, thinking back to how I'd arrived in the Outer Banks in search of my missing daughter. Fourteen years of not knowing where my baby was. Fourteen years of seeking the truth.

"Isn't that the craziest thing you ever heard?" Tracy went on to say, breaking my daze, her eyes round and bright, becoming lively again, a sign of her returning to her old self as though nothing had happened.

"Yeah, crazy." I kissed her forehead, an impossible idea weaving a fresh thread, one that I thought could materialize into a new lead for me to follow.

Closing my eyes, my heart swelling, I abandoned all disbelief for the moment, abandoned what was surely nothing more than a huge coincidence. For just a second, a fraction of a moment, I let myself imagine that Tracy was my Hannah. That she was my daughter, and that she'd been with me all this time.

A LETTER FROM B.R. SPANGLER

I want to say a huge thank you for choosing to read *The Crying House*. If you enjoyed it and want to keep up to date with all my latest releases, just sign up at the following link. Your email address will never be shared, and you can unsubscribe at any time.

www.bookouture.com/br-spangler

The Crying House was a terrifically fun one to write. The idea behind it literally began with the smell of salt while I was cooking dinner one evening. Of course, with an amazing setting like the Outer Banks, the smell of the sea is always there. But what if it was coming from a body? What if it was a serial killer that mummified the bodies?

Most all my stories begin with a question. Just one is all it takes. And then my mind starts spinning up a thousand different ideas until I can finally get a couple of them down on paper, stitching them together into a story.

I also loved revisiting Casey and Jericho's story, along with the rest of the characters, and even Cheryl. What do you think is going to happen next? What I can tell you it that while I sit here and write this, I've got a new chapter brewing for Casey White Book 5. Sign up with the link provided above to find out more about it, when the time comes.

If you want to help with the Detective Casey White series and *The Crying House*, I would be very grateful if you could write a review. I'd also love to hear what you think, and it makes such a difference helping new readers to discover one of my books for the first time.

I love hearing from my readers too. You can get in touch with me on my Facebook page, through Twitter or my website. I've added the links below.

Happy Reading,
B.R. Spangler

authorbrianspangler
@BR_Spangler
brspangler.com

ACKNOWLEDGMENTS

There are a few people who I would like to thank for their continued help and support with all the Detective Casey White books. They let me talk through new ideas and they read early drafts and they tell me what works and what doesn't work. Thank you to Ann Spangler, Chris Cornely Razzi and Monica Spangler.

From the team at Bookouture, thank you to the extremely talented Ellen Gleeson for her skillful editing, and for being able to see a story's strengths and weaknesses so I can work them in every draft.

Also, my immense appreciation and gratitude to all who work so hard at Bookouture to make every book a success.

Made in United States
Orlando, FL
26 March 2025